REHAB RUN

ALSO AVAILABLE FROM TITAN BOOKS AND BARBRA LESLIE

Cracked

BARBRA LESLIE

REHAB RUN

A DANNY CLEARY NOVEL

TITAN BOOKS

Rehab Run
Print edition ISBN: 9781783297009
Electronic edition ISBN: 9781783297016

Published by Titan Books
A division of Titan Publishing Group Ltd
144 Southwark Street, London SE1 0UP

First edition: November 2016
2 4 6 8 10 9 7 5 3 1

A CIP catalogue record for this title is available from the British Library.

Printed and bound in the United States.

What did you think of this book? We love to hear from our readers. Please email us
at: readerfeedback@titanemail.com, or write to us at the above address.

To receive advance information, news, competitions, and exclusive offers online,
please sign up for the Titan newsletter on our website:
www.titanbooks.com

For my brother
Aubrey Grant Leslie
The Cool

REHAB RUN

ONE

It was just my luck that I was the one who happened to find the severed hand in the mailbox.

On my very first day in rehab, they told me running would be therapeutic. An endorphin producer. A natural high, the perfect adjunct to individual counselling, twelve-step meetings, and basket weaving. Sorry: Occupational Therapy. Besides, it was this or yoga, and the yoga teacher they employed was so serene and reeking of self-fulfillment that I could feel my blood pressure rise to dangerous levels whenever I unfurled my borrowed yoga mat.

So, running.

I liked to count things as I ran. Cows in the farmer's field outside the gates I ran next to – twelve today, and I even slowed down in case I could see more. Bury your cows, we used to say when we were kids. Travelling in the car, every time we'd pass a farm we'd scramble to count as many as we could, then if we passed a cemetery whoever was the first to say "bury your cows" won. I wasn't sure why, but it always made me shiver. And what kind of sense did that make? Cows weren't exactly ominous creatures, and they weren't meat eaters either, unless you count what they fed all those poor cows in England to give them mad cow disease, making them eat the mushed-up products of their own sick, fallen brethren until their brains started to melt.

So I counted cows. And fence posts. On one particularly bad day, the amount of money I had passed to a Croatian crack dealer, whose wares I sucked greedily into my lungs. Or the number of days since my twin sister Ginger had been brutally murdered. Or since I had watched the love of my life bleed to death in front of me.

Or how many people I had killed in the white-hot sadness and rage that had followed.

Dr. Singh told me that the counting could be used in a productive way. Count the number of days since you've used, she said. Count how many people love you. Count your blessings.

I was trying. Some days it even worked.

And I had to admit, there were worse places I could have wound up in rehab. Rural Nova Scotia, the Annapolis Valley. It was spring, the apple blossoms were everywhere, and you could smell the clean sea air from the Bay of Fundy. I barely missed the city streets under my feet. And here, I could try to be a different person. No one knew me here, or knew what I had done, or what I had seen. I could be identified as the girl who laces up her running shoes after morning meeting and takes off for an hour trotting around the property, madly counting things. Or if I ever got it together in Occupational Therapy, I could be the girl who made the famous all-back collage.

I was almost smiling as I ran down the hill toward the front gates, where I planned to begin my ascent back up to the renovated Victorian house we called the dorms, and coffee and a shower. It was early morning, the birds were making their racket, and the air was sweet. I was clean. I could breathe. There are worse places to be, I told myself again. Count your blessings.

I reached the wooden fence at the bottom of the hill that acted as our gate, and held on, breathing hard. My ankle was aching, but it wasn't sharp pain, and it wasn't bad. It was only my fifth morning running. I was like Rocky in the early scenes, before he runs up those steps in Philadelphia. I was in training, but I didn't know what for yet. I thought for a good half second about getting back into fighting, but I thought about what Dr. Singh would say, and about the last times I had fought – for real, and to the death – and figured maybe running could be a goal in and of itself right now. Maybe a marathon, or even a triathlon? I would think about it.

I circled the old mailbox at the bottom of the hill. It was just inside the gate, painted bright red like a lot of the mailboxes around here, but wasn't used by the post office. Rose's Place used it as a sort of community mailbox: Residents could deposit their outside mail in there to be posted and staff would pick it up, or more fancifully, people could leave notes for each other, or staff, or anonymous complaints. It was meant to be cute, and a way to get people outside for a little exercise. The trek back up the hill would give addicts a bit of cardio and fresh air, and the old mailbox was supposed to add to the rural charm of our environment. If a resident was so inclined, they could amble down there and see if someone had left them a note. People rarely did that; it was a bit too twee for most of us hardcore addict types.

But despite myself, on that bright spring morning I found

myself opening the red mailbox to see what was inside.

I was already holding it before my brain fully registered what it was. For a couple of slow seconds as I was reaching in I thought it was a joke. A plastic freezer bag with red ribbons tied all around it – I thought maybe some kind local had stuck in some homemade baked goods for the poor addicts at Rose's.

Until I found myself holding it in both of my hands, registering the weight and meatiness of it. A hand. A man's hand. It wasn't a joke-shop plastic hand. It was real. The wedding ring was real. The nails had been chewed. A bad habit, biting your nails, I thought blankly as I put the hand carefully back into the mailbox and closed the door. So hard to get the cuticles to heal.

And then, with blood pumping in my ears, I ran up the hill toward the office as though the devil himself was chasing me.

They told me later that I ran into the office, picked up the phone from the desk and spoke to the 911 operator with a calm and steady voice, telling her what I had found and giving excellent and precise directions, while the staff looked on, stunned. Then, after hanging up, I fainted.

Brutal violence and fainting. Story of my life.

TWO

I had been at Rose's Place for fifteen days. Fifteen days straight without crack, or even a bump of coke. Nothing stronger than caffeine and e-cigarettes.

I'd been recuperating with my brother Skipper and his wife Marie after what happened in Maine, after the face-off with the evil people who had killed my twin sister and my husband. And during which I was nearly killed by an arrow from a crossbow, had my lower leg shattered by a fall downstairs, and had taken a beating with a fire poker by a psycho bitch who had impersonated me and kidnapped my nephews. I wound up shooting a good portion of her head off and accidentally burning her in a fireplace, though, so in the end I got the better deal. At Skipper and Marie's, what with January snow in rural Maine and me in a cast after a fun-time operation on my leg, I was pretty much housebound. But I did have a bit of a stash, which I snuck hits of here and there, in my closet or in the bathroom. Not much, and not even every day. But when the demons came to call, when I woke up sweating and teary after seeing my husband Jack die in my dreams or woke up thinking my nephews were gone, that I hadn't found them – well, if anybody wanted to blame me for a little self-medication in the form of my old friend crack cocaine, they could go right ahead, and fuck them very much.

I knew all along that I would do what my siblings wanted and take the spot at Rose's Place that my brother Laurence had reserved for me. But, like any sensible addict about to start getting clean, I planned a going-away party with two guests: me and crack. I'd phoned D-Man, one of my old dealers, paid him everything I owed him, and stocked up for one last binge. That's what addicts do: We think we have to get back to rock bottom before we climb out.

But I knew this was it for me. I wouldn't hurt the people who loved me any longer. It wasn't an option. And I certainly wasn't going to spend any more of Jack's hard-earned money on it. But unlike when I was drug-free in the previous months, this time there were no glasses of wine to take the edge off. At Rose's Place, we were allowed to be addicted to caffeine and nicotine. And as nearly all addicts smoke, everyone is given, as part of their welcome bag of goodies, an e-cigarette starter kit, with flavors ranging from Lemon Meringue Pie to Marlboro.

It's a brave new world.

Rose had been the late wife of the owner-slash-benefactor of the place, Dickie Doyle. Her addiction to prescription pain meds after a riding accident had found the poor woman wandering the streets of Halifax in search of men who might need some company and have some drugs to spare. After she died an ignominious death by overdose in a rooming house in the South End, her husband Dickie founded Rose's Place.

Drugs make some of us take a funny turn. In my case, I did manage to avoid such measures; but then, I had a bit of disposable income when I got into the life. By the time I got out of it, I owed a small sum to a few unpleasant drug dealers, but in the aftermath of what followed, that was the least of my worries.

I sat in the office at Rose's Place with Evan and Mary, two of the staffers, waiting for the police and an ambulance. The ambulance had been called for me, as my fainting spell had happened immediately after I got off the phone with emergency services. My head was pounding afterwards, as per usual. Mary was looking at the coffee maker as though she had never seen one before.

"Do you want me to do that?" I said. "Sit down, Mary. You've had a shock." Mary was prolifically tattooed, fifty-ish, and seemed to get her fashion sense from television shows about biker gangs. I never knew what her title was, but she ruled the roost at Rose's Place through a haze of Marlboro smoke, with a voice like a profane Lauren Bacall and the heart of Mother Theresa.

She was like my sober soul mate. Minus the Mother Theresa part, of course.

She sat down abruptly, putting her head between her knees slowly and deliberately, breathing like she was in labor.

"A hand?" she said. Or croaked. Her long red hair was muffling her voice.

"A big hand," I said. I remembered the weight of it, the fleshiness of it, and shivered.

In the last six months I had seen far more than my fair share of blood, guts, and all things disgusting. And while I was prone to what neurologists call syncope – i.e. fainting – I was pretty sure that it had something to do with an adrenaline spike and my flawed brain's inability to handle it. Before I go down, I feel a sensation almost like carbonation in my head, like bubbles in my brain, and everything goes black. But the hand had been so unexpected and so... human, in my hands.

"Whose hand was it?" Mary said. She sat back up slowly and patted the desk in front of her. I pushed her cigarettes toward her, and she patted my hand.

"I didn't ask it, Mary," I said. "And it didn't introduce itself." I looked at Evan who was staring blankly at the coffee maker. Apparently severed hands made people in these parts forget how to operate simple appliances. He hadn't said a word yet. He was only a kid, probably twenty-three years old, and looked like this was the worst thing that had ever happened to him. Which I hoped it was. He was doing night duty as a security guard at Rose's, and I had come down in the middle of the night more than once in the last couple of weeks to find him studying. He was quiet and smart, and there was something about him made me want to protect him. I pushed him out of the way and grabbed a coffee filter, idly musing as I scooped coffee that finding a body part in a mailbox at rehab should sort of give one a pass to relapse. They'd have to give me a discount, right? Next visit free?

We heard sirens coming from the main road. It was still early morning, and rush hour in these parts was non-existent, so the sound seemed louder and more alarming than it does in the city. Mary sat up and ran to the window, energized by the noise, and Evan said something about telling the staff and calling Dickie, the centre's owner.

"This is bad," Mary said. "People are going to be leaving. People who shouldn't be leaving." She was right of course, but in my shock of taking a severed hand out of the mailbox, I had neglected to consider what it might mean for the facility itself.

"Maybe not," I said. "Some people might even stay longer than they would have. Addicts love drama."

Mary snorted and flicked the switch on the coffee maker. She scratched her flat belly and slapped it a couple of times. Mary was a former anorexic – or recovering anorexic, as they said around these parts – and it hadn't taken more than a couple of days for me to notice that whenever she wasn't being mindful of her surroundings she was prone to gently slapping or patting parts of her body that on most people tended to gather body fat. I really hoped this kind of stress didn't start her cutting each mouthful thirty-two times, or whatever weird food rituals were particularly hers.

"Poor Dickie," Mary said. "Like he doesn't have enough to deal with." She looked out the window, over the oddly beautiful, marshy shore of the Bay of Fundy. I didn't know what Dickie had to deal with, other than having a dead wife, but I figured it was none of my business. There was enough openness at the morning meetings, with people telling each other the kinds of details that don't normally get aired in public. I hadn't been able to Share yet. Partially because I hated the word in that context, so when the group leader said, "Danny, would you like to share with us at this meeting?" I would smile and shake my head and look at my lap like a junior high wallflower. I respect people for being able to open up to complete strangers, and I can see how it would be valuable. There were issues that made me start doing drugs in

17

the first place, about Jack and the end of my marriage and not feeling alive anymore, and how crack made me feel euphoric and actually normal. Until it didn't. I was starting to talk to Dr. Singh about these things, but I wasn't ready to let a bunch of strangers poke into my psyche.

So whatever Dickie's problems were, I figured that if he didn't tell me himself, then I didn't need to know. And as the only reason I was here at Rose's Place, as opposed to some other pricey secluded facility catering to the sad and addicted, was that Dickie Doyle was a college friend of my brother Laurence. Laurence had gone to Bennington College and had one of those liberal arts educations that people like the Clearys normally didn't get – we were the kids of a small-town dry cleaner and a housewife from rural Maine. But Laurence was a special case, a star in high school, and a musical prodigy. So a scholarship landed in his lap, and he went off to learn how to mix with people who didn't shoot guns at cans in the gravel pit down the road. But Laurence never forgot us little folk – like the rest of us, he was both completely annoyed but also ridiculously besotted with his family. When we lost Mom and Dad after a drunk driver hit them head-on coming back from their yearly Florida trip, Laurence was the one who took it the hardest. He stopped playing piano, said he couldn't bear it anymore; if he played Chopin one more time he would want to commit some grand self-destructive gesture. So he switched streams at school and when he moved to New York, he started working in television. He had come out as gay in high school, which in and of itself was a brave act where we grew up, but at six-five – he claimed six-six, but we had our doubts – and with the shoulders of a linebacker, people tended not to mess with Laurence. Especially with the fierce Cleary clan backing him up. Rumor in town had it that we all carried guns everywhere we went. And then of course in high school I got arrested for breaking the nose of a girl who broke my little brother Darren's heart.

When Laurence moved to New York he dated a series of inappropriately older men, none of whom the rest of us met. "Oh, Danny, you really don't want to spend an evening with Edward," Laurence would say, after I'd spent an hour getting ready to meet them at some restaurant or other when I was visiting. Jack and I would go down sometimes for fun and stay at funky hotels because it was one of Jack's hobbies, hotels. "He's so old, and his hearing aid is on the fritz again. It will really slow down the conversation at dinner. Another time." Of course that other time never came, and then Laurence would have moved on to the next old man.

Dickie Doyle was Laurence's assigned roommate at Bennington, a random pairing that wound up surprising them both, and everyone else, by lasting through all four years of school. Dick was straight, an economics major, and on the lacrosse team, and although his family was full of drunken micks just like ours was, his drank at country clubs instead of the Legion. Despite the sports, Dickie was quiet, introspective, and a bad fit at Bennington, but his parents had hopes that mixing with all the artsy types would smooth out some of Dickie's rough edges. And they were right. By the end of his second year, Dick had taken to sporting pink shirts with bow ties and knew the lyrics to several Sondheim songs. Then Dickie met and married Rose, and after a few high-flying years in New York, they'd decamped to Nova Scotia to live the quiet life.

Then Rose, an avid horsewoman, was thrown from her mount and broke her leg. She was prescribed OxyContin for the pain, and like many good people before and after her, became addicted and needed the drugs long after her leg had healed. And when she eventually found it too difficult to cop pills in this rural area, she realized that everything she wanted was easier to get in Halifax.

Dickie was never the same. Rumor had it that he came by the facility once a month or so to check in, but otherwise he kept to himself in a cabin he'd built on a small lake a few miles away. While the addicts recovering at his centre showered in beautiful bathrooms and ate fresh, locally sourced food, Dick lived in a small cabin with only sporadic running water and a compost toilet. He chopped down trees for the woodstove, the only source of heat he had, year round. He poured all his money – what he had left from his family, which he had parlayed mostly successfully after a few years of day trading – into Rose's Place.

Locals thought he was either a saint or a lunatic. I thought he was probably both.

"This place is what keeps him going, I swear to motherfucking God," Mary was saying. Mary could swear better than I could, a feat in and of itself.

"Maybe it's a mistake," I said lamely. "Maybe it's fake and I was just hysterical." I knew it wasn't true. A severed hand is a severed hand, and you don't have to have hung out in a morgue to recognize one. "The hand, I mean. Like a Halloween thing."

"It's May, Danny." Mary was looking at the coffee pot. "Fuck, we're out of creamers I think."

I was about to say something about liking it black like my men, some stupid joke, but Evan was walking in the door with two cops from the Royal Canadian Mounted Police. I heard another siren and saw what seemed like a dozen emergency vehicles coming up the long drive.

"Armageddon," Mary said. She crossed herself.

"Not again," I said.

I crossed myself too. I'm not Catholic, but you can never be too careful.

While the police talked to Mary first, I ran up to my room, grabbed my cell, and called Laurence to tell him the news.

"I heard," he greeted me, when he picked up the phone.

"You can't say hello, like a normal person?" Like many of my family's quirks, it both annoyed and amused me. Never once had Laurence uttered a greeting into the telephone, either when answering or calling, and I never got used to it. In person he has the manners of a courtly, if snarky, Edwardian gentleman, but on the phone, he's like a curmudgeonly uncle who's being charged by the word. Yours and his.

"Dickie just called." I could hear him light a cigarette. "Someone called Evan called him."

"Since when do you still smoke?"

"Since always. I just don't do it much," he said. "I'm coming up there."

"Here?" I said. My voice sounded high and funny. "Why?" I was easing into rehab. For once in my life I was following orders, doing the right thing, and being where I was supposed to be. I

21

was thinking about making collages, and I went for runs. I went to the meetings, even if I hadn't conquered the Sharing part. I ate with strangers and had not, as of yet, hit anyone. I hung out in the office with Mary and put my feet up and cursed. I did my cleaning rota and didn't complain. I practiced smiling in the mirror, and the day before at dinner I found myself actually tasting the food and laughing at something.

But I craved crack so much that sometimes the thought of having to live the rest of my life without it seemed like the cruellest thing I could do to myself. Even the dead parts of myself – my hair, my toenails – missed crack. I would look at my fingernails and think, I know how you feel. I miss it too. It was the hardest thing I had ever done, and if I saw one of my sibs, I thought I would just turn into a bucket of mush and beg for someone to take me home and fix me warm milk and cinnamon toast.

"I'm needed, Danny," he said. "I going to get a room at a B and B."

"Ha," I said. The Clearys hated B and Bs, the forced conversation in the morning and the generally uncomfortable feeling of staying at the home of a distant aunt. "I don't get it."

"Nevertheless." Even for Laurence, this was taking his telephone brevity thing a bit far. "I've got to run, Banany," he said, and I found myself breathing easier. Like the rest of the family, he rarely used my name. I was either Banany, or Beanpole. Or Bean. Or Pole. All this talk of smoking and B and Bs was making me feel like my big brother had been body-snatched. "I'll come see you tomorrow night." And he hung up without saying goodbye, like some character on a television show.

I looked at my phone, checking the number again to make

sure that my mind wasn't playing sober-person tricks on me and that it was my brother Laurence I had been speaking to. I considered calling Darren to mull over these events. Darren was the youngest, and at thirty a semi-retired musician. These days he was living back in Toronto with our brother-in-law Fred and our nephews, twins of nearly twelve. Fred and the boys had been through way too much in the last year, and Darren was busy being full-time uncle. He had enough on his plate. And I was supposed to be doing well in rehab, getting myself clean and perhaps even getting some perspective on the events of last fall. The last thing I wanted to do was phone him with news of a dead hand in a mailbox. This bit of news I would handle on my own. And of course, with Laurence, when he arrived.

When I went downstairs, the police seemed as highly strung about the whole thing as we all were. Clearly, in this rural idyll, severed body parts delivered into mailboxes weren't *de rigueur*. There was even an ambulance outside (to revive the hand? Mary and I wondered). But they wanted to take my blood pressure and look at my pupils and I consented, with the eagerness of the newly-sober, to take a breathalyzer. They explained that I would make a better witness in court, eventually, if they could prove I had been sober when I'd found the hand. I was pretty sure even the fire chief was there.

And Mounties. Several Mounties.

"Mrs. Cleary, let's just go over this one more time." I looked at the detective, or sergeant as he called himself. He was a tall, bald, slightly doughy man, whose ruddy complexion was even more flushed with what I could only take as excitement. "Starting from when you got up this morning."

"Ms. But call me Danny," I said automatically. We were in the office still, and I was high on caffeine. I studied the man – my experience with police was mixed, to say the least. One had nearly sacrificed his life to save me and my family, and another had seduced me, killed my sister, and shot my brother with a bow and arrow.

But despite my days of mayhem only months earlier, looking out the window at the kind of soft sunny May morning we were in right now, it was difficult to believe that anything bad could happen. Despite, you know, the severed hand in the mailbox. At least it had nothing to do with me this time, I thought. I'm just another addict here, another person trying to get her life together. Let go and let God, and all that.

I don't know anyone here, I kept repeating to myself. I don't know anyone here. That hand doesn't belong to anyone I know. It has nothing to do with me or mine. There are bad people everywhere but there are good people too. I looked over at Mary, who was sitting with her head between her legs again. I smiled.

"Miss?" the sergeant said, seeing my smile. "Something funny?"

"Oh God, no," I said. I sat up straighter. "I'm sorry." He looked at me, and I could practically see the cogs turning. He was trying to figure out whether I was just some spaced-out junkie, crazy, or had put the hand in there myself. After all, my fingerprints would be on the bag; I had handled it. Handled the hand. I tried not to smile again. "Too much caffeine. I'm having one of those weird opposite reaction moments, you know? Where you don't know whether to laugh or cry? I mean, how often do you find a hand in a mailbox, am I right? Or maybe you do. Maybe they get delivered all over town here." Out of the corner of my eye I could see that Mary was sitting up straight now, looking at me. She shook her head slightly, a "shut the fuck up" move if ever I saw one.

"Uh. No," the cop said. "Not so much." He looked at me and there was a kindness in his face. I smiled.

"What a relief," I said. "So what do you want to know?" I told him again about my run, probably adding too much detail about what a beautiful early morning it had been, and how peaceful I was feeling. Not relevant, but it was all spilling out. "So I thought, what the hell, I'll open the mailbox. I've been doing that on my runs these last days. It's become a habit."

The cop perked up. "Do you do this every morning?" he wanted to know.

"Well every morning for the past five or six days," I said. "I've only been here for two weeks." But who's counting. I saw the look on his face. "You think whoever did this knew I'd be the one to find the hand, don't you," I said flatly. "He wanted me to find it."

"Not so fast," the cop said, and patted my hand, which was shaking suddenly. His name badge read MURPHY. Another mick, I thought. This area is lousy with us. "He probably doesn't even know who you are. It's possible – probable, even – that he just knows that people check that box. Or even if he has been watching the place, I'm sure it's not about you, Mrs., or Miss – Danny."

"But it might be," I said.

"Oh I suppose it *might* be," he said, as though I'd said it was possible we'd be having a solar eclipse today. "Just to do our due diligence, Danny, I should ask you – do you have any enemies?"

I sighed. "Take out your notebook," I said. "We might be here for a while."

* * *

Murphy asked Mary to leave the room, and radioed for someone called Jones to come in from outside. There was a throng of first responders, and at the bottom of the hill I could see a CTV news van.

"Wow," I said. "Even here." Murphy looked at me. "Vultures," I said nodding at the van.

"Just doing their jobs, I guess," he said. I snorted.

I sat down and rooted around in Mary's desk, found her pack of Marlboros, and lit one.

"Sorry," I said. "I'm going to have to smoke for this." Murphy nodded and sat down as a young red-haired constable, Jones, I presumed, came in quietly.

"You may have heard some of this story on the news last year," I started. "*Reader's Digest* version. In November of last year my twin sister Ginger was murdered in California." Murphy started to say something but I stopped him. "You're sorry to hear that. I know. Just let me – anyway, I live in Toronto, and I flew down there with my brother Darren. You might have heard of him – Darren Cleary?" Murphy nodded, which surprised me. Redhead grinned, which didn't surprise me. He looked more like the demographic for Darren's brand of upbeat folksy rock. I smiled back at him. "Yeah, he's my little brother. Anyway, we went down to California, and before we got there, my sister's twin sons were kidnapped."

Murphy again looked as though he wanted to say something. I didn't let him. I wanted to get this part over with.

"Ginger's husband Fred was arrested for her murder, but of

course he didn't do it. He hired this lawyer, name of Chandler York."

"I heard about this," Jones said. I was already thinking of him as Red. "I thought it was down in Maine?"

"It ended there," I said. "Or at least I hope it's ended." I tapped my ash into a coffee cup. I had to tread a fine line here between full and frank truth, and what wouldn't get me arrested. "Chandler York was an alias of a man called Michael Vernon Smith. He was my husband's foster father back in the day. He had a sort of… cult, of his former foster kids. They targeted my family because my husband had become very wealthy, and so had my brother-in-law. They play sick, psycho games with people. They torture people, and if you're on their radar, you'll sell your soul to get them to go away." Murphy was scribbling away, not looking at me. "They killed my sister, they kidnapped my nephews, and when Jack – that's my husband – when Jack and I tried to get the boys back, Jack got killed." I took a deep drag, and felt a little sick. "They tried to kill me. One of them shot Darren in the chest with a bow and arrow. He nearly lost a lung. They kidnapped me and tried to get me to give them all of Jack's money, and I killed a couple of them. In self-defence," I added quickly. "It was investigated and everything. You can check."

"But I thought one of them is still at large," Red said.

"He is," I said. "Chandler York. Or Michael Vernon Smith. He got away that night and he hasn't been seen since. He's on the FBI's Most Wanted list." I dumped the cigarette into cold coffee and swished it around. "Look. He told me that he has people everywhere, and he holds grudges, to put it mildly. I think it's highly unlikely that today's…"

"Events," Murphy finished for me.

"Events. Yes. I doubt this has anything to do with me, but I thought you'd better be apprised of all the facts." I grabbed a piece of scrap paper from Mary's desk and wrote a phone number, passed it to Murphy. "This is my lawyer, Linda Patel in Toronto. She'll answer any other questions you might have. Or you could talk to Paul Belliveau, he's a staff sergeant with the Toronto Police. I forget which division. They can give you more information, should you need it."

It had taken five minutes to give my bare bones account of the events of last fall. I felt like I should get a gold star. I'd finally managed to Share.

Detective Murphy had stopped writing at some point, I noticed, and just stared at me. "I agree, it's probably unlikely it has anything to do with you," he said, stressing the *probably*. He looked at Red. "Did you get all that?"

"Probably not," the young man answered. "Wow."

Murphy glared at him and turned back to me. "We don't have the manpower to have a protective detail on you personally, Miss – Danny. Though I would like to. But we are going to see about bringing in extra men, or extra people I should say," he stumbled, looking at me. I wanted to pat his hand and tell him it was okay. "The Major Crime Unit may be coming in. But rest assured, we're going to be watching the centre here, that's for sure."

"Don't worry about me, Detective Murphy," I said. "I can take care of myself." I found myself scanning the office, looking for what I would use as a weapon if someone attacked me in this room.

I felt a slow sense of dread and sadness take me over. Would it ever be over? Would I always have to look over my shoulder, wondering if someone would be coming after me or the people

I loved? For a brief time I had been normal – well, normal for rehab – and didn't feel the need to look for weapons or think about being on my guard. Physically, at least. Now, I found myself wondering how and whether I could get a firearm out here – next to impossible, I didn't know anyone – and worrying about whether my presence here was putting other people in danger. People who couldn't defend themselves. It was highly unlikely that the hand had anything to do with me, but then again, how often does that level of violent crime happen in the Annapolis Valley of Nova Scotia?

Murphy handed me his card and wrote his phone number on the back. "This is my direct line, and my cell phone," he said. "Eyes and ears open, right?"

"Right," I said. As the two talked quietly together and mentioned something to me about coming into the station for a videotaped statement, I stared out at the mailbox. Something was bothering me, other than the obvious.

"Detective Murphy," I said. He turned at the door.

"Call me Des," he said. He smiled.

"Des then." I didn't smile back. "Shouldn't there have been a note? With the hand? I mean, wouldn't that make sense? I mean, wouldn't this guy want some kind of attention or acknowledgment? How will you find out whose hand it is?"

Red coughed.

"Yes, there was no note," Murphy said. "But we'll be checking for fingerprints."

"Two sets," I said.

"I'm sorry?" Murphy said. He was halfway out the door.

"Two sets of fingerprints," I said. "The doer and the hand

29

itself. Two sets. You have to find out whose hand it is."

The younger cop looked pale under his freckles.

"We'll find out, Danny," Murphy said. "You just concentrate on your recovery."

"Recovery," I said, and took an e-cigarette from Evan's desk. Might as well try to save my lungs. "Tell it to the hand."

Red laughed, and I gave him a smile. Better than crying.

THREE

Every year at the end of May, the Annapolis Valley hosts the Apple Blossom Festival. There's a parade, and each little town and village has princesses and one of them is crowned Queen Annapolisa.

"If this was a Shirley Jackson story, at the end of the weekend the locals would sacrifice the Queen to ensure the next year's apple harvest," Laurence said, reading a brochure he'd picked up at the airport. I reached over and patted his knee.

"Twisted," I said approvingly. I was driving Laurence to the Valley from the airport. Mary had loaned me her Mustang.

"You're a terrible driver," Laurence said. He attempted to stretch his long legs. "When did that happen?"

"I haven't driven a stick since I was eighteen," I said. "I'm getting the hang of it." Of course at that minute I managed to pop the clutch and momentarily stall us on the highway. Luckily, the only vehicle in sight was probably half a mile behind me.

"Does anyone actually live in this province?" Laurence wanted to know. "Seriously. Where's the traffic? It should be rush hour." Laurence lived in Manhattan and worked in television. He didn't know how to be around quiet for very long.

"It was like this back home, you may recall." We had grown

up in very rural Maine, and often the only vehicles on our back roads were logging trucks.

"It's creepy." Laurence had never liked rural living.

"It's refreshing," I said. I felt protective of the area already. "You can breathe here."

"I breathe just fine on the Upper West Side." Laurence cracked the window and lit a cigarette. "You said Mary doesn't mind if I smoke in her car, correct?"

"Correct." Every New Yorker talks about Central Park as though it's the be-all and end-all for green space. They probably found severed hands every other day in there. There was probably a whole police unit dedicated to following up on severed limbs found in the park. There should probably be a *Law & Order: Central Park Body Parts* franchise. Note to self: Call Dick Wolf.

But Laurence and I hadn't talked about why he was here yet. We'd smiled and hugged at the Halifax airport as though we hadn't seen each other in a lifetime, when in fact we had all spent New Year's together at our brother Skipper's place in Maine.

"You look good, Banany," Laurence said. I hated people staring at me as I drove, so I gave him the finger. "Filled out a bit. Skin looks better."

"Clean living," I said. "Watch the road."

"You're the driver," he said. "Why should I watch the road?"

"Just do it." Laurence obligingly faced forward and we drove in silence for a good five minutes. It was nice. Laurence was the only Cleary who knew how to keep his mouth shut. It was very restful. He patted my knee and started to sing George Michael's "Faith." We always sang together. I liked singing with Laurence. He didn't make fun of my lack of any tonal sense, and he sung well enough that he made me better.

We drove in silence for another minute or so. "How're the twins?" I said. I knew Laurence had been to Toronto recently to spend time with Darren and our nephews.

"In fine fiddle," he said. "If a bit…"

"Fucked up?" And why not. Their mother was dead. They had been kidnapped by a crazy woman who looked like me, who claimed to be me, and they had watched both her and their Uncle Jack die in front of them. They were bound to have scars that would never heal.

"Darren was absolutely meant for this," Laurence said. "Full-time unclehood. They love him and actually seem to respect him at the same time, which is…"

"Fantastic. Yeah," I said. "It is."

"Surprising, I was going to say. But yes, fantastic." I cut my eyes at Laurence.

"Why are you here, really?" I checked my rear view and the same car had been behind me since the airport. Other than a few vehicles in the other direction, I hadn't encountered anyone else heading north from the airport.

"Thought I'd give you a *hand*," Laurence said. When I didn't laugh, he said, "Too soon?"

"Why aren't you staying with Dickie?"

"Do the words compost toilet mean anything to you, Danny? Dickie has embraced country life in a way that in my view is totally unnecessary." Laurence lit another Marlboro. "Actually I might. He asked me to, but it sounds like he's become quite a hermit out there."

"Where is it? His cabin?"

"Somewhere called Ferryman Lake." Laurence enjoyed smoking so much that it made me want to buy a carton of Marlboro and re-commit. "Very Thoreau, if you ask me." He took a long drag. "And guess what? There are no ferries on this lake." He said it with such glee, the big city boy, finding everything quaint in the country.

"Hmm," I said. "I didn't know you and Dickie were still in such close contact."

"As a rule, we're not. But he knows my sister is a resident of his centre, and she happened to be the one who found the, you know, severed hand yesterday." I could feel, more than see, him looking at me. "You okay there, Banany?"

"Right as rain," I said. I cleared my throat. "The cop on the case was asking me about whether this could have anything to do with me. You know, since the mailbox was on my regular running route. If I was meant to see it."

Laurence shook his head. "For once, I don't think this is about you. I think it's about Dickie."

"Why would it be about Dickie?" I didn't wish any harm to Dickie, but I felt a rush of relief. Please God, don't let this be about me. Let me just get well, in peace. Let my loved ones be safe.

"I don't think I should go into this with you, Danny." He patted my head while I was driving, which he knows drives me nuts. Laurence took up a lot of room, even sitting down. "You've been through enough, little girl," he said. "I'm just here to lend a little moral support to Dickie, and to see my wee little sister."

"Wee," I said. "Ha. I'm five-ten, Laurence. I'm practically a genetic mutant."

"What does that make me then?" he said.

"A science experiment gone wrong," I said. We smiled at each other.

"God, you're a shitty driver," he said. "Pull over." Laurence had a Porsche in New York, which was ludicrous for a man of his size. Especially a gay man of his size.

"Screw that, homes," I said. "This is Mary's car, and she entrusted it to me. Besides, we're on the highway. I'm not pulling over."

Laurence motioned to the empty road. "Banany. This is not a highway. This is a country road. I'm half expecting to see a horse and buggy around the next corner. The Amish probably take this road when they're not in a rush to get somewhere."

I looked in my rear view. The car was still behind me, and I wasn't exactly exceeding the speed limit. It was dusk, and I've always hated driving at dusk.

"Yes, it's still there," Laurence said lightly. "Pull over."

I ignored him. "So where am I taking you, anyway? There's a hotel a few miles from Rose's. The Old Orchard Inn. It's supposed to be nice."

"I reserved a room at the Hillbilly Hotel, or the Hickville Inn, or something like that. But after we take you back to the nuthouse, maybe I'll go stay at Dickie's after all." He was drumming his fingers on the dashboard. "Danny, please pull over. I'm not kidding."

I knew not to argue with that voice, and I wanted to make sure the car behind us would zip past and out of my mind. I didn't want to be thinking like this again, looking over my shoulder and seeing danger everywhere. I really wanted to leave that behind. I wanted to believe that the hand had nothing to do with me, nothing to do with anyone but a crazy person wanting to scare a bunch of dopers. Maybe the loony had even chopped off his own hand. Stranger things, etc.

I could feel the tension in Laurence's body as I signalled and slowly pulled over by the side of the road. It was nearly dark, and the area all around us was forest.

"Wait," he said, after I'd stopped and put my hazards on. "Wait."

I found myself holding my breath. I looked at the glove compartment, wondering if Mary kept anything handy like a flashlight, or a flare gun.

I couldn't tell if I was catching my brother's nervous caution, or if it was coming from me.

The car behind us slowed, and I could see it was a pickup truck, painted canary yellow. An old model by the looks of it. Laurence had his hand on the door handle.

"What the fuck," I started to say, but as Laurence opened his door, the truck picked up speed and zoomed past us. I tried to see the driver, but couldn't.

"Tinted windows?" I said. "On that piece of crap?"

"I'm driving," Laurence said. I got out and changed places with Laurence, and waited silently for him to fold himself in and adjust the seat and the mirrors. I didn't know exactly what he was thinking, but I could tell I wasn't going to like it. "Buckle up."

Within seconds the Mustang was peeling out and going like a bat out of hell. We finally passed a couple of cars going the other way, probably heading to Halifax or the airport, and the highway wasn't separated here. At our rate of speed, if the yellow truck was going the speed limit or even a bit over, we would have caught him up by now.

"So he's taken an exit," I said. "We passed two."

"Do we stay on this highway now, into the Valley?"

"I think so. I don't remember. Just follow the signs, it's pretty simple." The mood in the car had changed. "Do you really think he was following us?"

"Don't know," he said.

"Are you going to tell me what's going on?"

"Unlikely," Laurence said.

"So do you want to slow down a bit? This is Mary's car, you know. She was nice enough to lend it to me."

"I like it," Laurence said. He looked over at me. "Think she'd rent it to me while I'm here?" I laughed until I saw he was serious.

"You're a freak," I said. "Obviously." But I sighed, and said, "We'll ask her. Satisfied?"

"Thanks, Banany."

We chatted about nothing for the rest of the drive. I talked about my new passion for making collages. Laurence told me about his new trust-fund intern and her ridiculous shoes. He said she seemed to think she was working at *Vogue*.

"You know, I could just buy you a car for while you're here," I said. "Then when you leave I could use it." Jack's will was still in probate, but the executor, someone from his bank, had advanced me a significant sum against it. I hadn't really touched much of it. I didn't know how to spend money properly anymore. Post-crack, that is. I knew I'd be putting a large amount into trust for the twins, and I was paying through the nose for my sojourn among the afflicted at Rose's. I'd sent some to each of the sibs, saying I'd send more later. Maybe a trust for them too? Some kind of family compound somewhere? But I hadn't so much as bought myself a t-shirt. I figured a brain free from crack would probably make better decisions. I wanted to do Jack proud, and I wanted to look for a charity that helped foster kids. After all, if it weren't for Jack's evil foster dad and the hold he'd had over his sick family, Jack would be alive today.

"Danny, if you want to buy a car, buy a car. You can afford it, you know. But so can I," Laurence said. "So don't buy one for me. Buy one for yourself." I let that sit for minute. "But do the world a favor and don't buy a stick."

"I want an orange car," I said.

"Orange."

"Like a Creamsicle, my brother."

"Then we will find you a Creamsicle car. In the meantime, maybe your Mary will still rent this to me."

We got off the highway and drove through Wolfville, a pretty university town filled with cute pubs and funky pizza joints and places that advertised their commitment to ethically traded coffee. It was a beautiful night, late May, and there were still students around. The summer session would have just started.

Laurence rolled down the window. "Oh my God," he said. "Smell that air!"

"I know, right?" It smelled like verdant green and sweet crisp apples and a bit of wood smoke, with a hint of seawater. "They should bottle that smell."

We drove past the Acadia University campus, which was so beautiful and stately and serene, it looked like a movie set.

"I've been running in the mornings," I said quietly, looking out the window.

Laurence squeezed my knee again. "You'll be able to do it

again, Danny. Just not yet. Not until we catch the psycho who delivered that hand."

"We? Are you high? This has nothing to do with me, remember? I am not going after any more psychopaths. I've really had my fair share. Fuck, Laurence." I was trying not to cry. I was tired. I hadn't slept well. I told myself that I wasn't going to get into that crying business again. I wanted crack. Or at least a glass of wine. Or a bottle.

"The royal We, Banany, not we as in you and me," Laurence said. He hated tears. "The fine law enforcement officials of this fair town."

"What in the name of fuckville are you hiding from me?"

He shook his head. "I'm just worried about Dickie," he said. "He sounded a bit paranoid the last couple of times we've talked. Not himself. Nothing for you to worry about." He leaned back and with his left arm resting on the open window of the Mustang, looked as much at his ease as I had ever seen him. So I relaxed.

We drove past a duck pond and continued along the Evangeline Trail, named for Longfellow's heroine. In 1755, the French settlers around the Bay of Fundy, the Acadians, were kicked out of the area by the mean Brits, and they went south and settled in Louisiana and started calling themselves Cajuns.

"Your grasp of history is breathtaking," Laurence said when I explained this to him. We were driving by the beautiful stately homes on the outskirts of town, heading to Grand-Pré, to Rose's. "You should really give lectures."

"Maybe I will," I said. "I'll go on the circuit. Bill Clinton makes a pretty penny that way, I've heard."

The spring night had closed in, and it couldn't have been

more perfect. I closed my eyes and put my hand lightly on top of Laurence's, on the gear shift. The windows were open, and I was where I was supposed to be. I was clean. I was with family. The worst was behind me. I would honor Ginger's memory, and Jack's, and help take care of the boys, and do the right thing, as often as I possibly could.

"This must be it," Laurence said. He pulled up the long driveway. There was one lone police car at the end of the drive, who stopped us. He smiled and shone a flashlight into the car.

"Evening," he said. "Ask you folks what your business is here tonight?"

"I'm a resident here," I said. "I just picked my brother up from the airport. He's a friend of Dickie's," I explained. I had learned enough in fifteen days to know that I could refer to just "Dickie" and everyone around here would know who I meant.

"Oh, good enough," the constable said. "Hey, you're the one Mary loaned the Beast to," he said. "She's been chewing on the furniture, wanting to get home. Dixie's sick." Dixie was Mary's bloodhound, and it charmed me that he would assume I would know that. Life in a small town, I guess.

"His plane was late."

Laurence thanked him, a bit abruptly I thought, but then again I had gotten used to Nova Scotia manners, which dictated that if someone wanted to chat, you chatted, no matter what.

"Great security," Laurence said, peering at the buildings as he approached the main house. "Barney Fife back there."

"He probably recognized me from yesterday," I said. "And we're driving Mary's car."

"Still." Laurence drove around to the small parking lot at the back of the main house, and I could see the glow of a cigarette by the back door.

"Shit, Mary's waiting. Damn," I said. She was crossing over to us, her high heels catching in the gravel as she walked.

"Don't worry, don't worry, she's home from the vet," Mary called out before I could say anything.

"What are you, psychic?" I said.

"Colin has been telling everybody about Dixie being sick. Colin's my nephew, didn't you know that?"

"No," I started to say, but Mary was shaking Laurence's hand.

"Mary Dowe," she said. "Dickie will be so glad to see you, Larry."

I winced. Nobody called Laurence Larry. But there it was, a huge smile on his face. "Call me Laurence, my family all tell me I'm too tall to be a Larry," he was saying. Since when, I wanted to know, but I also knew when to keep my mouth shut. "Is Dixie going to be okay?" Laurence also had an aversion to dogs. Clearly, I had entered bizarro world.

"Oh, hell yes," she said. "Got sprayed with some porcupine needles, but that'll teach her, I guess. Not the first time though. She's not too bright, but we love her."

"Funny," said Laurence. "That's how we feel about Danny." Mary laughed and punched his arm, and the two of them were automatic best friends. Laurence lit a cigarette and the two of them chatted as I wandered slowly to the back door. I sat on the swing on the back porch and reached for the pack of cigarettes I kept under a lone red rubber boot that sat there, and lit one with the lighter that was tucked inside. I was vaguely trying to quit, but wasn't being too hard on myself with it. Even Dr. Singh told me not to go overboard with worrying about perfection. Quitting crack, being clean, staying clean – that was enough of a challenge.

I looked around. The place was so peaceful, at least this side, facing the water, where you couldn't see the news vans. We spent more of our time where I was sitting now, by the dorms, which housed all twelve residents, a couple of common rooms – one of which had a ridiculously large TV with a projection screen for movies – and laundry facilities. And the small residents' kitchen, for late-night snacks and card games. There was a carriage house that served as the dining hall. On the other side of that was a newer building, an add-on, which housed the yoga studio and Wellness Centre, where we got our blood pressure and other vitals checked every other day by a very cheerful male nurse. Upstairs in that building were a couple of offices, I presumed. Everything was clean and tasteful and relaxing.

I smoked my cigarette, taking in the evening air. Forty feet away my brother and a woman who was becoming a friend were joking around next to the Mustang, and I could hear Laurence trying to talk her into renting it or selling it to him. Inside the house I could hear people laughing in the kitchen, and upstairs through one of the windows it sounded like someone was praying aloud. There was so much peace in the air, I couldn't imagine leaving this place. I swung my legs and smoked my cigarette and imagined what it would be like to live here, full-time, in this place. Go for runs and stay clean and healthy and maybe buy or build a house where my family could come and stay. I could read books and volunteer and research ways to make my money work in the world. Maybe I would chop wood and start a garden.

Grow my own vegetables, and learn to bake bread. I looked at my hands, white under the porch light, and had a moment of pure peace. It felt like a revelation.

"Your brother sure knows what he wants," Mary called over to me. "I think I just sold him the Beast." I laughed and Laurence gave me a thumbs up. "I'll clean my shit out but you guys have to drive me home." I carefully stubbed my cigarette in the sand-filled coffee can under the swing, and stood to go inside to wash my hands. I wondered which counsellor was on duty, so I could tell them I'd be out a little late to get Mary home and Laurence settled in at the inn or at Dickie's, though I had only a sketchy idea where either of those was.

I closed my eyes and smelled the air. I found myself saying a silent prayer for peace for all of us, but after all I had done, I wasn't sure how predisposed God would be to hear me.

Mary ran over and grabbed my hand and started pulling me back to the car. She was stronger than she looked. "Come on," she said. "You have to take me to my puppy."

"And then you can help me find Dickie's place," Laurence called over. I looked at Mary, and she ran inside to tell whoever was on duty that I would be signed out for another couple of hours. I was aware of the fact that finding the hand in the mailbox – and that Rose's Place was topsy-turvy as a result – had meant that favors like this would not be a problem. Only two residents had left in the last day. The others, as I had predicted, seemed to be vaguely enjoying the drama. But as I wasn't the most sociable person here, I wasn't privy to the gossip.

I was about to walk in, when Mary burst back through the door and tossed some hand sanitizer at me. "Okay, who's driving?" she said, and threw the keys in the air somewhere between my brother and me. Laurence's height meant that he got there first.

He opened the passenger door for Mary. "My dear," he said smoothly, helping her in. I looked at him. "You're in the back, Bean," he said. "Behind me." He patted me on the head and I lightly kicked his ankle.

I couldn't stop grinning, and neither could Laurence. I climbed in the back seat, and we sped back down the driveway. And I, for one, had no thoughts of any more severed hands.

FOUR

Mary chatted away a mile a minute all the way to her place, and Laurence seemed vastly entertained. I was just happy in the back seat, watching the world go by. Night had settled in, and if the car had been a four-door I would have had my head sticking out the window like a dog, enjoying the air and movement.

We drove west along the Evangeline Trail, the main thoroughfare through the Valley, until Mary directed us onto a side road across from a huge, abandoned brick building, which apparently used to be a high school. Weeds were everywhere, and a bunch of kids were having a bonfire on what looked like it was once a track field.

"Don't worry, they built a new school," Mary said, though nobody had mentioned anything. "Years and years ago. But they can't get rid of that land for love nor money." We drove down a road with markedly less affluence than those we had been on before. Patio lanterns strung between rusted trailers, and chicken pens sat close to the road.

"We call this Dogpatch," Mary said. "You know, after the old *L'il Abner* funnies?"

"I can see that," Laurence said. The road was all hairpin turns and the vehicles we did see were pickup trucks, whose drivers obviously knew the road better than we did.

"Back when I was little, I had cousins down here," Mary continued. "Moonshiners. Some of them are still around back here. Off the beaten path."

"Where did the rest of them go?" I said. I felt like Margaret Mead.

"Oh, jail, some of them," she said. "Died off. My cousin Charlotte has an apartment in Wolfville now though." We drove slowly past what looked like a big old industrial furnace, abandoned by the side of the road. Until you saw that someone had blowtorched a small window out and hung a curtain in it. "There's hardship everywhere," she said, after a pause.

We drove in silence, past a small lumber mill that made me think of Maine, and then down a steep hill. It was all forest here, until at the bottom of the hill we came to a river. People were still swimming, and there was another bonfire on a miniscule beach. Parents were packing up coolers and one little girl was wailing her disapproval. She stopped for a startled second as I stuck my hand out the front window and waved enthusiastically to her from the back seat. On the other side of the river, the road grew steep again, and I could tell Laurence was enjoying getting the chance to play with the Mustang.

"We're heading up the mountain now," Mary said.

"I'll say," Laurence said. For a mile or so the road seemed to go up at a sixty-degree angle. Houses were few and far between, but while modest, they were nothing like what we had seen in Mary's Dogpatch.

"Manure!" Mary said, rolling up her window. "You're not in New York City now, Larry!"

I laughed. It was so steep that my ears popped. I could see myself living here. More and more, I could see it. Maybe not year round, maybe only in the summer. Laurence and Mary were bickering in the front like old friends about his name, and I fantasized about us all spending time together in some house or other I would buy. Eating lobsters and going for walks. I wouldn't know any dealers here, and maybe this would be the place I could settle. Reminded me a bit of where I grew up in Maine, but not so much that it would bring back painful memories.

Mary directed us into the driveway of a neat little white house, covered in wooden butterflies in bright shades of turquoise and yellow and pink.

"Shut up. I know they're tacky, but I love them," she said. Neither of us, of course, had said a word.

"Follow your dreams, Mary," Laurence said, straight-faced. Mary laughed and hit him on the arm, and told him again to shut up. She invited us in for tea but it was obvious she wanted to be with her husband and the dog, and we still had to find Dickie's place.

"Cell service is unreliable once you get back into the woods," she said. "Just follow my map; you'll be fine." Mary had made it for me before I went to pick Laurence up at the airport, and it was so precise and pretty I wanted to frame it. It included landmarks in small, neat handwriting, such as "big ugly red house, don't knock on their door" and "Bill's Bait and Grocery, cheap milk." Dickie's cabin was highlighted with a big gold star, the same ones they used on a chart in the meeting room at Rose's Place to indicate when someone had made a breakthrough in their Share.

"We'll be fine," I said. Laurence helped me out of the narrow back seat. I could hear Dixie barking madly inside the house, recognizing the sound of Mary's car door closing. I was curious about her husband, but that would be for another day.

Mary hugged us both and tugged her house keys off the key chain Laurence handed her and gave the car keys back to him. "I'll bring you the spare set tomorrow," she said. She gestured at the house. "I should..."

"We're leaving," I said. "Thanks so much, Mary." She patted her hip absently, smiled, and trotted into the house. Laurence and I pulled out of her driveway back onto the road and drove for a few minutes in companionable silence. I turned the light on and looked at the map.

"So this road will sort of take us around the lake," I said. "It looks like we have to turn once, but then it just follows the lake around, so it shouldn't be hard."

"It'll be weird to see Dickie," Laurence said. He passed his pack of cigarettes to me, the universal sign for *I'm driving, light me a cigarette*. So I did, and one for myself. Windows down, crickets chirping, elbow out the window, smoking cigarettes. I felt sixteen again. I was the happiest I had been since Ginger was murdered. Since long, long before that, in fact. "I hope he's okay." He glanced at his cell. "No bars."

"When was the last time you saw him?"

"Rose's funeral." He smoked in silence. "Before that? About a dozen years ago. Rose was already addicted but I didn't know about it."

"Everybody seems to love him," I said. "They all seem very protective of Dickie."

"He has always inspired that in people. Even when he was

earning close to a million a year. It's probably his greatest strength."

"You make it sound like it's fake, that he does that on purpose," I said. "Like he's conning people."

"No, Dickie's genuine. But in business, I would imagine he was savvy enough to know how he was perceived." I nodded. "But those days are over. He says he'll never set foot in an office again."

"Look," I said. We were now driving parallel to the lake now, and through the modest cottages you could see the water. More patio lanterns in the distance on several cabins. "It's beautiful."

"It is." Laurence slowed down and stopped. We watched the lake for a minute.

"Mosquitos," I said. I slapped one on my arm, and immediately became aware that I had been bitten several times. I'm one of those people whose pheromones attract them. I'd spent half my childhood summers covered in pink calamine lotion.

"Fucking nature," Laurence said brightly.

"I know, right?"

"Didn't you say something about wanting to move out here?" Laurence said. "You wouldn't last a summer."

"I'd stay indoors in the summer maybe," I said. "Views look pretty good from an air-conditioned room through floor-to-ceiling glass." We drove slowly on the narrow dirt road, enjoying each other's company. But I was actually starting to get a bit nervous about what state Dickie would be in. My own state of mind had been precarious enough of late.

"Car," Laurence called, and I laughed. We could hear a vehicle probably three hundred yards away, around a corner. When we were growing up, Mom and Dad had always yelled out "car" to us when that happened back in Maine. Used to crack us up.

Laurence pulled over to the side of the road and moved at a snail's pace, not wanting to surprise whatever was approaching. It was the first car we'd seen since leaving Mary's place, and with these corners we were an accident waiting to happen.

It was a yellow truck. A yellow pickup was heading for us.

"Jesus!" I heard Laurence yell, but my heart was pounding so hard it was muffled in my ears.

The truck had its high beams on and was taking the corner at speed. Laurence pulled sharply off the road and laid on the Mustang's horn. The truck didn't slow down, but didn't hit us either. I tried to see the driver when the truck was parallel with us. I caught a glimpse. The tinted driver's-side window was rolled halfway down.

"Did you see him," Laurence wanted to know.

"Red baseball cap," I said. "Dark hair."

"Man?"

"Probably," I said. I shook my head and shook out my hands, which were still holding onto the dash. "I don't know."

"Think it was the same one?" Laurence said and I knew what he meant. The same one from the highway back from the airport.

"Probably."

"Follow him or get to Dickie's?"

"Dickie," I said. "I really think we should get to Dickie's."

It was automatic. We had to get to Dickie's. Until this moment, even after finding the hand, I hadn't felt a sense of danger. Not until now.

After Ginger was murdered, I experienced some strange things that I hadn't faced yet. Dreams where she was talking to me. Everybody has dreams, but a couple of times I had felt like she was inhabiting my body, or I hers, moments before her death. Despite being fraternal and not identical twins, Ginger and I did have some of that twin telepathy that people always talk about. And I had encountered a couple of random strangers who seemed to recognize something in me, some sensitivity or that, if it existed, I had always ignored or explained away to myself. I had long ago sworn that the next person who used the word "psychic" in my presence in any serious way was going to get a knuckle sandwich.

But I was feeling something now. Something dark, something pulling me across the lake to Dickie.

Laurence was checking the rear view, but the road was deserted. "How much further?" he said.

"According to Mary's map we have to look for a cottage painted with lilac and green stripes. Then Dickie is on the right somewhere past that. He has a sign that says 'Rose' at the end of the driveway." I hadn't noticed that on the map before.

"God," Laurence said. "The poor bastard."

"Look," I said, a few minutes later. Ahead on the right, closer to the road than the lake, was the place Mary had described. Despite the feeling of foreboding I couldn't shake, I had to laugh. Even in the dark, it looked like something a five-year-old might color. But I loved it.

"That takes courage," Laurence said. "They're really letting the freak flag fly with that one."

A bit further down, the road veered away from the lake, so the cottages were hidden from view by thick forest. Most people had hammered cutesy signs into trees: MOTHER'S MANSION, or BIDE-A-WEE.

But within another minute we found Dickie's sign. ROSE.

Simple black lettering, small white sign.

There were no lights, and the night was now pitch black. Laurence flipped on the high beams and we turned onto a narrow, rutted road. There was still mud from the rain days ago. After about fifty yards was a yellow sign indicating a turn to the right, and then we saw the cabin.

It was bigger than I had been expecting, and in the dark at least, nicer looking. A simple clapboard cabin though, no crazy paint jobs. I immediately noticed an outhouse, and nudged Laurence.

"You're staying here?" I said, pointing at it. "This ain't Central Park West, baby."

"No shit," he replied.

I snorted. "You hope," I said, and Laurence grinned.

"Outhouse and a compost toilet inside," he said. "I'll be able to dine out on this for a while."

The levity was slightly nervous and definitely short-lived. The cabin was dark with no sign of life.

"Car's here," Laurence said.

"He could be sleeping." I looked at Laurence. "Well, so we knock on the door, right? Isn't he expecting you?"

"I thought so."

We got out of the car, and I found myself shutting the door quietly. For no reason other than my continued feeling of unease I found myself scanning the ground for something to use as a weapon. I picked up a rock the size of my fist.

And to my surprise, Laurence followed my lead. I looked at him.

"It was good enough for the cavemen," he said.

I snorted. "Yeah, and look what happened to them."

We went to the back door, which was fronted by a little porch with some plants on it, and even a welcome mat. I noticed that there was an outdoor light by the door, and the fact that it wasn't on, particularly when Dickie knew Laurence was probably coming tonight, made me reach into my back pocket and put my cell phone in my free hand.

Laurence knocked and we waited in silence. I stood flat against the building to the left of the door. There was nothing; no sound, no sign of life.

"So what now? Should I take you to the hotel?" My feeling of something wrong hadn't eased up; in fact it had ratcheted up a notch. But I had had enough bounding through doors where I wasn't expected to last me a lifetime. There never seemed to be birthday cake and balloons on the other side.

Laurence shook his head. He hesitated for a moment, then tried the door.

It was open.

"Dickie!" Laurence called without stepping inside. "It's Laurence. Are you here?" The direct approach, I suppose. No sound. "I've got Danny with me. We're coming in, buddy."

Were we now. Yes, I supposed we were.

Laurence groped around inside the door and flipped on a light, and we stepped inside.

FIVE

The first thing I noticed was the smell of meat cooking. Well, burning. Obviously, so had Laurence. He rushed over to a stove, picked up a frying pan and put it in the sink.

"It's turned off, but it's still warm," he said quietly. "Steak."

I quickly glanced to my left and saw the open bathroom door, and flipped on the light. Compost toilet, basic shower with the curtain open, sink. Nobody there. I scanned the kitchen area and grabbed the largest knife from a block on the counter, and motioned for Laurence to do the same.

My instinct was to remain quiet until we got the lay of the land, but of course Laurence had already loudly announced our presence.

Laurence was perfectly still. He was staring at the counter, where a cutting board sat, a lone tomato partially sliced into. A glass of beer beside it, which when I touched it was still cold.

No signs of a struggle. Nothing knocked over.

The cabin was one large room with a bedroom at the far end. It was neat, if shabby, and not in a fashionable way. No television or radio that I could see. Lots of books. A gun rack on the wall with a single-barrel shotgun. I touched the barrel, which was cold. Not recently fired, then. I started toward the bedroom but Laurence put his hand on my shoulder.

"Let me," he said.

I looked at my hands as though they belonged to someone else. A large knife in one, and a rock in the other. I had put my cell down somewhere, obviously. I didn't remember doing that.

"Dickie?" Laurence said and stuck his head into the bedroom. I heard Laurence's breath stop.

Before I could think, I was in front of my brother and pushing him behind me. Every muscle in my body was ready, and I found I was holding the knife in an overhand grip. No way was I going to lose another sibling. No fucking way.

Behind me Laurence had flipped on the overhead light.

And I knew why he had stopped breathing.

The body of a man was lying on top of the bed. Neatly wrapped in what looked, at first glance, like shiny butcher paper and twine. The only things visible were his head and his hands and feet.

His head was intact.

One hand was missing. And one foot was gone.

Laurence marched up to the bed. "It's not him," he said in a strange voice. "It's not Dickie."

"So where is Dickie then?" I said. "And who the fuck is that?"

"He might have been in the truck," Laurence said. He was still staring at the face of the man on the bed.

"Yes," I said. "But he definitely wasn't driving."

"Dickie…" Laurence started to say, but I stopped him.

"I know," I said. "I know."

* * *

I was never so happy to see a rotary dial telephone.

The 911 operator was a little impatient with my inability to give her clear directions, but once she heard me say the magic words – "Dickie Doyle's place" – everything went a lot more smoothly. I assured her that the body on Dickie's bed was not, in fact, Dickie, and gave her as good a description as I could of the yellow pickup. She told me to stay put and not touch anything else, and emergency services would be here as soon as they could. I imagined they would have to start pulling people from other counties at this point.

Laurence was standing in the kitchen and I could tell that it was all he could do not to start doing dishes. It was his fall-back position when things got hairy: rubber gloves and lots of soap and water.

"Don't touch anything," I said.

"I know that, Danny," he said. "Jesus."

We were silent for a minute. Laurence standing stock-still at the kitchen end of the cabin, and me perched on the edge of the couch. We both stared at the bedroom door, as if the neatly wrapped body on the bed might get up at any minute.

"Who do you think it is?" I said.

Laurence shook his head. "We'll talk about that later," he said.

"We just missed them," I said. Laurence nodded. I saw him glance at the kitchen counter, where one of us had put our rock down. I imagined fighting off a killer with it, someone who was going around cutting off people's hands and feet. I thought for a second about what tool would have been used for that. Definitely not a rock. "Do you think Dickie…?" I couldn't finish. I had met

Dickie once, when I was a kid and Laurence was rooming with Dickie at Bennington. But Laurence had known him for well over twenty years. They might not be best friends any longer, but that's a long time to keep up a college friendship.

"What, has something to do with this?"

I nodded.

Laurence looked at me like he wasn't even going to bother answering that one. Then he said, "Danny, when we were in school I used to host movie nights. Remember?" I did. Growing up, we were one of the first families in town to get a VCR, and before any video stores came to town, Laurence would be writing away to get movies sent to us. Classics, but he also had a penchant for teenager-in-peril slasher films. When Mom and Dad went into Boston for a weekend once, Laurence made Darren, Ginger, and me watch all of the *Friday the 13th* films with him. Ginger had spent most of that weekend with a pillow in front of her face. "Bean, trust me: Dickie got so sick at even the idea of blood and violence he would put his headphones on if he couldn't find anything else to do to get him out of there. He had to drop Bio in first year because he couldn't dissect anything. I'm surprised he even eats meat, come to think of it." He nodded to the sink, where the steak was still sitting in the pan.

In the distance, through the quiet night, I could hear sirens. "So Dickie definitely didn't do this."

"No," Laurence said. "Absolutely not." I believed him, but I knew there was something he wasn't telling me yet.

"But someone wants to fuck with him enough to leave a severed hand on his property, and a dead guy trussed up in his bed like an Easter ham," I said.

"And kidnap him," Laurence said.

I didn't say it, but I was hoping that's what had happened. It was dark out there. It occurred to me that Dickie could be out there somewhere, dead or dying. He might not have been in the yellow truck at all. And the yellow truck could just be a coincidence – the population was pretty small, chances are you would notice a vehicle like that around, doesn't mean it had anything to do with this. But of course it did, I knew it did. I knew that whoever was driving that truck had taken the hand and the foot of the dead man in the bed not fifteen feet from me. And he probably had Dickie.

The sirens were on top of us now, and before cops could bust through the door with guns drawn I ran outside and waved my hands in the air frantically. I hoped that no nervous trigger-happy rookie took me for the hand stealer. Be calm, move slowly, and let them see your hands, until they're sure you're one of the good guys.

And if you're not? Make like a tree and leave.

I glanced at the woods to my left, suppressing a sudden urge to do just that – run into the woods and avoid this whole mess of police and body bags and death. I didn't ask for this, not this time. I kept telling myself it had nothing to do with me.

And yet here I was.

"Fuck me," I said out loud. Someone was there. I saw something move in a sliver of moonlight. I was sure I'd seen a flash of red in the woods to my left, between Dickie's cottage and the next one down the lake. I saw it again, something red bobbing, definitely higher than animal height. Unless the deer in these parts had taken to wearing baseball caps.

And I ran.

Not back into the cottage, or up the driveway toward the sirens, like any sane person.

I ran into the woods. I ran toward the red hat in the dark.

SIX

For once when running toward danger, I wanted to make as much noise as possible.

I squatted to grab another rock on the ground and retied my Keds, keeping my eyes trained on where I had seen what I thought was the hat.

I couldn't see the flash of red any longer, now that I was ten feet into the brush. There was probably an acre or so of it between Dickie's and the next cabin, which I had noticed driving in had been dark.

I stopped moving and listened, glad I had spent my childhood playing in the Maine woods. I knew that as soon as the pounding of blood in my ears subsided, I would begin to hear life all around me – crickets and the wind moving softly through the trees, the small, distinct sounds of the creatures who lived in the woods all around. I measured the weight of the rock in my hand and stepped further in.

I wanted this to be over. I would fight whoever this was, fight and at least slow him down until the police caught up to us. Nobody deserved what had happened to that man in the cabin, whoever he was. And if this man was allowed to continue,

Dickie could be his next victim. And by extension, all the people who loved Dickie. Including my brother.

Enough pain. Enough killing. Especially of people I loved.

I heard Laurence calling my name, though even this small distance away it sounded a bit muffled. I had limited hearing in my right ear, after a fight with a bow and arrow in Maine. I had to concentrate to tell in which direction sound came from. I willed Laurence to stay where he was. I could hear the commotion of sirens and loud voices behind me near the cabin.

He was here. I could feel it, and somewhere at the base of my skull a shiver formed.

My brain told my muscles to be ready, and I quickly tensed and then consciously relaxed, like I used to do before a fight.

I took another step and heard it, the softest voice, nearly a whisper.

"Danielle," it said. And what I could have sworn was, "Go home, dear."

Something came flying through the trees and landed somewhere near me.

"In here!" I yelled over my shoulder, toward Laurence and the men with guns, and I moved carefully in the direction I thought it had come from. Closer to the lake. I saw the flash of red again, or thought I did, and then it was gone. And behind me the woods were lit up as men with powerful flashlights followed me, calling my name.

"I'm here, right here. I'm wearing a light shirt," I called. I stopped and put my hands on my head. I was glad I was wearing a white t-shirt, and hoped that my warning would mean that nobody would nervously shoot into the darkness thinking they had seen the killer.

I walked lightly back the way I had come. In the way that I sometimes knew things I couldn't explain, I knew the killer was out of my grasp for now. I kept my hands on my head and walked carefully and slowly, retracing my steps, looking for whatever had been thrown at me. From the sound it had made when it landed, it wasn't a rock. I more than half expected to see a neatly wrapped package that contained a severed foot. We're still missing a foot, I thought, looking down. I'm giving the police a hand finding the foot. Ha, ha.

But this time it wasn't a foot. And it wasn't wrapped in butcher paper.

It was a head.

And in the time it took me to sink to the ground in a faint, I registered that it belonged to Evan.

Evan, the young security guard at Rose's Place. The kid who couldn't make coffee. He should be at work. He should be at Rose's.

I backed up a few steps and let myself sink to a sitting position. The carbonation in my brain had started, and that was the last I knew.

SEVEN

Laurence had explained to the men who carried me out of the woods that I was a fainter, and that there was nothing to worry about. But to be safe they had stuck me in the back of an ambulance with a crinkly foil blanket around my shoulders, drinking lukewarm hot chocolate. But other than a sore wrist and a scraped-up forehead from the fall in the woods, I was fine.

Physically, that is.

I had seen my fair share of dead bodies. And had even been responsible for making a couple of them dead. And only the morning before, I had pulled a severed hand out of an innocent-looking mailbox.

But a head? Another thing altogether. And the fact that it had belonged to an innocent kid I had talked with nearly every day for the past two weeks was icing on the cake.

"Are you going to throw up?" a cop near me asked. He had been given the unenviable task of guarding me while police swarmed the forest. The woods and the lake were lit up with floodlights, and I watched from my vantage point high up the driveway as a diver emerged from the lake.

The only miracle was that the media wasn't here yet.

"No," I said. I managed something like a smile. "Not yet."

"She usually does, though, after a good faint," Laurence chimed in. He put his arm around me. "Don't you, Beanpole?" I nearly cried then. I leaned into him and let myself rest for a second. I had failed to catch or even slow down the killer, and now he – probably – had Dickie.

Laurence was wrong this time. I didn't feel sick. I felt like I wanted to sleep, and then I wanted to find Dickie. And get my ass back to the big city, where there was less crime. If I needed any more help staying away from crack, I'd hire someone to be my sober companion or something. It was the newest thing, and I could afford it. I'd hire somebody who knew the value of restful silence, and who liked kids. We'd hang out with the twins and shoot some hoops.

But after. After I found Dickie. If I caught the killer in the process, fair enough, but as far as I was concerned, he was the police's problem. I'm no one-woman army. I wanted to take care of my own and stay out of trouble, but apparently I couldn't even manage to do that in rural Nova Scotia.

More police arrived, and more lights. I didn't know how many people would be at their cottages yet, but the weather had been clear and fine. I heard a uniformed woman fifteen feet away talking to someone about a house-to-house search of the area, which I thought was a good idea.

Eventually a familiar face approached us as Laurence and I stood a few feet away from the ambulance to avoid any nasty accidents with oxygen and smoked cigarettes. Detective Murphy.

"You seem to have a knack," he said to me, shaking my hand. "Wrong place at the wrong time."

"Story of my life, Des," I said, causing Laurence to look at me funny. He didn't know that Des and I were old friends by now.

"How you doing? That must have been one hell of a shock. Hell of a shock." He didn't look too well himself, in fact. I didn't blame him. I patted his arm.

Des had been one of the last cops to arrive on the scene, so he hadn't been in on the initial vetting process that Laurence and I had gone through. I made the introductions, and noticed how subdued Laurence was. His oldest friend was missing, possibly – probably – in the hands of a demented killer. Tends to make the charm a little thin on the ground.

"Well you folks can leave now," Des said. "Nothing more you can do tonight, and we have an initial statement from you both. We'll want you to come in tomorrow and give videotaped statements, if you don't mind."

I nodded. "But wait," I said. "I'm supposed to be staying at Rose's. Is everyone else okay? Evan was there when we left earlier tonight."

"Right," Des said. He looked around for a minute. "Look, for now the place is locked down. The property is being searched top to bottom and everyone's being questioned." He looked at the cabin for a minute. The body hadn't been carried out yet, that I had seen. He looked back at me. "You might have a problem finding a hotel at this point. We're pretty booked up for the Apple Blossom Festival around here, plus we've got police coming from all over, and our people here have booked up as many spare rooms as we could. This might take a while."

"I have a reservation at a B and B," Laurence said. "But who knows if they held it for me." He looked at his watch. "Danny can stay with me."

Des nodded. "Good enough. But if they gave the room away, I'll tell you what. Go back to Rose's and tell them the situation, and tell them I said to give you a place to sleep there. I'm sure they can make sure a couple of rooms are safe for you."

We agreed and I shrugged off my shock blanket. "Do you know who the…" I gestured into the cabin. "The guy on the bed is?"

Des looked around him. "I can't tell you that," he said.

"Which means you do know," I said. "Please. You know my history. I need to know if this is a local." I didn't finish. I wanted to make sure this had nothing to do with me and what had happened in Maine. It seemed beyond the pale that something like this could be happening in my vicinity and not have something to do with the man who had killed my loved ones and then disappeared. In the last hour, standing outside with Laurence, it had been all I could think about. If somehow I, or the demons in my past, had brought carnage to this corner of the world – and to Laurence's oldest friend – I needed to know.

"He's a local," Des said quietly. "Was. But if I hear that on the news later, I'm going to know it came from you. You keep that to yourself, you understand?"

"Is he a friend of Dickie's?" Laurence asked quietly. "I'm sorry, I know you aren't supposed to say anything. But you must have checked up on us." Des looked at the ground, and for a minute I had a flash, a vision of him at home reading to his kids. A gentle man in a tough job, he reminded me for a minute of Paul Belliveau, the Toronto cop who had saved my skin once before. The floodlights showed the dark circles under his eyes and, despite the cool night air out on the lake, the sheen of sweat on his bald head.

Des shook his head. "One of the boys recognized him. A, uh, businessman from Halifax. Known to us." Known to police – code for *he's got a record*. "Was a resident of Rose's last year. Patient, whatever. And that's *if* that's the right guy. And that's all I'm going to say on the subject. Shouldn't have said that." But he knew we needed to know.

"Thank you," I said. I touched his arm. "Nobody else will hear that from us." He nodded. He looked miserable. "Any ideas?"

"No," he said simply. "You?" He almost smiled.

"No," I said. "But they've got Dickie."

"Dickie Doyle has been my friend since we were eighteen years old," Laurence said. "We're going to find him."

Des and I looked at him for a minute. Laurence had spoken almost as though to himself. Des brought his shoulders back, and looked like a cop all of a sudden. "In case you hadn't noticed, we've got a lunatic running around chopping people up. You'll leave this to us, sir."

"You don't think it's Dickie?" Laurence said.

"No, he doesn't," I said. I wanted to get away and think. What I did not want was for my brother to lose his temper and treat the local police like bumpkins. Counterproductive, and I liked Des.

Besides, it would make sense that Dickie would be a possible suspect, as well as possibly being a victim. The body was found in his cabin. The body of a man who had been a resident of the rehab facility that Dickie owned. And Evan had been Dickie's employee.

And while everyone knew Dickie, and there seemed to be a lot of affection for him around these parts, a lot of people think he did go a little crazy after his wife died.

"I think that if you see Dickie Doyle, Mr. Cleary, you need to head in the other direction and call us," Des said. "That's what I think." He nodded at Mary's car – Laurence's car – which had somehow been moved to the end of the driveway. Another thing I had missed.

"You two go and get some rest. We'll find you tomorrow."

"Des," I said to his back. He turned around.

"They called me Danielle," I said. "The person. The killer. Nobody calls me that. Dickie would have called me Danny." The cop nodded. I added, "And I'm not sure, but it might have been a woman."

Des opened his mouth as if to say something but thought better of it, shook his head and tried to smile. He waved goodnight in our direction and disappeared into the cabin.

EIGHT

Laurence and I drove in silence, back toward Rose's. A police cruiser followed at a respectful distance, presumably keeping us safe from any more dismembered body parts being chucked in our direction.

Evan's head. Evan. I shivered and rolled the Mustang's window up, but it wasn't the night breeze that was bothering me.

"The yellow pickup," I started to say, but Laurence shook his head.

"Thinking," he said.

Great. Just when I needed him to be chatty, he'd disappeared somewhere in his head. Normally, I respected this, but my adrenaline was still pumping and I desperately wanted to do the post-mortem on what had happened. I held out my hand and he passed me his smokes.

All the way back into town, I glanced through the rear view. I knew the cop car was there, and the chances of the yellow truck making another appearance, with law enforcement blanketing the area, was pretty much nil, but I couldn't help feeling it – or its occupants – were close by.

"Tell me about this Evan kid," Laurence finally said. We had left the dirt road behind and were on the paved descent down into town.

"I don't know much." I passed him a cigarette. "I think it's his first job. I think he was a student, maybe a grad student? Psychology or something? Very quiet-spoken kid. Seemed nervous a lot, actually."

"Nervous?" Laurence said quickly. "How?"

"I don't know. Not the most social creature. Most of the staff and counsellors tend to be pretty chatty. Evan is security, though." I took the cigarette back from Laurence and inhaled deeply, rolling the window back down.

I tried not to think about crack. I tried not to wish that the smoke I was exhaling was going to make my ears ring and my brain burst with euphoria. Instead, I coughed.

"Was," Laurence said. He gripped the steering wheel. "Was security."

I nodded. I knew the memory of seeing his head tumbling toward me, not knowing what it was, and then, in that sickening moment, realizing what I was looking at, would stay with me forever. Especially without any help in making it go away.

Say what you will about narcotics, but they do make bad stuff easier to bear. For a little while, at least, until the high wears off, and then God help you when you have to face your demons.

"Beanpole," Laurence said. "Change of plan. I'm going to stay with you at Rose's."

"Uh. Okay," I said.

"I can't face a B and B," he said. "There must be a couch somewhere. And under the circumstances, I don't think I'm going to be letting you out of my sight for the foreseeable future."

I knew he was half reading my mind. An addict's sobriety is a delicate thing at such early stages; I had been told over and over again in the last couple of weeks. And I may not be an expert on addiction recovery, but even I know that having body parts chucked at you isn't ideal when one is trying to find a peaceful place to get one's head back on straight.

"Okay," I said. "Good." I looked straight ahead, but I saw Laurence glance at me. He was probably expecting me to put up a stink about my independence and my general toughness at handling situations like these. Had I not, mere months earlier, tracked down and exacted bloody revenge on some pretty bad guys? Yes, but not wholly successfully – Michael Vernon Smith was still a free man, living under who knew what name – and I hadn't been able to stop my husband from being killed by one of his acolytes.

I watched Laurence as he skillfully drove the car and dialed the B and B to cancel. Probably against the law here as most everywhere else, driving and talking on the phone. I was pretty sure we'd get a pass, though, under the circumstances.

I was doubly glad to be keeping my brother close. That yellow truck had followed us from the airport when I picked Laurence up. I hadn't noticed it on the way there, and I think I would have; as Laurence had said, traffic in these parts was light enough that a canary-yellow pickup with tinted windows would stand out. So whoever had sped past us at the lake knew that Laurence was coming here, in all probability. And Laurence might be big and tall, but he spent his life behind a desk or in a boardroom. Like the rest of the Clearys, he did have a natural athleticism (though as our mother had always liked to say, for such a supposedly athletic group, we sure were a bunch of klutzes; none of us had ever gotten through a winter without falling on ice in the middle of the street), but I doubted he did much in the way of working out. And of all the Cleary kids, he was always the least eager to learn to shoot with Dad at the gravel pit when we were kids.

I thought of Darren and me in California. Darren had trained with guns, gone to shooting ranges when he was on the road with his band. And he had the benefit of youth and rock-star vanity on his side; he cared very much about his body and spent a good amount of time in the gym and, nowadays, doing some light sparring. Laurence had always been more cerebral and quiet, lived in his head more. Even back in high school, he excelled at track and diving, uninterested in team sports. I hadn't worried quite as much about Darren, and besides, when things started down in California, I was blinded by my grief over Ginger's murder, and, of course, by my old pal, crack cocaine. But sitting in the car with Laurence, driving down a beautiful country road that a couple of hours earlier had seemed like paradise, all I could think about was keeping Laurence safe.

No more Clearys were going to die. Nobody else I loved was going to die of anything but old age. Preferably – very preferably – after me. And if that meant that Laurence was going to be my shadow until we found Dickie, and the authorities found the killer, then fine. There were worse people I could be stuck with.

For a minute, I thought of Dave. While we hadn't started off well – he had been undercover, and I did break his nose at one point when he was holding a gun on me – in the end, he had been an ally to me when I needed one. And while I didn't know exactly what he was – undercover cop, private citizen,

Interpol, spy, whatever – he had offered to help me if I ever needed it again. From the inside of my left knee up my thigh, I had a tattoo, a beautiful mandala of color, woven into which was a telephone number that only someone inspecting the artwork very closely would be able to notice. It was Dave's emergency contact number, and for reasons I didn't fully know, it could be given to no one. I trusted Dave without knowing what or who he was, and he trusted me. The rest of the world, including members of my family, thought he could somehow be involved with Michael Vernon Smith. I knew the number by heart, though I hadn't had to call it, but I also knew that if I was in a situation where I really needed to use it, I might not be able to remember it. I knew the man who wanted revenge on me, and I knew that if he got the upper hand, I could very well be in a state where I barely remembered my own name. The tattoo was insurance, and a talisman.

I hoped very much I wouldn't need to use it.

But sitting in the car next to Laurence, driving back to Rose's, I couldn't help but think how it would be great to have him with us. And this time, I would endeavour not to break his nose.

"Something funny, Bean?" Laurence said. "Do share." I must have snorted out loud. I may have a tendency to do that when I'm lost in my own wee brain.

"Just thinking about the time I broke Dave's nose with my elbow when we were at Joshua Tree with Darren, going to meet Fred and that fucking cop," I said. I never mentioned Miller's name.

"Good times," Laurence said. "Also, interesting. This Dave guy pops up in your thoughts often, does he? Hmm?" He wiggled his eyebrows, which made me happy. Things couldn't be too, too dire if my brother was wiggling his eyebrows at me. Fact.

"Phhhffft," I said, eloquent as usual. Note to self, I thought: Don't let Laurence see my thigh, ever. He was a puzzle-meister; if anybody could see a phone number in the pattern, it would be my big brother.

"You guys emailing? Keeping in touch? Exchanging recipes and so forth?"

"Drive the car, dickwad," I said. "And, no. We are not. So don't get any fancy ideas of hacking into my email and seeing if you can get his contact info to give to the Feds. And you know," I added, "if he really had anything to do with Michael Vernon Smith, I'd be dead by now. So put that in your pipe and smoke it." Then I laughed. Pipes. Smoking. Rehab.

"God," he said. "Everything comes down to drugs with you, doesn't it," he said, and I swatted his arm. He held out his hand for the cigarette pack. "Home sweet home," he said. We pulled into the driveway of Rose's, waved past by the cop at the end of the drive, past the news trucks and yet another ambulance.

"And the evening started so well," I said. "Welcome to Nova Scotia."

Laurence turned into the parking area and turned off the engine.

Two ambulance attendants were carrying a body bag on a gurney, out of the back door and into the back of their vehicle.

"No lights," I said, nodding at the ambulance. My mouth was dry. "It's a body."

"Dickie," Laurence said, and bolted from the car.

NINE

One of my fellow residents, a former dancer called Sarah who had a problem with pain meds after years of cartilage damage slaving away in the *corps de ballet*, had made her nightly pilgrimage to the basement to smoke a joint. Upon discovering that the light had burned out, she used the flashlight function on her phone to descend the stairs. Apparently she was planning to grab the joint and lighter she'd left in a baggie behind the canned goods and crouch on the stairs to have a quick toke before bed.

When she got to the foot of the rickety wooden stairs – the basement was more of a cellar, used for storage and supposedly off-limits to residents, with damp walls and a very low ceiling – poor Sarah made the mistake of shining her light straight ahead to where she was going, instead of the floor in front of her. She was used to the room, and moving quickly, she said.

Of course you were, dear, I wanted to say. You were on your way for your nightly fix.

"I tripped over something. I fell flat on my face," she said. We were sitting in the kitchen, all of us: three police, half a dozen residents, a female counsellor whose name I could never remember, and Laurence and me. She showed us her scraped elbows and forearms. She had a smear of blood on her forehead, but I didn't want to tell her. I doubted it was hers. "Well, on my arms. And then I thought I heard something behind me, some noise, and I have no idea why I didn't scream. No idea."

I didn't, either. When Sarah, terrified, had scrabbled around on the cement floor and found her phone, she turned it back to the foot of the stairs where she had fallen.

The noise she'd heard was a rat. A rat, feasting on what was left of the body of Evan Sinclair.

"I didn't know it was Evan, though," Sarah continued. She was chain smoking in the non-smoking kitchen, and shaking a bit, but I had to hand it to the girl; there were no hysterics, no tears. She'd probably had those kinds of emotions drilled out of her at ballet boot camp, I thought, looking at her. She was in her late twenties, a bit younger than me, and while she had the body of a fourteen-year-old gymnast, she had a face that had seen things.

Then again, at Rose's, most of us did.

"I don't remember getting up the stairs," she said. "I just know I was up here and calling 911 and then… everybody was here." She nodded at the police and looked outside, where the ambulance had been. "Why would somebody do that to Evan? Do you know?" She was looking at one of the cops in the room, the oldest one. Not friendly-looking. Not Des Murphy.

"Not yet, miss, but we will," he said. He looked long and hard at Laurence and me. He seemed to be sizing us up, wondering if we could have done the deed, driven out to Ferryman Lake and left Evan's head in the woods, while I pretended someone had thrown it in my direction. I looked back at him, keeping my face neutral. I wanted to say, *You can try to intimidate me all you want, honey, but I've had men a lot tougher than you try to shake me up.* I wanted to sit him down and tell him the whole story, from soup to nuts, but I'd already done that with Des, and I didn't feel much like getting into it again. A poor kid who didn't seem like he could do any harm to anybody had been killed, decapitated, directly underneath where we all sat.

When we had first arrived, once we learned that it was not, in fact, Dickie in the body bag, the cop had taken us aside and said he knew about what had happened at the cabin. I imagined that every cop and reporter in this part of the country probably knew all about this by now. I closed my eyes for a second, hoping that my name would be staying out of this story. Somehow, I knew I wouldn't be so lucky. I sighed out loud.

"Is Des coming here?" I asked.

"Sergeant Murphy is leading the search at Mr. Doyle's property at"—he looked at his notebook; he couldn't be a local—"Ferryman Lake."

"And no one has found Dickie?" Laurence said. He had already asked, and the cop looked like he resented being asked.

"No. Mr. Doyle is still at large."

"'At large' suggests that you think he's a suspect," Laurence said.

The cop didn't say anything, just kept staring. He really needed a new schtick. The long cold looks were getting pretty old already.

I thought of the rat in the basement, feasting on Evan, and I suddenly felt the carbonation start in my brain, the pre-faint nausea. I quickly stuck my head between my knees.

"Ms. Cleary?" the cop was saying, but I waved him away. I sat up quickly, my vision blurring a bit. I tried to bite down the nausea.

"Wait a minute," I said. "The forensics guys are down in the basement, right?" I obviously hadn't ventured down there – not that I'd wanted to; I was happy to take everybody else's word on what it looked like – but we could hear voices downstairs, and there were lights set up at the top of the basement stairs. "So they must know – was Evan killed here? Or somewhere else and brought here?"

"I'm afraid that's confidential to the investigation," he said. He smiled, a nasty sort of smirk. "You might have a reputation down south, but you do know that you have nothing official to do with this investigation. We don't want any Nancy-Drew-meets-the-Manson-family antics here."

My heart started pounding, and I wanted to punch him. For a minute, it took every single ounce of whatever limited self-control I possessed to stay in my chair. Great, I thought. He's heard about the freak show that happened in Maine, and he's one of those law enforcement types who hates private investigators. I didn't even bother pointing out that I wasn't one; half the papers had identified me that way, and who was I to argue with the media. Or maybe he just hated women who could handle themselves. In any event, he was obviously a jackass.

And either way, I didn't trust myself to speak without saying things that could get me into trouble. And trouble was something I didn't need any more of.

Crack, however, I could use. I would be very, very happy to have some crack.

"Excuse me?" Laurence said quietly. He sounded remarkably

like our father when he was about to tear a strip off somebody. "Listen, I am not sure who you think you are, or who you're talking to here." He held his hand up to stop the man from interjecting. "You are either a rude idiot, or simply misinformed. So let me help you out, and make a couple of things clear." The hairs on the back of my neck stood up. This was my brother, the power broker. This was his boardroom voice. He hadn't risen quickly through the ranks of high-end cable television in New York City because he was a pushover. "My sister was a hero, and risked her own life to save the lives of our nephews, who had been kidnapped by an evil man and his followers. Our sister – her *twin*," he continued, and I couldn't look at him, I knew I would cry if I did, "was brutally murdered by these people, and her husband Jack MacRae was also killed by them, in front of her, while trying to rescue our nephews. Our other brother was nearly fatally wounded by these people, and Danielle was kidnapped and drugged, along with our late sister's husband and their sons. She managed to rescue both of our twin nephews – children, we're talking about here – from these people. So don't you dare speak to her that way again. Officer." He said the word with the same inflection I might use to call someone a fuckwad. I glanced up and it looked like everyone in the room, residents and cops, had their mouths hanging open. I could feel eyes on me, and tried to refrain from sticking my head back between my knees.

Crack, please.

"We, her family, helped choose this particular place for her to recover, after everything she has endured, because I roomed with Richard Doyle at Bennington, and we kept up a friendship over the years."

Oh, he was *Richard* Doyle now. From Bennington. And I was Danielle, all of a sudden. I thanked God Laurence was on my side. And found myself thinking he was wasted on the cable TV world; he should have been a lawyer.

"After my sister discovered the… body part on the property here, I wanted to come and be close to her. She has gone through far too much in the last year to be handling such a shock on her own." Now, I was trying not to sob like a baby. I thought it would look bad, though, since that Sarah chick had managed to keep her composure after tripping over a headless corpse being eaten by a rat.

"And in my communications with Mr. Doyle in the last months, while securing a place for Danielle here at Rose's, he had mentioned to me that he thinks he is being followed."

I looked at Laurence quickly. This was what he wasn't telling me. Why hadn't he told me this?

The arrogant cop started to say something, but Laurence held up his hand. "He didn't advise the authorities, no. Mr. Doyle has suffered with major depression and anxiety since his wife died. He finds it difficult to talk to anyone at the best of times, and he is aware that because of his lifestyle choices and what have you, he may have a reputation around here as… eccentric."

Lifestyle choices. For some people, living in that little cabin with an outhouse, when he could afford nearly anything he wanted, would be enough to deem him crazy. And I was pretty sure that Laurence was a bit worried about that himself, whatever he might be saying now.

Laurence leaned across the table and grabbed Sarah's pack of cigarettes, shot her one of his smiles, lit one for himself, and another for her. Sarah gazed at him like she wanted to eat him for breakfast. With whipped cream.

"Richard Doyle is one of the most gentle people I have ever had the pleasure of knowing, and would never – could never – hurt anyone. He built this place to help people. Not only would he never kill anyone, he would not disappear from his home like that, knowing I was coming to visit. With, by the way, dinner still cooking. He's very sensitive to the feelings of others, particularly since his wife died. If you are making him your only suspect, instead of looking for him as a, I don't know, hostage, or a victim of this madman who's killing and dismembering people, then you are lazy and even more stupid than you look."

Ouch. I may be a hothead, but even I knew that was going a bit far and wouldn't do anybody any favors. Fortunately, I was pretty sure it wasn't against the law to call a police officer stupid and lazy. Reckless and counterproductive, abso-fucking-lutely, but illegal, no.

One of the other cops in the room cleared his throat, and I looked up from the table, where I had been curling and uncurling a bamboo placemat instead of running around turning the house upside down in case some previous addict-slash-resident had left a wee rock of crack lying around. It was a novelty for me, not being the person in the room who went too far. I snuck a glance at our new cop friend, but he was looking at the door.

"Thank you, Mr. Cleary," Des said. I didn't know how long he had been standing there; my hearing loss in one ear made me miss sound behind me sometimes, and there was noise still coming from the open basement door. "I'm sure you've given Staff Sergeant Lester a lot to think about." He looked like he was trying to hide a flicker of amusement, and I got the impression he and Lester weren't beer buddies. But more, he looked haggard, and even possibly a little scared. "For the time being, Mr. Doyle is a missing person. Not a person of interest. At this time," he added. Person of interest. Cop speak for suspect.

Lester looked like he wanted to belt Des, but he said nothing.

Laurence stood up. He was white. "What did you find?" he said.

Des shook his head slightly, and spoke to the group in the kitchen, the residents – and I didn't know if anybody else was upstairs; there had been a dozen of us before I'd found the hand in the mailbox. Probably some people had already cleared out.

"Thank you all for your patience. We know this has been a horrific and trying time for all of you." He rubbed his forehead. He looked exhausted. "The house has been cleared – there is no one here that shouldn't be, and you can rest assured that there will be a police presence inside and on the grounds in the days to come, both from local detachments and from our Major Crime Unit." I didn't know about anybody else, but I was glad to hear it. Unless the police presence was going to include this Lester character, in which case I might be happier pitching a tent in the woods, killer or no killer. "We've gotten initial statements from those of you who are here, but I'm afraid there will also be formal statements taken at the station in the next day or two. We'll inform you of that schedule tomorrow. Those of you who have other places you can stay in the area are free to do so, as long as you give that information to one of the men here and you don't stray too far."

So much for my sober-living companion back in Toronto.

"Ideally, we would put you all up at a local hotel, but as you may be aware, there's no room at the inn. Inns," he said. He almost laughed. One of the cops did; a short yelping giggle which made him go red. "This is the number one tourist holiday of the year in the Valley here, with the Apple Blossom Festival on. So while this is a crime scene, we would ask you to confine yourselves to your rooms and the bathrooms and what have you, the kitchen here. And the dining hall, of course. The other buildings will be off limits for the time being. Your meetings or group… things, perhaps you could hold here in this room, or in the living room.

"Needless to say, the, uh, cellar is off limits."

"No worries there," one guy said. He had tattoos on his neck and a thick Australian accent. I didn't think I'd ever heard him speak before. He obviously wasn't good at Sharing either.

Des clapped his hands once, a meeting-over gesture. "Thank you all for your cooperation, and as I say, you'll all be safe. There'll be law enforcement everywhere you look, and no doubt this situation will be resolved lickety-split."

People started to slowly rise from chairs, and the counsellor – Janet, that was her name – herded some of the residents into the living room for a chat. I declined. Laurence was still standing, still looking at Des for answers.

"Go upstairs, would you, and have a look around," Des said to the uniforms. "Answer any questions, be visible." They looked relieved to have something to do.

Lester, Laurence, Des, and I remained in the kitchen.

"What happened?" Laurence said again. "Please."

Des motioned for us all to follow him outside onto the back porch. It was much colder now, and late. Laurence put his arm around me, and I leaned into him. I hated the reason he was here, but was grateful he had come.

Des pulled a pack of American cigarettes from his breast pocket. He lit one and looked at the sky.

"I know Dickie Doyle myself, you know," he said to Laurence. "Not well, not like you do. But back in the day, my wife Sheila and his Rose became friends. They used to swim together at the Acadia pool." I could tell Laurence wanted to hurry him up, and I pressed his arm and shook my head a bit. "Four of us used to go camping sometimes, down to Keji. Canoeing, bonfires, the whole bit. Never knew he went to Bennington." Lester looked like he was trying to suppress a yawn. Theatrically.

"Anyway, I've seen Dickie without his shirt on, when we were out on the lake. I've seen his tattoo."

"I didn't know he had a tattoo," Laurence said. "It never came up. I mean, I haven't seen him with his shirt off since we roomed together."

"Well, it would have been since then. He got it when he married Rose. A big letter R, right here," Des said, and indicated his chest, over his heart. "Sheila was after me to get one, and I said, 'Honey, why do you want me to get an R on my chest?'" I smiled at him. I knew something bad was coming, but I smiled at Des. You had to like him.

"We found that tattoo tonight, Mr. Cleary," Des said. He cleared his throat. "We found it, and a good chunk of flesh around it, stapled to the sign at the end of Dickie's driveway at the lake."

Oh God. "The 'Rose' sign," I said.

"Yes," Des said. "'Rose', with skin tattooed with the letter R stapled neatly underneath." Nobody moved. I felt like I couldn't breathe for a minute. "And you want to know the oddest goddamn thing? When the crime scene techs came out there, they photographed everything, including that sign on their way in. They're damn anal, those people. And that's good, they're supposed to be. It wasn't until I was leaving to come here that something made me turn around and look, and I saw it." He lit another cigarette off the first one.

"Jesus, Mary, and Joseph," I said. "So when all those cops and everybody was there…"

"How's that for you?" Des said. "Bold as brass. I got the forensic people out there right away and in the meantime I must have taken a dozen pictures of that thing. And I looked at the photos they took a while earlier, and sure enough, the damn thing wasn't there. Checked it myself."

"Fuck me," Lester said, and it sounded like the least snarky thing he'd said all night. He looked up at Laurence, who was about a foot taller than he was. "You okay there, sir?" He reached for Laurence's arm.

Suddenly I was supporting some of my brother's weight. "No, but thank you," Laurence said. "And I'm sorry for the way I spoke to you earlier."

He started to cry, quietly. I realized I had never seen anything make Laurence cry. Not when our parents died. Not when Ginger was murdered. But this had. Dickie Doyle had.

TEN

By the time my head hit the pillow, the sky was starting to turn from black to a faint gray. I lay still and listened to hear if Laurence's breathing had changed, whether he was asleep yet.

He had called the B and B and told them he wouldn't be coming, but told them to bill his credit card anyway. In the end, he phoned them again and transferred it to Sarah the dancer, with his compliments. He and I were going to stay together, and apparently at the inn they only had one queen bed per room. I love my brother, but sharing a bed with him, unless under duress, was pushing it. At Rose's, I had a large private room – all the rooms were private, each with its own en suite bath – but we wheeled in a bed from one of the abandoned rooms. When we were sure we were settled in for the night, Laurence moved his bed length-wise against the door and fiddled with the castors so it wouldn't move, all without a word.

I wasn't complaining. In the last two days I'd seen and heard enough to know that Rose's Place was about as safe as a psychiatric hospital during a power cut. Police presence or not, I had no gun and no idea who I was up against. My big brother barring the door and a purloined screwdriver, snatched from a drawer in the resident's kitchen before bed, tucked into a fanny pack under my t-shirt made me feel a bit better. A nice little automatic handgun would have done the trick even better. Though considering what we seemed to be dealing with here, perhaps something with a blade was the order of the day.

Note to self: See where one could buy a machete in town.

Of course, unlike some of my past adventures, this time it didn't feel strictly personal to me – whoever killed Evan and the man in Dickie's cabin – not to mention maimed Dickie – could probably have taken me out before now if I was a target. Instead, I got a head hurled in my direction and – was my newly clean brain playing tricks on me? – almost kind-sounding words about going home. But whatever was going on, it was centred around Rose's Place and Dickie Doyle. Not only was I a resident of Rose's, but my brother was one of Dickie's oldest friends.

"You asleep?" Laurence said.

"No." I stared at the ceiling in the dark, deciding whether to go downstairs and have a cigarette on the porch.

"It's not what you think, Danny," he said. I saw something blue glow in the dark. Laurence was using my e-cig.

"Isn't it?" I said. "*Larry.*" And for some reason I started giggling. I turned over onto my side, facing his bed.

"I really wanted the Mustang," he said, and started laughing too. It felt so good to hear him laugh. Then I thought of Evan, and the laughter seemed to die in my throat.

"Did you and Dickie ever fool around?" I asked quietly. Laurence was quiet. "You know. Back at Bennington. Some drunken night, sharing a room." I thought of his tears. I wondered.

I heard him sigh. "Straight people seem to think all gay

people want to have sex with them, all the time." I didn't say anything, just watched the blue end of the cigarette and waited for my brother to talk. "No. That's not fair. Dickie actually wasn't like that. Back at school, I mean," he added quickly, and I knew what he meant. He didn't want to refer to Dickie in the past tense. Bad juju. "For a guy coming from such a blue-blooded family, a guy who played rugby and all that, he wasn't what I expected."

"So. Did you ever…?" I wouldn't normally be so delicate, but this was new territory, and as we lay in our beds on Dickie Doyle's property, where earlier tonight, a couple of floors below us, a young man's headless body had been discovered, the chances of him still being among the living seemed slim indeed.

Particularly after the news about the R tattoo on the sign.

"God, no," my brother said. "Danny, it's not like that. Really. I don't love Dickie like that. Not sexually." He sat up. "Is that really what you were thinking? You know I have a type."

"Old?" I said.

"We don't get to choose what turns our crank, little sister," he said.

"True."

"But I do love him. Almost… romantically."

"Jesus, Laurence. Do you want to spoon him? What? I don't get it."

"Romantic, as in the knights. With a k," he hastened to add. "Just let me— Look, Dickie and I were in a class together first year. Or no, it must have been second. Whatever. Chivalric romance, medieval notions of courtly love and so on. Feudal bonds of loyalty and tribalism and staying true in adversity." It was getting lighter in the room, and if you could ignore the horrific events of the past days, there was something comforting about this, lying in the early dawn light, listening to my brother – not the most forthcoming of creatures – talk like this. We were both propped up on our elbows.

"I remember the class itself less than I remember Dickie and I sitting up talking about it," he said. "We were both outsiders in our own ways, and this idea of two men being bonded by something like honor and fealty, loyalty in the face of any adversity – well, for whatever reason it resonated with both of us. Filial love."

"Like family," I said.

"Like *we* see family," Laurence said. "Most families aren't like us. Especially like you."

"And if you choose someone, when you're young like that, and make a pledge to them or whatever it is you and Dickie did – I get it," I said. "I think. It could be even stronger than family, especially if you're not close to family. Or stronger than a marriage, since there isn't a sexual component, so this loyalty, this bond, is a choice. A test of your word and your worth as a man."

"Like men who go into battle together," Laurence said. "Look, the point is, I'm glad you understand. If anybody should understand loyalty, it's you, Beanpole."

"Suppose so," I said quietly, looking out the window. I didn't want to think anymore. I wanted to go to sleep, and not see blood. Anyone's blood. Or bloody human skin attached to signs in the woods. I sighed, closed my eyes.

"Bean," Laurence was saying. "Do you trust this Murphy guy? Des?"

"Mmm," I said. I wanted to be fully asleep before the room

became any more light, and my circadian rhythm told me it was time for my run. "Think so."

"Because Dickie – he's been sounding paranoid lately. Well, I thought he was paranoid. Apparently not. He told me he's been seeing Rose," he said. "At the lake. And feeling like he's being followed, like I said."

I could feel blessed sleep crawling into my body. I'm still recovering, I wanted to say. I wanted to say it to Laurence, to the police downstairs, to the person who threw a dismembered head at me. I'm still recovering. I'm in rehab to get better. I'm supposed to sleep ten hours a day, and eat healthy food, and go for easy runs and do bad art projects. I'm supposed to get used to my leg being in pain, and not being able to take anything for it. I'm supposed to get used to the fact that I can only hear properly on one side. That my twin sister is dead, and my husband is dead, and I've killed people, and I'm not supposed to be able to smoke crack anymore to escape any of this.

No, I thought. For probably the first time in my life, I wanted to cover my ears against my brother. I just wanted to be left alone, to sleep, to escape. If I couldn't sleep to escape, I was going to need drugs. Simple as that. It came into my head just like that, almost with a cartoon light bulb. If anyone expects me to handle any other fucking thing, I am going to need crack to do it. Otherwise, world, leave me the fuck alone to recover.

Here I was, in rural fucking Nova Scotia, and this shit had found me here. Where did I have to go to get away from blood and death and murder? Iceland? Ant-fucking-arctica?

"Bean?" Laurence was whispering. I played dead. I breathed deeply and let sleep take me. Someone else could stand watch over the dawn. This wasn't my fight. But I would help. I would help tomorrow.

When I woke up, the sun was high in the sky.

Someone, somewhere, screamed. I sat up.

Laurence was up and out; his bed was neatly made and moved out of the way of the door.

Footsteps were coming for my room, and I could tell they were too light to be my brother's. It sounded like they were trying to be quiet. They paused outside the door, and I waited for a knock.

Instead, I saw the doorknob turn.

ELEVEN

Laurence had locked the door behind him.

I patted my waist to make sure the screwdriver was still in the fanny pack, and went for the window silently, barefoot, grateful that I had removed the screen on the first night, when I wanted to sit in the window to smoke, not wanting to sit outside with the others to socialize.

I swung myself out of the window and hoisted myself onto the steeply pitched dormer arch above it, my feet quickly getting hot from the shingles. All I had on was a Joy Division t-shirt and an old pair of Jack's boxers that I liked to sleep in. And a fanny pack. I perched on my hands and knees then, and for one hysterical moment I realized how ridiculous I must look, trying to surf the roof barely clothed, thinking a screwdriver was going to be lethal enough to defend myself against whoever was cutting people's bodies up.

I looked at the ground. For one mad second, I just wanted to take a header. I wasn't high enough to guarantee anything but broken bones any other way but head first. Then again, even a header from the second floor might just mean a broken neck and a lifetime of eating all my food through a straw. I had

had enough of this, of adrenaline and death and wondering if someone was trying to kill me, or worse, the people I loved. Of struggling through my days without Ginger or Jack. Or crack.

No, Danny. Fight.

Ginger's voice, as clear as if she was perched next to me.

I felt shame, then, as though I had run from a burning building, leaving people inside to die. I closed my eyes and felt it again, the rage that had gotten me through my time in southern California, my time in Maine, when Ginger and Jack were dead and I had to find the boys. I couldn't be sure that what was happening right now wasn't my fault, somehow. Would any of this be happening if I hadn't come here? So far it didn't seem like it, but this was the place that my family had sent me. Pain and death followed me, this I knew. This was a fact. And my brother needed me, not only to help find Dickie, but possibly to save his own skin.

And I had climbed out a window, sitting above it all on a roof like a coward, when people around me were dropping like flies.

I looked out. My room was at the back of the building, looking toward the Bay of Fundy. There was nothing to see but a beautiful early summer day and Cape Blomidon in the distance. A couple of cars were parked below me – I could see The Beast, Mary's Mustang, below, so Laurence was probably still here. I breathed deeply, trying to calm myself. There was one police cruiser, but no officers calling me off the roof, no residents pointing up at me. No people.

Except, perhaps, for someone in my room, directly below me.

Whatever was happening was happening – whatever had

made someone scream – around the front of the building, or at least off where I couldn't see. I turned my head and put a hand over my bad right ear to see if I could better isolate the sounds. No more screaming, but I could hear a siren in the distance – another one; the events around Rose's were certainly giving first responders in the Valley a hopping week – and lots of excited voices. Someone was crying. At least I thought so.

I could hear nothing from my room below me. I crept forward and leaned down, hoping to be able to see in without falling off the roof.

Then a head popped out my window, with a dark-red ponytail.

"Mary," I called out, and she let out a short shriek and looked up, too much of her body outside the safety of the window. "Get inside, I'm coming in," I said.

"Jesus fucking Christ, what are you doing up there?" she said. "You just about gave me a coronary."

"The view," I said. I smiled at her, both of us looking at each other upside down. I was calm. I climbed out of windows barely clothed every day, as far as she knew. "Gorgeous day." I looked into the distance with a hand over my eyes as though to block the sun, Lewis and Clark-style. Yes. So cool.

"Are you trying to kill yourself or something? Please tell me you're not up there to kill yourself." Mary leaned even further to see, and I was worried she would slide out, all ninety pounds of her, down to the paving stones below.

"Get inside! No, I'm not trying to kill myself!" I started to move, to adjust my position so I could climb down and swing my legs inside the window once she moved out of the way. At which point, of course, I realized that a couple of the shingles were loose, and the gutter piping was rusty and full of wet leaves from who knew how long ago.

Note to self: If we all live through this, tell Dickie he needs to drop a few bucks on some maintenance around here. In the meantime, however, it was clear that getting in might be harder than getting out was, and that climbing out windows before I had a chance to fully wake up and assess the situation was not, perhaps, my smartest move.

"Stay there, Danny, don't you budge," Mary yelled out, as though I was a hundred feet away. "I'll get the fire department. We need the ladder. We need some men. You try to climb back in here, you'll break your goddamn neck."

"I'll be fine," I started to say, but her head popped back inside. And the window slammed shut.

Great. No ledge under the window meant no way to open it from the outside. Couldn't swing myself in, even if I had been able to manage it, without taking a header after all. Which would be ironic, and probably what I deserved.

Mary had probably just come in to see if I was there and to tell me about whatever was happening. Probably sent by Laurence, in fact. And now, whatever was going on around front would be disturbed by the need to come and rescue one of the residents from the roof. It would probably get written up in the local paper as a suicide attempt. And with my luck, my name would be on the front page: NOTORIOUS P.I. ATTEMPTS SUICIDE AT REHAB.

My name in the papers again. Michael Vernon Smith possibly knowing where I was. Presuming, as I was, that he was hopefully thousands of miles away and had nothing to do with what was going on with Dickie Doyle and Rose's Place, I'm sure he had all his search engines set to ding him if my name popped up anywhere. He would always want to know where I was, just as I would always be looking for him around every corner.

I sat on the roof and cursed the security consultants we had hired. Shouldn't someone have told me that I should have booked in here – registered anywhere, in fact – under a false name? I thought of Darren and Fred and the boys in Toronto. They were as safe as money could make them, but I knew that Darren would probably never relax until we knew Michael Vernon Smith was behind bars. Or preferably, six feet under.

I crossed myself. I didn't want to wish death on anyone else, ever again. I didn't want to have anything to do with making anyone else dead. Sometimes I thought about my soul, if it would be possible to wash myself clean of what I had done. And then I would remind myself that I'm not Catholic; but with the amount of sin I knew I had to be forgiven for, I sometimes thought about converting. I daydreamed, sometimes, about how comforting it would be to go to confession and pay penance and be forgiven.

But then again, I figured I paid penance every day, with Ginger and Jack dead, and my constant desire for crack cocaine whispering in my ear. I sat on the roof and thought about it. I could try to be good. I would try to be good. But there are those of us in life whose job is to carry the burden of others. I never wanted Darren to do what he had done in California; he carried a burden too. But if I could help it, I would spare Laurence – and for that matter, anyone else I cared for, anyone good, whose life had never been tainted like mine had – from seeing and doing evil.

Not doing crack was a penance. It was pain. But it was pain

I would endure, as long and as much as I could, to make the people who loved me happier. We all have that responsibility, to try to spare our loved ones pain, or even to spare good people pain. Mary was good, of that I was sure, even after our short acquaintance. I was pretty sure Dickie Doyle was good – my brother was an excellent judge of character, and from what I knew about Dickie, with him living in his little cabin and pouring his money into a rehab facility to help others, he was living his own penance for what had happened to his wife. And having had the monkey on my back myself for so long, I was the first to know that no one can be responsible for another person's addiction. Rose Doyle had died an unnecessary and ignominious death because of her own predilections – whatever may have gone on in their marriage, no one starts hooking for opiate money unless they have that special cocktail of psychology and brain chemistry that makes pain reduction in the form of narcotics or alcohol seem as necessary to survival as air.

I heard Laurence calling my name, and I looked down.

He was lighting a cigarette. From where I sat, I thought I could see his hands shaking, but his voice was even. "Nice day," he called up.

"Beautiful," I said, and nodded. "Thought I'd catch some sun."

"It's true, you're a little pale," Laurence said. He didn't take his eyes off me.

"What's happening?" I said. I jerked my arm behind me, indicating the commotion at the front of the building, and two of the shingles I was sitting on started sliding, taking me with them. I caught myself easily with my feet on the slanted roof. "Whoopsie," I said.

"Let's just get you down," another voice called up, and there was Mary's nephew Colin the cop, with another cop and someone who looked like an EMT. They were carrying a long ladder.

"Place needs new shingles," I called down. Des appeared around the corner and I waved at him. "Just wanted to get a better look at your beautiful view here." Mary came trotting toward Laurence in her heels and grabbed his arm. She said something to him I couldn't hear, and he smiled.

"Mary wants to know if you're accident prone," Laurence called up to me, as Colin and the other men extended the ladder and put it in place.

"No offence, Danny," Mary yelled up, again like she was shouting across a great distance. She slapped Laurence's arm. "He wasn't supposed to repeat that. I just meant with the fainting and everything."

Colin was climbing up the ladder as though he was going to lift me off the roof himself, fireman-style. Two other men stood at the bottom of the ladder and looked up. The EMT, I could not help noticing, was very good-looking. Of course. And me in my dead husband's boxers. Very revealing, unflattering boxers at that. I've never tried to be a sex bomb, but this was ridiculous.

"Not to worry, Mary," I said. "Nothing I haven't heard before." As a matter of fact, despite my general physical confidence, I did have an aversion to going down ladders. Or, in general, to climbing down things. I was always a climber as a kid, unable to resist the urge to scramble up trees as high as I could go, but I always had to talk myself into the climbing down part. I used to love to climb the ladder on the high diving board at the pool, and got a rush out of sailing through the air, off the board. But climbing down the same ladder? Pass.

I had a moment of pure embarrassment, during which I debated scrambling across to the front of the building – which would mean climbing higher, across more potentially sketchy shingles and who knew what else – and just jumping from some unobtrusive spot on the other side. But then I remembered my healing leg, and the thought of re-breaking it – and the embarrassment of not getting over there to jump before the group assembled below me could run over to witness it – made me move. I crab-walked down to the ladder, waved Colin down ahead of me, and managed to swing myself onto it, hoping my face wasn't as red as it felt.

"Well, that was fun," I said, when I reached the bottom, trying not to sound shaky. "Seriously? The roof needs repairs, and the gutters really need cleaning."

"Oh, Lord, Geoffrey was supposed to be taking care of all that," Mary said. She looked pale, for her. Mary was the type of woman who liked a year-round tan. "My husband? But he's been laid up lately. He has MS," she said to me. "Some days are better than others."

Colin looked at the ground, I sputtered an apology, and the EMT just stood there looking uncomfortable. Des was there, pacing.

"Never mind that," Mary said. "We all have our troubles. Poor Sarah."

"Sarah?" My heart started to pound. "What happened to Sarah? Isn't she at the B and B?" The young dancer who had found Evan last night. Laurence had given her his room, so she'd feel safe.

"She never made it there," Des said. He looked at me. "One

of my men drove her there and watched while she walked up to the place. It's sort of on a hill. There's a staircase to get up there, and then the house, the B and B, is back about fifty, sixty yards. She waved when she got to the top of the stairs to say she got there safely."

"When I woke up, I checked my messages," Laurence cut in. "The woman who runs the place had called, wondering where her guest was. She'd heard about all the troubles out here, I guess, and she didn't want to sound too irate, but she obviously wanted to go to bed."

"Somewhere between the top of those stairs and the front door of the house, she disappeared," Des finished. "The officer who took her there is – well, he's very upset. He knew he should have walked her right in, but he was tired, worked a double yesterday, and his knee has been giving him troubles lately, he said. He didn't want to do the stairs." It was pretty obvious what Des thought about that. He looked like murder.

I felt a flash of pity for whoever this poor cop was. If Sarah didn't turn up alive and well – and really, what were the chances of that; she'd been exhausted, didn't know the area, and didn't have a vehicle – he was going to have to live with that guilt for the rest of his life. Forget his career, which would go nowhere even if he managed to keep his job. But knowing that his moment of laziness may have cost a young woman her life would never leave him.

"No sign of her?" My voice sounded funny to myself. Harder than it had been in a while. Maybe it was my wonky hearing, but the voice I heard was the one I used when I was on my rampage months earlier. The voice that had softened, in the past couple of months of recuperating at Skip and Marie's, and then being here.

Des shook his head. "We've got teams searching everywhere. We'll have volunteers searching by nightfall."

"Where?" I said. "Where are you looking?"

"That's the problem, isn't it," he said. "We've got very little. This place, and the area at the lake around Dickie's cabin. The area around where she was probably taken."

"There's a fair amount of wild land around here," Colin said.

I looked at Laurence. "This ends now," I said. "No more." Laurence locked eyes with me. He knew what I meant. He knew I'd decided to do whatever I could to stop this. Just like I could read his body language, he knew me inside and out. I could feel that my posture was different. My breathing, even. I twirled my bad ankle around a bit as I stood there, testing how strong it was, what I could make it do. I was glad I'd been running and improving my cardio a bit. All of this went through my mind in the time it took me to say the words.

No more death. No more chaos. No more killing. Not around me and mine.

Luckily, no one else standing there, on that beautiful day, could read me like my brother could.

"Maybe you two could join the search later today," Des was saying. "We're going to need a lot of volunteers."

"Absolutely," I said. "Count us in." I started walking toward the back door.

"Where are you going?" Mary said. "I think we should be on a buddy system. Nobody should go anywhere alone."

I smiled at her. "I'm going to get dressed and see if there's some food left in the dining hall," I said, nodding at the smaller building about two hundred feet from the dorms.

"I couldn't eat a thing," Mary said. "I'd like to throw up. All this…"

"Get something to eat, Auntie," Colin said to her. "You need to keep up your strength."

"Listen to him, Mare," Laurence said, as I strode toward the back door. "We'll meet you over there in a bit. I'm going to take care of some things while she gets changed."

Laurence followed me inside and when we were alone in the kitchen, I turned to him. I spoke in a low voice. "Quickly. Grab a few sharp knives, but not too big, and preferably ones that have sleeves or sheaths, if you can find them. Put them in your pockets, but make sure nobody sees you." I headed toward the stairs and turned. "And a corkscrew if there is one," I added quietly. "If they have more than one, grab them all."

"You want wine at a time like this?" he said. "Danny."

"No, fuckbrain, I don't." I turned and looked at him, and just nodded.

I took the stairs two at a time, and went to get ready.

TWELVE

I was grateful, looking through the things I'd thrown into the drawers in my room when I'd arrived, that I was a little high when I got packed, and angry at the people who had broken my family. Since I'd been at Rose's I'd been living in leggings, band tees, hoodies, and my running shoes. But I'd also packed jeans and Docs and some fighting gear – wraps and gloves and even shin guards, in case I found a decent gym in the area.

Or in case I needed to fight.

A two-minute shower with a shim firmly under my locked bathroom door, then I threw on black cargo pants and steel-toes and a tank with a long-sleeve shirt over the top. Layers aren't only good for changing weather, but can protect you from things that can slow you down; anything from cuts and scrapes to providing an extra layer of padding in case of any kind of hand-to-hand combat. Not to mention, I didn't know what kind of terrain I'd encounter in the search for Sarah. This area had everything from rocky beaches and boggy marshes to green farmland and dense woods going up the mountains that bracketed the Valley. Versatility was the order of the day.

I was aware, when packing, that everything I brought would

be carefully inspected when I got to Rose's Place, a rule of thumb at any detox or rehab: Addicts are creative about where they hide their emergency stash. I threw in some fighting gear I doubted I'd use or need, because I had also packed some weighted gloves that Jack had given me years ago, regular-looking work or gardening gloves made of Kevlar – impervious to knife strikes – with about eight ounces of steel across the knuckles of each glove to pack that extra punch. And to top it all off, a black baseball cap that, though it looked as streamlined as any normal cap, was engineered to act as a sap, a weapon, if I took it off and hit somebody with it.

Should I need it. Or get a chance to use it against whatever axe- or machete-wielding crazy person I might encounter in this peaceful little valley. Sarah was now missing. The odds of me finding trouble – especially since I was going to be looking for it – seemed high.

Fully dressed, I caught a glimpse of myself in the full-length mirror. Definitely not as scrawny as I was six months earlier, some of which had come from lying in bed being fed by Skip and Marie in Maine, maybe a bit added since I'd been at Rose's. The food was fantastic here: healthy, insanely good, and plentiful – it wasn't a fat farm, so the portions were suited to compulsive addicts who needed an alternative to their drug of choice. I'd never actually seen the chef, but apparently he was some kind of hot-shot in that world, having been a finalist on some chef competition on TV, and according to Mary, he had taken this job so that his kids could live in a beautiful, peaceful part of the world. Boy, had he chosen wrong. I wondered if he had decamped to safer pastures by now.

But here I was, and from what I was seeing in the mirror, I was ready.

Two taps on the door, and Laurence said, "Can I come in?" I opened the door and he entered quickly, shutting the door behind him. He smiled when he looked at me, raised his eyebrows and nodded at my ensemble, and started emptying his pockets on the bed.

"No corkscrews," he said.

"Well, probably not a good idea in a rehab," I said.

"Sends the wrong message," he said. I looked at the bed. My brother had relieved the kitchen of half a dozen steak knives in what looked like the plastic sheaths they were bought in, one lone serrated bread knife, and a hammer.

"It's not a cooking kitchen," he said, defensive. "I could have brought you tons of teaspoons and butter knives. People obviously only eat toast and take-out in there."

"And the hammer?"

"The bottom drawer has a few tools in it." He looked at what he was wearing, his neat flat-front khakis and white Oxford cloth button-down. He stuck the business end of the hammer in his right front pocket and looked at himself in the mirror.

"Subtle," I said. "But you might get some male attention."

"That ginger cop is cute," he said. "Young. But cute. Oh, but he's Mary's nephew, isn't he. Yikes, I take that back."

"Excuse me, sir. Is that a hammer in your pocket or…" Laurence adjusted the hammer, pushing it deeper into his pocket, and the effect made him look like he had the world's hugest – if slightly oddly shaped – erection.

"Well," he said, "I do dress right."

I laughed so hard my cheeks hurt, watching Laurence strike poses in the mirror with his hammer hard-on. It was so good to laugh that I felt it border into something close to hysteria.

"You are such a fucking tool," I said, and that sent us both over the edge. Laurence took the hammer out and threw it onto the bed next to where I was sitting. We calmed down and sat in silence for a minute.

"I'm scared," he said. He was looking at me in the mirror.

"I know," I said.

"For us, and for Dickie. And Sarah."

"I know," I said. "Me too." I wanted to tell him to get in the car and drive to Halifax, drive back to the airport and let me handle this. I wanted him to get away from here, away from this. None of us were safe; that was obvious. But I knew he wouldn't go, and I also didn't want to leave him alone, even for the drive, even just to the airport.

The yellow pickup had followed us from the airport. There wasn't enough traffic on sections of that highway, and I didn't want to hear that Mary's Mustang had been found abandoned by the side of the road, with no sign of Laurence. Except maybe a body part.

I shivered and felt sick. Literally a bit sick, as though I was coming down with something. "We need to eat something," I said. "Even if we don't want to, we need to." We hadn't had dinner last night. I took off my weighted baseball cap and hit myself in the palm with it a couple of times so Laurence could hear its weight. "Wear this," I said. "Doesn't pack the same punch as your buddy there," I looked at the hammer, "but, what the fuck, it can slow somebody down for a minute." I put it on his head.

"I'm staying with you, Danny," he said. "Until they catch this guy." His nose went a bit red, and I realized he was trying not to tear up. Then I remembered: I wasn't the only one who had lost Ginger. Darren, Laurence, and Skipper had, too. And just because I had never seen Laurence cry before last night, didn't mean he hadn't shed his fair share of tears privately.

"Yes, you are." I kissed his cheek. "Let's eat. Maybe if we have pancakes, by the time we're finished Sarah will have been found alive and well, and the crazy psycho axe murderer will have been caught."

"And Dickie found too," he said.

"And Dickie," I said, standing up. Maybe even alive, I said in my head, but I think Laurence heard it anyway.

The day was clouding over and cooler than it had been when I had been doing my unexpected sunbathing on the roof.

"We'll need our jackets later," Laurence said. We walked the thirty or so yards to the converted carriage house that acted as Rose's dining hall. I looked at the sky, at the storm clouds that seemed to be gathering out over the Bay of Fundy, and thought of Sarah. I hoped that she had managed to live through the night, and that she was at least inside somewhere. Then again, that would make her harder to find. I glanced at my brother, who was staring at his shoes as he walked. I figured he was thinking about Dickie.

Laurence was one of the most honorable people I'd ever known. He could be difficult, testy, stubborn, and a bit of a curmudgeon at times, which Ginger and I had always chalked up to his dating men who were generations older than he was. If he had sworn this filial oath to Dickie Doyle, no matter that it was the kind of romantic gesture that undergraduates everywhere indulge in and few actually think about twenty years later, he took it seriously. He wasn't a man with a ton of friends.

He would be worried to death about Dickie right now, first and foremost.

And I owed him. I owed all my siblings, for what I'd put them through. On top of which, if it hadn't been for my lifestyle, Ginger would probably still be alive. I needed to protect Laurence, and if the police didn't find the killer – or killers? Wouldn't it make sense that this was more than one person? – very soon, then I was going to have to act.

The carriage house had a large picture window facing the water, but now the view was gray and dismal. The minute we stepped through the door into the steamy warmth, the rain began behind us.

There were only three people in the dining hall, other than Laurence and me: the counsellor Janet, who was standing looking at the food in the steam trays, unmoving; Colin the cop, Mary's nephew, who was drinking a coffee; and the tattooed Australian resident. I didn't know his name, but in my head I was calling him Aussie Rules.

No kitchen staff or servers, and none of the usual bustle. We were late for lunch, but I had the feeling that it wouldn't have mattered. The place was losing people by the hour. Some of them with all their body parts intact.

Colin nodded at us, looking grim. The Australian was reading something on his phone, and Janet still hadn't moved.

I grabbed a tray and looked at the food with her. Half a dozen grilled cheese and tomato sandwiches, a soup with a handwritten label that said Barley, and some fresh greens, with a couple of containers of crumbled bacon and grape tomatoes and feta cheese. Not terrible, but nothing like the breadth of fresh, elegant food I'd become used to.

"Chef left," Janet said. Her voice sounded tight and loud in the quiet room, with its high ceiling. "One of his assistants put this together a few hours ago, but I think she's left as well."

"Nobody can blame them," Laurence said behind me. He put his hand gently on the woman's shoulder. "Can I help you carry something?" His voice was quiet and kind, and Janet pulled a tissue out of her pocket and wiped her eyes.

"Oh!" she said. "Thank you, but I'm okay. Just need some soup, I think. Need to warm up. The day's turning. Can't trust the weather here, at this time of year." Her movements were slow, and I looked more carefully at her. I knew that many addiction counsellors were former or "recovering" addicts themselves, and it wouldn't surprise me if the fear and stress in the air had made more than one person turn back to their drug of choice. I hadn't paid much attention to Janet before now – she was the kind of earnest do-gooder who generally bored me stupid, and I found it hard to believe she'd taken anything stronger than cold medication in her life. And even that, exactly as the directions on the box stated. Not a huge sense of humor, that one. One thing you can say about sober addicts: We tend to be able to poke fun at ourselves. Janet always looked like her eyes would turn pink and she would wilt if anyone chided her. About anything. I hadn't really spoken to her since I'd been here, and then I realized that was a pretty shitty thing. She was doing her best in this life, like the rest of us. Or most of us, anyway.

"Eat with us," I found myself saying, and Laurence looked at me with genuine surprise. "I think I'll try the soup too." I did ladle myself out a bowl, but also fixed myself a plate with a sandwich and some greens. I might need the fuel later. And nutrients.

For half a second looking at my tray, I thought, I hope when they do my autopsy, this isn't the last food in my stomach. I watched as Laurence carried Janet's soup and his own sandwich over to a table, like a gentleman, and thought, better me than him. Any day of the week.

Oh God, for some crack. I wondered what the Australian's drug of choice was. He was probably a meth-head, I decided. Maybe heroin. I wanted to put my food down and run back inside the house and search all the rooms for hidden spots for drugs. Sarah had hidden some weed in the basement; maybe other people had had a similar idea. Maybe there were nooks and crannies in there with little baggies and spoons and all kinds of illicit paraphernalia.

Then I thought of Sarah, who had tripped over Evan's headless body in that basement, and the fact that she was very probably in pieces somewhere.

As soon as we had finished eating, I would ask Colin where the searchers were meeting. And if I had enough time, I might leave Laurence in his company – I could see he carried a sidearm, and there were people in this room; Laurence would be safe here – run inside pleading gastrointestinal issues, and do a quick search of the place.

"This is it," Janet was saying as I sat down. She nodded at

Aussie Rules and us. "The people in this room. And Sarah," she added. "Everyone else has left, or is leaving. Gone to hotels in the city until the police let them leave the province, I guess." Halifax was the only city of size in the province, and it was about an hour or so away. "Well, Mary is still around, of course, but she doesn't sleep here. No other staff. I'm the only live-in."

"Why haven't you left?" Laurence asked her gently.

Janet played with her soup spoon. I wanted to tell her to eat already. I wanted to make her a steak. Then I realized that I wanted a steak. I took a bite of my cheese sandwich and, without intending to, exhaled in audible disappointment. Janet looked up at me, mistaking my sigh for impatience.

"I'm sorry," she said. "This is all so…" She reached into her pocket and fished out a Kleenex.

"Yes, it is," I said. "Sorry, Janet. This must be awful for you. How long have you been here?" It occurred to me that while I'd gotten to know Mary very well, and Evan a bit, I knew absolutely nothing about Janet's life at all.

"Oh, I'm from the Valley here," she said. I tried to guess how old she was, whether she would have parents or family waiting for her, worrying. "I mean, I was born in Halifax, but my parents adopted me when I was a baby. They're gone now."

I wanted to ask her if she meant gone as in dead, or gone to Europe or somewhere, but I could see Laurence shaking his head slightly and frowning at me. My social skills around the nice people sometimes left a little bit to be desired.

"I can stay at the house," she said. She blew her nose surprisingly loudly, and the Australian dropped his phone, which made me jump. "But I don't feel safe there either, with all this." She pointed at the house. Fair enough. If she felt safe, she'd be either an idiot or the killer. Ipso fatso.

"I'm sure the police will get this sorted out quickly," Laurence said. I hated when people said things like that. We had no idea what was going to happen, and when someone said something patronizing and mundane like that to me, I usually wanted to slap them silly. How can you be prepared for the crap in life if everything is sugar-coated for you? After Ginger died, I'd gotten a sympathy card from someone I used to train with who said my sister was in "a better place." I was reading the cards when I got back to my apartment in Toronto from my two-month convalescence in Maine, after I'd gotten a big fat delivery from D-Man, my friendly Eastern European drug dealer. I debated calling the stupid cow and giving her a blow-by-blow about the "better place" Ginger had been in during the hours before her death, but then I thought, no. I am, for a change, going to take the high road. Try to take on some of Ginger's good qualities. She'd been all smarts and sweetness and goodness, and I was the one in school who'd punch anyone who looked at her wrong. Division of responsibilities, I used to say to her. I had plenty of love, but it just came out differently than Ginger's did. As we were twins, our dad used to say that when the egg split, I was probably swimming around in there, making sure Ginger got all the good nutrients and cushioning her against any blows from the outside world. We were born very close together, only three minutes separating us, because, as Dad said, I wasn't going to let her out there on her own.

I tried to look at Janet and feel the same protective urges toward her. She looked like she needed protecting desperately, far more than Ginger – who may have been gentle, but was tall and athletic – ever did. She looked like a bunny rabbit, pink nose and eyes and all.

"It's not just this," Janet said. She toyed with her food. "I have a little sister, also adopted, and she stays at the house sometimes, and she – well, it's awful to say, but I don't like her."

Laurence looked at me. We were getting the full-on life story. I tried to make myself more comfortable in my chair. I thought about whether I should have taken more salad. "Well, you don't have to like her," I said. "But staying there sounds better than staying here at the moment, right?"

"I just don't feel safe there either," she repeated. She looked utterly miserable, and for a minute I wanted to shake her. But I was trying to be nice.

"Janet, I think you should go into Halifax like everybody else," I said. "Or do you have anybody who can come and stay with you? A boyfriend? Girlfriend?" Laurence looked down at the table and smiled. Janet went bright red.

"No! I'm not gay or anything!" She looked at my brother and got redder. "Not that there's anything wrong with that, of course!" Well, at least she had better gaydar than Sarah.

"Of course not," Laurence said, all soothing. Another Cleary who went out of his way to be kind to the needy, whereas I seemed to make people either want to cry or kill me. "Danny is just concerned about you. I think she meant 'girlfriend' as in female friend?"

"Yes, whatever," I said. There was an axe – or whatever – murderer on the loose. Social nuances were going to give me a sinus headache any minute. "A good friend, someone you trust.

Or someone whose house you can stay in."

Janet shook her head. "Not really," she said. "Just from the old days. You know, my friends who aren't sober, and I can't stay with them." I nodded. This, I understood. "Mary's got her husband, and of course he's in a wheelchair some of the time so he needs her. Dickie needs me to keep an eye on things."

Laurence looked at me. I shrugged about three millimetres. Mary's husband was that disabled? She was a dark horse; I had no idea. I knew MS could get that bad, I supposed, but I was surprised Mary hadn't mentioned it if Geoffrey's illness was that advanced. Still, as chummy as Mary and I may have gotten, there are things we all keep to ourselves, and it had only been just over two weeks since I'd met her. And we all have tough lives, one way or another. Scratch the surface of any beauty queen or billionaire, and you'll find dark secrets and areas of pain. It's the human condition. And without pain, we wouldn't appreciate the joy as much.

At least, that's what I liked to tell myself.

"Honey, for all intents and purposes, Rose's Place is closed for now," Laurence said to her, the soul of gentleness. "Dickie is missing too. Danny and I are staying in the dorms for now, as I'm Dickie's oldest friend, so I'm going to keep an eye on things for him." He looked at the Australian and lowered his voice. "We can check, but I bet that one's booking his hotel online as we speak. Or his ticket back to Oz. There are no more classes, or whatever you call them, for the time being."

"Meetings," Janet said. "And therapy."

"What about Dr. Singh?" I said. I'd just thought of her. I ...h. She was one of the rare strangers who seemed to ...aining.

"She lives in Halifax, commutes in three times a week," Janet said. She finally brought herself to take a mouthful of barley soup. "I'm sure Mary's talked to her, or the police have."

"So will you go somewhere?" I said. I'd eaten my sandwich and salad, and so had Laurence. I was about to start my soup, but I turned around and eyed the hot plates, keeping a mental note of how many sandwiches were left.

She shook her head. "I can't," she said. "I owe money. But maybe I'll go back to my house after all, I guess." She looked at me straight on, the first time she had. "It's on the mountain," she said. "Dad farmed for a while until he got sick. But it's a big property, and the house is old."

"Isolated?" I said. God. I couldn't imagine this poor woman living there at the best of times, let alone with a killer targeting people who had anything to do with Rose's. And a mean little sister. It would be *What Ever Happened to Baby Jane* up there. The incredibly boring version.

She nodded. "Kind of. There's a farm about a half-mile down, but it's up for sale. Has been for a year." She'd stopped eating. I pushed the bowl an inch closer to her. I wanted to take her outside and teach her a few self-defence moves, but knew I'd probably just scare the life out of her. You're either ready, or you're not. Like getting clean. Had I been ready? At this very minute, it didn't seem like it, as a third of my brain was already inside searching for drugs.

"I'll pay for a nice hotel for you," I said. "Don't worry about it and don't thank me." Her spoon hung in the air, and her mouth was open as she stared at me. "Seriously, Janet, I'm going to find a nice, safe hotel in the city for you and give them a credit card and you stay there as long as you need to. And I won't hear another word about it." I nodded at her soup, and she dutifully took another spoonful. Her face was crimson.

"But you have to tell me, because I'm dying to know," I said.

"What?" she said. Or squeaked. I found myself saying a little prayer for her safety, somewhere in the back of my brain. This one, for whatever reason, had no defences.

"What was your drug of choice?"

She actually smiled, and for a minute it was like the sun came out, she was that beautiful. "Oh! I guess you weren't listening in meetings."

"Yeah, I'm not good at groups," I said. "So?"

"Booze!" she said. "I was a terrible wino." She swallowed a spoonful of soup, and Laurence laughed. Janet joined in, and sitting opposite them, I hoped the moment would last. I looked at Colin, who seemed to be making notes in one of those little police notebooks while he nursed his coffee, and glanced at Aussie Rules, who was speaking quietly on his phone, pulling a card out of his wallet. I was right, I thought. Reservations. Janet and Laurence were saying something, but for a minute I thought about going and introducing myself – finally – asking him what hotel he was staying in. For Janet's sake, of course, and to ask whether he knew if I could score any coke or crack anywhere in this town.

Just idle speculation, mind you.

Colin got up from his table and headed over to ours. He met my eye. He looked like he wanted to talk about something.

Something outside the window caught my eye.

A red cap outside, maybe twenty yards away. A red cap

and tan jacket. A red cap and a tan jacket, pointing a rifle in our direction.

"Down, everybody down!" I yelled, and shoved Laurence's and Janet's heads into the table before I could think.

In the space of time it took for my heart to beat, the picture window shattered inwards at us, and I dove head-first toward Colin and the sidearm on his hip.

THIRTEEN

Rifle blasts are loud. Especially when you're calmly eating barley soup and talking about winos. Especially when said rifle blasts are through a large picture window in your direction.

Colin was on top of me, and for half a second I was relieved – someone else was in charge. Someone else – a cop! – had the situation covered.

Then I felt his blood on my neck, and saw that Colin was missing some of his head.

Time slowed. I could hear Janet making some kind of high-pitched keening sound, and I glanced at them. Laurence was on the floor, covering her. There didn't seem to be any blood on them. Thank God. My brother was fine. He had his entire head. Thank God. He nodded at me.

I flipped Colin over and unsnapped his holster, trying not to look at his head, moving myself to a crouch. There was glass everywhere. I waited to hear shouts and sirens. Where was everybody? Had it been half an hour, or half a second? Aussie Rules was on all fours beside his table across the room, staring at me. He stuck his head up about a foot to look outside, and another blast – seemed closer this time – broke more glass.

Aussie Rules was flat on the floor now, but I could see his eyes wide open, and judging by the panic in them, he was definitely still alive.

I checked Colin's ammo, crab-walked to the wall next to the window and fired a couple of rounds out without looking, hoping I wouldn't hit any civilians. In the context, however, it seemed unlikely. I just wanted the – hopefully lone – gunman to back the fuck away before he could see our positions inside and start picking the rest of us off like ducks in a barrel.

One more blast from the rifle outside, but this time not in our direction – at least, it didn't sound like it. I held my breath, and was about to fire more shots.

Then, the glorious sound of sirens, and police and more gunshots, other guns, all of which seemed to be moving away from the dining hall.

I carefully put Colin's weapon down within easy reach and kneeled with my hands on my head, feet underneath me in position to let me spring forward or out of the way if I needed to.

I was covered in blood, with a dead cop only a few feet away. And I had just fired his gun. Unless I needed to move, I was going to keep my hands on my head and stay as still as possible. If more shots came whizzing in here, I would be ready.

Colin was gone. Long gone. No amount of first aid was going to help him. I closed my eyes and said a quick prayer. Laurence was still covering Janet, who was sobbing, and who could blame her. Aussie Rules was flat on the floor in perp position, head down, hands laced behind his head. Yup. I would have guessed – he knew that if a couple of nervous young cops came into a scene of carnage like this, with his tattoos, he wouldn't necessarily look like the innocent bystander. Whereas Laurence and Janet, the khaki twins, had their preppy armor to keep them safe.

Hey, the world isn't a fair place. Of course, killers may be just as likely to be in khakis as they are to look like bikers. But we all have ingrained prejudices, and anyone who isn't white and middle class gets used to operating in defensive mode.

Colin was a kid. No more than twenty-six, if that. Mary's nephew. Smart, and struck me that he would have made – he *was* – a good police officer.

"Shit," I said out loud. Everything above Colin's eyes was gone. A good deal of it felt like it was on my neck and chest and abdomen. I stripped off my top layer, my long-sleeved cotton shirt, covered in gore, and arranged it gently, covering the poor boy's head. "Shit." I knew I probably shouldn't, I should probably be preserving the crime scene or whatever, but Mary wouldn't want him to be lying there like that, uncovered. If he had been one of my nephews – well, that didn't bear thinking about. I looked at Colin again, and fought it, but I couldn't.

Of course, I fainted. Of course I did.

FOURTEEN

I was lying in shards of glass, but my brother's face was staring down at me.

"Okay?" he said.

"Yes," I said, though I wanted to vomit. "You? Did you get cut?"

He nodded. "I did," he said. "My ass." There were people moving around us, and walkie-talkies. Someone was crying, a man was crying. I didn't want to know who. I closed my eyes.

"Is Colin still here?" I whispered. I didn't want to move my head; my eyes locked on Laurence. I felt tears leaking down the sides of my face, around my ears. Poor Colin. Poor Mary.

"Yes," he said. "You've only been out for a couple of minutes, max."

"Did you say your ass got cut?" I said. "Are you okay?"

"Just a sliver," he said. He wasn't smiling, but I know my brother, and I knew he was nearly giddy with relief that I was okay. Ish. His giddy could look like other people's morose.

"Will it scar, do you think?" I said.

"Deformed for life," he said quietly. Any cops listening to us would probably want to arrest us on the spot for being callous, insensitive monsters, with Colin's body a couple of feet away, but they didn't know us. Deflection? Who, us?

I closed my eyes. My nausea passed.

"I don't think I'm going to throw up," I said. There was a surprise.

"My little girl is growing up," he said, but very quietly. I looked at him. I didn't want to move my head. There was glass everywhere – how had I not really noticed that before? – and if I let my peripheral vision take over, I would see Colin. Blood. Red everywhere. Bits of bone and brain matter.

"Did you get him?" I said loudly. I started to sit up, but someone behind me held me down gently. "The man in the red hat, the shooter. Did you get him?"

There was a single quiet moment. Nobody said anything to me, but voices resumed behind me. I was facing the blown-out window, with Laurence crouching over me. It was pouring rain out there, the sky a dark gray.

"Danny, there's a paramedic here. She's going to make sure you're okay," Laurence said. I didn't protest, as I knew there was no point, and it would only take a minute. I was fine. Between the EMT behind me and Laurence, they got me to a sitting position without cutting me. I could feel someone pressing the back of my head gingerly.

"Am I all there?" I said, and immediately regretted it. "Oh God, I'm sorry." Someone was snapping pictures of Colin's body, which I could reach out and touch if I wanted to. Which I sort of did, as though I could comfort him. I remembered holding my husband as he choked on his own blood. He died trying to save me and my family. He had died hard.

At least Colin didn't see it coming, I thought. He didn't feel any pain. He didn't have pieces of himself cut away first. I hoped I would be so lucky.

I felt the person behind me pulling at my head, and a couple of small, sharp pains.

"Glass," a woman's voice said. "But superficial. You won't need stitches." Her touch was gentle; it was almost like a massage. Then I thought that the fact that having glass removed from my scalp by a paramedic felt like a massage to me might mean I should rethink my lifestyle choices. Laurence was holding my hand.

"Janet?" I said. "She okay?" He nodded. "Did you see the shooter?" I asked him.

"No. I was trying to hold onto her," he said. He nodded toward the other side of the room, and as soon as he did I could hear Janet's light voice, talking quickly to someone. I didn't even try to listen to what she was saying. "She wanted to run. Stronger than she looks, that one."

Something was stinging a bit. Alcohol or something, maybe, on my head where the glass had cut me. "Aussie Rules?" I said to Laurence.

"I beg your pardon?"

"The Australian guy. He okay?"

"Oh! Yes, I think so. He's gone."

"Gone? What do you mean, gone?"

"Outside with one of the officers," Laurence said. "He was a little hysterical." Probably he was the one who'd been crying. Male or female, it's a normal response to what had just happened.

I couldn't move my head with the paramedic working on it. I watched boots approach me slowly and the bottoms of uniform pants with that distinctive yellow stripe. Someone patted my shoulder.

"Hi, Des," I said. I felt tears in my eyes. Laurence felt around in his pocket for a handkerchief. Yes, he carried handkerchiefs. He dabbed at my face, which of course made me want to cry more. "Did you get him?" Des squatted down next to me, and the paramedic let go of my head.

"No," he said, and for a minute I thought I was going to crumble, just stop existing. Not again. Someone trying to kill me, or my brother, or even having us caught in the crossfire – it was too close for comfort, and I realized quickly that I had not had enough rest since what had happened in California, and Maine. I was only beginning, at the very earliest stages of recovering from losing my twin sister and my husband, and from killing people and being pretty badly hurt myself. So, I had gone running a handful of times. I had no crack in my system – though I wanted it; God, did I want it. I had sort of made a friend in Mary, and I was eating and sleeping well.

Two weeks in rehab. Apparently that's what I was going to get. Two weeks.

"The other resident said he thought it was a woman," Des was saying. "That the shooter was a woman."

"A woman?" I closed my eyes for a second. "I saw a red cap. Tan jacket. And a gun." The gun. I would be a very happy woman if I never had to see a gun again, unless it was in my own hand, at a shooting range. "In the woods yesterday, at the lake," I said. "The voice I heard. It sounded like a woman. At least, I think. I'm not sure." The head. Evan's head. "I didn't see a face. Just the red hat. And the gun. But I thought it was a man. I mean, I registered the figure as male, anyway."

Des nodded. "He said he wasn't sure, but he thought it was a large woman." I could hear more cars arriving, and someone was saying something over a bullhorn, but I didn't catch it.

"Tactical team," Des said to us. "They were on their way anyway to lend a hand."

"Why would somebody take that chance, to walk right up on the property in broad daylight?" Laurence said to him. I could hear the strain in his voice. "This whole area has been crawling with police."

"We got a call that someone had found a body," Des said. "That someone found Sarah Gilbert's body, and a bunch of other, uh, remains, in an abandoned hunting cabin. Call was anonymous, untraceable."

"Let me guess," I said. "You never found anything."

"If that cabin exists, we haven't found it yet," Des said.

The paramedic patted my shoulder and stood up behind me. Laurence and Des each grabbed one of my hands and helped me stand. My legs seemed to be working. Rubbery and shaky, but working.

"They were trying to lure police away from here," Laurence said. He looked at Des like he wanted to hit him.

"We had a couple of officers here, of course. But they were busy putting out a fire – literally, somebody set a small fire in the kitchen in the main house there." The residents' kitchen, which faced the road, was the farthest point from the dining hall on the grounds. "Look. In case you hadn't noticed, this isn't a big city police force. We don't have things like this happen here."

"Things like this don't really happen anywhere," I said.

"Well, not unless I'm around." I regretted saying it right away. It sounded self-pitying and self-aggrandizing at the same time.

"Danny, this isn't about you," my brother said. "This is about Dickie somehow."

"Possibly," Des said, "or just about Rose's Place in general, Mr. Cleary." He said it gently, but he had a point. The man in the cabin, Sarah, Evan, and now this. If Dickie had gone off the deep end, he could even have cut off his own tattoo and put it on that sign. Stranger things, etc.

"Please just call me Laurence." He looked outside. "I need a cigarette." The rain had stopped.

"Me too," Des and I said in unison, and he smiled at me. "Don't tell my wife," Des said. "I'm supposed to have quit."

Glass crunched under my feet as the three of us walked around Colin's body, and I saw Des cross himself. I wondered if the poor man had slept at all; with his girth and red face, he looked like a heart attack waiting to happen. I followed the men, looking at the mess at my feet, and stepped into the afternoon gloom. The grass outside was wet, and there was a distinct chill in the air. Hard to believe I'd been warm perched on the roof in my underwear just a few hours ago. If I closed my eyes, though, and ignored the sight of RCMP officers combing the property, the air, chill as it was, felt more like home. Like Maine. And in that instant I felt a wave of homesickness for my childhood that felt like a punch. When my parents were still living. When I still had my twin sister.

Loss can creep up on you and nearly make you dizzy with the sadness of it. Just the feel of the air on your skin can transport you to a time you'd almost rather forget. Dr. Singh said this was normal. She said it was more normal to go nearly crazy with grief, especially after suffering the double-barrelled loss that I had, than to not experience it. And that it could come suddenly like this, without warning, months after the event. Years, even. I doubted I could handle that. I doubted I could stay sane.

Des and Laurence were talking, and I had a cigarette in my hand I didn't remember accepting or lighting. Maybe this was it, then. Maybe I would just go mad with grief, lose time, crawl around on strange rooftops in my underwear now and then. I thought it had started raining again, but then I realized I had tears streaming down my face. I wasn't sobbing, but tears were just rolling from my eyes, unchecked. I was glad my brother and Des were talking together so intently, a few feet away. I didn't want to have to speak. Behind me, inside that carriage house, was the dead body of a young man who'd dedicated his life to service. I didn't know him well, but he seemed like a good kid. Mary had mentioned a week or so ago that he was talking about asking his girlfriend to marry him. But now more lives would be touched by this kind of horror and sadness, and because of what? A lunatic enacting some kind of psycho, pseudo-*Friday the 13th* fantasy on this place, this pretty, semi-remote facility dedicated to helping people get better. And why? I was, at this point, despite just having been shot at, willing to believe that I wasn't the target. The voice in the woods had sounded nearly kind, telling me to go home. Did she – was it a she? – call me dear?

Why Rose's Place? It couldn't just be about Dickie, not at this point. Not after today. Dickie Doyle was probably dead, though I wasn't going to voice that opinion to Laurence.

Or he was doing it. The cabin had been just recently deserted when we got there – cold beer, warm pan, and a trussed-up man missing some of his appendages on Dickie's bed. Laurence would never believe it. That I knew. I wouldn't even bother mentioning it to him; I didn't want him to go off without me somewhere in anger.

I turned my back on the men and walked a few feet away, smoking furiously. The man in Dickie's bed had been a resident here. And quiet, shy Evan. Sarah, wherever she was. And now Colin, though the fact that he was the only one of us killed in the dining hall – and that he, who had been neither staff nor resident, happened to be there at all – was probably a coincidence. Whoever had shot at us would not have been expecting shots back, and that would have slowed him – her? – down a bit. Colin had been sitting out of sight of the window, and it was only a fluke that he stood at the second those first shots were fired.

At least, I thought so. Hard to gauge seconds and order of events after something like that, but I happened to see Red Cap as he was taking aim, and I was pretty sure Colin was out of his sight at that second.

If he hadn't stood up to come talk to us, he'd probably still be alive.

"Drugs," I said, and turned around. I walked to Laurence and Des. "Addicts." They looked at me. "You have to look at everyone who's ever been a resident here, or worked here," I said to Des. "Or, I don't know, anyone who may have gotten kicked out because they were caught using, or who may have OD'd after they got out." I looked at Laurence. "I don't think it's about Dickie, Laurence," I said. "It's someone with a grudge to settle against this place. I think."

"Whatever happens now, this place will be shut down,"

Laurence said. "No one will ever want to come here again. For anything, as a matter of fact. I mean, even if Dickie managed to sell the property, would this be where you'd want to come on a relaxing holiday?" He lit another cigarette. "If shutting Rose's Place down was someone's goal, I'd say they've already succeeded, with today's... events."

I shook my head. "It's more than that. This is more personal. To someone," I said.

Des looked at me. "Danny, I agree, and there are people looking into that. Mary was and will be helping a couple of our people, sorting through files, telling anything she can remember about each and every resident who's ever been here. It's been open for just a few years, and it only houses a dozen residents at a time. She knows where all the bodies are buried." Then Des looked at the ground. "Jesus Christ. My mouth."

"Don't worry about it, I do that all the time," I said. I touched his arm. I wanted to hug him suddenly. Then I realized: He reminded me a bit of our late father.

"She does," Laurence said. "Think nothing of it, Sergeant."

"Des. My God. Des, please." Des looked like he wanted to be anywhere but here. He'd mentioned something about being so happy to be posted here, this beautiful part of the world. He and his wife had dreamed of their retirement here.

Mary. "Where is she now?" I said. "Mary." Crime scene people, some of whom I recognized from being at Ferryman Lake the night before, were unloading equipment. Colin's body probably wouldn't be removed for a while yet. I wasn't sure what the procedure was vis-à-vis the coroner, but I hoped it would all get wrapped up before Mary came anywhere near here.

"Home, thank God," Des said. "She was up half the night going through those files, and her husband was calling. He worries about her, and she worries about him. He wanted her home for a nap, 'cause he knew he wouldn't be able to keep her away from the search party."

The search party. *Party.* I almost asked if I should bring a bottle or some cupcakes, and nearly laughed. Would there be a DJ? I nearly let out a hysterical bark of laughter, but somehow managed to keep it in, for once.

"Who will tell her?"

"I will. Going to drive up there very shortly," he said. "I was Colin's sergeant." Nobody said anything for a minute.

"You're both covered in evidence, by the way," he continued. "We'll get someone to escort you back so you can change and we can bag your clothes. And of course we still have to do formal statements."

Evidence. Colin's blood and brain matter was all over me, despite the fact that I'd taken my outer shirt off. My cargo pants were black, but as soon as Des mentioned evidence, I could feel the blood weighing them down, soaking into my skin underneath.

"Yes, I need to change," I said. It seemed urgent, now, to get these clothes off. "But we need to be included on that search. Or I do," I added, looking at Laurence. Behind him, I could count more than a dozen red uniforms. And after this snafu, I highly doubted this property would be left without at least that many of them hanging around. Especially now that a cop had been killed here.

For better or worse, I was pretty sure that this property would be the safest place in the Valley for miles, just now.

"I'll have to think about that," Des said. "Talk to one or two people. You were both in that room. You could have been targets."

"We weren't," I said. For once, I actually mostly believed it, too. "Wrong place, wrong time."

"You have to let us help," Laurence said. He stepped forward, and stood, I thought, too close to Des. Very tall people have to be aware of their physical presence; it can be seen as confrontational to stand too close while speaking, as if you're exerting your size. "Please. Dickie is my oldest friend. And I'm the one who gave Sarah my reservation at the B and B."

Shut up, Laurence, I wanted to say. Des looked at him, and really for the first time I could see him as the tough law enforcement leader. "I'll get back to you," he said eventually. He motioned for two constables to come over, and instructed them to escort us into the dorms and wait while we changed.

"I'm heading up the mountain to see Mary," Des said. "I'll be back in an hour or so. In the meantime, I'm instructing you to stay in the dorms. Like I said last night: the kitchen, your rooms, bathroom, whatever. Nobody is getting in or out of here. Not this time."

Laurence and I trudged back to the dorms in silence under the forbidding sky, flanked on either side by our bodyguards with guns. I didn't have to ask my brother what he was thinking, because I was thinking the same thing.

We were going to search for Sarah. And Dickie. And if we weren't allowed on the volunteer search, we would go alone.

FIFTEEN

Constable MacLean kept her back turned while I stripped out of my bloody clothes. Layer by layer, I handed each item back to her until she had everything bagged and I had nothing but a towel wrapped around me. I managed to take the Kevlar gloves out of my pocket and throw them on the floor along with the mess that was already there. They wouldn't tell the police anything, except that I had possibly been expecting trouble when I came to rehab, and that was a kettle of fish I didn't want to deal with. Laurence was in one of the abandoned resident rooms close by, doing the same thing with the male constable.

When I was left alone I immediately got into the shower for the second time that day. I kept my eyes closed, not wanting to look at what I washed out of my hair and off my skin. The small cuts on the back of my head stung under the hot water, and I was almost glad. I brushed my teeth while the mirror was still steamy, happy I couldn't see my reflection properly. I often found seeing my reflection jarring, especially after I'd seen or participated in any kind of violence. I expected to look different, for the experience to have made more of an impact on my appearance. But unless I'd been hit in the face, I always seemed to look the same. Something about that made me feel empty, bereft. I sometimes wished my outside matched the chaos of what went on inside me and around me, at times like this.

I sat on the bed with the towel around me and ran my hand along the tattoo on my inner thigh. Dave's number, in my tattoo. And by now, tattooed into my brain as well.

I wondered if I should call it.

And then I wondered if I would get out of this with my tattoo still attached to me.

Ten minutes later, I was dressed again, and wishing I'd packed differently. I wore jeans and my last clean t-shirt, with a ratty old cardigan. They had even taken away my Docs with the rest of my clothes, so I was down to my running shoes, flip-flops in case the showers had been communal – ha, it was a nicer bathroom than I'd ever had – and a pair of ancient knock-off Uggs I'd thrown into my bag at the last minute. I'd really expected to be shuffling around from basket weaving to food hall to dorms.

I wondered whether there was time to check out the shopping in the area. See if I could find some new boots. And maybe, I don't know, a couple of machetes. They go well with any ensemble.

I made sure I had my keys, and grabbed the keys to the Beast from where Laurence had tossed them on the dresser. It would be safe to leave Laurence here now, just for a little while, just so I could run into town and pick up a couple of things, and be away from my brother for half an hour while I thought a bit more about Dickie Doyle. I could hear footsteps all over the house, and when I opened the door to my room, Constable MacLean was standing there. It looked like I had caught her mid-pace.

"Hi," I said. "Are you on bodyguard duty?" I really didn't want the company, and I thought I'd be pretty safe in town for a little while.

She shook her head, and I could see that she was trying not to cry.

Of course, I thought. She looked to be about Colin's age. They were probably friends. All the police around here were probably good friends, or at least had worked together closely. "I'm so sorry for your loss," I found myself saying. "Were you and Colin very close?" She nodded, and something made me hug her. Unlike me, yes, but the woman had been in the room while I stripped naked. That tends to form a bit of a sisterhood bond, whether you want it to or not.

But she was a professional. She patted my back briefly but pulled away. We were almost exactly the same height.

"I know who you are," she said quietly. "Everybody knows who you are. Well, we do, I mean." The RCMP, I presumed she meant. I nodded. She lowered her voice further, and I had to lean in.

"If we don't catch him, you have to," she said. "A few of us – well, we hope you find him first."

"Him?"

"Dickie Doyle," she said. "Whoever's working for him."

Well, I no longer had to wonder what law enforcement's take on all this was. I opened my mouth to speak, but she shut me down.

"No," she said. She was calm again, calm and angry. I knew that look. I've had that look myself before. She was nearly whispering. "If you catch him, you shut him down. Do you understand? Shut him down." I didn't have to ask what that meant. And I didn't blame her for the sentiment. And she couldn't do it; none of them could. They were sworn officers of the law, and this wasn't some corrupt big-city American police force. These people had gone through extensive training, as I understood it, and were educated. Civilized.

Above the kind of mayhem, therefore, that she was hoping I would unleash on the person responsible for the death of her friend. But from what she knew about me, she was pretty sure that I was not.

"I don't even know where to begin," I said, my voice as low as hers. "I'm not from here. I was going to join the search party for Sarah."

Constable MacLean shook her head and stepped into my room, pulling me inside with her. She shut the door behind us, but she kept her voice low and spoke quickly. "Don't bother with that search. There will be dozens and dozens of locals searching the farmland and beaches in concentric circles from where she was taken. They may find Ms. Gilbert's body, but not Dickie Doyle."

"Why are you sure it's Dickie?" I said. I grabbed a pack of Laurence's cigarettes from the dresser and lit one, breaking the rules about smoking in the dorms, but I was willing to take the risk.

"I'm *not* sure. None of us is sure," she said. She looked at my cigarette longingly, but didn't ask for one. "But it seems the most likely answer, and at the very least, whoever is doing this has something to do with him. Go back to Ferryman Lake. Go back to the cabin, except don't go all the way in by car. A couple of our guys are still out there." She pulled a keyring out of her pocket, with two keys. "There's a cabin a few doors down from Dickie's," she said. "It belongs to my family. It's got a weird paint job, with stripes…" she started to say, and I stopped her.

"I know it. We passed it." The lavender cottage. And her, a constable of the RCMP. People always surprise you.

"Nobody is there," she said. "You can stay there, you and your brother."

"Why?" I said.

"Dickie is somewhere out there," she said. "Nobody has found him, but because of the yellow pickup you guys saw, the assumption is that he's gone or been taken away – he's certainly not at the lake anymore. But he's always in the woods. He basically spends more time wandering around in the woods than he does in his cottage, from what we can tell." I looked at her, eyebrows raised. "I don't have time to explain. But we've been distant neighbors since he moved out there."

"This is…" I stopped. I didn't know what to say. "Why are you trusting me with keys to your home?" I was starting to think that perhaps this woman was, in the parlance of my adolescent nephews, cray-cray. And yet, with a day that started with me crawling out the window and continued with getting shot at, it was really par for the course. "You just want my brother and I to what, go there as bait, and for me to kill him if I see him?"

"No! I don't know what I mean. But knowing what I do about you, I trust you to do the right thing." I stared at her. "Besides, it's not home, it's just a cottage." She sounded impatient, as though she had expected me to take the keys and run, no questions asked. "We wouldn't be going there this early in the season anyway. And I read about your story. I don't know all of it but I know you went after the people who killed your sister and your husband. And you got away with it."

"It's more complicated than that," I started to say, but someone was walking around in the hallway. Sounded like Laurence, from his heavy footsteps.

"I know it is," she whispered. She pushed the keyring into my hand and leaned in, whispering in my ear. She smelled like lilac perfume and bubble gum. "The smaller key is to the gun safe. It's under the bed in the first bedroom on your left upstairs. My room. If someone stops you, I gave you the keys to give you somewhere safe to stay. Nobody will question it."

Laurence knocked at the door. "Danny?"

"Just a second, finishing getting dressed," I called out. I took the keys and put them in my pack. "Thanks, Constable," I said, in a normal voice. "And again, sorry for your loss."

"Thank you, Ms. Cleary," she said, just slightly too loudly. She handed me her card. "If I'm off shift, don't hesitate to call with any concerns or questions." Her cell number was written on the back. She turned and opened the door, and motioned for Laurence to step in before she walked out.

"Don't forget, both of you, leave your cell numbers with the constable by the gate if you leave the property, and your estimated time of return."

"We will," Laurence said. Constable MacLean shut the door on her way out, and I sat down on the bed. I wanted a few minutes alone to process that strange encounter, but it didn't seem as though I was going to get it. Laurence took the cigarette from my hand and took a last drag before walking to the window and flipping it outside.

"I gave Janet a couple of blank cheques and a credit card," he said. "She was pretty hysterical."

"She'll probably rob you blind," I said, flopping down on my back.

"Undoubtedly," he said. He sank onto the other bed and stretched out. "Hookers and heroin."

"Things of that nature," I agreed. "Shenanigans of the illegal and immoral kind."

"It's always the quiet ones." We smiled at each other. He wiggled his eyebrows.

"Let's stay in tonight, dear," I said. "Play gin rummy." I looked out the window. There would be no sunset tonight; the sky was too dark with clouds. I looked at my watch.

"Do you think they're doing the volunteer search tonight?" Laurence said. "In this weather? After what happened today? Nobody seemed to have an answer yet, when I went downstairs." He sounded very tired.

"I think they're crazy if they do." I did, actually. The Apple Blossom parade was scheduled for the next day, and the area was thick with tourists. Not that we saw many, cloistered as we were on the grounds at Rose's. But no matter how many floodlights they set up, having volunteers who didn't know the terrain searching in the cold, dark, and wet while a killer or killers were not only slicing people up, but now shooting at them? I doubted they'd be keeping that plan.

"I'm not going to lie to you, kid," Laurence said. "I am as exhausted as I've ever been in my life."

I looked over at him. He was ten years older than me, in his forties now, a smoker, and not fighting fit. And he wasn't used to the adrenaline spikes we had had over the last twenty-four hours. The mental strain would be almost as exhausting.

"Only a day," I said. "Do you realize you've only been here a day?"

"Jesus," he said. "I should call Antonio." His current flame, a retired restaurateur who'd had three children with his ex-wife before he came out as gay in his fifties. Now he divided his time equally between Manhattan and Key West.

"Am I going to meet him?" I snapped my fingers for the cigarettes and Laurence tossed them over.

"You could buy your own, Danielle," Laurence said.

"Yours taste better, *Larry*," I said. I was smoking too much, but it seemed like the thing to do. Helped me think. "So. No meeting Tony?"

"Antonio. Please. Whenever I hear 'Tony' I think of his ex, who, by the way, I have had the honor of meeting on several occasions now. They've been very civilized about it all. But she's so…"

"Jersey? Carmela Soprano?" I was obsessed with *The Sopranos*. Smoking crack, I would watch the series from beginning to end two or three times a year.

"Not at all. She's more of a Dr. Melfi. All muted good taste and political correctness."

"Huh," I said. Part of me wished we could lie here all evening and riff on pop culture, play cards, and go to sleep by nine o'clock. And that's what I intended that Laurence do, once I made sure for myself that the house was safe. I hadn't wanted to let him out of my sight, but he was safer here at this point than he would be with me. And while I didn't know what I was going to do yet – I didn't fancy driving out to the lake tonight and creeping through strange woods in the dark – I knew I wanted to get this over with.

I didn't know if I should be looking for Dickie alive or dead. And if alive, was he carrying a rifle? Wearing a red cap? Running around with an axe? Driving a yellow pickup? Between Des's oversharing and Constable MacLean's bizarre request, I couldn't really know what the police's plans were. Finding Sarah Gilbert would probably be the priority, if only because she had been abducted while supposedly under RCMP protection.

I just wanted it to be over. I wanted Dickie to be found alive, and innocent, and for the police to find some lead with the old resident records. Maybe by morning they'd make an arrest, the bad guy or guys would give something away about what they had done with Dickie and Sarah, and I could go home to Toronto and see Darren and the boys, hire a sober companion after all. Maybe even visit Laurence and Antonio in New York before it got too hot in Manhattan. Kick back, sort out the rest of what I was going to do with Jack's money, and try to live some kind of life.

I closed my eyes for a minute, but they flew back open a second later.

Mary. Des was going to tell Mary about Colin, and Mary was looking at the records. I could find Mary's place again. I just had to look for the butterflies. It wasn't fully dark out.

Laurence had fallen asleep. I tiptoed to the window, closed it, and locked it. I grabbed my bag, which had the car keys, MacLean's freak-flag cottage keys, and my wallet. I grabbed the hammer and threw it in. Between that and the screwdriver, I'd be all set if I saw some emergency repairs that needed doing.

I grabbed my jacket from the chair and let myself out. I whispered something about making toast, in case Laurence would register it.

In the kitchen, two officers were chatting quietly. I had passed two more walking through the house, one with his gun drawn but at his side.

"Hi," I said. I pointed to myself, like an idiot. Walking into a roomful of cops was not something I would ever get used to. "Danny Cleary."

"What can we do for you, Miss Cleary?" They both looked jangly, and I didn't blame them. I was glad they had all the lights on, though I wished Rose's Place had more window coverings.

"Not a thing," I said. "I'm just going to go into town, buy some cigarettes, get my brother something for dinner."

"Don't forget to leave your cell number with the…"

"Officer at the gate," I finished. I smiled at him. "I will. I won't be long." I was about to walk out the back door, but stopped. "Is the search going ahead?"

"Law enforcement and auxiliary officers only," one of them said.

"Good idea," I said. "Hey. Is Aussie Ru— Is the Australian guy still here, or did he leave? Was he okay?"

"He's here. He said he's not coming out of his room until we take him for his statement tomorrow, and to the airport from there." I nodded, and stepped outside. Maybe I should figure out what room Aussie Rules was in, pay him a visit, commiserate about our shared horrible experience earlier, and see if he had any nice, illegal narcotics he wanted to rid himself of, before boarding a probably international flight.

The night was still young.

It was warmer than it had been a few hours earlier, almost muggy. Nothing like the east coast for changeable weather patterns. I slowly walked to the Mustang, wishing that it was an automatic. I wasn't in the mood to wrestle with the clutch. And once I got to town there would probably be traffic – not city traffic, but sightseers and the like. I stood outside for a second, debating asking one of the cops to give me a lift into town and actually doing what I just said I was going to – pick up smokes, some food, and come back and reread *Jane Eyre* until I fell asleep. Laurence wasn't the only one who was exhausted. I'd become a bit flabby, as it turned out, both mentally and physically. And I was the one Constable MacLean thought was going to hunt down and kill Dickie Doyle? I doubted I had the wherewithal to hunt down a pizza at that moment.

Something pale caught my eye against the dark fence next to the parking lot. I walked slowly toward it.

Something pale and small, with blonde hair.

Sarah.

I yelled for help, dropped my bag, and ran toward her.

SIXTEEN

A lot of her was missing, but it didn't look like a human had done it.

I was squatting down next to where she had been tied to the fence, nude, her head down, hair covering her face, when I saw that some of her fingers and parts of her feet had been raggedly removed. It looked like they'd been chewed off. Someone had wrapped her to the fence around her waist and neck with wire, and I was grateful her hair was covering her face once I saw the rest of her.

Then there were lights, lots of lights, and someone was pulling me away from Sarah. He didn't have to pull very hard. I'd gone from a squat next to her, to landing backward on my butt and pushing myself away from her, scrambling to get to my feet.

Oddly, I didn't faint. Fourth body in twenty-four hours, if you counted poor Evan's head being thrown at me in the woods. Perhaps I was building up immunity.

I almost hoped not. No one should get used to this. Not even me.

I pulled my phone from my pocket and shone the flashlight away from the cops, away from Sarah. Someone had left her there, and it had to have been in a very narrow window of time. He had to still be close. I wanted a machete. I wanted a gun, not a fucking hammer and a screwdriver. I started screaming into the darkness. Not words, just rage and frustration. Someone was trying to hold me, restrain me, and without checking who it was, I jerked my head back, hard, to hit his face – he was an inch or two shorter than me – and went limp so I slid out of his arms, elbowed him in the groin on my way down, and crawled a few feet away.

It was a cop, and he was howling, and there was blood all over his face as he lay curled in a ball on the ground. And I was glad. He really should have known better than to try to restrain someone from behind in the current situation, with a woman's desecrated body fifteen feet away and a killer in the vicinity. Especially since all these police apparently knew what I was capable of.

If I'd had my screwdriver in my hand, it would be lodged in his scrotum right now, and then we'd really hear screaming.

Then somebody was saying something to me. Laurence was there, and he was speaking to me. I wasn't screaming any longer. I was just sitting on the ground cross-legged, watching the cop writhe around in pain, shout obscenities at me, and then puke onto the grass. Laurence started toward where all the cops were gathered around Sarah's body. I was on my feet again, covering the ground between us.

"No!" I was yelling again. My primordial crocodile brain took over and I grabbed Laurence's arm as hard as I could and pulled him back to me. Don't let him see that, was all I could think. You can do this, at least. Two of the cops came toward us, trying to block Laurence from getting too close. Aside from anything else, it was a crime scene. "Don't look. Don't look. Do not look at her." I couldn't seem to stop yelling. Even as I was doing it, I knew this wasn't me, this wasn't the way I behaved. I hadn't fainted, but I'd lost control of myself nonetheless.

Then I thought, Ginger. Sarah had long blonde hair like my twin sister. Someone had killed Sarah, killed her horribly, and I had done nothing to stop them, nothing to help look for her earlier. I could have grabbed an energy bar from the kitchen after getting off the roof, instead of going to the dining hall, and insisted on joining the search then. And if they hadn't let me do that, I could have gone to see Mary and talked to her – and maybe if Colin hadn't gotten up from the table at that second to come talk to us, he would still be alive. Or I could have driven to the lake and searched the woods, where Evan's head had been thrown at me. Instead, I'd sat on my ass, had a stupid sandwich and felt sorry for insipid little Janet, when Ginger was dying.

Sarah. When Sarah was dying.

I was crying. I think I was crying. Laurence picked me up in his arms and carried me to the porch and set me down out of sight of the commotion.

Even though I'd made a total hysterical fool of myself, I was glad, later, that I did that. Laurence never saw Sarah's body, not really. By the time he'd fully woken up and run downstairs and outside, there were several cops around the body and more running toward us. He just wanted to get me out of the way. He said he registered a bit of a shoulder, maybe some blonde hair, but that was it. And that was good, because you can't unsee things like that. Better me than him, any day.

It had become my mantra.

"Come on," I said to Laurence. I walked toward the Mustang, grabbing my bag from the ground as I went. "We're getting out of here. Now."

Laurence didn't try to stop me, or make any sounds about going back inside to grab his things. He just followed me to the car, but when I headed to the driver's side, he held out his hand.

"Keys," he said, and I knew he was right. I fished them out of my bag, tossed them across the car to him, and we changed sides. None of the cops tried to stop us, and at the foot of the drive, the one cop left guarding the front gate was talking on a walkie-talkie.

"We're going to find somewhere else to stay," Laurence said, not coming to a full stop. "We'll let Sergeant Murphy know where we wind up."

The cop just nodded, and mouthed what I thought might have been "good luck."

We peeled out of the driveway and drove.

I was never to set foot inside Rose's Place again.

SEVENTEEN

I could tell how worked up Laurence was by how calm he seemed.

"Good thing you didn't have a knife in your pocket," he said. He rolled down our windows as he lit a cigarette. He didn't ask me to do it, I couldn't help but notice. Probably thought I might set fire to the car, in my crazy frame of mind.

"Oh, snap!" I said. "I was thinking the exact same thing before. When the cop was puking."

"So what did he do? I missed that part. I just got there in time for the aftermath."

"Gave me the old reverse bear-hug," I said. "I was being a hysterical female."

"Gracious. How dare you?" he said.

"That's what *he* said." Laurence grinned. We couldn't have been more than three-quarters of a mile from Rose's, and I already felt better. I wanted to drive all night. Maybe drive right back to Toronto. Between us, we could do it in about twenty hours, I thought. See some Canadian countryside. Embarrass ourselves in French in Quebec on the way. I could call Detective Paul Belliveau in Toronto, my guardian angel, and get him to smooth things over with the RCMP out here. Shouldn't be too hard, seeing as how my brother and I had been stalked by a murderous psychopath for the best part of twenty-four hours.

This was not in the Nova Scotia guidebook.

I saw that Laurence's cigarette pack was nearly empty, just as we were about to pass a tiny wood shack that seemed to double as a convenience store. "Stop here." Laurence swung in and for the first time I saw why he liked driving his Porsche so much in Manhattan. With barely a check in the rear view, he pulled in front of the store and stopped about half an inch short of hitting the building, but with such ease and grace that I, Queen of Carsickness, barely felt it. Laurence patted his pockets.

"Hope you've got more than good intentions in that bag, little sister," he said. "Wherever we're going, it's on you."

"I got you covered, sunshine," I said. "Don't you worry your pretty little head."

I went into the store just as the teenage boy working there was about to flip the Closed sign. "I'll be two minutes," I said. He looked at me with a total lack of expression on his face, which felt a bit weird. Every other person I'd dealt with in this part of the world had bent over backward to be friendly.

But at least he didn't shut the door in my face. It would not have bode well for the road trip I was pretending we were on.

I walked to the back of the tiny store and grabbed a few bottles of water and a few huge cans of energy drink. I dumped them on the counter and then grabbed big bags of chips and nuts and even some dried cranberries, as a concession to vitamins. The packet of cranberries was very dusty, and I decided not to check the expiry date.

"Can you give me a carton of something? Do you have Marlboro Lights here?"

"Nope." The kid looked at me, not moving. I doubted he was going to be photographed for the Nova Scotia tourism brochure.

"Okie dokie then," I said. I smiled. He seemed unmoved. "Just give me a carton of whatever's your most popular brand, I guess." The kid looked at me for a long moment, during which I was torn between chucking a chocolate bar at his head to get him to move or walking out the door. It was dark outside, and only a couple of cars had passed us. But Laurence was out front in the car – I could see the light of his last cigarette.

In a few minutes, the kid was taking my money and he even gave me a bag to put the stuff in, after I asked him twice. Before I left I grabbed a lighter from a display and left a five-dollar bill on the counter. "Buy yourself something pretty," I said. "Cheer yourself up."

The kid winked slowly at me and nodded as I turned to leave. He was either the driest comedian of all time, or I was in *The Twilight Zone*.

In the car, Laurence was excited about all the junk food. "Antonio says I should gain a little weight," he said. "What, no licorice?"

"I, too, am fond of a larger guy," I said, throwing the bag of cranberries at him, "but leaner is better for your health." I ripped open a bag of chips. I couldn't believe I was eating. And suddenly ravenous.

"I was reading about donairs," Laurence said. "It's a local junk food delicacy. But I don't know if they have them outside the city." We were going to drive through Wolfville, and if anyplace was going to have easy, cheap food, it was a university town.

"Okay," I said. "But we're getting them to go." I could feel my brother looking at me, but I shoved chips in my mouth. Chips: okay. Pasta, carbs, egg salad sandwich: whatever. Anything with meat, I was going to give a pass. Possibly forever, after what I'd seen tonight.

"You have a plan?" he said. "Because if it involves leaving the province, you can forget about it. Aside from the fact that we have to be around to give statements, we still have to find Dickie."

I had to find Dickie. At the moment, as far as I was concerned, Dickie was just as likely to be involved in all this as not, and I didn't want Laurence getting to him before I did. "I know," I said. "I have a plan. Trust me?"

Laurence grunted something that I guessed was supposed to be his assent, and as soon as we hit Wolfville – all two or three blocks of the downtown Main Street area – the traffic was bumper to bumper.

"Tourists," I said. "I almost forgot about the festival." The parade would be tomorrow. Or had it already happened? Time seemed to be so slow. I wanted to sleep for a month. Correction: Smoke crack for a couple of hours, then sleep for a month. I looked around the streets of Wolfville and thought about how trying to score crack here would probably (and hopefully for the residents) be futile. Halifax might be different. Dickie's wife Rose had done that at the end, I remembered: gone to Halifax to be alone with her drug. And she'd died there.

"Wait," I said. "Did I dream it, or did you tell me that Dickie had mentioned to you that he thought he was seeing his dead wife following him around?"

"You didn't dream it," he said. He reached for the chips, as we were at a standstill while a young couple kissed goodbye in the middle of the street – with no one honking their horns. "Look at that," he said, nodding at them. "Young love."

"Do you think he was going crazy? Seriously. Did he sound like he was mentally ill?" After what I'd gone through with Jack, my family had had a crash course in mental illness.

"He's never been the same, since Rose died," Laurence said, after a long pause. "Well, after he figured out that she'd become addicted to the pain meds, and he didn't know how to deal with it."

"No," I said. "It's awful what addiction can do to couples." Not to mention mental illness. Jack's had come long before my drug use. If I hadn't been so devastated by leaving Jack, in so much pain and guilt, I wouldn't have sought out that escape. Or been as self-destructive.

"To families, Danny."

"You don't have to remind me," I said. "I'm very aware." Without a word, I pointed to a sign ahead, in front of a pizza joint, that advertised donairs. And by some miracle, someone pulled out of a spot right in front of it. I handed Laurence a couple of twenties, asked for a veggie slice, and sunk down into the seat to wait. And think of the plan I had promised Laurence.

I checked my bag, just a medium-sized nylon tote I carried around a lot in the city. My fanny pack was inside, with the screwdriver and extra cash, and my wallet with cards and emergency numbers. My phone was in my pocket. The hammer was at the bottom, giving the bag a bit of extra heft, which I appreciated.

And where we were going, there was going to be at least one gun. And beds to sleep in, because I was going to need to get my head down. The adrenaline was wearing off a bit. I'd get us settled in, and I would tell my body to wake up just before dawn. I was able to do that, if I needed to.

I kept glancing at the pizza joint, checking to make sure Laurence was still in there, safely in line. He stood out among the young students, ready for their summer session, and the town kids, who looked a tiny bit tougher but with whom I immediately identified.

Maybe someday I would go back to school. I'd always thought of Ginger as the academic, both Ginger and Laurence. Skipper, Darren, and I had been more streetwise, more eager to start our real lives, no matter how ephemeral those lives had seemed at the time.

Now, my brother Skipper owned a few car lots and was living a happy, comfortable life with his wife Marie back home, marred only by their infertility. They were starting the process of becoming foster parents, and while nobody had said so to me, I knew that what had happened in their home in December – the fact that I, Skipper's crack addict sister, had murdered a cop in cold blood in their foyer – might affect their chances. Everybody knew that Harry Miller was a murderous cop, but that's a pretty high hurdle for potential foster parents. Helping them somehow was on my to-do list. It was a long list, and at least with the money Jack had left me, maybe I could actually do some good.

The night was pretty now, warm, the cold rain of the afternoon behind us. I leaned my head out the car window and tried to get the same joy from the smell of the air that I'd had only, what, yesterday afternoon. All I smelled was donair, pizza, and the faint but unmistakable tang of skunk weed. My fantasy of twenty-four hours earlier, of buying a summer property here, had dwindled markedly after the events of the last day. Being shot at and being in close proximity to so many dead bodies will do that to a girl. But I looked around and envied the people walking by, the cars full of teenagers with their windows rolled down, enjoying their Saturday night. Wolfville was a lot more cosmopolitan than Downs Falls ever was – we didn't have a university, and that changes a place. And even now, Downs Falls didn't have places advertising organic fair trade coffee and poetry slams.

I put my hand on my thigh, thinking about when I had got the tattoo done there in Maine, back when I still had the cast on my leg. After I'd gotten the letter from Dave, which I'd memorized and then burned in Marie's sink. And then immediately smoked a little rock with the bathroom fan on.

It had been in the back of my mind for the past twenty-four hours to call Dave. I was supposed to call him if I encountered our mutual nemesis, Michael Vernon Smith, but also if I just needed help. And really, what with getting a severed head thrown at me in the woods last night, having a dead cop's brains decorating my clothing this afternoon – not to mention getting shot at – and finding poor Sarah earlier, I was fairly sure that this met the criteria for "needing help," by anyone's standards.

And at this point, I really couldn't be sure that this had nothing to do with what had happened to us all in California, in Toronto, in Maine. It seemed unlikely – I hadn't had enough time to process all this, but whether or not Dickie Doyle was behind what was happening, this was a madman on a particularly grisly spree, and I was just in the wrong place at the wrong time. I was a bit more worried about Laurence, after the yellow pickup from the airport, and the fact that he was Dickie's only confidante.

Laurence was at the counter now. I didn't really want pizza, I wanted a couple of glasses of Prosecco. Not even crack – I could get by without it tonight. Just a glass of wine, to take the edge off.

Two weeks. I had had two weeks in rehab, before people started dying. I resolved that if I did hire a sober companion back in Toronto, that I would provide him or her with their own bodyguard. Then I started laughing, alone in the car, thinking about me, my security, my sober companion and her security, all heading out to walk the dog I was thinking of getting. A rescue dog, one other people had given up on. Jack had been allergic and after him, I was in no shape to take care of anything.

When Laurence walked out of the take-out place, I was almost cheerful. We were going to get through this. Laurence would go home to his very own Tony Soprano, Senior, and I would go back to Toronto and surround myself with dogs and security people and nephews and would do Good Deeds with my new money.

But first things first.

"There's a liquor store, next street over," I said. "I've passed it before." Laurence looked at me, but under the current circumstances even he couldn't muster any real disapproval. He was probably gagging for a drink as much as I was. "Rehab is over, for the time being," I said. I put my hand up. "I'm not asking to be let loose to wander the Acadia campus inquiring after crack. A civilized, adult beverage. You know booze isn't my issue." And he did know it. I didn't think about it, didn't think about not being able to abstain in rehab, as it had never been part of my daily life. But if a woman isn't allowed to get a bit tiddly on white wine after she's had the kind of twenty-four hours I'd had, then I didn't know what.

"Lead on," Laurence said. Before we pulled into traffic, he looked at me. "I got you a donair, just in case."

"What about my veggie slice?"

He rolled his eyes. "That too."

I patted his arm. "Good man."

First thing tomorrow morning, I was going to call Dave, and I was going to end this.

EIGHTEEN

After we loaded more booze than was necessary into the Beast, I told Laurence to head back to Ferryman Lake. I told him about Constable MacLean and the freak flag cottage, just leaving out the part where she encouraged me to assassinate his oldest friend.

"Really? She just gave you the keys to her family's cottage?"

"Small town," I said. "Besides, she's a cop, and she knows about our family, and who knows, maybe her family and the Doyles were friends." I regretted saying it as soon as it came out of my mouth. "Anyway. Don't forget, I practically got naked in front of this woman. That shit breeds intimacy."

"And she probably feels sorry for you," Laurence said, seriously, and then after a second we both laughed.

"Indeed, after almost seeing me naked and all," I said. "Aside from my obvious physical malformations."

"All you people are malformed, you ask me," he said.

"You people?"

"Women."

"Badum tish," I said. "Jackass."

"I'm here all week."

Laurence didn't have to be reminded where to turn off

the main drag, as I knew he wouldn't. He had a crazy accurate sense of direction. We drove the same route we had the night before, when we dropped Mary off at her house. Neither of us said anything, but I knew we were both wondering if we should stop in and pay our respects, give our condolences about Colin. I knew I didn't really want to, selfishly, not tonight. That kind of grief is private, for family only, and the fact that I, especially, had been so up close and personal with her nephew in the second he died would make things worse.

"We don't have anything to bring anyway," Laurence said, reading my thoughts. "You can't show up to a house in mourning without some food." He was right, and I doubted two donairs and a slice of pizza were quite the thing. But, conveniently, neither of us had remembered to pick anything up when we were driving through town.

"Tomorrow," I said. "We need rest. I'm sure Mary does too."

We did. And I also wanted to check out the cabin we were going to, make sure I managed to claim the bed with the gun safe underneath, eat and get to sleep early. I was going to wake up at dawn and if I couldn't get a signal on my phone and the cabin didn't have a landline, I was going to take the Mustang and drive far enough into civilization that I could call Dave.

No. First, I would call the cops and make sure nothing else extreme had happened, and maybe they'd even have made an arrest overnight. Failing that, I'd call Dave, park the Mustang by the main road, leave a note for Laurence and go for a little walk in the woods. This time, with a gun in my hand instead of a rock.

As we approached Mary's house, Laurence slowed a little bit. All the lights were on. A squad car was parked in the driveway. I wondered if Des was still there, or if he had gone back. I hadn't seen him since he'd left to tell Mary about Colin earlier in the day.

From the road, we could hear yelling. Men screaming at each other. I didn't hear Mary's voice, or any female voice. It made my heart beat faster.

Laurence picked up speed.

"Was that Des?" he said.

"I have no idea," I said. "It could be anybody." My fucking hearing. I didn't know if I was ever going to get used to it. "I heard men, and that was it. My bet is no, however." We drove on for a couple of minutes until the house was out of sight.

"Do you think we should go back?" he said. "Make sure Mary's okay?"

"No," I said. "It's her house. There's a cop car there. Her husband and somebody else are arguing. She's probably in bed, about to yell at them to shut up." I thought for a second. "It's family business, Laurence."

I didn't believe what I was saying, not a bit. Whatever weird intuition thing I had was telling me that something wrong was happening there, but also that Laurence and I should be away from it, and fast.

Suddenly I wanted to smoke crack so badly I wanted to weep. I wouldn't have to listen to the voices in my brain that made me do or not do things. On crack, I was just bliss incarnate. No conscience, no rage, no sadness.

I wanted to talk to Dr. Singh right now.

I knew she'd been told about all this, but was anybody making sure she was alright? Hadn't somebody told me she lived in the city and commuted in a few days a week? She was as tied to Rose's Place as anybody else, certainly more than somebody like Sarah, who'd only been there a couple of weeks. And look at what had happened to her.

But this was not my job here. My only job was taking care of my brother and my brother's friend – or at least finding my brother's friend, even if he was involved. Keeping Laurence safe and putting his mind at rest, one way or another. They had a whole police force full of people who could take care of the rest of it.

"Keep driving. Please. Mary's fine, I know it."

Laurence kept driving. He knew me well enough to know that if I really thought Mary was in trouble I would have made him stop. But right now, I wasn't sure that was true. The past days had been horrific, and as much as I liked Mary and felt awful for her and her family, keeping Laurence safe was my priority. It had to be. "We'll visit tomorrow," I said. "And maybe call first."

We drove the rest of the way in silence. I knew Laurence was worried about Dickie or Mary or both. So was I, but I had to figure out a plan for the next day that would keep my brother safely occupied.

"So this is really it?" Laurence pulled into the MacLeans' driveway slowly. It was pitch black up here, and while we could see through the trees that a few places around the lake had patio lanterns and lights on, things on this part of the lake seemed deserted. "I've got to take pictures of this tomorrow. Antonio will flip."

He was right. And I was going to take pictures too, for our nephews. I hoped I could pass off this time as a fun little holiday, Aunt Danny and Uncle Laurence doing silly things together and taking pictures. Note to self: buy them souvenirs.

The cottage was much bigger than it looked through the trees from the road. Definitely bigger than Dickie Doyle's cabin by some order of magnitude. The part that was visible, the crazy lavender stripes, was actually the second story. The ground floor was like a different place altogether, a tasteful cedar with what looked like wrought-iron trim painted white. It was hard to tell just by the headlights, but the place looked as though someone had put one cottage on top of a very different one.

"I guess they're pretty lax with the old planning permissions out here," I said. "Wow." But I dug it. I've always been drawn to things that don't look like they belong together – which, my brothers always said, explained my dress sense.

"Are you sure this is okay?" Laurence said. We were still sitting in the car. I had the keys clenched in my hand, and I handed him the hammer.

"Yes, it's fine," I said. "Swear to God. She gave me the keys and told us to stay here. No hotels, remember?" I was not strictly lying, and Laurence would forgive me later. I hoped.

"So why am I holding a hammer?" he said.

"Because, in case you hadn't noticed, we've been surrounded by dead bodies since you stepped off the plane, and a hammer beats a rock." I laced the keys through my fingers and cracked my neck. I checked that my running shoes were laced properly and wished I had my Docs. "Just hang on a second." I took the fanny pack out of my bag and grabbed the screwdriver. I'd come back for the bag once we'd checked the place out. I debated telling Laurence to stay in the car while I walked around the property, but I knew it would be useless.

No motion-sensor lights had come on when we pulled into the drive, like I'd been hoping, so I was counting on there being one by the door. But if the family hadn't officially opened the place for the season, it could all be shut down. "Turn the lights off," I said. The headlights might help us stop from tripping over something, but they would also screw with our night vision. I'd memorized exactly where the door was as we'd been sitting there. There was a bit of moonlight. We'd be fine. "Just follow right behind me," I said. "Remember, my hearing is wonky. If you can stick right to my back and walk backward with your phone flashlight on, do that."

"I can barely walk forward," he reminded me.

"Bullshit, Mr. Track and Field," I said. "You move like a cat." This made him laugh, which I was hoping for. I wanted him relaxed enough to be able to move and not be paralyzed by whatever paranoia I was instilling in him.

We got out of the car and moved quickly to the door. Nothing seemed amiss. No body parts – that I could see in the dark, anyway – and no gunshots. I could hear Laurence breathing close behind me.

I nearly tripped on the stairs up to the door, because I'm graceful that way. An owl hooted not too far away, and I nearly jumped out of my skin, which made Laurence make a sound that was close to a giggle.

There were two keys on the ring Constable MacLean had given me. One was bigger than the other and obviously for the door. I found the lock, and it turned easily. I wished Laurence was safely in the car, but just now it didn't feel like anywhere was safe, so I'd rather he was close to me.

I swung the door open and stepped back, nearly knocking Laurence over. I'd almost expected to be met with a gun or an axe, but nothing. It was quiet, and it was dark. I leaned inside and felt around for a light switch, found it, and flipped it on.

There was light. There was a homey-looking kitchen. There was nothing on the stove and no cold, newly poured glasses of beer, like at Dickie's. The place smelled a little musty, like the windows hadn't been opened for a good while, but I didn't smell the coppery scent of blood that I'd come to know so well. No stench of decomposition. It was just a cottage. And so far, it seemed empty of anything but us, and possibly whatever mice had made it their home over the winter.

"Okay," I said. "Come in, and lock the door behind you."

While Laurence rummaged around in the kitchen for plates for the donairs and pulled the fridge out to plug it in, I made the excuse of having to find the bathroom and did a swift check of the place, screwdriver in hand. I turned on every light and opened every closet, quickly. There were no sheets on any of the beds in the three bedrooms so I was spared having to whip them down to check for stray body parts.

Laurence yelled something from downstairs.

I took the stairs two at a time, heart pounding. I paused while running through the living room to grab a heavy-looking copper lamp, ripping the cord from the wall.

In the kitchen, Laurence was whistling. He took one look at me with the lamp in one hand and the screwdriver in another, standing in the doorway, and nearly dropped the plates he was holding.

"What the fuck," he said. "Is somebody here?" He slid the

plates onto the counter and grabbed his hammer with both hands, like a tennis racket.

"No! You were yelling," I said. My heart was slowing down.

"Oh!" he said. "Don't scare me like that." He put the hammer down. "I said, there's no water." He nodded at the sink. "Nada."

"Jesus," I said. I looked at the lamp I was holding. I'd managed to break part of the cord out of the base. Leave me alone for five minutes and I break the house. No wonder I rarely got invited anywhere.

Well, that, and being a degenerate crack addict.

"The place hasn't been opened for the season yet," I said. "Constable MacLean gave me her card. I guess I can call her and ask if it's okay to turn it on. In the basement I guess." There was a door off the kitchen.

"Funny the power was on, though," he said. He was right, and it bothered me. And if the power was on in the cottage, shouldn't the lights at the top of the lane and outside be turned on? Then again, I was no electrician, and most things had a very simple explanation. Occam's razor. But after the last couple of days, all horses were going to look like zebras to us.

I looked again at the basement door, and looked at Laurence. He was looking at it too.

"Shit," I said. "You stay here. I'll be two minutes." I really wanted a glass of wine, a few bites of food, and to find where they kept the sheets. I hesitated a minute, debating running upstairs and getting the gun under MacLean's bed. But despite everything, I felt almost safe, and I wanted this done quickly.

"Danny," Laurence said. "Look."

Behind the kitchen door, hanging neatly on hooks in the

wall was an axe. The handle looked old and sturdy, but the blade was clean, with no rust that I could see.

"Woodstove in the living room," I said. "They chop wood." My mouth was dry.

"Sure," he said.

"We chopped wood at our cottage," I said. "Dad kept it right beside the back door like this, too."

"Yes, he did."

"Fuck this," I said. I grabbed the axe off the wall, tested its weight. "Open the wine," I said.

"I'm coming with you," Laurence said, and grabbed his hammer.

"Don't be stupid. There is nothing down there." I put my hand on the doorknob, and turned back. "But if you hear me screaming or anything, you know..."

"Run for the hills," he said.

"I was going to say come and rescue me."

"Oh," he said. He nodded. "Okay."

The second I started to open the door, a phone rang. An old-fashioned telephone ring. I believe I may have screamed a little, startled, but Laurence had more presence of mind. There was a telephone hanging on the wall.

"MacLean residence," he said. He sounded like a butler. Definitely not like he was watching his little sister about to descend into a strange basement holding an axe. "Oh, hello, Constable," he said, friendly. "Thank you, we did, we found it fine." He was listening. "I know she's sorry about that, but he probably shouldn't have come up behind her and restrained her when she had just seen a dead body, under the..." He listened some more. "Well, she is that. She's right here."

It seemed so normal. "Hello?" I said, taking the phone from him.

"Hi, Ms. Cleary," Constable MacLean said. She sounded friendly enough, if tired. "I just wanted to make sure you were both okay and all that."

"Please call me Danny," I said. "After all, I'm going to be sleeping in your bed tonight." And then I blushed. I did get a vaguely lesbian vibe from her, but I wasn't meaning to flirt. However, as I seem to have no ability to speak normally when I'm stressed or nervous, half the population probably thinks I'm either a sex addict or that I have Tourette's.

"You're trying to let me know that you found the right room," she said. Wow. She understood. I looked at my brother, who was wiggling his eyebrows at me. "Good."

"Yes, thanks," I said. "Listen, we just got here, and it seems the water is off."

"That's the other reason I was phoning," she said. "We keep the power turned on year round – Dad has a nerdy reason for that, but don't ask me, 'cause I don't listen. But we always turn the water on and off if we go in off-season. Do you want me to walk you through turning it on?"

"I'm going to let Laurence do that," I said. Now that Debbie was on the phone, my fear of the basement seemed silly. I wasn't nuts about admitting I was making my brother do the manly work, but I was the product of fairly traditional parents, and Jack and I had always lived in apartments. I had wanted to go into the basement to save Laurence from any machete-wielding boogeymen, but if I tried to turn the water on, I'd probably wind up extinguishing a pilot light somehow and blowing us both up.

"Before you hand me over to him, I just want to thank you," she said. "I'm sorry if I put you in an awkward position today. I shouldn't have said what I said. I was upset."

"I get it," I said. "Really." I did. I'd said as bad or worse to people I shouldn't have when Ginger and Jack died. "And thanks again for letting us stay here. It's really very nice of you."

"Yes, it is," Laurence said loudly in the background, for her to hear. He was looking for a corkscrew and seemed much more relaxed. Constable MacLean laughed.

"Use the phone as much as you want, don't worry about it," she said. "Nobody can get cell reception in that spot. About a half mile as the crow flies in either direction you're fine, but we're in a dead zone there."

"Nice choice of words, Constable," I said.

"God, call me Debbie," she said. "Now, let me talk to your brother so you guys can relax and try to get some sleep."

I stood at the top of the stairs holding the phone while Laurence went down to turn the water on. MacLean – Debbie – was quiet on the other end. I think she knew I would be nervous until he got back up.

"Danny," she said. She sounded like she was being careful. "You saw Sarah, obviously, yes?"

"Not her face," I said. "Just some of her body. Enough."

She sighed into the phone. "You're not particularly squeamish, after everything you've been through?"

"I don't know about that. No, I guess."

She spoke quietly and quickly. "Sarah didn't die in that spot. Well, we knew that."

"Right."

"The ME said… well, she said that Sarah suffered from exposure and dehydration as well as her wounds. Her hands – well, her wrists were severely abraded." She didn't have a lot of her hands left, which was what Debbie was trying not to say.

"What happened to her?" I said. I was being quiet, trying to hear downstairs as well as into the phone.

"The working theory is that she was tied to a tree or a rock – probably a tree, had something stuffed in her mouth so she couldn't scream, and she was left there for the animals." I could hear MacLean lighting a cigarette.

"Holy mother of God," I said. "In one night? That happened to her in one night?"

"One night and one day, yes," she said. "We've got more wildlife in some areas than people realize. Wolves, we've had a few black bear maulings over the years… even stray or feral dogs could have done what was done to her." We were both silent for a minute. It didn't bear to be considered too much.

She had been sitting with us just last night. Sitting around the table with us.

"Danny, try the water," Laurence yelled up from the basement. I walked over to the sink, got some noisy air, then rusty water. I let it run, just as Debbie was telling me to let it run.

"I got it," I said. I yelled to Laurence he could come back up. "I feel sick," I said to Debbie.

"We all do," she said. "And listen – what I told you today, about the woods? Stay away from there. Stay in the cottage, play board games. There's no TV, but there's a radio and stuff. My stepmom is a huge reader, there's tons of books. I'll pop in tomorrow afternoon sometime and bring you guys some food, but I'll call first. You know what the other key is for, but don't go looking for any trouble. This is too much. Just stay safe."

"Thanks," I said automatically. Laurence came into the kitchen with a big smile on his face, as though he had dug the well himself.

"And, Danny? Just to keep my mind easy, maybe tonight keep the curtains closed and don't keep all the lights on."

"Oh," I said. "Right." Of course. If Dickie had anything to do with this, he'd be able to see the lights from the woods, if he liked tramping around in there as much as she seemed to think. If he was still alive, that is. Had Sarah died in these woods? Surely it would have to have been even more remote than this?

I waited until after he'd eaten to tell Laurence about Sarah, and even then I didn't mention the animals. But he wasn't stupid. We drank two bottles of wine quietly, in the semi-dark, checked the locks on all the windows, and quietly made up our beds. Laurence was in the room next to mine, and I told him to put a chair under his door. The bedroom doors didn't lock.

Why should they? This was rural Nova Scotia. The safest place in the world.

NINETEEN

I set my internal clock to wake up half an hour before sunrise. I wanted to be out early, in case Laurence woke up with the sun. New places can do that to a person.

Just after five a.m., I was up, quietly bathed, and dressed in somebody else's clothes.

Not only did Debbie MacLean's room have the gun safe, it also had a few things in the drawers – a couple of bikinis, an old pair of Seven jeans and a few pairs of denim cut-offs, and an oversized Acadia University sweatshirt. I was glad that the jeans fit, and were even the right length, more or less. After a second's thought, I took them off and put a bikini on underneath as underwear – I hadn't worn a bra last night and I had nothing with me, and I wanted as much on as possible. Why a bikini under my clothes should make me feel safer, I couldn't tell you, but after sleeping in my t-shirt and jeans – the furnace wasn't turned on yet, and the nights were still cool – I felt like the layers were armor. I put my t-shirt back on over the bikini top and pulled the Acadia sweatshirt over the top. I tiptoed to the bathroom and pulled my hair into a ponytail. It had been a long time since I'd kept it that long.

From a distance, if you didn't see the Glock stuck down the back of my jeans or the frown lines etched between my eyebrows, I could be a student on a late-spring stroll. Gathering mushrooms, perhaps.

I listened at Laurence's door, glad he was a loud snorer. He was fine. He would be fine. I'd listened to the radio before bed and the day was promising to be warm and sunny. Nothing bad would happen today.

Downstairs, I used the landline to call the detachment. I kept my fingers crossed, hoping they had made an arrest while Laurence and I slept.

They hadn't. Plan B: walk up the road until I could get cell reception, and call Dave out of earshot of Laurence, if he woke up and wandered downstairs.

The thought made me feel better. I had a gun, and it was loaded, and I had extra ammo in my fanny pack. My phone was charged, even if it wasn't getting a signal here. I'd written a note to my brother saying I'd be right back, that I was armed, and for him to sit tight. I taped it to my closed bedroom door, which he'd have to pass on his way to the bathroom.

I'd hesitated for long minutes about telling him about the gun, but I figured he'd worry less if he knew I had it. I'd deal with the flak later. And that's if I didn't get back before he woke up.

Just before I left the house, I grabbed a bottle of the energy drink that I'd put in the fridge the night before. I thought of Sarah, thirsty, scared, cold. And then the animals.

I had to sit down on a chair for a minute with my head between my legs.

Then I said a quick prayer that Laurence would sleep for

hours, soundly and safely, and I quietly left, locking the door behind me.

The sun was coming up, and the birds were making a racket. Twenty feet from the cottage, I took the Glock from my waistband and carried it in my hand.

I had no permit, and even if I did, I was pretty sure Nova Scotia would be like Ontario – no open carry, anywhere. Canada took its gun laws seriously, and there should be Mounties posted somewhere on the main road near Dickie's cabin. But I was planning on walking the other way, and with the quiet, I figured I would hear any car in plenty of time to hide or toss the gun. Besides, with what I'd seen in the last couple of days, I knew there were worse things than the possibility of a weapons charge.

If I could only block out what I thought might be lurking in the woods, it was a beautiful morning. The road had been freshly gravelled, and crunched pleasingly underfoot. It felt good to be moving my body again. It was cool – it wouldn't warm up for a few hours – but the sweatshirt was warm, and even with tight jeans on I was tempted to break into a slow run. But my ankle was aching a bit already from lack of use in the last days, and I couldn't risk injury. I hoped nobody else had been killed in the hours I'd slept. I hoped the police had made an arrest.

How could someone have carried Sarah's body onto the grounds of Rose's and left her there, so close to the main house, with no one seeing? It spoke not only of an incomprehensible amount of luck and/or skill, but also dangerous confidence. Overconfidence. Nobody could take that many risks and continue to evade police. Not to mention the media, who had been camped at the end of Rose's driveway for days. I hadn't listened to enough radio to hear more than basic details last night, but they had the news about the shooting on the grounds. Impossible to quash that story; it would have been heard. They hadn't released Colin's name, or even mentioned a fatality. I was glad I wasn't on the RCMP Communications team this weekend. But as far as I was concerned, the less information that got out immediately, the better. The killer, or killers, didn't seem to want to target anybody who wasn't involved with Rose's Place. So far, at least, the general public seemed to be safe.

I just hoped there wasn't anybody on staff or with the police who had loose lips about the names of residents. My notoriety after the events in Maine in December may have died down, but here on the east coast, they might still be fresh in people's minds. And having Michael Vernon Smith know my whereabouts when I was this exposed was not something I wanted to add to the mix.

More reason to get hold of Dave.

After fifteen minutes or so of walking, I tried my phone. There was only a faint signal, but enough. I'd put the local RCMP detachment in my contacts, and after hesitating for a moment, I called them back. I decided to try to speak to Des. The other officer had confirmed no arrests, but maybe they had more information, a lead of some kind, and I wouldn't have to bother Dave. It was a beautiful morning. Something good had to happen today.

I moved to the centre of the road, furthest from the trees on either side. I'd hear and see a car coming, but if I was distracted on the phone and trying to hear what someone was saying, I might not hear anyone – anything – approaching me from the bush. I longed, at that moment, for city streets, the first time I had since I had arrived in Nova Scotia.

Someone at the detachment answered on the first ring. It was a different cop, and he sounded more awake than the one I'd just spoken to.

"Miss Cleary," the cop said. "We've met. I'm Constable Gordon."

"Okay," I said. I had no idea which one he was.

"Have you seen Sergeant Murphy since yesterday afternoon?" Oh, no. Des.

"No," I said. "The last I saw, he was going to inform Mary about Colin. Uh, Constable LeBlanc." I was aware my voice was tight. "I was calling to see if he was on duty. Why?"

There was a pause. "He left there – Mary's, that is – after a couple hours. And… well, he never came back here, or to Rose's. And he didn't go home last night, either."

"Oh, fuck," I said.

"Yes, ma'am," he said. "I know you and the sarge became friendly, and he was watching out for you. If you hear from him?"

"Of course," I said. "Thanks, Constable."

I hung up, and felt like my head was going to explode. Not him. Not Des. If Des didn't turn up, alive, today, then I was going to get Laurence into the car, and we were going to drive as far away from here as we could get, Dickie or no Dickie.

I was about to phone Dave, phone the number that was tattooed into my thigh and into my brain, when I heard a vehicle some distance away. It was a long way around the bend, but not many people at this hour observed speed limits.

Immediately I chucked the Glock, underhand, a few feet into the woods.

On impulse, I followed it, darting into the woods and

flattening myself into the muddy ground.

The vehicle approached without slowing, and when it passed I peeked up.

Canary yellow pickup. Tinted windows, rolled up this time. Coming from the direction of both Dickie's and the MacLean cottage.

Laurence.

I waited a couple of beats until I was sure it was out of sight, grabbed the Glock from where it was, under my body, and then I turned and ran, back toward my brother.

TWENTY

I got twenty yards. Before I was out of cell range, I stopped and hit redial. The same cop answered, and in a breathless rush, I told him what had just happened.

Leaving aside the Glock, of course.

He wanted to know what road I was on, and I couldn't tell him the name of it.

"A few kilometres past where Mary lives," I said. "On Ferryman Lake."

"We're on our way," the cop said, all business. "Miss Cleary, I want you to stay exactly where you are, by the side of the road. Someone will be right with you. Do not step back into the woods, and don't go back the way you came. Stay exactly where you are."

"No," I said. "My brother. We're staying at Constable MacLean's cottage. She gave me the keys, somewhere safe to stay. He was asleep when I left."

"Oh, good," he said. "I know it. We'll be there in two shakes. But stay where you are. And if you see the truck again, then get off the road."

Which? I wanted to say. Stay out of the woods, or get into the woods? "Hurry," I said. I hung up, and continued to run. As

I did, I put the Glock into my fanny pack, in case I released the safety while running and shot myself in the foot. Stranger things have been known, etc.

I ran, full tilt, and cursed my hearing. I could only hear my breathing, which was too labored for such a short run, and my feet hitting the gravel, which no longer felt so pleasant. I didn't know whether to pray for the sound of a car – the police – or dread it – the pickup.

I ran down the drive and fumbled for the keys. My hands were shaking. No lights were on, but it might be bright enough inside now. I'd only been gone for what? Half an hour? A bit more?

I ran up the steps to the porch, and accidentally dropped the keys.

They landed on a small box, wrapped in red tissue paper, that was sitting by the door. There was a white card on top that said "Lawrence." Spelled incorrectly. Couldn't be Dickie. Unless he didn't want people to think it was him.

I grabbed the keys gingerly, trying not to touch the box. It was about the size of a shoebox, but flatter. I unlocked the door, but before I walked in, I looked over my shoulder. No police. I took the Glock out of my fanny pack and went in, closing and locking the door quickly behind me.

"Where the fuck did you get that?" Laurence said, looking at the gun. I jumped out of my skin. He was standing in the kitchen with a can of energy drink in his hand, wearing a robe.

"Come with me, quickly," I said. I grabbed his hand and pulled, and he moved.

We ran up the stairs and into my – Debbie MacLean's – room. I unlocked the gun safe and wiped the gun clean of my fingerprints with the sweatshirt while Laurence watched. After I locked it back in the safe, I wiped the safe. I stepped around Laurence, who was standing with his mouth open staring at me, and shut the bedroom door behind us, putting a flimsy wicker chair under the handle. I took the screwdriver out of my bag, wishing I had thought to tell Laurence to grab the hammer.

The police were on their way, yes. Constable Gordon had promised "in two shakes." But I had found Sarah's body right under their noses, and very probably whoever had left the box outside this door had shot and killed a cop through a window with us in the room. I whipped the curtains shut from the side, without standing directly in front of the window, and told Laurence to sit on the bed.

"How long have you been up?" I said.

"Ten minutes," he said. "About."

"Did you hear anyone? See anything by the back door?"

"Danny. No." He paused. "But something woke me up. Some noise."

I told him about the truck, and the package, and it was all I could do to keep him in the room.

"The police are coming. That package could be a trap to get you to open the door. Get you shot. Or worse." I paced, and thought better of walking back and forth in front of the window, curtains or no. I debated taking the gun back out of the safe.

I thought of Sarah.

I sat next to Laurence on the bed. He grabbed my hand. "So, we wait," he said.

"Not my forte," I said. I felt like a coward. I don't sit. This needed to be over with. And I hadn't had a chance to call Dave.

"I'm aware," he said. "But while you might be a fighting demon, I'm bigger than you are, and you're not going to try to hurt me. You're staying in this room until Sergeant Murphy knocks on that door."

"That might be a problem," I said. I told him what the cop had told me, about Des being missing. Laurence thought for a bit.

"Dickie is dead," he said. "He must be."

"Not necessarily," I said. "Laurence. You said that Dickie's been seeing Rose around. He must think she's alive. But presumably it was easy enough to identify her body when she died, so it's not like there was some mistake at the morgue or something. The woman is dead." God, what I wouldn't have given for a cigarette. Not even crack. Just a simple cigarette. But they were downstairs.

"Yes," he said.

"Dead people don't wander around," I said. "Dickie is not well."

"I know that's what you've been thinking," he said. "It's been written all over your face." Oh. So much for my poker face. "But you're wrong. I don't know how else to say it." He looked like he was trying not to wring his hands.

"Did she have any sisters? Twins? Ha?"

Laurence shook his head. "Her father came to the funeral. No siblings, at least none there, and none that I know of. Her mother died in childbirth."

"And her father is where?" I felt guilty that I didn't know this; he'd probably told me.

"New Hampshire, I think. Rhode Island? Somewhere like that. Bad health. I'm not even sure if he's still alive."

He put his hand up. "Cars in the drive," he said. I heard it right after he said it, but we were the other side of the building, facing the lake.

Moments later, there was a racket at the back door, and noise at the front door as well.

"Danny?" I heard a female voice calling out. Debbie. Constable MacLean.

"The cavalry is here," I said. I exhaled. We went downstairs.

It was chaos, but under the circumstances, very welcome chaos. There were two cops inside and one outside. One of them was putting on some kind of protective gear; to handle the box, I presumed. Laurence and I had been relegated to the couch in the living room and told not to move. And despite the sunny morning, the cops kept the curtains shut.

These were fresh faces. I wondered how many Mounties worked around here, of it these were reinforcements.

"Has anyone seen Mary?" I asked the room. Constable MacLean came over and perched on the couch next to me.

"I just talked to her," she said, "and to Geoffrey, her husband. She's taken to her bed, pretty much. Colin is her sister's boy, and her sister died years ago. They were very close."

I paused to let that sink in. "But Des was there yesterday," I said. I thought of the squad car sat outside when Laurence and I passed in the evening, and the yelling. "What time did he leave?"

"Late afternoon, according to Geoffrey. He thinks about five."

I looked at Laurence, and spoke. "We passed there last night on our way here. Not sure the time. Maybe ten? And there was a squad car there, and we heard men's voices yelling."

"Yes," she said. She looked like she hadn't slept since yesterday. "I heard. Geoffrey and one of the other sergeants. Geoffrey was upset about Colin, about how we could have let this happen. You know. Et cetera."

"But Mary's okay?" Laurence looked at her. I wanted to put him in the car and drive away. I wanted to feel safe for five minutes.

"She is. And she isn't. You know. But she's safe, if that's what you mean."

"As much as anybody else is," I said. MacLean sort of smiled at me. It must have been weird for her to have all these people in her private space. No doubt she was regretting giving me those keys about now.

"Everything locked up safe?" she said quietly to me.

"Yes, clean, safe, all good."

She smiled at me for real. "Those are my clothes."

I felt myself go red. "Oh my God, I'm so sorry. I didn't go back in for my things." I didn't tell her I was wearing one of her bikinis for underwear. Hospitality only goes so far.

"No, it's fine," she said. "They look better on you." More blushing. No way was I going to look at my brother, whose eyebrows were probably going a mile a minute. I didn't even feel like she was flirting with me, but after my experience with Miller, and my general social awkwardness without drugs or violence, I felt silly. "If you like, I can pick up your things from Rose's. Or I can bring you other things to wear." Now, this time I did feel like she was flirting, because of the way she said it. I opened my mouth to say something that would undoubtedly have been stupid, when there was a small commotion in the kitchen. MacLean excused herself and told us to stay put.

"So. How's your holiday so far?" I said to Laurence.

"Beautiful scenery," he said. "Of course, it's a bit quiet around here, after the hectic pace in New York." I nodded. We sat in silence.

There was a hushed conversation going on in the kitchen and I, for one, wanted to hear it. But of course couldn't, due to my stupid bad ear. After a few minutes, two of the officers came in, the two I didn't recognize.

"Mr. Cleary," one of them said, his hands behind his back, "I understand that you and Dickie Doyle are good friends."

"Since university," Laurence said. He'd been asked this a million times already, but he sounded patient. Certainly more than I would be.

The cop nodded. "I'd like to ask you to look at something for us, and I'll be honest: It's going to be upsetting."

Laurence just nodded. The cop signalled to one of the other ones, who disappeared and came back in with the box. The lid was on.

"The box was addressed to you, but there was no note," the cop continued. "I'm going to show you the contents of this box, and I'd like you to identify it for me if you can."

They put the box on the coffee table in front of us, instructing us not to touch it. One of them took the lid off.

Inside the box was a man's ring finger. With a ring on it. And a lot of blood. I knew what that meant.

"He's alive," I said. "That was taken off him when he was alive." I looked at my brother, who had no expression on his face. He was bent over, looking closely at the finger without touching it.

"That's the ring," he said. "That's Dickie's ring. I was his best man. I carried it around for him for two days." He leaned back on the couch. "How does that mean he's alive?"

"If it had been taken after he was dead, it would be cleaner, less bloody," I said.

"That's partially true," one of the cops said. "We'll be analyzing it, obviously, but we just wanted your initial identification."

"He can't have done this," Laurence said. "Dickie Doyle could not have done this." There was a second of silence. Seemed not everyone in the room agreed.

"If it is Dickie Doyle's – well, it is possible for someone to cut off their own finger," one of the men said, gently. "Nothing about this case has been normal. Someone who could do what happened to that girl…" he started to say, but someone shushed him.

"No," Laurence said. "I mean, he literally couldn't have done this." He pointed to the box. "Dickie is left-handed. Very left-handed; and he has severe nerve damage in his right hand since surgery after a rugby match at Bennington." I didn't know this. I wondered if Laurence was making it up to get the police to believe in Dickie's innocence. But it would be easy to disprove; anyone close enough to him – Mary – would know if this was true. "Dickie could barely hold a fork in his right hand, let alone manage to cut off his own finger with it." I could tell that Laurence didn't know whether to be happy or even more upset.

Someone was holding Dickie Doyle and cutting pieces off him. And wanted Laurence to know it.

"We are leaving today," I said, to the room at large. "If you people need formal statements, we'll come in now and give them. And then we're going back to Toronto. We can answer any further questions from there."

"That's a very good idea," one of the cops said.

"You leave today," Laurence said to me. He looked at the cop who'd shown him the box. "I'm searching for Dickie. I won't get in anyone's way. And if you have a problem with that, I will give you my lawyer's number."

I could try to find a way to drug him and get him on a plane, I supposed, but he would just come back.

"I guess we're staying," I said. "Hey. Does the RCMP have any kind of deputization program? You know, so we can carry guns? We're both proficient." I smiled at the room. "What could possibly go wrong?"

Nobody seemed to find me very funny, but a couple of the younger cops almost seemed to think it wasn't a bad idea – Colin was dead and Des was missing. Warm bodies, people you know are innocent, who know their way around a gun? Why not? One of them even took the time to explain the citizen's arrest laws in Canada.

Laurence eventually went to take a shower while MacLean took me upstairs to look for spare clothes he could put on. Her dad was really tall, she said. They'd find something, but not what "somebody like your brother" would normally wear. I wasn't sure if she meant gay or a TV exec from New York City. Seeing as I was pretty sure Debbie MacLean was gay, I decided she meant New York.

"Don't worry," I said, following her up the stairs. "He'll just be grateful if the bottom third of his legs are covered." While she went into another room to look for clothes, I made the bed – her bed – and sat on it.

There had to be at least two people doing all this. At least. And if Dickie wasn't involved, then it was somebody who hated him and what he had been trying to do at Rose's very much. Des had said Mary was going over old files to tell one of the investigators what she could remember about previous residents.

If what Laurence said was true – if Dickie really couldn't have cut off his own finger – it was always possible that he had a partner in crime do it for him.

Or maybe it wasn't his finger at all. It could be Des Murphy's finger, with Dickie's ring on it.

The first thing I wanted to do was go see Mary. Alone. If her husband Geoffrey had a problem with the RCMP, then I didn't want to be showing up with one. Or two, or ten. Just little old me, and a homemade banana bread. But since that didn't seem possible, I'd take one or two of the bottles Laurence and I had picked up at the liquor store. Mary was a woman's woman – she and I had bonded in my first week there, and while we weren't best friends or anything, I knew she'd be more comfortable talking to me alone. Without Laurence. She adored him, but with him she was her public self. I needed her to talk to me honestly.

She knew about my past, or some of it. About my twin sister. She knew that I was aware of how important family was.

Laurence came into my room a few minutes later, wearing sweatpants that made him look like Pee-wee Herman. Constable MacLean was behind him, trying not to laugh.

"Okay, so maybe Dad isn't quite your height," she said.

"My dear Constable MacLean," Laurence started to say, but Debbie stopped him.

"You're my guest. Debbie, please."

"Debbie. We are taking such advantage of your hospitality and kindness. But I'm afraid I'm going to ask you for one more favor." He looked down at himself. "Do you think you could take us back to Rose's? Just a quick stop in to get our things. I'm not leaving the area until we find Dickie Doyle," he said, "but of course as soon as hotels free up we'll move to one."

"Excellent idea," I said. "But, Laurence, I really don't want to go back there. Can you pick my things up for me? I didn't get enough sleep, and I'm sure you'll be leaving someone or other around here?" I looked at Debbie. There was a lot in that look. She knew I wanted to get back to the gun and possibly to the woods. I wanted to tell her not to worry, that I was just planning on a quick visit to Mary's. "And you can bring back a few groceries maybe?"

Half an hour later, Laurence and Debbie, along with a couple of the other police, pulled out of the drive.

I went to the bathroom and cleaned up a bit – turns out I had mud on my face the whole time, from my dive into the woods when I heard the pickup – and grabbed one of Debbie's dad's t-shirts, swapped it with the Acadia sweatshirt, which was covered in dirt, leaves, and a couple of things that crawled. With Debbie's bedroom door closed and my security chair in place, I quickly took the Glock back out and put it into my fanny pack, and put the whole thing into my nylon tote. I sailed downstairs, smiled at one of the cops, and grabbed a bottle of vodka from our shop the night before. I took a bottle of water from the fridge, and let myself out the back door. No one questioned me. I wasn't a prisoner. I had the impression that the police there were just waiting for something to happen, maybe for crime scene techs to show up; I wasn't their concern.

This made me happy. Not much had made me happy in the last couple of days.

I started the Mustang, adjusted the seat and mirrors, and managed to get on the road without popping the clutch once.

I took it as a good omen.

Boy, was I wrong.

TWENTY-ONE

The day was the warmest we'd had so far, and I drove with the windows down. I still had the carton of cigarettes in my tote bag, and there was a bottle of vodka in the passenger seat. I figured that was good enough for a visit, seeing as how I couldn't get my hands on any homemade food.

I would make Mary something to eat at her place, and for myself too. Then after visiting with her – presuming, of course, that she would see me – maybe I would go for a drive. Peace. Nobody shooting at me, nobody leaving body parts for me, like a cat leaving dead mice as offerings for its owners.

I hadn't driven this road in daylight. Once you left the treed area, at the top of the hill you could see so much of the Valley. It was breathtaking. Green fields and the Bay of Fundy way in the distance. You could even see all the way to Cape Blomidon from here.

Laurence would be safe today. Every instinct I had told me that. And despite everything, for a few minutes I was able to put Sarah out of my head, and Evan, and Colin. Maybe after visiting Mary and meeting her husband, I would even drive onto the campus. Maybe I could even score a little coke. Not crack, and

I wouldn't cook it. Just a few bumps of coke to get my synapses firing. I had been cheated out of rehab, after all.

I would find the diviest tavern in town, preferably not one in town proper, and see what I could see.

I pulled into Mary's driveway and heard a dog inside barking like mad. Dixie. There was no vehicle in the drive, but then again, I was in Mary's car. And maybe her husband was out, or didn't drive.

I walked to the house, swinging the bottle of vodka from my hand as I did. I felt a bit edgy suddenly, but the sunny day and the feeling of peace could never have lasted anyway. I was about to visit a woman whose beloved nephew had been killed in cold blood, twenty-four hours earlier.

I rang the doorbell and waited a minute or two. What's the polite amount of time to wait when you've shown up to someone's house unannounced under these circumstances? But Mary and I had a conversation one day, about how people around here don't call first, they just pop in if they're driving by. It hadn't even been like that in Downs Falls where I grew up, and I found it quaint and charming when she told me about it. I would find it hellish to live in – give me notice before you show up at my door – but in theory, quaint and charming.

I was about to walk back to the car, when the door swung open, and a very large, very happy dog was being restrained from giving me a whole lot of puppy love.

"Danny," Mary said. Her voice was quiet. "I'm so glad you're okay. Well, they told me you were."

This wasn't the Mary I knew. She was subdued and had no makeup on. She was wearing loose shorts and a heavy wool sweater despite the warm day. She had, of cou

"Oh, Mary," I said. "I'm sorry to just dr
to see you." I held up the vodka in my han
you don't want company, or if you're sleeping or whatever." She
seemed to think about it for a minute, but her eyes kept going
to the bottle.

It occurred to me, suddenly, that Mary could quite possibly have
been an alcoholic. She wasn't a counsellor at Rose's, but she could
have gotten the job from Dickie because of her own experience
with addiction, or some twelve-step organization. Being a former
anorexic might not be the only monkey on her back.

Shit. Too late now. She took the bottle from my hand and
waved me in. "Thanks," she said. "Sorry for Dixie," she said.
"She's feeling better, though."

"I can see that," I said. Mary waited until I'd stuck my hand
out and Dixie licked it, then she let go of her collar. Suddenly I
was getting a face bath from a dog who didn't weigh much less
than I did. I laughed. There's nothing like a bit of doggie love to
change your mood. I was definitely going to find a rescue dog
when I got back to Toronto.

If I got back. Despite the slight uptake in my mood after
my brief, blessedly solitary drive in the sun, I put my chances
at about 50-50, if Laurence was insisting on staying until Dickie
was found. And I wouldn't leave Laurence here alone.

If I had thought about what the inside of Mary's house
might look like, it would be this. A mix of traditional, worn
country furniture with some rock-and-roll touches thrown in.
A well-aged La-Z-Boy covered in some kind of faded plaid, but
with a removable headrest that had the Playboy Bunny logo on

..t. Some photos on the wall of smiling families that looked years old, side by side with a black velvet Elvis. I wasn't quite sure if Elvis was meant to be ironic, but either way, the effect made me feel oddly at home. I'd never lived in a home like it, mind you, but it was Mary.

I followed her into the kitchen. It was painted bright pink with black borders, almost like a 1950s bathroom, and a retro pin-up was on the wall over the small table, like an old Vargas print.

"Very cute," I said. "I love your house." Mary was sitting at the table, an ashtray overflowing and her cigarettes on the table. The only part of the house that seemed out of place was the sink. It was overflowing with dirty dishes, and I didn't see a dishwasher.

"Sorry about the mess," Mary said.

"Oh God, Mary, no," I said. She was looking at the bottle on the counter but didn't open it. "Do you want me to make us some coffee? Or do you want a drink?"

"There's 7-Up in the fridge," she said. "Lots of ice, please." She lit a cigarette and looked at the table. I wondered again whether the vodka was the right idea, but too late now.

I found the glasses, put a few ice cubes in each, and filled them three-quarters of the way with 7-Up. When I brought Mary hers, she took a long draw of the soft drink, then topped up the glass with vodka, and stirred it with a finger. I poured a bit in mine to be sociable, but hard liquor was never my bag. The vodka was Laurence's buy. Not to mention, I was driving.

"My sister's son," she said.

"I know," I said. "Oh, Mary, I am so sorry."

"Des said he didn't suffer."

"No, he didn't," I said. "He never knew what hit him." We

drank in silence for a minute, and then I pl
cigarettes out of my bag.

"Your husband not around?" I said. He should be here with
her, I thought, but then again, he'd gotten in some kind of fight
with one of the cops last night. Maybe he was off licking his
wounds, or maybe she'd kicked him out.

"Working," she said. "He does odd jobs for people. When
he's having a good day, he has to take advantage of it and get out
and work. The good days are getting fewer." I remembered what
Janet had said about Mary's husband being in a wheelchair, and
sure enough, I glanced into the hallway and saw one outside the
door to what must be a bedroom. People have pain. More and
more, I was reminded that I wasn't the only one with troubles.
When you're in the midst of active addiction, all you can think
about is getting more of your drug of choice, and planning
when, where, and how you'll do it. Then in the white-hot grief
after losing Ginger and Jack, all I could think of was revenge. No
one else's pain had felt real to me. Active addiction is the most
selfish state in the world.

I had wanted to talk to Mary about any theories she might
have about who was doing this, about anything that may have
occurred to her after going through the old files from Rose's
Place with the police. But it seemed a tricky subject to bring up.

"When was he diagnosed? Geoffrey, that is?"

"Must be about six, seven years ago now," she said. "He
was getting numbness in his hands and feet that wouldn't quit.
Couple of times he fell. Anyway, that was the start."

"Does he have any family around, or is it all down to you?"

"He's got a mother, but she comes and goes. Doesn't spend

too much time around here. Rest of his family is dead. Cousins somewhere, I think, but..." She waved her hand, indicating that they were far away, maybe geographically or just far removed, not in the picture. "He's a good man, though, is Geoffrey," she said, as though I had said he wasn't.

"He must be, if he caught you," I said. "You're one in a million, Mary." I put my hand over hers, and for a second she let it stay there, then patted my hand with her other hand and pulled away.

"Thank you, Danny," she said. "I'm so sorry you had to come here while this is all happening. It's a beautiful area, around here. I liked the other night, when you were talking about buying a place here. That would be nice." She drained her drink, tipped a bit more vodka into my glass, and filled hers about halfway with it. I got up to get the 7-Up. "Don't bother," she said. She looked at me. "I know what you're thinking. All you addicts do. You're probably thinking I'm a drunk, right?"

"No," I said. I was lying, of course. She looked at that bottle the way I looked at a pretty rock of crack. "If you didn't want to get a buzz on while you're grieving, then I'd be worried."

"Damn straight," she said. "Damn fucking straight." She took another swig, and so did I. One thing I am not a fan of is being the only sober person in a room. If anything would make me want to get crack, it would be that. "Tell that to Geoffrey, though. You'd think I was, I don't know, shooting kittens, the way he carries on if I want so much as a beer, lately." Her voice rose at the end. This sounded more like the Mary I knew.

"Ah," I said. "Is he a recovering addict or something? Can't stand to be around it?" Lots were like that. Former addicts are like former smokers – buzzkills if you want to have a little fun.

"No," she said. "He used to enjoy a drink now and again, but never extreme. Nowadays, though…"

"Did he get religion or something?" I remembered that phrase from Maine. Mom and Dad used to talk about people "getting religion" as though it was the flu. They sent us to Jesuit Catholic schools for the good education, but neither of them were believers.

"No, he just turned judgmental. I blame the pain he's in. And his medication is expensive, I don't get benefits, and God forbid he should apply for assistance so he could get them. Well, if he did I'd have to quit my job anyway. Even though I don't make that much, he wouldn't qualify for benefits if I'm working."

I closed my eyes. This made sense. People had problems. It had been a long time since I had really had to worry about money, other than for crack. If I hadn't spent all my money on it, I would have been quite comfortable. But I never went without the things I needed. And now, of course, I was in a position to do something. I took a breath. "Let me help you," I said. "You helped me so much, Mary, when I got to Rose's. I was a mess. Meeting you was what kept me there."

She smiled at me, but there was a lot of sadness behind that smile. "Well then, I wish you'd never met me. Hasn't exactly worked out for you, has it?"

"Got me there," I said. "But, you know my husband died. He left me money. I've been thinking about what I'm going to do with it, and I figured I might as well try to do some good. I caused a lot of pain, back when I was using." I took a long swallow of the vodka, and wondered why I'd never appreciated it before. It felt clean, going down, but with a bit of a burn so you knew it was doing its job. For me, alcohol would never be a replacement for crack cocaine, but just at the moment, it was good enough. "That's why my sister died, you know. Was because of me. And my husband, too." I realized my voice was too loud. Vodka and grief. And I wanted, I needed her to understand why I wanted to help her.

"Don't say that, Danny," Mary said. Her voice was raised, and she looked almost alarmed. "All addicts feel that way. It's just the guilt talking." She waved her hands as if to shut me up. "I won't hear it. And whatever happened, you did the right thing. You got yourself together and got yourself clean." She stood up and went to the sink and started taking things out of it, piling them on the stove, making what seemed like a deliberate racket. She definitely didn't want to hear my troubles, not today.

"I'm sorry, Mary," I said. "You sit down. I'll do that. I love doing dishes. I'll top your drink up, and you put your feet up." I approached her at the sink, and very quickly she turned and hugged me tight.

"Run," she whispered in my ear. In my right ear, my bad ear. I thought I had heard wrong.

"What did you say?"

"Get in the car and go. Run. Now. Please, quickly."

I pulled back and looked into her face. She looked terrified. Sweat started along my hairline, and adrenaline was pounding through me.

"You're coming with me," I said. I grabbed my bag and pulled her arm.

Someone was in the house. I couldn't tell where the noise

was coming from with my bad ear and the pounding in my chest.

"No, I won't," she said, loudly. "Just go, Danny. We need to be alone."

I grabbed my bag from the floor and headed to the door. Someone was walking behind me, but didn't seem to be hurrying. Still, I didn't have time to fumble around for the gun in my bag. Why hadn't I carried it on my body? What kind of idiot was I?

Dixie ran outside with me, excited and bounding, thinking we were going to play. Not today, puppy. Not today.

The Mustang's hood was up. Why was the hood up? I had my keys in my hand and as I started across the lawn, away from the car – I couldn't see who or what might be on the other side of the hood – I threaded them through my fingers to use as a weapon.

Then something hit me in the head from behind; something large and heavy hit me harder than I have ever been hit. I saw the ground coming at me, and that was all I knew.

TWENTY-TWO

I was freezing cold. I was outside, and I was freezing cold.

And, as far as I could tell, my right hand was missing.

Before I was able to open my eyes, I started to panic. I couldn't breathe. *Be calm, Danny. Be calm.* Ginger's voice, not mine. I slowed my breathing, four counts on inhale, four on exhale. My mouth was taped shut. If I panicked and started to cry, my nose might get stuffed. Suffocation was one of my biggest fears. I breathed in four counts through my nose, and out for four counts, until I was calm enough to open my eyes.

It was dark. The kind of dark that felt like it was going to be light soon. Which meant that I had been out for maybe twelve hours or more. Good. People would be looking for me.

I was sitting on a rock, and I could smell water, and hear it lapping, close to me. Then a light went on somewhere not far away – a business or a house, or even a lighthouse? A boat? My arms were chained to something behind me, something I was leaning against. I was sitting up, my legs stretched out in front of me, tied together with duct tape. Lots of it. My right shoulder hurt like hell, but I was going to ignore it. I couldn't give in to pain; I had to think quickly.

I was tied to something hard and immovable behind me, and I was pretty sure I didn't have my right hand. I could wiggle the fingers of my left hand, but not my right. But no. I had to have my hand, because otherwise I would be able to slip out of the chains that were binding me to… something. I just couldn't feel it. It was asleep. If it had been cut off, I would be in pain. More pain than I was in, even, with my shoulder, and the cold, and a head injury that was making it difficult to see, even leaving aside the dark. I was wearing Debbie MacLean's jeans still and just a t-shirt.

I was on a rocky shoreline, and there was something above me, some structure. It was rough and hard, and as hard as I pulled, it wasn't going to give. My feet were bare, and the water was lapping at them. More than it had been a couple of minutes ago.

A pier. I was tied under a pier.

I watched as my feet became submerged.

The Bay of Fundy. I had read that it had the fastest moving tides in the world, rising a few metres in an hour in some spots.

I was tied to a pier of some sort, a dock, and the tide was coming in quickly. Sitting up as I was, if the tide was moving as fast as it seemed, I probably had twenty or thirty minutes before I would be immersed. That's what I figured, doing some crude math in my head, and watching the water. I had never thought of water as alive before, but this water was, and rising as surely as the sun rises in the morning. And much quicker.

I was going to drown.

People would be looking in the woods, probably, not along shorelines. And who knew how far I had been taken, in all that time? It was a blank; I hadn't come to once, as far as I could remember.

I thought of Laurence and how unutterably horrible this would be for him. I had wanted to leave, and he had insisted that he, at least, was staying. He would never get over this. And my nephews, Ginger's boys Matthew and Luke – they had been through so much trauma already. This would scar them even more, having their auntie murdered, just like their mother was, like their uncle Jack was. You don't get over that. Nobody gets over that.

Fuck that. No. No fucking way. Nobody gets to do that to them.

In that moment, if the person who had been doing this – who had done this to me – had been standing in front of me, I think I would have been able to burst through the chains, I felt such rage. I screamed, made as much noise as I could somewhere deep in my chest, my throat, but even if there was someone around, nobody would hear me over the water. Not to mention through the duct tape.

Then I realized I was starting to cry, which would mean less air, a clogged nose. I sat for a while eyes closed, and breathed as evenly as I could, trying to be calm. Trying to think over the pain and the panic.

The water was past my waist.

I thought about Ginger and her boys, and about Jack, but just for a minute. I couldn't let myself think about Jack.

Instead I thought about my brothers.

And then I thought about what I wanted to do to the person who had done this. Mary's husband. I wanted to tie him to a tree and watch him die. I waited for the water to rise.

When the water was high enough, I took a breath and stuck

my face in it. I came up a second later, panicking, trying to blow saltwater out of my nose. I breathed again, trying to be calm. Then I leaned over as far as I could and let the water run over the bottom part of my face. I did that four or five times, each time thinking this was the one that was going to kill me, where I wouldn't be able to breathe air when I came up.

Then I raised my good shoulder and rubbed my chin, as hard as I could, back and forth across it. The pain in my other shoulder nearly caused me to pass out, but I was lucky. The cold water kept me conscious.

I don't know how long it had been. And I was tired. So tired. It hurt to move my head. My shoulder was broken. It hurt to try to move anything.

I put my face in the water one last time – easier now, as the water was higher – and then rubbed my face raw along my shoulder.

The duct tape that had been covering my mouth came away. On one side only, but enough that I could make noise.

I took a deep breath and screamed, as loudly as I ever have. I don't know what words I said, but I know I used words.

And because Mary's husband wasn't as smart as he thought he was, some men who were getting ready to go out lobster fishing heard me.

They got me free, even before the water had reached my chin.

If Mary's husband had used better quality duct tape, the saltwater and rubbing probably wouldn't have loosened the adhesive enough.

If the fishermen hadn't had those rusty bolt cutters on their boat, finding me wouldn't have done any good. They would have just had to watch me drown; the tide was coming in too quickly.

All I remember about the following time is panic, and pain, and cold. Panic because I still couldn't feel my right hand, even though I could see it. Pain, excruciating pain, as my body was warmed carefully in the ambulance. They didn't give me anything for pain then, because of the head injury and my confusion. I screamed when they moved me into the ambulance, when someone tried to pick me up by my shoulder to put me on the gurney.

At some point at the hospital, before I drifted away on a morphine cloud, I told someone who I was, and that Mary's husband was the killer. But nothing else mattered, because I was warm and alive and there was no more panic or pain.

You're missing something, I thought, or heard, but then, merciful sleep.

TWENTY-THREE

The headache of my life. That's what I felt when I woke up. Laurence was sitting beside my bed, chin on chest, sound asleep. It was bright outside, and it was nice to have the curtains open. That's one of the first things I thought – the curtains are open; they must have caught him. They're not worried we'll be shot at through the windows.

Debbie MacLean was there too, in street clothes. She smiled at me when I looked at her, then jumped out of her chair and ran out into the hallway. She came back with a woman in scrubs and a white coat.

Laurence was standing next to me then, kissing my forehead. His eyes were swollen and he hadn't shaved.

"You look like shit," I said, and found I was raspy.

"You aren't going to win any pageants today either," he said quietly. He was crying, and one of his tears dropped onto my face.

The doctor told me I had a concussion from whatever hit the back of my head and kept me knocked out for the better part of a day, a dislocated shoulder which would be sore for a while, mild hypothermia from the time in the water, and I was covered in abrasions. Especially my wrists, which had been tied very tightly.

"I still don't really feel my right hand," I said. I didn't want to talk. It hurt my throat, and my head hurt even more. But I must have been on some kind of happy drug, because the idea of having no feeling in my dominant hand didn't seem to bother me too much.

Then again, escaping a horrible death by drowning will put things in perspective.

"You may have some compressed nerves," the doctor said. "You managed to get through your ordeal with no broken bones, but your shoulder was dislocated when they brought you in." In a raspy whisper I told them about dunking my head in the saltwater and working my face against my shoulder to get the tape off so I could make some noise.

The doctor looked at me, and then at Laurence and Debbie. "That's remarkable," she said. "The pain must have been – how did you do it?"

Laurence saw that I couldn't speak any longer, or didn't want to. "My sister is well-trained in self-defence and, uh, survival," he said. "I think she's able to put her pain to one side until later." I closed my eyes. Everybody was staring at me. The pain was bad. The thirst was even worse.

I moved my arm and pointed at the water next to the bed, and whispered something about my head. Laurence brought the water and a bendy straw, and the doctor said she'd send a nurse in with some more pain meds.

"Go back to sleep, Danielle," the doctor said. "Your body has a lot of healing to do."

I looked at Debbie. "Mary?"

She nodded. "Everything is fine, Danny. You just sleep,

okay? It's over. Mary is alive and well."

I turned toward Laurence and stuck out my hand. He sat back down and held it, and I drifted off again.

I was tied to a tree. My shoulder was killing me, but it was secondary to the fact that I couldn't loosen the bonds. I knew there was something in the woods, something large and evil and worse than anything I had met before. I couldn't yell. I tried, but someone had taken my voice.

I knew that if I could smoke some crack, I would be fine. I would be able to handle the pain, and I would have the strength to get away.

Then Ginger was there. My sister was there, and so was Gene, my old partner in crime from the crack days. I hadn't seen Gene in so long. But he was with Ginger, and they were going to help me. They couldn't untie me, of course, because they had no hands. But somehow they managed to light the crack pipe that I had in my mouth, because they knew that was what was important. I had to get out of this myself, but they knew I needed crack to do it.

The pipe wouldn't light, or the crack was no good. I was inhaling and inhaling but nothing was happening. And something was crashing through the woods toward me. Gene was gone, and Ginger was crying. "Do what you need to do, Danny," she said. "You'll know what to do. Do what you need to do."

I needed to get the crack into my lungs. I was powerless without it.

Then I heard the rumbling, and I looked up.

A wall of water was coming for me. A tsunami. I could feel the cold of the water as it rushed at me.

I was in a different room. There were glass walls. My throat was coated in broken glass, and my skin felt like it was burning. A nurse put ice chips in my mouth.

Sometime later, Laurence was sitting on the bed, and he looked different. He had a beard. I had never seen him with a beard. I was glad he was there, but it was alarming. Years had gone by. My hand was burning. I tried to speak, but Laurence said something to the nurse, and someone put something in my IV drip. I watched it and closed my eyes, waiting for it to work. Whatever it was.

I woke in the semi-dark and tried to get up. I started screaming when I realized I didn't have any feet. Then Laurence was there and someone else was there, a nurse, and Laurence held up a mirror and showed me that I had feet.

Then one morning I woke up and I felt different. I felt like I had lost weight, body mass, muscle I didn't want to lose. My whole body felt floppy and weak. I was in some pain – my hand hurt like hell, but my throat didn't hurt, at least not much, and I could breathe properly.

Something else was different, but I couldn't put my finger on it.

And I wasn't in the glass-walled room any longer. I was in a private room. The curtains were drawn. I wanted the curtains open. Laurence wasn't there, or Debbie. Or anybody.

But I was alive, and my hand was no longer invisible under the mummy wrappings. My wrists were still bandaged, so I looked like a failed suicide case, but I could feel my fingers on both hands. And my feet, too. The door to my room was closed, which felt a bit weird. Don't they usually keep the doors open? Where was everybody?

I was feeling around for a call button when a flower delivery guy came in with a huge pink and white arrangement.

"Ms. Cleary?" I watched the man walk toward me and for a second I braced myself to fight, looking around for something to hit him with. But no. I knew that voice.

I blinked. I thought I must still be in a fever dream. "Dave?" He was dressed in a delivery uniform, with a cap low over his eyes. He put his finger over his lips.

"No, ma'am, they said they were gonna send Dave but he had a flat, so…" He fiddled with the flowers.

It *was* Dave. He winked at me. "This place is lousy with cops," he said cheerfully. "I guess there's been a lot of crime lately, so it's good they're watching over everybody, miss." Okay. He thought somebody was listening.

I had too many questions. I needed water. I reached for it, and Dave poured me a glass. He didn't give me a bendy straw. I took a long sip, which felt nearly as good as a hit of crack, at that minute. "How are you here?" Had I called him and forgotten? It was possible.

"Darren," he whispered, his voice low and quick. "I heard about some goings-on in this neck of the woods, and I've been keeping tabs. I got in touch with him. He decided to trust me, probably because he's been going out of his mind with worry." He looked at the door. "But I can't be sure he didn't change his mind after we talked and called in people I don't really want to talk to right now."

"He wouldn't," I said. "I don't think."

"I'm renting a house. Airbnb," he said. I laughed. Why hadn't we thought of that when the hotels were all full during the Apple Blossom Festival? Still, the short-term rentals had probably been full too.

"What's the date?" I said. Something was odd. Everything was too clear.

"June second, I think," he said. "You've been really sick."

"Am I okay now?"

"Do you feel okay?" I did. Not much of a headache, a little sore, but I'd been lying in bed for days.

"Oh my God!" I said. "I can hear!" That was what was different. The hearing in my right ear was back. Normal. Dave smiled at me, and I realized I'd missed him. Despite the fact that he'd conned me and held me at gunpoint once upon a time, I trusted him.

He smiled at me. "It's safe," he said. "The house. I've made some modifications to the property." He scratched his ear and grinned. "Upgraded for the owners."

"But it's all over, isn't it? They arrested Geoffrey? Mary's husband? Isn't it over? Where's Laurence?"

"Laurence is fine," he said. "He's at my place right now, getting some rest." Well, that was bizarre. Laurence had not been on the pro-Dave bandwagon. "But, Danny, I'm sorry. It's not over."

Oh, no. No. "What do you mean? Is Mary safe?" I didn't want to ask if anyone else was dead. I didn't want to ask what I had missed.

"I'm sorry, Danny, I've got to go," he said. "I'll tell Laurence you're awake, and he'll fill you in, and they'll let you out soon. You'll be staying with me, both of you." He pulled his cap down further and started to leave, but he came back to my bed. He pretended to be moving the flowers to the other side of the bed, in case someone was watching somehow. "Danny, don't trust anyone. Anyone, not even the cops. Just your brother."

"And you," I said. I hoped so. I hoped so, with every fiber of my being. If this wasn't over, I was going to need help. The kind of help that my brother, wonderful as he was, couldn't provide. The kind that came with weapons, fake IDs and a shitload of experience and resources.

"And me," he said. He touched my hand lightly, as though by accident, and then he was gone.

TWENTY-FOUR

I had gotten an infection in my hand after cutting it at some point while in captivity under restraint, some superbug that didn't respond to the first antibiotics. Combined with the concussion, hypothermia, and being only a few weeks past a not-insignificant crack binge before coming to Rose's, my immune system wasn't what it should have been.

The doctors credited the return of full hearing in my right ear to the heavy-duty antibiotics I'd been on.

My hand didn't hurt any longer, or not much, and I could move my fingers. But I still had an odd numbness in the middle two fingers on that hand. It would probably, I was told, heal itself. Or it wouldn't, and I could look forward to therapy and possibly surgery down the road.

They'd told me that about my ear.

I was to be kept in for another day or two, especially now that I could eat solid food. And I had my suspicions that someone had had a word in the doctor's ear, advising her not to release me yet. I was both a target, if this wasn't over, and a thorn in someone's side. Plus, someone else who needed to be protected.

Not anymore, I wouldn't. With Dave here, and after having

been left to a horrible death, my desire to act, to bring this killer or killers to some kind of justice, was at a high. My family would have suffered in the last days, wondering if I was going to live or die. Nobody was going to put us through that again. It needed to be shut down.

The phrase made me think of Debbie MacLean. She had said that to me the day I met her, back at Rose's. She had wanted me to "shut down" Dickie Doyle. I hadn't seen her since my fever had broken, and I hoped she was okay. I hoped she had taken a nice long holiday. Quit her job, if that's what it came to. And Des Murphy – I didn't know if he had been found safely.

When I finally had Laurence in my room, alone, with no doctors or student doctors taking my vital signs and bending my hands and feet in various directions, I wasted no time. "Tell me everything," I said to him. He smiled at me, and the sadness in his face made my heart break.

"Let's get you better," he said. "Then we can get you back to Toronto. The boys made you a video. Let's just say neither of them is ever going to win a Grammy."

"What the fuck? Laurence, please." I was going crazy with the waiting. I needed to know.

He looked at me, grabbed my chin, and made me look into his face. "Later. Trust me. I promise. Play along." He was speaking very quietly, nearly in a whisper. My heart started to pound. We weren't safe in here. He didn't think we were safe, in the hospital.

He started smoothing my sheets and making me sit up so he could, ostensibly, rearrange the pillows behind my back. "You gave us a real scare, Danny. But, you know what? First things first, you need to eat. And I mean eat. You need your protein."

He squeezed my arm gently, my bicep. He was telling me I was going to need my strength.

"I am fucking hungry, actually," I said. I was.

"You must be starting to feel better. First F-bomb in days!" He finished basically taking my bed apart around me in the guise of making it neat and tidy. "God, I can't stand a mess."

Then I knew something was amiss. Laurence was a slob. He said he was like that on purpose, because he couldn't bear all the gay stereotypes, but really he was just lazy. Doing dishes, he loved, but he once told me he had never, in his adult life, made his bed.

"Such a queen," I said. I was trying to sound natural, which of course made me feel like I was in a school play. With a knife at my throat. "Can we get room service or what? In this establishment?"

"Danny, you are in a hospital, not the Four Seasons. They will bring your gruel around at five p.m." The clock on the wall said just after three.

"Let's go to the cafeteria," I said. "That must be open. And I have got to get out of this bed. The faster I'm on my feet, the faster we blow this town."

"Good idea," he said. I was hooked up to an IV still, but Laurence helped me get out of bed.

"Whoa," I said. I had to sit down again. I hadn't been on my feet since – well, since I ran from Mary's house and saw the hood of the Mustang propped open. And had gotten brained, a minute later.

I stopped and looked at my brother, thinking, wanting to speak.

Back at Mary's, I'd heard something behind me, but someone

had to have been outside to open the hood, and the house wasn't so big that I wouldn't have noticed someone coming and going. And I doubted Mary could have hit me as hard as I was hit. But my head was fuzzy, and the timeline was still a bit unclear. They'd told me my memory of the incident might be gone altogether, or off-kilter, due to the concussion and the trauma after.

Then I realized that having that concussion might be useful.

Laurence got me a wheelchair so I could get out of the room and get some solid food into me, before I tried any real walking. He brought me a new hospital gown and a robe to put over the top, so I wasn't flashing anybody, and I managed to change in the bathroom in my room.

I tried to avoid looking in the mirror, but, really, there's not much else in there. I needed to wash my hair and brush my teeth. The right side of my face from my cheekbone down was red and raw from trying to work the duct tape off in the saltwater. My jaw was bandaged; the abrasion there must have been worse. I looked skinnier than I should; my cheekbones and clavicles were too pronounced. I'm not a fan of that look on anyone, least of all myself. I wanted to look strong as well as be strong.

I looked much like I had when Ginger died – gaunt and sick. I needed food, and a shower, and more food. Still, it was a hospital, and I doubted I was being scouted to be Gina Carano's stand-in for her next film, so I guessed I'd do.

The hospital seemed like a new one. There were tons of windows, and everything seemed spacious and fairly modern, considering. "It's the hospital for the whole Annapolis Valley," Laurence told me. He wheeled me past some oil paintings that locals had done to raise money for the facility.

My heart sunk a bit, as I'd been hoping that I'd been taken to Halifax at some point when I was in my fevered state. Somewhere a bit further from the action, in other words.

I was so hungry, the smell of hospital cafeteria food made me almost giddy with joy.

"Park me by a table," I said to Laurence, "and get me one of everything." He looked at me. "Just get me a lot, okay?" I waited semi-patiently until he brought food over on three trays, taking two trips. There was a Salisbury steak-looking thing, which, despite my hunger, I found I couldn't touch. I wondered how long it would take me to embrace meat again, after seeing Sarah's body, or if I was going to morph into a vegetarian. I might. But I ate a plate of French fries with gusto, and an egg salad on whole wheat bread. Plus a bottle of orange juice and a bottle of cranberry juice. Laurence didn't talk much while we ate. Well, while I ate; he drank coffee and picked at the steak I didn't want.

"How do you feel?" he asked.

"Extremely full," I said. I ate a couple of the peas off his plate, in a concession to having something green. It was the first solid food I'd had since eating a couple of bites of donair and a couple of bites of veggie pizza the night we'd left Rose's. My stomach was objecting a bit, and I hoped I could keep it down. "Talk."

My brother looked ragged, suddenly, as if he'd used up all his energy in the last twenty minutes. "I'm so glad you're okay, Danny. It was all my fault. We should have left. I put loyalty to Dickie over your safety, and I will never forgive myself. Never." He started to cry then. Not a couple of tears, but quiet, wracking sobs. One table of people in white coats nearby looked politely away.

"No," I said. "I could have forced you. And I don't blame you.

212

I understand loyalty, God knows." I squeezed his hand quickly, and let go. I wanted him to collect himself, not send him further into self-flagellation. "And I was so stupid that morning. I put myself in a stupid situation, and I didn't react the way I should have. I should have fought – my God, the man has multiple sclerosis. Even on one of his good days, I should have been able to do something to defend myself." I thought of the Glock in my bag and wondered what had become of my things. But we'd deal with that later.

"Who has MS?" Laurence said. He grabbed a couple more paper napkins from the dispenser and wiped his face.

"Geoffrey," I said. "Mary's husband."

"Did you see him?" Laurence asked. He was staring at me and he grabbed my wrist. It hurt, and I pulled away. "Sorry. Danny, did you see Geoffrey?"

"No," I said. I remembered the footsteps behind me. They were heavy, sure. I cursed myself for not having looked back. "But I heard him, and it was definitely a man. He was in the house when I was in the kitchen with Mary. And I saw his wheelchair in the hall."

"God, I need a fucking cigarette," Laurence said. He looked at me. "The police think Mary must have helped her husband. Neither of them could have done all this on their own."

"No," I said. "No way. And Mary couldn't have hit me that hard. There's no way she weighs a hundred pounds. And I was hit – and I know this, Laurence – I was hit by somebody who was at least my height. I could... feel it." I pushed the empty tray away. "Besides, the Mustang. The hood. I was with Mary every second I was in that house."

"Look, I know. I do believe you," he said. "And really, who would believe that Mary could have transported you and tied you like that? She had to have help."

"But… Mary? Are you sure? She was scared, Laurence. She was scared of whoever was in that house." We sat in silence for a minute. I didn't ask about Dickie. I knew he would have led with that, if there had been any news, and I didn't want to reopen that wound just now. "Whatever is going on, Mary isn't involved. Or at least, she's a victim too. Somehow."

"I'd like to believe that myself," he said. "But she's gone. She took the car, and she's gone. And Geoffrey is gone too. Missing, or gone with Mary. Nobody knows."

I let that sit a minute. "Gone? As in, on the run?"

Laurence chewed on a straw. He wanted a cigarette badly; it was obvious.

"In the wind, my sister," he said. "They are in the goddamn wind."

TWENTY-FIVE

The next day, I was released from the hospital with a prescription for oral antibiotics I was to keep taking. Other than that, I was cleared to go. Debbie had come to visit, again in her street clothes, bringing with her the few personal items Laurence and I had left at her family's cottage. As far as she knew, Laurence and I were going to take it slow, drive a rental car back to Toronto, and sightsee along the way.

I didn't like lying to her. But if I had learned one thing, it was that my instincts about people sucked. Family, I could trust. Dave, I had wound up trusting, but certainly not at the beginning. And I had been so blindly wrong about certain people in the past –Michael Vernon Smith, Harry Miller – that I decided, for once, to follow directions and just be cautious.

"I'm sorry about your jeans," I said to Debbie as we chatted in my room. "I don't know if you're going to want to wear them after I, you know, spent a day unconscious and restrained who knows where in them, and then wore them in the Bay of Fundy while nearly drowning."

"Actually," she said, taking a plastic bag out of the huge tote she carried, "I've decided you should have them."

"Oh," I said. "A souvenir!" I laughed. She had gotten them back from the hospital, she said, and washed them several times, and actually ironed them.

"Like new," she said. "Don't think of them as bad luck. These jeans brought you good luck. When you were wearing these, you survived something that you really shouldn't have."

"Yikes," I said. I looked at the jeans. "Not sure I like that phrasing. But thank you."

"I've got to bust a move," she said. "I'm due on shift in a couple of hours." She stood and stretched, and something in the way she did it told me she was doing it for my benefit. I wanted to tell her that while I have nothing against girl-on-girl action, it's also not really my particular thing. Even if I had any desire to play around, with anyone. Which I didn't. But, I did like her, and flirting is harmless. I let it pass. "So don't think you're going to get away from us forever," she said. My senses were so highly tuned, it almost sounded like a threat. "We'll catch Mary Dowe and her husband, and whoever else was involved in this, and you'll have to come and testify, most likely. You can stay at the cottage again. It won't be so scary next time," she said. "And now you know you don't need an axe to go into our basement."

"That would be great," I said. "I never got to go for a swim."

"Think you'll be able to stay away from drugs when you get home?" She was delaying leaving.

"I don't know," I said. "I'm going to try."

"Honest, at least."

"At least." Then she did what I knew she'd been working up to. She walked over and kissed me, gently, on the mouth. And I did the thing you do when someone you like kisses you and you don't really want it – not exactly responding but not pushing her away either. Letting her save face, but at the same time not leading her on.

Oh yeah. That's me. A chick magnet. But really, men and women aren't that different, in my opinion. A few different body parts here, hormones there, but most people just want a connection with another human being. I was attracted to what I was attracted to, which usually came in a package with a penis and more testosterone.

Of course, that was the exact moment Laurence chose to walk in. Because that's the way my life works.

"Oh, gracious me," he said. "Sorry, girls." He hesitated in the doorway, but it was for show. He didn't want to miss a minute of my discomfort. Brothers.

"Get in here, you asshole," I said. "Debbie was just saying goodbye."

"I was saying see you later," she said. She was acting cool, but she was blushing. She grabbed her tote, hesitated, then kissed Laurence on the cheek. "I'm sorry you two had to go through this. It really is a nice place to live."

She was halfway out the door, and I called her name. She turned around.

"Why is your cottage traditional on the ground floor and painted lilac and green stripes on the second?" I couldn't believe I hadn't asked her yet, but there had been more pressing matters.

She smiled, a real genuine smile, and it made me really hope she had nothing to do with any of the violence. "It was a gift from my dad. I came out a couple of years ago. He had a really hard time with it for a few months. But then he went to a couple of support groups and tried to embrace the whole 'having a gay kid' thing, so he did that."

"That's… lovely," Laurence said. He had a huge grin on his face.

"I didn't have the heart to tell him it was hideous and clichéd. He's a good dad."

"You're lucky," I said. "Thanks again for everything."

She waved, and was gone. Laurence just looked at me, his eyebrows waggling like crazy.

"Oh, shut up," I said. He started singing the Katy Perry song, "I Kissed A Girl," and I threw my jeans at him.

"Never mind your sordid love life," he said, clapping his hands. "Let's hit the road. Blow this pop stand. Make like trees and leave."

On the way out to the car, Laurence told me that until we got back to the house, we should be careful what we said. He had just rented it, but it had sat alone in the parking lot for half an hour, and Dave was urging extreme caution. He had some kind of device that detected bugs, or whatever, he said, and once we got there we'd be able to talk freely. He warned me that we'd be taking a long route to the house Dave had rented, to make sure nobody was following us. But there were so few cars on the road, he said, especially now that the tourists had mostly gone, that anybody tailing us would stick out.

It was another gorgeous day, and I was alive. Laurence seemed in good spirits, despite everything, and I felt more secure knowing that Dave was with us. It was the most relaxed I'd been since the morning I found the hand in the mailbox. It felt like a year ago.

And, I could hear. I could hear perfectly, in both ears. I

wouldn't say it was worth what had happened to me, but it did make me feel more alive. And safer. Definitely safer.

Laurence had rented an SUV, a black Chevy Tahoe.

"This isn't your normal kind of ride, brother," I said. "But it fits you better."

"I didn't want to be on a long drive with you in a sports car," he said, and winked. I knew it would also be because it would be less conspicuous around here. I had vaguely noticed that in my limited experience thus far, the east coast of Canada was like Maine – the residents liked their cars domestic.

We drove out of the town of Kentville, and seemed to be in no particular hurry and with no agenda in mind. I didn't care much. It was a beautiful drive. I closed my eyes and daydreamed, lulled into a blessed feeling of safety. We drove into a pretty little area called Hall's Harbor. It was on the water, and there was a place selling lobsters. The beach was rocky, and the tide was out.

"Let's go for a walk," Laurence said. "Buy a lobster. I came all this way." There were no other cars in the parking lot.

"It wasn't far from here," he said as we walked across gravel toward the restaurant and gift shop. I stopped.

"That they found me?" I looked around, not that it would do me any good at all. Laurence nodded.

We stood looking out at the water like tourists, but I wanted to leave. Get back in the car and leave. I owed my life to those lobster fishermen, and I was going to do something to thank them before I left the Valley, but I didn't want to go into this place. I could have been food for the lobsters if the killers had had their way, and I doubted I'd ever eat one again.

"Why are we here?" I said. It felt almost cruel, for Laurence to bring me close to where I'd almost died, so recently.

"A couple of reasons." Laurence lit a cigarette, and I took one from his pack and lit it too. It tasted disgusting; I hadn't had one for a while. But I was enjoying it nonetheless. Ah, addiction, thy name is Danny. "I wanted to see if anyone was following us. And I wanted to see if you recognized anything, or felt anything, or… anything."

I stepped away from him and walked a bit. I smoked my cigarette and tried to clear my mind, let my crocodile brain take over. I closed my eyes and smelled the air.

I walked back to Laurence, shaking my head, but he was checking out a car that had pulled in to the small parking area. A minute later, a nice-looking young couple got out, and released three small children from their tethers in the back seat.

"Nope," I said. "They didn't do it. I'm fairly sure. Though that kid, he's got a look about him." One of them, about three years old, had obviously been confined in the car too long. He was picking gravel up and flinging it in the air like Mary Tyler Moore with her beret. "I'd watch that one."

Laurence asked if I minded if he ran into the gift shop. He needed to pick something up for Antonio, he said, some souvenir, and what better place?

"Than where I was nearly murdered? You sentimentalist." I took his cigarettes from him and snapped my fingers for the lighter. The healthy-looking couple frowned at me. How dare I smoke, in the open air, where their precious children might catch half a whiff as they walked by? I had a sudden urge to flick a lit cigarette at the woman, but I refrained. I'm classy that way.

While Laurence went inside, I wandered back to the car. I

realized I still had dressings on my wrists, and my face looked like I had road rash. Combined with the smoking, all I needed was a neck tattoo and this woman would probably be hustling her progeny back into the car.

I knew we weren't going to leave until we had more answers or until Dickie was found. Now Dave was with us, at least. And if I was going to be of any help at all, I needed to get my synapses firing properly. My rehab experience had been less than stellar, to put it mildly, and I knew I would have to deal with the problem later. I still wanted crack. I wanted it like I wanted water. Not as badly as I did once, it was true. The need was less, but the desire was just as strong.

Crack wasn't the best drug for thinking. Sometimes I could do it. I could react quickly. I had proven that in Maine, but I had also done my best to curtail what could have been an all-out binge.

Cocaine, however – powdered coke – was what I needed now. If I wanted to get this over with, Laurence and Dave were just going to have to deal with it. My "recovery" could wait. Dickie was still missing, as was Des Murphy, Laurence had told me. Mary was gone, and I wasn't yet fully convinced she had any real part in anything. And for whatever reason, Dave wasn't trusting the police.

In the last week I had been shot at, found a dead body, plus a severed hand, had a severed head thrown at me, been covered in a dead cop's blood, found an acquaintance who'd been eaten alive by animals, and been kidnapped and nearly horribly drowned. I'd suffered a dislocated shoulder, nerve damage in my hand, and contracted an infection that could have killed me in itself.

If anybody wanted me to be useful, I was going to need help.

And the kind of help that I was used to.

When Laurence came out of the store clutching a plastic bag and waving a large stuffed lobster, I stopped him before we got into the car.

"You do not have the option of saying no," I said to him. I gripped his arm and looked into his eyes. "If we're going to do this, I am going to need some cocaine."

To my great surprise, he only nodded. Sadly, but he nodded. "I know," he said. "Dave's taking care of it. In case you needed it," he added.

"Oh," I said. I'd had my argument all prepared, and I was so shocked, I found I had nothing to say.

He handed me the stuffed lobster, we got in the car, and drove.

TWENTY-SIX

We were silent in the car, Laurence and I. I was thinking about cocaine. I knew it was wrong, to be putting that thought above all else, the lives that were hanging in the balance. But, like any good addict, I rationalized my excitement. It would make me feel better. It would take away the body aches and pains that were distracting me.

And, for better or worse, as long as I didn't overconsume, I would be sharper on it. My instincts were better. My brain made connections more quickly, and maybe, just maybe, we could get all of this over with.

And if Laurence and Dave were agreeing to this – and if Dave had indeed procured some cocaine for me – they knew it too.

We drove up one of the mountains that bracketed the Valley, but I didn't recognize this area. More farmland, less forest. More manure smell, which made me think of taking the drive with Mary, the first night Laurence had arrived.

I would think about Mary later.

Laurence pulled into a driveway lined with cedar trees, past a Cape Cod-style house nestled well back from the road. I didn't see another vehicle. Laurence put his fingers to his lips and got out of the car. I followed. I was tired. My throat was hurting again a bit, and I wondered if the infection was coming back. I wanted some tea with honey.

Laurence approached the back door and opened the case of a small touchpad with a key. He pushed in some digits and the door swung open.

And then I realized what Dave had meant by "modifications." I highly doubted the homeowner had a security system that included a massive steel door that, until it swung open, looked like a regular, albeit large, wooden door. Laurence ushered me in, and, at first sight, the place was what one would expect. Pleasantly modern kitchen, with the usual granite countertops and stainless-steel appliances.

Laurence led me down into the sunken living room – the house was obviously built in the 70s – and pointed out the wireless security cameras. "That's just the beginning," he said. "Dave will explain the rest." I heard a noise coming from down the hall where the bedrooms seemed to be. I grabbed Laurence's arm and ran back to the kitchen to look for a knife.

"No, Danny," he said. "That's just Jonas."

Now it was my turn to raise my eyebrows. I just couldn't do it as well as he could.

We walked down the hall, and despite Laurence's obvious relaxation now that we were inside, I was tensing and relaxing my muscles, getting ready to fight. I made my breathing shallow to get my adrenaline pumping.

At the end of the hall, Laurence led me into what was obviously once a master bedroom. Now, it looked like Command Central, a mini war room. Jonas was a ridiculously handsome young guy in white denim overalls, who looked like he was about to go to his shift as a male stripper. He was on his hands and knees on the floor, doing something with cables.

"Hello," I said. I'm witty like that, when faced with impossibly good-looking people.

"Oh, hey! You're Danny!" Not only was he eye candy, but he was a gee-shucks nice guy. My instincts about people might not always work, but I had a feeling this kid was going to be making me herbal tea and begging me to eat a kale and quinoa salad very soon. He jumped to his feet nimbly and crossed the room, shaking my hand with both of his. "So, so great to meet you. Dave has told me so much about you, and of course we've been wondering if you would call. So eventually he took the bull by the horns, you know, and got in touch with your brother. Your other brother," he said, flashing the smile at Laurence.

I was glad for all of us that Laurence was attracted to the elderly, because this much wattage could blind a person.

"We?" I said. I couldn't help but like the guy. How could you not? It would be like disliking puppies or sunshine. But, we? "You and Dave, are you…?"

"I'm his partner, yeah," he said. He went back to his cables; things were obviously moving quickly around here.

Laurence was looking at me very closely. I hoped my face didn't betray the weird disappointment I felt, and didn't want to feel, and in fact didn't want to think about.

And where was my cocaine?

"Cool," I said. "How long have you two been together?" *And where is my cocaine?*

"Oh, dude! Whoa. Not that kind of partner. Though as an

enlightened, feminist male, I am not insulted that you would think that." More smiles. More teeth that must have been whitened five minutes ago. "No, we just do our stuff together." He indicated the room, the house, the situation as a whole, I supposed. "We have our areas of expertise. Dave's the boss. He chooses what we're doing, where we're going, and why."

"And Jonas is the *savant* when it comes to all things electronic, security… the stuff that keeps us – and our clients – alive."

Dave was standing in the doorway. I hadn't heard a thing, and supposedly my hearing was back up to par. But he was a pro, and my guard was totally down. In the last couple of minutes I felt safer than I had since… well, since before I got the call that my twin sister had died. My radar had gone quiet. What a blessed relief.

As far as I was concerned, I was moving into this house and never leaving. Get Skipper and Marie and Darren and the boys and even Fred out here. We'd build an extension. Get dogs.

Of course, the house was a rental. And we had the small matter of missing people and killers to find before we were safe. Before anybody around here was safe, as far as we knew.

Dave and I hugged, and I ignored Laurence's eyebrows, which were threatening to fly off his face. Dave pulled away and held me at arm's length, studying my face. "I can't believe you got out of that," he said. "You're one tough cookie, Cleary."

"Bullshit," I said. "I have done nothing but fuck this up from start to finish." And to top off the Best Week Ever, without warning, I burst into tears. And before I knew it, Laurence was hugging me and rocking me, and then Jonas was also hugging me, and Dave was patting me on my head.

Not my proudest moment.

"I'm so sorry," I said. "It's just been…"

"No doubt," Jonas said. He was rubbing my back. Normally I hate when strangers touch me, but sure enough, I found it soothing. I felt tea and kale coming any minute.

"And this is the first time in a long time that I've felt anything like safe. Or that I didn't have to be on full alert. With all you guys here," I finished lamely. "And I'm not that kind of woman," I added. I looked at Dave. "You know that. It's not about men taking care of me."

I needed to shut up before I curled into the fetal position on the floor and begged them all to do just that.

"Danny," Dave said slowly. "Do you remember what happened when you and I and Darren were in the desert?"

"When you conned us and took us prisoner? Hard to forget, buddy."

"Yeah. And despite the fact that you had no weapon and I was holding a significant piece of hardware to your heads, you managed in a matter of seconds to break my nose and take my gun." Then he tapped me on my face, lightly, where the abrasion was from working off the duct tape. "And a few days ago you managed, with a dislocated shoulder and no use of your limbs, to free yourself from certain death. You kept your head, and you survived."

I didn't want to tell him that I did the opposite of keeping my head. I had been operating on rage at the idea of leaving another legacy of violent death for my nephews.

Laurence hugged me again, and he was trying not to cry. "She's always been like this. Almost always." Almost meaning the years I gave up and sat in my apartment doing crack with Gene.

Jonas clapped his hands. "We've got work to do, lovely people," he said.

"We do have work to do," Dave said. "Here's what I propose. Laurence, you get Danny settled into her room." He looked at me. "Laurence got you some new things to wear and some fun little bits of disguise."

"I'm going to make dinner," Jonas said. "No meat. I'm sorry, and you seem like nice people, but I cook animal flesh for no man. Or woman."

"Absolutely fine," I said. Quinoa, here I come. And I surprised myself by looking forward to it.

"Danny, have a bath, relax, lie down for a bit. I've got some more work to do around here, and we've got a couple of guys coming to do some more…"

"Modifications?" I said.

He grinned and scratched his ear. I liked that habit. "Yeah. But I've got the place for a few months at least, and the owners may be amenable to an offer."

A few months. "Do you think this is going to take that long?"

"God, no," he said. "But once we do something like this—" he indicated the house "—it's done. It can be a safe house for us, for our friends. A vacation house, whatever. This is a nice part of the world."

"And the other thing?" I asked Dave, and he nodded.

"Yes. I have coke for you. But it's sort of… medicinal only. A tool. Laurence and I will have it; you won't be storing it up in your room. You do it in front of us, or not at all."

"I can live with that," I said, all calm, as though I wasn't jumping up and down on the inside.

* * *

My room was bare-bones, like the rest of the place, but comfortable. I'm not exactly a Kardashian. Laurence had a few bags of clothes for me, and he'd chosen well. Though when I looked through some of what was there, I thought Dave must have chosen. Tactical stuff: good boots with excellent treads, with a steel toe but still light enough. A couple of pairs of good-quality black combat pants that wouldn't look out of place anywhere. A pair of what looked to be ballistics sunglasses. In pink; a bizarre concession to femininity, I supposed. Some gloves, which made me mourn the loss of the Kevlar gloves. A very cool leather purse/fanny pack deal which, after playing with it for a bit, I realized could be strapped to me in a bunch of different ways, including around the thigh to use as a holster.

Yes. Dave and Jonas definitely had to have supplied this stuff. Other bags had underwear and sports bras, and I really hoped Laurence had bought those. And then there were a couple of wigs, some makeup and simple jewellery, and studenty shorts and t-shirts.

I was relieved. When Dave had said something about disguise, I had visions of high heels and spandex, but this was a university town in early summer. If I had to be incognito anywhere around here – and I couldn't see why that would be necessary, but I was out of the loop, obviously – blending in as part of the university or a basic townie would be more effective than anything elaborate.

Besides, I had never once been able to walk convincingly in heels.

I collapsed on the bed and shut my eyes for a few minutes.

I was happy, or as happy as I was going to get until this was all over. I had the kind of support I would have killed for a week ago, I had cheated death, and, a little later, I was going to be allowed to get high. And still be productive.

I let myself put Des and Mary and Dickie out of my mind for now. We would be brainstorming later, obviously. And I did have a touch of a sore throat. Rest.

A while later, there was a quiet tapping on my bedroom door. "Danny, dinner's ready! Your presence is requested, man!" Jonas. I really liked Jonas. I bet the boys would like him, Matty and Luke. In my head, I had somehow already adopted Jonas into the family circle.

Dave? That was a little more complicated.

I got off the bed and stuck my feet into a pair of flip-flops that were in one of the bags, and headed down the hall.

I walked through the kitchen into the dining room.

"Surprise," they were all yelling. There was wine, and candles, and the smell of good food. Some spices I couldn't place, maybe saffron? And in the middle of the table, a cake.

"Happy birthday Danny," Laurence said. He looked emotional, and a bit nervous at my reaction.

So it was. For the first time in my life, I had forgotten my own birthday. It was the first time Ginger hadn't woken me up with a phone call. It was my first birthday without my twin.

"Wow," I said softly. "Thank you." I felt shy suddenly, and moved. But there was no way I was going to start crying in front of these guys. Not twice in one day.

"No, no! Happy day! Take a load off and eat." Dave pulled out a chair for me, and I sat down, feeling touched and awkward and also bereft. My twin sister wasn't here.

Jonas started bringing out food, and Laurence poured me a glass of wine. A small glass. "It's going to be a long night," he whispered.

"We should be working," I said. "You guys didn't have to do this."

"We'll work later," Dave said. He raised his wine glass, and the others followed. "Danielle Jacinta Cleary, you have survived this year, against the odds. First we celebrate a bit, then we'll get down to work."

I couldn't believe it. I looked at Laurence. "You told him my middle name? You shit!"

Dave smiled. "He didn't."

"I didn't, I swear to God!" Laurence said. He was grinning. He looked happy.

"Would you people please eat?" Jonas said. "You all need fuel, especially this one," he said, nodding at me. "I used to be a private chef, in another life. Don't let it all get cold."

"A private *vegan* chef," Dave said. "I'm not sure that counts." Jonas flipped him the bird.

"Did you make the cake?" It was pretty, black and white frosting with one big pink rose in the middle.

"Dude! That sugar bomb? No. But you know, go ahead and enjoy, once you eat something that's actually good for you."

I started to eat. Ginger, I thought, I miss you so much it's like an amputation. But I've got this, and I have to try to be happy.

I felt a pleasant breeze along my brow that felt like a kiss. But it was probably just the fan.

TWENTY-SEVEN

There was a young woman and an older guy I hadn't seen earlier working on putting some kind of film over all the windows while we were eating, and at one point Jonas excused himself to go to the back room to check on some system he had set up. Dave apologized several times for having to check his phone when it beeped. But as far as I was concerned, the less attention on me and my birthday, the better. It's not an age thing – I couldn't give a rat's ass about that, and frankly I couldn't believe, in a way, that I was only thirty-three. In some ways I felt like I had lived enough for three lifetimes.

But being the centre of attention has never been my bag, and I love a bit of bustle going on around me. Especially when I know it's to keep us all safe. Especially my brother. Having this birthday without Ginger was more than I could really handle thinking about. Nothing was going to happen to Laurence on my watch, and I wasn't the only one making sure of that now. Having all these people here was going to help me end this shit, and hopefully bring Dickie back safely. If not in one piece, I was hoping to at least get him back alive.

Plus, it was kind of exciting. I had never entered the world of high-tech security before.

"It's not that high-tech, but don't tell Jonas," Dave said. "We're doing what we can in a short space of time, in an area that isn't rife with resources for this kind of thing." He nodded at the couple in the living room. "That film is reinforcing the glass, making it more or less shatterproof. Not bulletproof, though. We just didn't have time." He grabbed his wine glass and leaned back. "It's also rare, in that the tint will make it impossible for anyone outside to see in."

"Dave," Laurence said, "what is it that you actually do?"

Dave smiled. "If I told you, I'd have to kill you." He looked at his phone, but it hadn't beeped.

"Bitch, please," I said. "I am beyond grateful that you're here. And that we're here," I added. "And I wouldn't be sitting here with my brother if I didn't trust you."

"I know," Dave said. He sounded serious. "Thank you for that."

"But we are, quite literally, putting our lives in your hands. Are you former military? You sell security systems? A private investigator? MI6? CIA? CSIS?"

"Mossad?" Laurence said. He was flushed with wine and quite enjoying himself. I was obviously not the only one who felt a bit giddy to not be so afraid. "Hezbollah?" We laughed.

"You left out the A-Team," Dave said.

"Don't forget the Black Panthers," Jonas said, coming back into the room with bottles of water. "We're having a resurgence. Dave's a bit pale, but I vouched for him at the door." The people in the living room finished the last window there, and said hi cheerfully to us, as they crossed through to head down the hall.

"Grab food," Dave yelled after them.

"I left you guys some downstairs," Jonas added, louder.

"Downstairs?" I asked.

"Mm-hmm," he said. "The basement."

"The basement," I said. I closed my eyes. I felt giddy for a minute, nearly faint. "Oh my God."

Dave was looking at me. "Yes," he said slowly.

"What's up, buttercup?" Laurence said. Yeah, he was definitely a little drunk. But that didn't matter now.

"Can we move in there?" I said, indicating the living room. I indicated the messy table, the plates that we hadn't yet cleared. "We need to talk, now. We'll do this later. Okay?"

Dave and Jonas moved efficiently. Jonas took a thin laptop from the small table behind him and indicated that I should grab the bottles of water he'd just brought in. Dave went into the kitchen, where I heard him making coffee.

"Dave?" I said. I wanted the cocaine now, and it really was so I could do what I needed to do.

Mostly.

"I'm bringing it, Danny," he said. "Laurence, no more wine. Start on the water. Coffee's coming."

Jonas had closed all the shutters in the living room and sat on the floor with his laptop. "There are motion sensors all over the property," he said. "It's the first thing we did. But those windows aren't bulletproof, and I don't take unnecessary chances." Laurence went down the hall and came back with his head soaking wet, a towel around his neck, and a couple of packs of cigarettes.

"We're smoking," he said to Jonas.

"Dude, I'm used to it," Jonas said. He was tapping away at his laptop.

"I soaked my head in cold water," Laurence said to me.

"Smart," I said. I tried sitting on the floor like Jonas had, but I couldn't stay still. I had to pace. We were all silent.

Dave came into the room a few minutes later with coffee for him and for Laurence, and he handed me a small baggie of coke. Probably about two grams. "Coffee table," he said. It was glass. I felt my pockets, but I had no wallet, no cards on me. Dave rifled through his, and I could tell he was holding back impatience. He handed me a driver's license and a twenty-dollar bill.

It probably speaks to how much I wanted to get going that I didn't even glance at the name on the driver's license, or where it was from. It wouldn't have been real, anyway.

I didn't waste time. My hands were steady, and I poured a bit of coke onto the table, cut a couple of fat lines with the card, and quickly rolled the twenty into a tight straw.

I snorted both lines, one into each nostril, and sat back. I felt the coke at the back of my throat, that feeling that tells you it's decent, not overly stepped on – cut with too much baby laxative or whatever other substance dealers are using nowadays – and that things will be just fine.

I took a sip of water, then dabbed a bit of water into both nostrils and snorted it back.

Junkie trick. Don't ask.

Laurence wasn't looking at me, but Dave was. Jonas didn't seem to even care; he was immersed in his laptop.

"Okay," I said. "There have been two occasions, and two places, where the killer or killers have appeared and disappeared seemingly out of nowhere, when police were everywhere. Rose's, and the woods near Dickie Doyle's cabin." I took another long swig of water. Coke makes you thirsty. "The day we were shot at in the dining hall, Laurence, the day Colin was killed? Whoever did that managed to get in and out. Like magic." I was trying not to talk too quickly. I needed them to take me seriously and not think these were the ramblings of a drug-addled mind. "And Sarah Gilbert's body appeared there, when there were media everywhere on the road and cops all over the grounds."

Dave was nodding slowly. Laurence just stared at me and gulped his coffee.

"There has got to be an underground bunker of some kind there," I said. "Maybe not in the woods; I don't know. We need to talk about that. But my guess is that there is some kind of underground structure, a bomb shelter or just some kind of large cellar, I don't know, but there is something on the property, or close enough to it, that the killer has been using. And if that's the case, then who knows. Dickie could be held there. Or Des Murphy, or both." I leaned over and grabbed Laurence's cigarettes and lighter, and lit one for me, and one for him.

"That's insane," Laurence said.

"And what has been happening isn't insane? How on earth did anybody get Sarah's body onto the property? Even if one of the cops was the killer, there were other cops there. The killer had to have brought Sarah from close by, close enough that he could get in and out very quickly."

I smoked furiously. I wished Dave would say something.

"And what about a vehicle? That yellow pickup? Getting to and from the property, if this is the case?" Dave was looking at the ground. I had a flash, just then, of the guy I thought he was when we first met in southern California. The slacker who worked at a pawn shop. Ha.

"I don't know. Maybe this structure is larger than we think."

Dave shook his head. "No. If there was a door big enough for a car to drive through, someone would have seen it by now." He paused. "But a simple hatch in the ground, covered in leaves or whatever – and it's possible that if something like that existed, it's existed for a very long time."

"You know the Underground Railroad was active in the Annapolis Valley," Jonas said. He wasn't looking up from his laptop. "My grandmother used to tell me stories she'd heard about landowners right here in this Valley, who would hide slaves on their property."

"Why did they have to hide once they got here?" Laurence said. "They were free here."

Jonas looked at my brother. "Dude, didn't you guys learn about this in school? There were agents, slavers who came up here to basically hunt escaped slaves after they passed the Fugitive Slave Act in the U.S. It was dangerous for them. The slaves, I mean."

"I did not know that," Laurence said slowly.

"No worries, bud," Jonas said. "But it would not surprise me at all if there were these underground bunker things Danny's talking about." He went back to his laptop. Dave grinned and pulled his ear.

In case I had been wondering if Jonas was paying attention to things other than tech, I had my answer.

"Look," I said. I slowly started cutting a bit more coke into lines. It was soothing. And compared to my crack habit, cocaine felt almost wholesome. "There has got to be more than one person involved in this, and obviously it's been planned for a long, long time. Killing all these people, doing all these things suddenly, out of the blue? No way. It's precise. It's like a military strike."

"And on the holiday weekend," Dave said. "That festival thing they have."

"The Apple Blossom Festival," Laurence said.

"It would cause maximum media impact, and maximum damage to Rose's Place."

"Here's another fun fact," Jonas piped up, still looking at his laptop. "Rose Doyle, née Carlisle, was named Queen Annapolisa in 1992. I've got pictures here, if anybody wants to see them."

"What?" I said. "Holy Fuck City. Laurence, did you know this?" Jonas was giggling, and I was about to glare at him when I realized he was laughing at my potty mouth. So I just smiled.

"No," he said. "I didn't. But really, why would I? I knew she grew up around here, but she went down to the States when her father did, when she was about twenty. That's when she went to Bennington, and she and Dickie met."

"Well," Dave said, "somebody remembers Rose Doyle, née…?"

"Carlisle," Jonas said.

"Carlisle. That's for damn sure. Danny's right. The timing is no coincidence."

I leaned over and snorted a line. My brain was working. I felt no pain. My brother was sitting eight feet from me, safe.

Now, we were getting somewhere.

My phone beeped. I had a text. "Weird," I said. My old phone was gone, lost somewhere between getting knocked out at Mary's place and winding up tied to a pier. Laurence had replaced it for me; there was a new one waiting for me at the hospital. But I couldn't care less about gadgets, and I hadn't even checked to see if it was the same number. I hadn't thought to ask him. I'd already talked to everybody in the family, and I didn't have many close friends. Okay, any. Not since Gene, and since I stopped going to the local watering hole where I'd met him.

The men all looked at me. I started to laugh before I looked at my phone: Sitting around the kidney-shaped glass coffee table, all of us on the floor to avoid getting shot through the windows, and lines of cocaine spread out, we looked like the last guests at a key party in 1979.

"Check your phone," Laurence said. "Could be the police."

"They think we're gone," I said.

"We hope," Dave said. "That was the idea, anyway."

I took the phone out of my pocket. I didn't want to stop what we were doing. This was the first time I felt on top of things since it all started happening.

I looked at my phone. "Huh," I said, before reading the text aloud. "'That wasn't supposed to happen to you. Very sorry. Get well soon.' No idea. Mary?"

"What's the number?" Jonas asked. I read it out to him, a 902 number. Local, in other words. Jonas did what he did, while we watched.

"It's a pay-as-you-go, bought at a mall out of town, registered to Richard Doyle," Jonas said. "Today. It was bought today."

"Can we get the security footage of where it was bought?" Laurence said. He was flushed, leaning forward. I knew he was hoping it was actually Dickie, but after the missing tattoo and the severed finger delivery, I deemed it unlikely.

"Working on it," Jonas said. His fingers were flying across the keyboard.

"Danny, didn't anyone tell you to turn off your phone? Get rid of the SIM card?" Dave was looking very serious.

I looked at Laurence, who shrugged.

"Oh, wow, my bad," Jonas said. "I really thought you would have told them. And I keep thinking they're professionals. Or at least that she is," he said, nodding at me.

"Oh, shit," I said. "Laurence, give me your phone." He took it out of his pocket and handed it over. I was going to start taking both our iPhones apart to take the SIM out, but Jonas just gave me a look and held his hand out.

"Why is this an issue?" Laurence said. "If we don't recognize a number, we won't answer the phone."

"If anyone in the RCMP is involved in this somehow, they could track your whereabouts using these," Jonas said. He spoke with the patience of someone who is constantly surprised at how childlike most people are.

"Which means," I said, picking up the twenty I was using as a straw, "that your safe house is no longer as safe as we were hoping." I snorted a line and rubbed some into my gums.

"I think it's time for a quick tour of the weapons," Dave said. He rubbed his hands together, like he was eager to get started. He motioned for us all to get up and follow him.

"Now we're talking," I said.

Dave looked at me. "You're not touching anything tonight. You can look, but hands off."

"That's what *he* said," Laurence and I said at exactly the same moment, and after a one-second pause at the perfection in our timing, we all cracked up. As I am often prone to a touch of hysteria when it is least appropriate, it was nice to see that I was not alone.

Jonas then showed us the CCTV camera from the mall where the phone was bought.

It was grainy, and it was black and white. A woman. A thin woman in jeans and a long-sleeved shirt, with a baseball cap covering her hair. She spent less than five minutes at a kiosk in the mall making a purchase, and then she walked away, head down.

"Mary," Laurence said. We were all quiet.

"Or anybody," I said. "I have never seen Mary wear long sleeves."

"And you have never known Mary to try to avoid detection before, either," Dave said, but gently. "And you've only known her a very short time."

No one said anything.

At that moment, a very loud alarm started ringing throughout the house.

"We've got guests," Dave said. "Get down." And he dove for the floor – or more precisely, the gun he had secured under the couch – just as someone banged at the back door.

"They'd better not want any of my cake," I said, but I seemed to be the only one who found it funny.

Cocaine. It's a hell of a drug.

I heard the two people in the basement come running up the stairs, and Dave motioned for Laurence and I to sit where we were and not move. Laurence had crawled closer to me, as though I was going to let him block me from whatever might happen.

Fat chance.

Jonas, however, was calm. "Hey, hey! It's just Ned. Everybody chill." I scooched over to where he was sitting with his back against the couch. Sure enough, he was looking at video images of cameras that had been installed all around the perimeter of the house.

"Jesus," Dave said, and went to the back door. But I noticed he kept his gun in his hand, at his side, instead of tucking it into his pants or leaving it. I couldn't see the back door from the living room, but I watched on the video with Jonas as Dave opened the door and a big guy came in. The two men hugged briefly, and I watched as the two from the basement exchanged what looked like friendly words with him. I couldn't make out his face, but something about him was familiar.

Everybody traipsed into the living room. Dave, followed by the older guy and younger woman who had been putting the film on the windows.

And then Aussie Rules walked in, hands in his jeans pockets.

TWENTY-EIGHT

"**H**ey there," he said, with no trace of an Australian accent. He walked over and shook Laurence's hand. "We haven't been formally introduced. Ned." My brain was exploding slightly, but I played it cool.

"Aussie Rules, right?" he said. He sounded pure Yankee. "Yeah, I heard you say that once."

"So much for my ear for accents," I said. Even though it was clear that this guy was a plant of Dave's and therefore not actually in need of rehab, I felt embarrassed about the coke in front of me. For a minute, anyway.

"Ned likes to really go, like, undercover," Jonas said. He held his hand up for Ned to slap, without moving from his spot. "Totally unnecessary, but whatever floats his boat."

"What can I say, I'm a frustrated actor," Ned said. "Listen. I'm starving, and we've got to talk."

"Were you followed?" Dave said.

"Bitch, please," Ned said. "I wound up walking half the way up here."

While everybody else went into the kitchen to scavenge for food, I sat with Jonas. He actually looked away from his laptop for a minute and patted my knee. "How you doing, little sister?"

"Oh," I said. "Fan-fucking-tastic."

"A lot to take in, right?"

"You can say that again." I started cutting a couple more lines.

"I don't suppose I should ask you to take it a bit easy with that?"

I started to say something snarky, but stopped myself. These people were all here to help me. I didn't have any idea how all of this worked for them, but having a whole security team – or whatever they were – come to my aid was not something I wanted to take for granted. And Jonas was just being kind.

"I will," I said. "I just have a feeling this isn't going to be an early night."

"You might want to have a glass of wine now, along with the water," he said. "So you don't get too jangly. Am I right?"

"Actually, yes." Before I could move, Jonas jumped up with the ease of a six-year-old and came back with an unopened bottle of white and two glasses.

"I'm going to join you," he said. "I don't drink much, though, so if I get silly just slap me." I grinned at him. Matthew and Luke were going to love him. I wondered if I'd ever be able to tear him away from Dave. Maybe he could be my sober companion and security guy, all in one! The thought made me ridiculously happy, under the circumstances.

Ten minutes later, all of us were sitting around on the living room floor. The young woman was Lydia, and the older guy was her uncle Bert. They were both Brits. Laurence had brought the cake down and everybody sang "Happy Birthday" to me, and then Laurence handed out plates of cake.

It was, by far, the strangest birthday party I'd ever had.

Aussie Rules – Ned – was eating Jonas's leftovers and studying me. More carefully than I felt comfortable with.

"So, this is weird," I said. "Did you know about this?" I said to my brother, indicating Ned.

"Nope," he said. "To be honest, it would have been nice if we had been told. How did you know Danny was going to be there? And why did you feel the need to have her watched?" He was drinking wine again, and despite everything, he seemed to be mistrusting Dave again.

"It's complicated, but Danny knows that she and I have a mutual… enemy."

"Michael Vernon Smith. I'm aware, yes."

Dave looked at Laurence. "So I feel responsible for the fact that I wasn't able to stop what happened to Jack MacRae in Toronto. And to Darren in Maine. I have my own reasons for keeping an eye on Smith, and keeping an eye on him means keeping an eye on Danny." He looked at the floor, and I realized like lightning that he had other reasons for keeping tabs on me. I buried my face as far as I could into my wine glass, as though I was appreciating its bouquet. Or whatever wine snobs call it.

"Because you think Smith is keeping tabs on her?"

Dave nodded. "He doesn't give up. It may be years before we hear from him again, but I have no doubt that we will."

"That's great," I said. "But let's get back to matters at hand." I looked at Ned. "What happened?"

"So, as these characters know," he said, indicating everyone in the room except for me and Laurence, "I've been the last resident left."

"How did they let you stay?"

"Well, it got complicated for them. I made a bit of a stink, because, you know, I'm a paid-up resident, and the owner is missing. I said I had changed my mind about going back to Oz," he said, slipping into his Aussie Rules accent, "and with all of them there, I felt safe."

"Did you?" Laurence said. "Feel safe."

"Pfft," he said, and grinned. "Safe is boring."

"These dudes are all adrenaline junkies," Jonas explained to me. I nodded. I knew the type. I *was* the type. At least, I used to be.

"I found out a couple of things," Ned continued. "One, Evan wasn't such a lily-white young man. He was dealing weed and pills. Perfect place to do it, really."

"Wow," I said. "He never approached me."

"No," Ned said. "Well, he knew what your drug of choice was, and let us just say, your reputation preceded you. He wasn't going to try anything with you." He pushed his empty plate aside and started on his cake as though he hadn't eaten in a year. "But it was penny ante stuff, at any rate. Like I said, weed and pills."

"Opiates aren't penny ante," I said. "That's how Rose Doyle started down her road. People can get hooked on that shit, then they to go fentanyl, or heroin… it's awful stuff." There was a small silence as people looked at me, with cocaine laid out in front of me in neat lines. "You guys know what I mean."

Laurence spoke up. "Wait a minute," he said. "So Evan was dealing, and we know that Sarah had gone into the basement to smoke weed the night she left. The night she was abducted."

"So the killer hates drug users?" I said. "The whole place was full of drug users. Kind of the point."

Dave shook his head. "No, Laurence is right. It's one thing to be there and getting your shit together. It's another thing to be, what, throwing that chance away by using or selling. If that's a motive, I mean."

"Holy shit," I said. I snorted a line and dabbed water into my nose. Amazing, to be doing that in front of everybody. And so far, I actually hadn't craved crack. But I knew I couldn't keep this up. Dave and Laurence were right – this felt too good, and if I kept going, I would be right back where I started. "Des said the cops were going to go through files with Mary, old patient records, to see if there were any, I don't know, disgruntled or particularly... weird former residents." I was talking too fast. I needed to slow down. "And the day I went to see Mary. I told you she got really upset when I was talking about all the harm I had caused, being an addict. How my sister's death, and my husband's death, could both be attributed to my stupidity. She tried to get me to stop talking like that, and she got up and started making noise. Maybe she was trying to stop someone from overhearing me."

"If that's true, Mary is innocent," Laurence said. "She was trying to save Danny." We all sat with that for a minute. Jonas was on his laptop again.

"I don't think you could say she's innocent," Ned said slowly. "I didn't get to know her like you did, and I agree she – well, I would never have put her down as a killer, that's for sure. But the truth of the matter is, she's missing." He finished his cake. "But here's the piece I really wanted to get to. I've been keeping my ears open and hanging out with some of the Mounties who are on the grounds." He cleared his throat.

"Mary kept her own name when she married Geoffrey."

"Mary Dowe, yeah," I said. "So?"

"So," Jonas said, looking at his computer screen, "Geoffrey's last name is Carlisle."

"He's Rose's brother," Ned said. He looked slightly put out that Jonas had stolen his thunder.

"You didn't know this?" I said to Laurence.

"Obviously not," he said. He looked pale. "And I don't think Dickie did either. Geoffrey wasn't at the wedding – it was a small wedding, I remember who was there. And Dickie would have mentioned it. I know he would have mentioned it."

"Laurence, you may have to face that you possibly didn't know Dickie Doyle as well as you thought you did," Dave said. "What are the chances that Dickie hired Mary to run Rose's Place just out of the blue, without a family connection of some kind?"

"Maybe not," Jonas said. "Geoffrey Carlisle spent a number of years in a psychiatric hospital when he was in his twenties and into his thirties, but I don't know why. Yet. And he's that much older than Rose – he was born in sixty-seven, Rose in seventy-five. So when she was in her late teens, he was hospitalized."

"So, what are you saying? That Rose kept her crazy brother a secret from her husband?" I said.

"Not every family is like the Clearys, Danny," Dave said. "People have secrets. She was, what, Queen Bee…"

"Queen Annapolisa," I said.

"Right. And then when her father moved to the States, Rose went down there too and went to Bennington and married a smart man from a good family. She might not have wanted to advertise the skeleton in her closet." He shrugged. "Devil's advocate. We have to look at all possibilities."

I hoped that wasn't it. I hoped Rose wasn't that petty. I couldn't imagine abandoning my family. Then again, when I was holed up in my apartment doing crack, that's exactly what I had, effectively, done.

"Either Dickie knew about Geoffrey being Rose's brother or he didn't," Dave continued. "But where does that leave us? Geoffrey and Mary are still missing, yes?" He looked at Ned, who nodded. "Sergeant Murphy and Dickie Doyle are, as well."

"So who are the bad guys and who are the good guys?" Lydia piped up. I noticed she had pulled a gun out of somewhere and was cleaning it slowly and carefully. I probably would have smelled the oil, but my nose had been otherwise occupied.

"Well, I think it's safe to say that whoever bashed me on the head and left me tied to a pier to drown in high tide isn't a good guy," I said. "And I was knocked out at Geoffrey's house."

"Still, we make no assumptions. Not yet," Dave said. "First things first: We need to find out if there are hidden bunkers anywhere around Rose's place."

"Or Dickie's cabin," I said.

"Or Geoffrey and Mary's house," Laurence added. "But how, exactly, do we do that? Show up there with shovels and start digging?"

"Every question has a creative solution, brother," Jonas said. "You've entered my territory now." He and Dave started talking about ground-penetrating radar, people they knew who could be up here by morning, and I started to drift. Jonas was simultaneously hacking the local planning office. Ned and Bert went to the kitchen and brought back a few cold beers for the non-wine drinkers, and Lydia started cleaning another gun.

I just wanted to get moving. The police, according to Ned, had finished the search at Geoffrey and Mary's house, and it was sealed. The media had spent a day camped out front during the search, but had moved on, still hanging out down by Rose's. And by some miracle, they hadn't found Dickie's cabin. It had been registered under a numbered company, and so far neither police nor locals had spilled the beans.

And, sadly, a university shooting in Tucson with a high body count had taken some of the attention off what was happening in this sleepy backwater.

I knew that what Jonas and Dave and the rest of the crew did was important. And sitting around like this exchanging information had been invaluable. But it was dark, it was late, and wasn't this the best time to get off our asses and do some actual looking? Some leg-work?

I looked at Laurence, who seemed ready to pass out. He was never much of a drinker, and he probably hadn't had much sleep while I was in hospital.

"Listen," I said. "I think Laurence needs to crash, and Ned, you probably do too, after that walk. I'm obviously going to be up for a while—" I gestured to the cocaine "—but I think a lot of what we have to do now is down to Jonas, before we decide on how to act."

I glanced at Dave, hoping he could read that I didn't mean a word of what I had just said. I just wanted to get Laurence away and safely tucked in. And to prove it, I neatly scraped the remaining coke back into the baggie Dave had given me, leaving myself one small line on the table. And maybe a few crumbs here and there.

"I'm a civilian," Laurence said. He ran his hand over his face, his sandy blond hair. I felt such a surge of love for him. "I can't pretend to be as superhuman as the rest of you." He started to get to his feet. "These old bones are creaking."

"You're, what, forty-three? Forty-four? You're hardly a pensioner, my brother."

"I'm a desk jockey, Danny, as you well know." On his way past, he picked up the little baggie I was going to give back to Dave, and made the delivery himself. I got up and followed him, to use the bathroom and check that he was okay.

"You feel safe?" I said, standing in the doorway of his room.

"As safe as I can feel, under the circumstances," he said. He paused. "Yeah, actually. I do feel safe."

"One way or another, we'll find Dickie," I said.

"I think so," he said. "But now that you're out of hospital, my goal is really to get you back home safely."

"Sleep," I said. "And drink some water, or you're going to have a mighty hangover."

I went back to the living room and sat on the floor between Ned and Dave.

"Back to the lake," I said. "Tonight. Now." I had a feeling about something, and there were people missing. There was no time to waste. I looked at Dave. "Do I seem fucked up to you? Too high to function?" I knew I wasn't. I would want a bump in half an hour, but then again, adrenaline is a powerful force. I might not need it.

Dave looked at me and nodded at Ned, who smiled like he was game for anything.

"Jonas," Dave said, "we're going to the cabin. The three of you stay here."

"Call," Jonas said. "Every ten."

"Nope," I said. "It's a dead zone there. No cell reception."

"Crap. Of course it is," Dave said. "We'll take the walkies."

"Really?" Ned said.

"Actually, from two high places like this, in a rural setting, it can go up to thirty miles, depending on weather and other interference. I put the chances at fifty-fifty." Jonas looked over his glasses at Dave. Who looked at me. I looked at Ned.

"Fifty-fifty isn't so bad," I said.

"We're tough," Ned said. "I have tattoos and everything."

"Plus, you can do accents," I said.

"That, too," Ned said. "I'd say we're golden."

Lydia fitted the holster thing onto me, quickly adjusting it around my hips and thigh like she'd done it a million times. I felt like an outlaw, a gunslinger, with it on. She stuck one of the guns she had cleaned earlier into the holster, after making sure I knew how to use it. Another Glock. I hoped very much I wouldn't need it. I felt much better, but a couple of fingers were still a bit numb, though functional, and, despite the cocaine-fuelled adrenaline, I knew I wasn't at my fighting best with my shoulder either. I went to the kitchen and, for luck, took a corkscrew and stuck it into my pocket.

A corkscrew had been the tool that had taken down Michael Vernon Smith back in Maine. It hadn't killed him, but it had saved the lives of people I loved, and, for me, it had become a talisman.

The three of us stood in the kitchen and agreed quickly on a plan of action. We all changed into black clothing, and I was wearing my new gloves and my thigh holster. My nervous system was coursing with cocaine.

Despite the awful reason we were there, and doing what we were doing, I've had worse evenings. And I could tell that Dave and Ned felt the same way.

We slipped out the back door and into the night.

TWENTY-NINE

It was after one a.m., and we didn't run into a single car on our way to the lake. We took a route that circled around the lake in the opposite direction from the way I'd always come. The road had more potholes, and if it weren't for the seatbelts, we'd have been tossed around like dice in a cup.

We were in a four-wheel-drive Jeep, with me in the back. In the front, Ned and Dave were calm, but the jokey attitude we'd all had back at the safe house was gone. They were all business, testing the walkies with Jonas, changing channels, and quietly discussing strategy, too low for me to hear over the truck.

"Hey," I said. "I'm back here. Want to let a girl know what the plan is?"

Dave turned around from the front passenger seat. "You and I are going into the cottage," he said. "We're looking for memorabilia, anything Dickie might have about his wedding, anything at all about their past as a couple, their young adulthood, yearbooks, whatever. I've got a hunch about something, and I want to see pictures. Also, any signs that anyone else has been there since the police cleared the scene."

"I'm going into the woods above the lake with a metal detector," Ned piped up.

"A metal detector?"

"See if there's anything underground, any hatch, door, whatever, covered with leaves."

"Oh," I said. "Smart."

"This ain't our first rodeo, little lady," Ned said.

"What's your hunch?" I asked Dave.

"Don't bother. He never tells us about his hunches," Ned said.

"Until I'm sure. Otherwise, it might taint how you see things."

We passed a police cruiser coming from the direction of the lake, and Dave calmly told me to get down. We had discussed this. I slithered to the floor and felt in my pocket.

I had a tiny bit of cocaine folded in tin foil in my front pocket. If I felt myself flagging, I was going to do a quick bump at some point. I was just hoping not to be caught with it by the police. The weapons were hidden so expertly inside a fake spare tire I felt sure we would pass any random inspection, but there was no use worrying about the police now.

Being arrested is one thing. Being stalked by psychopathic killers is another thing altogether. Most of us would rather be in a cell than a grave.

Ned turned onto a road that I wouldn't even have seen. It was unmarked, save a garbage collection shed at the end. We were deep into the woods now, though in one patch it looked like some clear-cutting had taken place.

Ugly, but harder for a killer to hide. Then again, harder for us to hide.

I didn't bother asking Ned how he knew the way. He'd

been at Rose's for a while, and no doubt had explored pretty extensively. He'd probably attended just enough of the group sessions to avoid getting kicked out. Then again, the rules at Rose's were so lax that I doubted he could have if he had tried. Not bringing drugs onto the property seemed to be the only one written in stone.

Evan apparently had. And Sarah. And they were both dead. And while I hadn't heard as much, I would have laid bets that the same had been true for the poor bastard Laurence and I had found trussed up on Dickie's bed.

"Wait a minute," I said.

"You can get up now," Dave said. I hoisted myself onto the backseat, then slipped and fell back down.

"Oof," I said. I righted myself. My face was red.

"You move like a cat, Danny," Dave said. "Smooth." He and Ned both had big grins on their faces. They both looked happier than pigs in the proverbial shit.

"Yeah, yeah, fuck you both," I said. "And I mean that with the utmost respect, of course."

I was grinning too. I realized I was happy, too. Sitting around puzzling things out was great and all, and God knows I had appreciated being able to have a little R & R in the form of cocaine. But this? Driving into the night, putting myself into the path of danger, with the added bonus of possibly helping people?

This is what I was made for. For better or worse. I felt it as surely as I felt love for my family, and as surely as I felt the presence of Ginger watching over me.

Dave stuck his hand back without turning around, and I grabbed it. He squeezed it and let it go. Ned met my eyes in the rear-view mirror and winked. We were in this together. It felt like such a luxury, to be doing this with people who had the same blip in their genetic makeup, the same predisposition for running toward danger instead of away from it. Luckily, we were the good guys. Our addiction to adrenaline and danger could be satisfied by this, instead of robbing banks or committing much worse crimes. This must be what firefighters feel like, I thought. Running into buildings that other people are running away from.

I wasn't sure if Dave and Ned had the same propensity toward violence that I did, however. Obviously they were ready for it, but I didn't know them well enough to know if they got the same visceral satisfaction out of it that I did.

"Hey. I'm sorry about your nose," I said to Dave. "Back in the desert, I mean."

"Danny, Dave's nose has been broken so many times, he's got a reward card with the plastic surgeon," Ned said. "Pay for nine surgeries, the tenth is free."

"Like you with the dentist," Dave said. He turned to me. "Ned's like a hockey player. He's been hit in the mouth so many times I think there's only one of his original teeth still in his mouth."

We laughed. The road was narrowing, the trees heavy here, old-growth evergreens. It was both beautiful, in the headlights, and menacing.

"Wait," I said. "How did anyone know Sarah was hiding weed in the basement? I mean, how did the killer know, unless she specifically told him?"

"Or her," Ned said. "But yeah. Good point. Sarah kept herself to herself. She wouldn't have shared that information with any of us. Not until the night she found Evan's body down there."

"And she told everyone in that room. The police, Laurence and me, you. But she was taken directly afterwards."

"So somebody either saw what she was doing because there was a hidden camera there..." Dave started.

"Or the killer, one of the killers, was one of the police there," I finished.

"Holy shit," Ned said. We were silent for a second.

"We don't even know we're right about all of this," I said. "This theory, I mean."

"No, we don't," Dave said. "But that's why, in situations like this, we only trust each other," Dave said. "Police are just like the regular population. Most of them are good, decent people, but pinning a badge on somebody doesn't make them exempt from doing horrific things."

At a fork in the narrow road, Ned turned right, away from where I judged the lake to be. We couldn't see it from here. He pulled the Jeep over as far as he could and cut the engine. We sat in silence in the dark car for a few moments, waiting for the night and the wildlife to adjust back to silence without the engine, and for us to get our night vision and hearing adjusted.

The fact that I could hear properly from both ears might, I knew, save my life tonight.

Dave passed me a headlamp, but told me to keep it off for now. As agreed earlier, we got out of the car as silently as we could, and Ned retrieved the weapons from the back. As I stuck mine back into the holster, Ned smeared some black stuff from a little tin onto my forehead, cheekbones and nose, and did the same with Dave. His touch was quick and businesslike.

Ned indicated the direction Dave and I would go, and where

he was heading, back into the woods with the metal detector. We each had flares, in case we got into trouble, and Dave passed me a walkie-talkie, but it was turned off while I was with him. If we split up for any reason, I would turn it on. It was set to the right frequency, agreed upon with Jonas. We had agreed to meet back at the car at four a.m., if nothing happened before then.

Ned and Dave exchanged some hand signals that I didn't understand, but looked practiced and rehearsed, and something like you might see in a military movie, or from a baseball catcher to his pitcher.

Then Ned disappeared into the trees, and I followed Dave in a slow, quiet jog down the middle of the dirt road, back to the fork.

Eyes and ears open, Danny. I heard Ginger's voice in my head. My body felt good, despite my time in the hospital. Our pace was slow, and I matched Dave's steps.

Then, around a bend, I could see the moonlight shining off the lake.

We were on.

THIRTY

I followed Dave. My breathing was easy enough, despite the cocaine and my recent brush with death. I tried to listen for anything in the woods, anything that shouldn't be there. I was thinking not only of a killer with a rifle, but of whatever animal or animals that had fed on poor Sarah Gilbert.

We hadn't gone far when Dave pointed ahead. Dickie's cabin was about a hundred yards away. The bush was thicker from this side; I wouldn't have noticed the driveway until we were on top of it. Dave slowed to a walk, and I followed his lead. The ground crunching under our feet sounded cacophonous to me, but I couldn't tell if that was an effect of the hearing having returned in my right ear. I touched the Glock strapped to my thigh, for comfort as much as anything else.

We walked slowly down Dickie's driveway. Dave had unholstered his weapon and was carrying it by his side. I opted to keep mine where it was – I wasn't quite as comfortable with guns as he was, and I hoped I wasn't going to have to use it.

Loons were calling to each other over the water, and the air smelled very faintly of woodsmoke. Someone on the lake had their stove going; it was a cool night. But there was no smoke coming from Dickie's cabin. It was dark. There were no police around. There was no one around. I couldn't even see any patio lanterns around the lake from here; it was midweek and the holiday weekend was over. Dave indicated that he was going to keep his eyes on the cabin and I was to watch the woods.

We reached the outhouse. Dave flung the door open and stood to one side, but judging by the smell emanating from its interior even from ten feet away, I doubted anybody would want to take refuge in there. The thought nearly made laughter bubble up out of my throat. My tendency to nervous or sad hysteria had to be quashed, and quickly. It was all so surreal.

I bent over at the waist and took a deep breath. I thought of Sarah, tied to a tree, in terror and pain, and my urge to laugh went away.

We walked in silence to the cabin. It seemed as deserted as deserted can get. There was police tape over the door, which I broke, while Dave took something from his pocket and unrolled it. Lock-picking tools. While he worked on the door, I wished I had the night-vision goggles as I scanned the woods. I half expected to see a red cap moving through the trees, but nothing.

I kept my hand on my holster, and tried to tune out my busy brain and just be part of the landscape, let my instinct and my primordial senses take over.

Something was wrong. I felt that something was wrong, but I couldn't see or hear anything. I unsnapped my holster and kept my hand resting lightly on the grip of the Glock. But for whatever reason, I didn't think the danger was coming from inside the cabin. There was someone out here that shouldn't be, but unless they moved or made a sound, me trampling through the forest in no particular direction wasn't going to do anybody any good.

I was worried about Ned. I wanted to get inside. I wanted Dave to walkie him, make sure he was okay.

I heard the lock turn. Dave turned on his headlamp and, with his gun extended in front of him, went in to make sure it was safe. I stood in the doorway, heart pounding, ready to run inside if Dave needed help, or run into the trees if I spotted anyone.

I had never felt so alive. And I was very glad that Laurence wasn't with us.

I heard Dave moving through the small cabin. Then in a quiet but normal voice, he told me to come in and lock the door behind me.

He was closing the curtains, for which I was grateful. I turned my own headlamp on, and went inside.

We had discussed protocol – well, Dave and Ned had, and I had listened. All our walkies were switched to silent and would vibrate with incoming messages. Dave and Ned had headsets for theirs so they could be hands-free, but they didn't have all their equipment with them, and there were only two headsets. I was told that if I was separated from Dave and in trouble, to just press the button and shout bloody murder into the walkie – and even without the walkie-talkies, I'd probably be heard. But if I was in a situation where making noise was not an option, we'd use Morse code, SOS.

Dave holstered his gun and radioed to Ned that we were in. We waited for his reply, his assurance that he was safe.

When it came, I realized I had been holding my breath.

"Okay," Dave said. "Closets, drawers, cubbyholes. Any place where people keep their papers, whatever. Keepsakes."

One thing I have never had is a desire to root through other people's stuff. I'd seen bits in films where a woman stays over at her boyfriend's place and as soon as he leaves, she starts rooting through his drawers or his laptop, trying to find dirt. Inevitably, she finds some, and that never leads to anything good. As far as I'm concerned, a certain amount of privacy should be allowed every human. Ginger and I had shared a bedroom growing up, and she wrote in a diary every day. She only hid it between her mattress and box spring because she knew Mom or one of the boys would find it irresistible. She could have plopped the thing open on my face while I was napping, and I wouldn't have read it.

As far as I'm concerned, what goes on in a person's head or in their past should be their own damn business. Unless, of course, that information could stop people from dying. Or losing bits of their body to somebody's knife. That's when all bets are off.

At least, that's what I told myself as I opened Dickie Doyle's closet, looking for skeletons. Metaphorical skeletons, that is: any literal ones would, hopefully, have been found by the police by now. They probably weren't interested in Dickie's credit card statements or the sympathy cards he'd received after Rose died. At least, if they were, they hadn't taken them, because that's what I found in the shoeboxes at the bottom of Dickie's closet. I put the sympathy cards to one side. Dave hadn't told me about his hunch yet, so I had to guess.

For a middle-aged man of means, Dickie sure didn't seem to own much. The sum total of his wardrobe took up about four feet in the closet and consisted mostly of white t-shirts, which looked ironed, and flannel work shirts. A couple of pairs of khakis – I checked the pockets; nothing but gum wrappers – and jeans, and one black suit. Probably the one he'd worn to Rose's funeral. He must have had more clothes, more… everything, when Rose was alive. He'd obviously gone all Walden Pond and gotten rid of most of his worldly goods. But someone who had loved his wife as much as Dickie Doyle had loved his must have mementoes.

I had gone through every pocket and even reached my hand into the toes of the two pairs of sneakers – small feet – that were at the bottom of the closet. Two shoeboxes of bills and cards were the sum total of personal shit.

I moved to the dresser and glanced outside to the main area, where Dave was taking every book out of the bookcase and leafing through, shaking them out.

The police and forensic people would have gone over this place pretty carefully. I'd avoided looking at the bed itself, which was stripped. The last time I'd been in this room, a dead man was trussed up on it, missing a hand and a foot. I made an executive decision and didn't move the mattress to look for diaries. The police had to have done that.

The top drawer of the dresser was full of mismatched sports socks and white boxers, which I didn't want to look at too closely. I was starting on the second drawer – oh my, t-shirts! – when Dave told me to come see something.

He was looking through a yearbook. I felt a chill up my spine. The police wouldn't have seen anything amiss in Dickie having Rose's high-school yearbooks around, but the information inside was worth more than its weight in gold. At least to Dave and his hunches.

He flipped to the grad pictures, the C's. Rose Carlisle. Beautiful, black hair, red lips, not too much makeup. Full face without being fat. Healthy-looking, red cheeks matching the red rose in her grad gown.

"Nice teeth," I said. Dave looked at me, the headlamp shining in my eyes. "Hey."

"You are one weird sister, Cleary," he said.

"Why, thank you," I said. I was debating taking the last bump of cocaine. It was burning a hole in my pocket.

Dave read Rose's yearbook bio aloud, quietly. "'Rose may not be the best at math, but we all agree that she brings the best blueberry muffins to Trig! Rose was launched into the world at six thirty-two a.m. on May 29th, 1975—'"

"May 29th," I said. "So it was her birthday around Apple Blossom weekend."

Dave nodded and continued. "'1975, at the old Wolfville Hospital. Her parents, Geoffrey and Pamela, were so taken aback at the beauty of their daughter that they immediately decided that perfection had been achieved and chose not to spoil things by having another.'"

"Geoffrey," I said. So Mary's husband had been named after his father. "And I thought Rose's mother died in childbirth."

Dave nodded. "'Rose spent some of her younger years in the United States, which explains her bad taste in music.' Whatever that means."

"Her father was from Connecticut," I said.

Dave continued. "'Many men have tried to win her heart, but she has, like many young women before her, given her heart forevermore to the captain of the hockey team.'" I snorted.

Forevermore, huh. But the prose reminded me of my own high-school yearbook, where the student staff wrote everybody's profiles, with input from the person's friends. "'Rose's greatest dream is to ride in the Olympics, and her greatest fear is to shovel manure for a living. Rose plans to head to Acadia, where she wants to study Early Childhood Education.'"

Sad. Eerie. And wouldn't she have known, near the end of her senior year, that she would be going to Bennington, and not Acadia?

Dave was flipping through the yearbook quickly, and I could almost hear his heart beating faster.

"Here," he said. "The hockey team." His fingers trailed over the names.

Captain: Desmond Murphy.

"Holy Fuckville," I said. "Des." Sergeant Des Murphy was Rose Doyle's high-school boyfriend.

We were silent for a second, the light from both our headlamps on the page, looking at a bunch of hormonal teenage boys, one of whom had been the love of Rose Carlisle's young life. And who had also come back here, in later years, to live. They had socialized together, the two couples.

I wondered if Dickie knew about Rose's history with Des. I doubted it.

I had to take this in. "Was this your hunch –" I started to say, but then I saw something at the back door. A woman in a white nightgown with long black hair, standing at the back door, looking through the glass.

Rose.

THIRTY-ONE

"**W**ait," Dave said, but I was nearly at the door.

I turned the lock and, my hand on the gun, copied Dave and stood to the side of the doorway.

When I looked, I saw a white nightdress disappearing into the woods, maybe twenty yards from the door. The same woods where someone had thrown Evan's head at me.

I felt Dave drag me back by my shoulder. My sore shoulder. He was talking into his headset and pushing me out of the way. He started running toward the woman in white.

I stopped for a second, moved behind the door and reached into my pocket. I wanted to do the line of coke that was there. I wanted it right now, to help fuel what was going to happen next. And I was irritated that Dave had pushed me out of the way.

Just go, idiot. Just go, I thought.

I ran after Dave, into the trees.

If she hadn't been wearing white, we never would have been able to see her. I thought I saw bare feet, and my mind rebelled. Rose was dead. Her body had been identified. And nobody could run through this dense undergrowth with bare feet.

Despite the fact that I heard my dead sister talking to me

almost daily, I'd never believed in ghosts. Humans could and did get up to enough evil on their own without bringing fairy tales into the mix. My parents were killed by a drunk driver. My twin sister and my husband were killed by an evil man and his brainwashed acolytes. I'd seen what had happened to Sarah Gilbert, and no ghost had eaten her hands and feet.

Either Rose Doyle wasn't dead, or this wasn't Rose Doyle.

I passed Dave. I was either a bit fitter than he was, or he was less reckless than I was.

I was gaining on her. She was a fairly big woman, I could tell. My height, if not taller, and definitely with more girth. If it was Rose, she'd be forty or so, and even in her high-school shot she looked like she would lean toward being big. But she ran with abandon. Her feet were bare, and must have been torn to shreds. As I got closer – ten feet, maybe fifteen – I could hear her breathing hard.

Ghosts don't have cardio issues.

When I was close enough that I thought I could take a shot, I unsnapped my holster as I ran. I could hear Dave behind me, but he was losing ground.

"Stop," I yelled. "Please. It's over now." I could see a cottage ahead in a clearing about fifty feet away. It was dark, and hopefully uninhabited, but I didn't want to take any chances.

The woman stopped abruptly. With her back to me, she raised her hands in the air and slowly turned to face me.

It wasn't Rose. She had to be in her sixties, maybe seventy years old, but she moved like a woman who had spent her life outdoors in the woods. I didn't recognize her. Her long black hair was matted, and streaked with gray.

I had my gun pointed at her, but for once I found myself

without anything to say. I wasn't going to shoot this woman. For all I knew, she was somebody's mother with dementia, lost in the woods. My brain was buzzing.

"Hello, Pamela," Dave said behind me. I let him pass me. He was moving slowly, his gun at his side. I put mine down. Her hands were in the air.

"I don't know who you are, young man, but I'm glad somebody has the sense God gave him," the woman said. Her voice was clear and strong, and in an instant I knew it was the same voice I had heard in the woods a week earlier. Just before Evan's head had come barreling at me.

She started to walk toward us, very slowly, then she feinted to her left and dove into a thick copse of trees.

Pamela. The name in Rose's yearbook. Her mother. Who had supposedly died in childbirth. At least that's what Rose had told Dickie.

"Pamela, you must want this to be over by now," Dave called. He moved very slowly in the direction she had gone, and before I thought about it, I ran ahead of him.

Dave was here because I had come here. It might have been because he was looking for our mutual enemy Michael Vernon Smith, but if I hadn't come to Nova Scotia, Dave would be wherever he had been before this. I didn't know if Pamela had a knife or an axe or a gun somewhere, but I wasn't going to let him be the first to find out, the hard way.

I ran into the trees and entered a clearing about eight feet wide.

Sitting tied to a tree was a man. A large man. I didn't recognize him.

Pamela had a gun pointed at his head.

"Come on, don't be shy," she said. "You two are safe. Unless you try to stop me."

I looked at the man, who had duct tape covering his mouth. His eyes were open, but he didn't look afraid. He looked resigned, and tired, and very sad.

It wasn't Des. It wasn't anybody I knew.

"Danielle, this is my son, Geoffrey," Pamela said. Geoffrey. Mary's husband. Rose's brother.

Where was Mary. My God, where was Mary?

"Hello, Geoffrey," I said softly. He nodded at me politely, as though we were being introduced at the hardware store. "Pamela, where's Mary?"

"Oh, she's around here somewhere," the woman said. "She doesn't matter." I looked at Geoffrey, who had tears streaming out of his eyes. I wanted to tell him to fight, to pull against the tape. He was twice my weight, probably. If he tried hard enough, he could do it.

Then I remembered that he had multiple sclerosis, and my heart sank. Who knew whether he was symptomatic at the moment, whether he had any strength in him to fight. And his body language told me he had no fight left in him, either way.

"She matters to me," I said. "She's my friend." I put my gun down, slid it into the holster, which I didn't snap closed. "Why are you doing this?"

"He knows," Pamela said. She had a huge smile on her face. She was smiling at someone behind me. "This one knows."

"I don't know why you have Geoffrey tied up, Pamela," Dave said. "I can guess about some of the others, but not your son."

"Where's Dickie, Pamela?" I said. "My brother went to

Bennington with Dickie. They were great friends. Laurence was Dickie's best man. He's worried about him."

"Dickie Doyle," she spat out. "The precious Dickie Doyle." She scratched her head with the barrel of her gun, hard, like there were things nesting in there. I knew Dave couldn't take a shot, though. We still didn't know where Des was, or Dickie. "What a pussy. He let her get sick, he didn't take care of her. Not a single goddamn man has done anything but fail my daughter, from day one."

"She had an accident, right?" I was stalling. I was trying to send Geoffrey some strength. I was trying to gauge whether I could get to him before she could shoot anybody.

"She was a fucking junkie," Pamela yelled, and creatures nearby scooted away. "People get one chance. You got a chance, and you took it. You came here to get better. You're a good girl," she said.

I didn't want to tell her about the tinfoil in my pocket.

"I saw you," she continued. "You didn't do anything wrong. You got up in the morning and got your exercise. You didn't have sex with boys, and you didn't go looking for any drugs." Have sex with boys? And how did she know how I behaved in rehab?

Cameras. There must have been secret cameras everywhere. That's how she knew about Evan, and about Sarah. And Geoffrey was the handyman there. He must have installed them for her.

I shot a glance to my right. Dave was parallel with me now, and I could practically read his thoughts.

"She is a good girl," Dave said. "So why did you try to kill her?"

"Oh, that was a misunderstanding. I'm sorry about that,

dear. But you were at the house asking questions, and Mary's weak, and if there's one thing we can't stand around here, it's a Nosy Nellie." She started hitting Geoffrey around the head with the gun, lightly and absently, as though she didn't realize what she was doing. His eyes were closed. He looked defeated, like he was waiting for the blow that would kill him.

"So is Dickie dead, then, Pamela? Because if he is, I don't blame you, really. I love my family more than anything, and if he's to blame for what happened to your daughter, then he probably got what he deserved."

"Damn right," she said. She looked at Geoffrey as though she had forgotten who he was.

"But it would be a great favor to me and my family if you could tell me where I could find his body," I said. "My brother is really fond of him, and he'll never know a moment's peace if I don't find Dickie."

"Your brother's a fairy, right?" Before I could answer, she put her hand up. "Never mind. That's none of my beeswax. And I don't mind the fairies. They're good to their mothers. Not like this one." She hit Geoffrey hard across the back of his head with a backhand that Venus Williams would be proud of. His head fell to his chest, his eyes closed. I couldn't tell if he was knocked out, or if the blow was strong enough to kill him. Probably not.

"I wasn't the best mother. I know that. But my daughter was used and mistreated by every single man in this Valley," she said. "This one didn't protect her." She put her hand on Geoffrey's shoulder, not looking at him. "And God knows, Dickie Doyle didn't have the stones to put a stop to it."

Dave inched forward. Literally, it felt like he was moving

an inch a minute in Pamela's direction. I could tell he wanted to take a shot, but she was moving quickly back and forth behind Geoffrey, one minute with the gun to his head, the next scratching herself with it.

"I hope if you ever have a daughter, Danielle, I hope that she's ugly."

"Oh?" I said. Really. My mouth can't stop at the worst moments, but when I should be smart, I can't count to ten.

"I was beautiful once, and look at me now." She paced back and forth behind her son, seemingly oblivious to what was underfoot. In bare feet. "Men fail you. Not all men. I don't know about that one," she said, gesturing to Dave with her gun, causing my heart to leap into my throat. "But they want to own you and then they throw you away, lock you up, ignore you."

Pamela leaned down suddenly and kissed the top of Geoffrey's head.

Then she put a bullet in it.

And before Dave or I could move, she put the gun to her own head and pulled the trigger.

THIRTY-TWO

I bent over at the waist, trying my damnedest not to puke, trying to stop my brain from failing me, my blood pressure from falling – whatever it was that made me faint.

Dave ran over to the bodies, and it looked like he was searching Geoffrey's pockets, patting him.

"Shit," he said. "Danny, we've got to move. Keep it together."

I followed Dave. I didn't think, I just followed him as he ran lightly back the way we had come. He headed into the cottage and told me to wait outside, listen for sirens or anyone coming.

But I knew no one was coming. The lake seemed deserted, and if there had been cops close by, we would have already seen them. But my senses were on high alert all the same.

All I could think was, she didn't tell us where Dickie was. If we couldn't find his body, Laurence would never rest. He could have been in the woods. At least if he was in the woods, tied to a tree – and I prayed he wasn't; I stood and said a prayer that Dickie hadn't met his end the way Sarah had – the police would find him. We would tell them where to look, at least.

Dave came back with his bag across his body.

"Yearbooks and shit," he said.

We ran back up the drive, faster than we had coming in. Dave was holding the walkie-talkie and saying something into his microphone to Ned. I couldn't hear him over the pounding of the blood in my ears.

This was who Dickie had been seeing in the woods. Pamela, Rose's mother. Not Rose. But at night, with his head and heart consumed with mourning his dead wife, I wouldn't blame him for thinking it was Rose that he saw. Hell, I had just looked at a picture of Rose and that's who I thought I'd seen peering in the door, too.

We ran back in the direction of the Jeep.

It was either Pamela or Geoffrey who had hit me and tried to drown me. Or both.

Mary was "around here somewhere"?

"I've got to go back," I said to Dave. I grabbed his arm to stop him. "I have to look for Mary. She could be tied to a tree back there. In here. Anywhere." The thought of Mary, so small and vulnerable, suffering the same fate as Sarah, made me want to be sick.

"Danny," Dave started to say, but his walkie must have vibrated. He grabbed it and pressed the button, spoke into his headset. "On our way back to the meeting point," he said. Why he couldn't just say "car," but whatever. He listened and responded with, "Ten-Four, Out."

"Ned has found Mary," Dave said. "He needs help with her. Follow me."

"Is she alive?" Oh please God, let her be alive.

"Sounds like it," Dave said. He started running again, and I followed.

A minute later Ned met us on the road, and we followed him

into the bush. We all turned our headlamps on. It was black here, the moonlight not reaching through the tree cover. Dave took the rear, letting me follow in Ned's footsteps, but I don't think any of us felt any danger now. There were tangled branches and vines underfoot, and it was still muddy in here. In this part of the woods, it probably didn't dry out until sometime in July.

Ned held his hand up and I stopped short behind him, nearly tripping over him.

In front of us was a metal door on the forest floor, like an old root cellar door. It was rusty with age.

"Jesus," Dave said. "In there?"

Ned nodded. "There's only room for two of us to get her out, and I think Danny should come down with me. She seems confused, and she knows Danny better than me. And she's a woman." Thank you, Captain Obvious.

"Of course I'm going down," I said. I watched as Ned and Dave opened the hatch. It was so loud, I'm almost surprised we didn't hear it from Dickie's place when Ned had found it before.

"Thank God for Jonas," Ned was saying. "A metal detector. Who'd have thought to bring a metal detector here with us?"

"Jonas," he and Dave said at the same time.

"It was well-hidden, covered in debris. I would have found it if I had stepped on it, of course, but that thing went crazy." He pointed at the small lawnmower-looking thing on the ground a few feet away.

I looked at the rusty ladder. Did I mention how much I hate ladders? I peered down into the hole, and couldn't see anything but darkness, and the ground at the bottom.

"She doesn't have a light down there?" I said. "They put her down there in the dark? She must have thought she was being buried alive." Oh God. Poor Mary.

"She was," Ned said. He was grim. "She must have been there for days. There are a few empty water bottles. And the smell – well, I hope you have a strong stomach."

I looked at Dave and he looked at me. He knew that having a strong stomach was not exactly what I was known for. He probably didn't know about my ladder aversion, however, and a girl likes to keep a few things to herself.

"Maybe I should go," he said.

"She doesn't know you, man," Ned said. "It's got to be Danny. She's like a terrified little animal down there."

"We don't know for sure that Mary wasn't the one who hit Danny," Dave said, but I stopped him.

"It wasn't Mary," I said. "I told you. It was someone tall. Pamela or Geoffrey. Besides, no matter what she did, she's in no shape to do any damage now." Enough talking. Bull-by-the-horns time.

"Give me your weapon," Ned said as I hesitated at the top of the stairs. "If you have an accident and it goes off down there, somebody's going to get hurt. Not to mention your hearing." I handed him the Glock and looked down into the darkness.

"Mary?" I called. I waited a second. I heard nothing. "Mary, it's Danny. I'm coming to get you."

After a minute, I heard her. "Danny?" she was saying. "Be careful."

"I'm coming down," I said. I put my foot on the first rung of the ladder and felt rust fall away under my boot. Jesus. "How deep is it?" I said to Ned.

"Maybe fifteen feet," he said. "Too far to jump safely in the dark."

"Just take it one step at a time, Danny. You'll be fine." I looked up at Dave as I started down the ladder. "I'll chuck you down a bottle of water when you get to the bottom. Try to get some in her before we bring her up. Just a little bit."

"I have to wait until you get to the bottom, Danny," Ned said. "I don't trust that ladder with both of our weight."

"Peachy," I said. "That's just great." I took a minute, clutching for dear life onto the ladder while taking my gloves out of a pocket and putting them on. I wasn't sure if I'd gotten a tetanus shot in the hospital, but I was pretty sure with all this rust and my luck, I was going to need one. "Okay. I'm going down, boys," I said.

"That's what *she* said," Dave and Ned said at the same time, and I couldn't help but laugh with them. Which made me feel immensely better. If we were laughing, I was going to be okay.

I took the ladder slowly. The rungs were unusually far apart, or so it seemed to me. I was careful to get a firm footing before I took the next one, like a scared kid on the monkey bars.

The smell hit me about a third of the way down. Feces, and something else. Blood, maybe, and vomit. Poor Mary.

I put my foot down on the next rung. Then my other foot. My walkie squawked and startled me – hadn't it been on silent? On impulse, I went to grab for it to silence it, and it fell.

Then the ladder collapsed from under me, and I fell the rest of the way down, chunks of rust falling like bloody hail all around me.

THIRTY-THREE

I heard the boys calling down, but the wind had been knocked out of me, and something was tearing into me somewhere. I closed my eyes and concentrated on being calm. I felt Ginger, patting my forehead, telling me everything was going to be fine. *Breathe*, she said.

I felt rather than heard Mary crawling behind me.

"Danny," she was saying. Her voice was weak, so weak I couldn't believe she could speak at all. "Is anything broken?"

Good question. As soon as I thought about it, I felt a burning in my right hamstring. And then the burning turned into a searing pain. I opened my eyes and tried to move my head to get my lamp to illuminate my leg.

Lovely. From what I could tell, a chunk of rusty metal had impaled my right leg, gone right through. Looking at it, my mind and stomach rebelled. I tried not to vomit from the shock and pain. Between the pain and trying to get air back into my lungs, I was pretty sure I was going to pass out.

"She's hurt," Mary was trying to call up. She was beside me. I was so grateful she was beside me. I could feel how hard it was for her to speak. She tried to swallow, and she called louder, "She's hurt."

"Danny, I'm coming down." Dave's voice. Then I could hear Dave and Ned up top. More rust fell down on me as one of them was testing the strength of the bit of ladder that remained.

"Danny, it's Ned." I still couldn't talk. Mary took my hand, and I squeezed it. "I don't think Dave should try it. The ladder's integrity is gone, and if he falls, he's going to fall right on you. You shouldn't move."

"I'm going down there," I heard Dave say. I heard it clearly.

"We have to get help," Ned was saying. "Buddy, it won't take long. Half an hour…" Then their voices either lowered, or I lost some time.

I opened my eyes, and I could see Dave's face peering down at me. He seemed so far away. Was it that far? Ned had said fifteen feet. This had to be thirty feet. Didn't it?

"Danny, Ned is going to get on the road and call for help."

Ned stuck his head over the side. Looking up felt like far too much work. My eyes wanted badly to be shut. "Danny, I think I should just go and get Bert and Lydia and a ladder. We shouldn't be around here when police come. Dave told me what happened. We'll have a lot of explaining to do. We'll take you right to the hospital."

"You're calling 911," Dave said. His voice sounded hard, and I tuned them both out. I let my eyes close and concentrated on the pain. Or at least, not screaming. I tried counting my breath to calm myself, like I had done in the water when the tide was rushing in at me, but it wasn't working.

I couldn't look at my leg. Seeing the bar sticking through it might make me sick.

"Danny," I heard Dave saying again. "Ned is gone. He's taken the vehicle and the walkies and the bag with the yearbooks, and when he's in range he'll call for the ambulance." I nodded. I knew he couldn't see me properly, but I nodded. "I'll stay here with you. It won't be long. You're going to be fine. I promise you, you're going to be fine."

Oh really, I wanted to say. Let me stick a rusty bar through your leg and tell me how fine everything is.

"I'm throwing down a bottle of water now. I've only got one, so you have to share it. Mary, can you hear me?"

"Yes," she croaked.

A plastic water bottle came tumbling down and, because I'm lucky that way, hit the bar sticking out of my leg.

I screamed. At least I had my breath back.

"Fuck," I heard Dave say. Mary was moving around me and I felt her put the bottle to my lips.

"No," I said. "Mary, you have some. You need it. I don't need water." She paused for a second, then I heard her take a tentative sip. Then a long chug. "No more right now," I said. "You might just throw it up. Let it settle." The pain was settling into something I could almost feel that I could live through. It was nauseating, but it was a thudding nausea, as opposed to the searing, screaming pain it had been. But I had no intentions of moving anytime soon.

I was glad Dave was there. He was talking to me, and I let his words wash over and around me. The pain was incredible, but it was less if I stayed absolutely still. I tried not to envision the blood gushing from my femoral artery, or the bar puncturing my sciatic nerve so that even if I lived, I'd never walk again. I felt tears leaking from my closed eyelids, and I did my best to think about Darren and the boys, and getting back to Toronto. Buying a big, very safe place where we could all live together. I could hear Dave above me, just talking calmly, and his voice was soothing.

I had just had my birthday. Ginger's birthday. We were thirty-three now. No, I was thirty-three. The age when Jesus died. Or was it Hamlet? Or both? I remember Ginger telling me it was supposed to be a very important year in a person's life. Or was that thirty-two? I hoped not. Thirty-two had gone by in a haze of crack smoke and sadness and death.

I heard a commotion up top. It seemed like a long way away. I heard a voice, or voices, and a cracking sound. Nothing good would make that sound.

I opened my eyes and looked up, and Dave wasn't there anymore. I didn't hear Dave, and I couldn't see him.

"Dave?" I called up. Gathering the energy to speak that loudly made me move my leg, and I tried not to shriek.

I heard footsteps, and I was pretty sure I saw black boots.

Then one of the metal doors slammed shut above me, and after a minute, the other. I thought I might have heard some rustling – someone moving Dave's body? Covering the doors with branches? – then I heard nothing else.

Mary and I were closed into the hole, alone in the dark, with only the faltering light from my headlamp. I was severely injured, and I was pretty sure that if I tried to move much, I was going to lose too much blood. Besides, the ladder was broken from about a third of the way down, and even had I been uninjured, I couldn't have scaled the wall to get to it. We had what, half a bottle of water between us. Mary was already severely dehydrated, and who knew what else.

The phrase "silent as the tomb" went through my mind.

This definitely wasn't in the brochures, I thought, and nearly laughed. I bit my lip. I had to avoid hysteria. If I passed out now, if I had one of my stupid fits, I was pretty sure I'd never wake up again.

"We're never getting out of here, are we," Mary said. Her voice sounded a bit better, a little bit stronger. Either that, or I was engaging in some heavy-duty wishful thinking.

"Of course we are," I said. "You heard him. Ned went to call 911. They'll find us. I have friends who will look for us." I hoped they would. Oh God, Dave. I couldn't think straight.

"No," she said. "We're not." She sounded almost dreamy, like whatever excitement and adrenaline having us come in had caused had drifted away from her.

I tried to shift my position a bit so I could see her better, and I ground my teeth against the pain. Mary wasn't moving, and I couldn't tell if she was holding her breath and staying still, or if she was passed out.

Or worse. But I wouldn't think about that.

I closed my eyes. I prayed that I would be out of this hole in the ground before Laurence even knew I was gone. I prayed that Dave was somehow okay. I prayed that Ned had gotten away and called 911, and that I would hear sirens very soon. I prayed that very soon both Mary and I would be in a nice clean hospital, surrounded by nice clean doctors and nurses.

I drifted for a bit. I don't know if I was disassociating to stay away from the pain or if I was feverish. I'd had a sore throat even since coming out of hospital; my infection was probably not gone. It was going to take hold of me anew, lying here with a rusty pipe in my leg, on dirt, surrounded by feces and who knew what else.

Wake up, Danny, Ginger was saying. *I'm sorry. Wake up.*

When I opened my eyes, it seemed to me that there was a bit of daylight trying to get through one side of the door, where the ground had probably eroded. I'd been out for hours. I tried to calculate past the fuzziness in my brain. We'd gotten out of the car at about one-thirty a.m. I'd probably come down into this hole at two-thirty? Maybe three? Daybreak at this time of year here was at around five-thirty, I was pretty sure.

Hours. I'd been down here for hours.

Ned couldn't have called 911. He couldn't even have decided not to, and made it back to the safe house to get help. They would have been here long before this. Somebody had stopped Ned, somehow.

And then I realized with a brutal, sickening clarity what must have happened.

Nobody had stopped Ned. Ned had never intended to get help. Ned had found this, what, root cellar or half-finished fallout shelter so quickly because he knew where it was. He was involved somehow. He had to be. He had circled back and come behind Dave and surprised him, killing him. Or knocking him out. Something. I had no idea how long Ned had been working with Dave. Ned could be working with Dickie, if Dickie was somehow behind this. Dickie had money, and Ned struck me as more of a mercenary or soldier of fortune than the rest of them. Ned had been here before Dave and the rest had come. He could have learned a lot in that time. He could be blackmailing Dickie, even.

My mind was on fire. I couldn't think of any other explanation. Pamela and Geoffrey were dead. I had seen them die. Nobody had come to rescue us, which meant Ned hadn't made the call, or hadn't told anyone where we were. But he couldn't go back to the safe house and tell Jonas and the others that Dave and I had just disappeared, and oh hey, where's the peanut butter?

Or maybe Ned hadn't made it out of the dead zone, the cell dead zone. Maybe whoever had taken Dave had also taken Ned.

I couldn't decide which scenario was worse. Either way, Mary and I were very, very alone.

I was dizzy. Literally dizzy. Despite the fact that I was pretty sure I wasn't going to make it out of the hole, I had to figure out what had happened. I had seen Pamela and Geoffrey die before my eyes. Or had I? Dave had approached them, but I had stayed a good fifteen feet away. I knew Pamela was dead; I'd seen her head explode. I thought I had. Had I dreamed that? She'd shot her son first. Geoffrey. Geoffrey was her son. Mary was Geoffrey's wife.

I looked over at Mary. She wasn't moving.

I steeled myself to move. I had to move. My mind was slowing down, my faculties dimming, and I thought if I let myself, I would just die sitting there, while the fear and fever ate away at my brain. I had to see if there was any water left. I had a fever. I was freezing, shaking, and my eyes were doing some funny things at their edges. I was seeing lights at the periphery of my vision.

With every bit of will I had, I used my abdominal muscles to pull myself to a sitting position without jarring the bar sticking through my right leg. I leaned against the wall, so I could see the space. Mary was at one end. She had crawled a few feet from me, like an animal, to die. She was clutching the water bottle in her hand. I tried to train my headlamp on the bottle to see if there was any water left. I wouldn't last long without water. Two days, max. Less if I had a fever. I had a fever.

There was water left, but I would have to get to it. I would rest first. I looked at Mary's chest to see if it was moving. I couldn't see any movement. I didn't feel her there anymore.

Mary was gone.

I was trapped underground. Nobody but Dave and Ned knew exactly where I was, and if help hadn't gotten here by now, I doubted it was coming.

I had a fever. I thought I was already dead. But Ginger would come for me. I waited for the doors above me to open, for Ginger to rescue me. I hadn't been able to rescue her, I hadn't been there when she needed me at the end, but she would come for me. I was freezing to death, and Rose and Geoffrey were in the hole with me. We all needed help.

I think I slept for a time. Something woke me, some noise.

Something crawled out of the darkness to my right. I could hear it coming.

I was in a nightmare. I swung my head to the right, my headlamp losing its power as I did.

Something large was crawling toward me. Something covered in blood, which moved like a person, but wasn't a person.

I screamed. I think I screamed. I wasn't going to die, eaten by an animal like Sarah.

I leaned forward to pull the rusty metal pole out of my leg. I could fight the thing off with it, and at least the blood I lost when the pipe was removed would hasten my death. I was not going to be tortured and mauled in a hole in the ground. This was *my* life, and if it was going to end, it would be on my terms.

THIRTY-FOUR

I leaned forward to get a good hold of the pipe.

"No, no, no," the thing said. "Stop screaming."

I hadn't realized I was still screaming.

And then, through my fever, I realized that animals don't talk.

It wasn't a creature, it was a man, and he was a prisoner like I was. I tried to hang onto that thought. He wasn't a monster. I opened my eyes and tried to catch sight of him with the fading headlamp, but he had scurried back into a corner.

My headlamp was down to nearly nothing. Very soon we would be in total darkness, other than the thin strip of light that was getting in from the door.

The pain was beyond bearing. I wasn't going to get through this. I'd been through so much, but I wasn't going to get through this. If Dave and Ned had been killed, Jonas would come down here. He would have people searching. But I didn't have days, and I knew it. I doubted I would live to the end of today. I knew with a sudden clarity that I hadn't gotten a tetanus shot at the hospital. That the sore throat I had was tetanus developing, and with the rusty pipe sticking out of my leg, the bacteria would be invading my bloodstream like hordes of killers. My jaw would lock. I couldn't remember what else was supposed to happen with tetanus, but I already had the fever.

I was going to die painfully in a hole in the ground, and Laurence would never, ever be able to forgive himself or live a normal life again. And my nephews, and Darren and Skipper.

For some time, I forgot there was anyone else down here with me.

I was glad. I didn't want to see him. The glimpse I had gotten was enough.

"Dickie?" I said. "Are you Dickie Doyle?" My voice sounded high, panicked. I tried to breathe. I had to get to Mary, to the water.

"Yes," the voice came back. "Who are you?"

"Danny Cleary," I said. Tears leaked from my eyes. "Laurence's sister."

Well, I had finally found Dickie Doyle. That was something, at least.

"Oh my God," he said, and suddenly he sounded like a man. "Oh my God." I heard him moving. "I'm coming toward you," he said. "Please don't scream again."

"Okay," I said. "Do you have any water?"

I heard him trying to crawl. I could tell the hole was high enough to stand in, so he must be very injured. "No," he said. "We drank the last of it a while ago."

"How long ago?" I asked. I wanted to know how long he had left.

"Last night, maybe. I'm not sure. How's Laurence?"

I nearly laughed. Such a normal question. We could be running into each other at the bank.

"He's here," I said. "Well, not here. But he flew up. You knew that, right?"

"I knew he was coming. But they took me."

"Dickie, Mary has a bottle of water in her hand," I said. "I don't know if she's still, uh, with us." The tears were making their way freely down my face now. I tried to stop them. I couldn't afford to lose any liquid. "But I have a high fever." I was trying to speak as clearly as I could. I couldn't hear my own voice in my head. My vision was doing that funny thing again, where I could see little sparks of light at the corners of my eyes. "And you need water. We need to make that water last. I can't get to it."

I steeled myself, and looked at my leg.

Whatever damage the rust was doing to my bloodstream was already done; I doubted I would help matters by pulling it out now, and I was very sure that it would kill me pretty quickly. I would save that, then, if dying from thirst was becoming too painful. I looked at the leg as though it belonged to someone else, for a minute. It was fascinating, looking at it that way. If it belonged to someone else, I'd tell them to get a tourniquet on that, and fast.

But it was my leg.

Fight, Danny. You have to fight.

Ginger.

For the first time, I felt the leather bag that was attached to my hip, which Lydia had strapped to me. It was the bag that the holster was fixed to, and I knew there was stuff in it, but I had forgotten it.

Dickie Doyle was crawling toward us, toward Mary, and I didn't let myself look at him. Something was wrong with him when I looked at him before, and right now I wanted to focus on my body, on stabilizing myself.

I unzipped the bag. When I felt inside, I thought that if I lived to get out of here, I would take care of Lydia and her uncle for the rest of their lives.

Antibiotic wipes. A handful of them. A pair of nitrile gloves. Some gum and hard candy. A small bottle of aspirin. And best of all, four pouches of water with electrolytes.

And a flare.

For a second I almost forgot about the pain.

And when I felt my leg, the holster, I realized that it was at exactly the right spot to act as a tourniquet, a few inches above where the piece of metal was sticking out of my leg. I just had to tighten it. Maybe Dave had said that, when he was talking to me, before something had taken him away. He might have been telling me to tie off my leg, but I wasn't listening to words. I was lost in pain, and just listening to the sound his voice made.

"Dickie," I said. "There's some water in my bag. They put water in my bag." I wasn't sure I was making sense. He wasn't responding.

I looked up, and by the sliver of light overhead, I could see him feeling for Mary's pulse.

"Take a sip of water first," I said. "Help yourself to that water. And I have candies. They'll help your mouth make –" I couldn't think of the word for it "– saliva."

I was ripping open one of the water pouches and emptying some of it, as slowly as I could manage, into my mouth. It was warm and slightly salty, but the best thing I had ever tasted. Until I opened the tin of candies.

I looked at Dickie. He was dressed in what appeared to be

a white t-shirt and a pair of boxer shorts. He sat down with his back to the wall facing me, as he drank the water, and I saw what had scared me earlier.

Someone had scalped him. At least, that's what it looked like. There was blood covering his face. He was missing fingers, more than one, I thought, and the front of his t-shirt was almost totally dark with what must have been blood.

The tattoo they had cut off.

He must be in agonizing pain.

I tried not to react, but he wouldn't be able to see me well, anyway.

"Is she gone?" I asked. I shook the aspirin bottle. I couldn't see it well enough, but I got it open and counted. There were eight pills. "Mary."

"I can't tell," he said. "Probably." He sounded odd. But then again, I'm sure I did too. And he'd been down here a lot longer.

"I have eight aspirin here," I said. "Do you have any water left?"

"Yes," he said.

"Can you come closer to me? I'll give you a few aspirin for the pain." He crawled over to me slowly, and I tried not to look too closely at his face. I'd been right the first time. He didn't look fully human. But my fever was making everything go from clear and bright to nightmarish.

He got close enough, and I held out my open palm, with a few pills in. With a shaking hand, he plucked them out of mine, one by one, and swallowed them slowly.

"Try to stay sitting up for a little bit," I said. "Let the pills go down." I swallowed three, wishing they didn't have a coating so I could chew them. I swallowed the last of one pouch of water, and handed Dickie a couple of hard candies. Then I let myself lean back.

If the aspirin could reduce my fever a bit, I would be able to think more clearly. I could speak to Dickie more. But he was in much worse shape than I was, and he didn't look like he had much left in him either.

I closed my eyes and did a mental inventory. I had three more pouches of water. Two aspirin. However many little candies. The gloves and the antibiotic wipes, which would have been great if I had, say, scraped my pinky finger on the ladder, maybe. But still, they were there. A flare, which I might use if the darkness started to drive me crazy. A bag with a holster strap I was going to try to tighten, as soon as I could.

And a walkie-talkie.

"Oh my God," I said out loud. Wasn't that how I'd fallen? Reaching for it when there was static or something? I doubted it would work this far underground. I felt my hip, and it wasn't there. Not in my pockets.

I had dropped it. It was on the floor somewhere here, and it couldn't be far.

It was darker in here now. I could hear rain hitting the metal door up above. An overcast, rainy day, then, which would lead to a pitch-black night.

I was going to get us out of here. Something clicked, something turned over; whatever survival mechanism that had helped me get the duct tape off my mouth in the Bay of Fundy was going to get us out of this stinking fucking hole and back into daylight.

I was feeling around on the floor when I remembered one

other thing I had, deep in my pocket. The small fold of tinfoil with a wee bit of cocaine. Cocaine is one of the best painkillers there is, and it would help chase the fever fog away. It was only a tiny amount; the buzz would only last a very short time. Ten minutes, maybe fifteen? I decided to wait for a few minutes, wait to see if the aspirin would help at all. But I had to stay conscious and not drift away into a fever fugue again.

"Who took you?" I said. "Which one of them took you?" I couldn't see anything now. The rain above seemed to be picking up, and what little light there had been was nearly gone. "Dickie?"

I crossed my fingers. They couldn't both be dead. If they were both dead, and I was stuck down here with two corpses, I thought I might go mad. My fingers felt around in the dirt, and I picked up a couple of small bits of what I hoped were pebbles. I chucked one in Dickie's direction. "Dickie," I said, more loudly.

"Rose," he said. His voice sounded like it was coming from a long way away. "Rose came and got me. We went for a drive."

"No, Rose is dead," I said. "Remember? Rose died. It was her mother, Pamela." More silence. Maybe I should just leave him be, I thought. Let him drift away, remembering his wife. What was the point in making him relive all of this again? What was the point?

I tried to think clearly. Dave wouldn't have left me down here if he had any choice. He had either been shot, or he was being held. Maybe tied to a tree in the rain. But by whom? Was it really possible Geoffrey hadn't been shot?

A headache started, the kind of headache I didn't experience very often. It was the fever, I knew, the infection in my blood.

Ned had insisted that only one of us could be on the ladder

at a time. He told me it was fifteen feet, when it was clearly much more than that. Could it be possible that my trust in him was yet another one of my famously bad errors in judgment? Could I really be that stupid?

Or maybe he was working for Michael Vernon Smith, the man responsible for the deaths of the people I loved most in the world, my twin and my husband. Could it be possible that my past had come back to haunt me so soon?

I had to get out. I was going to get out. I wasn't going to die wondering.

I took a breath and started dragging myself, inch by painful inch, to my left, to where I thought the walkie-talkie might have landed. Feeling around on the floor was an exercise in disgust. I felt what were probably the bones of some small, dead animal, and something else that was moving, crawling with worms. I bit in the inside of my cheek and recoiled, knocking my right leg into the floor. I screamed.

I could hear Mary stirring. Thank God.

"Mary," I said. "Speak to me, honey." My face felt it was soaking wet. Sweat, tears, and drops of rain getting through from above. She moaned. I needed to get more water into her. "Dickie! Wake up!" I picked up a handful of whatever I could find and threw it in his general direction. I think there were worms in there, but I didn't care. "Dickie!"

"Yes," he said. "I'm here. I'm here."

They were both alive. I was going to keep them both alive. And myself. I was going to keep us all alive. "Dickie, is there any water left?" Silence for a second.

"Yes," he said.

"I need you to get it to Mary. Try to get some water into Mary." Dickie was moving in her direction, and I renewed my frantic patting of the ground and inching left, trying to get to the walkie-talkie.

This was the moment. I stopped and took the square of tinfoil out of my pocket and carefully unfolded it. I didn't have fingernails or keys to snort it with, so I just brought the tinfoil to my face and snorted.

I figured neither Dickie nor Mary were in any position to either notice or care.

The rain stopped, and a minute later, a bit of daylight came streaming down into the hole.

Dickie was supporting Mary's head and slowly streaming water into her mouth. She looked like a tiny bird, but she was getting water. I'd had a tiny bump of coke. Baby steps. We were going to get out of here. I just had to figure out how.

In the light, I could see all of Dickie for the first time, and I saw why he was crawling.

They had taken one of his feet.

I forced myself to try to make sense of what I was seeing. I was pretty sure the fever had subsided somewhat. The aspirin had done something, anyway. Dickie's leg ended in a large bandage. A large dressing that had at one time been white, but was now just brown with dirt and blood. How could he have survived that, down here? They couldn't have done that right away; he would have died of shock or infection, something. Had they kept him in the cabin some of the time, on an IV?

"Did they put dressings on your chest as well?" I said to Dickie. "Where they sliced off your, uh, tattoo." They hadn't made any attempts to do anything about his head, which looked like it was missing the top couple of inches. I closed my eyes for a second. It felt like every word I said cost me, like I had a finite amount of breath and energy and it was running out.

But I had to talk.

"My tattoo?" Dickie said.

"The R," I said. "For Rose."

"Oh," he said. "My tattoo. Rose hated that tattoo, you know."

"Did she?" I said. I wanted to keep him awake, keep him verbal, but I thought if I heard another word about Rose fucking Doyle I was going to kill somebody.

"He never stopped loving her," Dickie said. "All those years. She told me it was over, but I don't know if it ever was. Not really." He sounded drugged. He must have been drugged; no one could manage the kind of pain he would be feeling otherwise.

The yearbook. "Des Murphy," I said. Oh God. Oh my God. "Sergeant Desmond Murphy."

In the faint light, I could see Dickie look at me quizzically. "Yes," he said. "But it was me Rose came back for."

Des Murphy. Rose's high-school sweetheart, the captain of the hockey team.

Oh, no. "Dave," I whispered. And Ned.

And then I heard the sirens. Even from deep in this hole, I heard the sirens. As soon as they stopped, it sounded like close by, I started yelling for help. Dickie tried, but he didn't have the strength, and Mary was barely alive. I screamed until my sore throat nearly exploded. I screamed until I saw stars.

Then the doors opened, and there was light.

I looked directly up and I saw white, and then I could make

out more than one set of feet and blue uniform pants.

And then Dave's voice. I had to shield my eyes against the direct light, but it was his voice. It sounded funny, nasal, but it was him.

"Dave? Are you alright?"

"Am *I* alright?" His voice did sound off, but not enough that I couldn't tell it was him. He sounded almost like he'd been crying. "Oh my God. Thank God."

"Get us out of here," I said. I wasn't in the mood for a long conversation.

"Just a minute, Danny," he said. I could see other faces and heard people talking behind him. "They're figuring out the logistics up here."

"Get us the hell out of here, fuckwads," I yelled up.

"Thatta girl," Dave said. He was laughing. But I thought he might have been crying, too.

Idiot could have been a Cleary, I swear.

I heard people above moving around, getting ready to get us out, and fuck the cynics: Heaven is for real.

THIRTY-FIVE

If there is any more blissful feeling than knowing you're going to be rescued when you think you're going to die, when you are absolutely sure that your life is going to end in a dark hole in the ground, then I don't know what it is. Better than crack, even. Although having a paramedic descend from the sky and inject a kick-ass dose of morphine into your veins before you're lifted onto a gurney and pulled into the daylight is a close second.

Seeing Dave's concerned face when I was being carried into the ambulance was pretty great, too. Even though his face was so swollen he looked like Al Pacino in *The Godfather* after he's had his jaw broken by the crooked cop, and he had his arm in a sling. But he was smiling that goofy smile, and I was on a morphine cloud, and the pain in my leg and in the rest of my body from the fever was fading away. I was on a boat, waves lapping at the sides, my hand dipping in and out of the water, and the pain was back at the shore.

And then my brother Laurence was with me; he was crying, really crying, and I was so happy because he was fine, nobody had gone to the safe house to chop his feet off, and I had found his friend for him. "Dickie is alive," I said.

"I know, Bean, I know. But the most important thing is that you're alive."

"We're all alive," I said. I was so happy. I loved everybody.

But I was forgetting something important. I knew I was.

Laurence was with me in the ambulance. According to him, I was singing "Lucy In The Sky With Diamonds." I don't know whether to believe him or not, as his poker face is pretty good.

I was lucky Laurence was with me at the hospital.

When I was a kid, my nervous parents would call an ambulance when I fainted – until epilepsy was ruled out, two separate MRIs had shown that there was nothing wrong with my brain (at least, no diseases that would cause spontaneous fainting and vomiting). Some neurologist told my parents I probably had a rare form of migraine that doesn't present with headaches, but with blacking out. Another doctor told them that I was just high-strung. Whatever it was, after a certain point, the syncope – my "fits," as my family called them – were just a genetic quirk and nothing to worry about. (They felt the same way when Laurence told them he was gay. We were lucky in our parents. They were pretty normal people who both had a dark sense of humor, and we were all taught not to take ourselves too seriously.) In any event, I had my share of doctor and hospital visits as a kid, and then later when I was training and fighting, I had a few trips to the ER with injuries here and there. While I wasn't a fan of pain, I'd always seen it as part of life, part of the package if you wanted to pursue certain things. I knew I could take physical pain. In the same way, my split with Jack and my ensuing affair with crack cocaine had taught me that I can't endure emotional pain. Stab me in the gut before you hurt anyone I love; it's much easier for me to bear. This is not because I'm heroic or impervious to physical pain, it's because I am more equipped to handle it than the emotional kind. I've lost both my parents, my husband, and my twin sister. This, I know.

Physical pain is a message from the brain that something is wrong. For a time, that message can be ignored, if necessary. Adrenaline does a good temporary job with that. Trying to defend yourself or someone you love also works well. But when the immediate danger has passed and you and your loved ones are safe, that pain will come back and tell you what's what.

When the hefty dose of morphine that had been used to get me out of the hole and into the ambulance started to wear off, I knew I was in for trouble. Not only was the physical pain getting worse, but the urgency with which I was being prepped for surgery made me realize that this might be a bit more serious than a broken ankle.

But Laurence kept a steady stream of love in the form of dry humour coming my way. He told me that Darren, Matty,and Luke were in the process of doing another homemade music video about my time in the hole, and the hole in my leg. They were calling it, fittingly enough, "The Hole."

I was laughing so hard that one of the nurses joked that maybe I didn't need any more pain meds, but a few choice words from Laurence meant that I was soon watching the nice morphine going down the nice tube into my arm.

Before the surgery, I didn't ask about Dickie or Mary, and Laurence didn't volunteer anything. I could sort of handle having a rusty pipe sticking out of my leg, but I wasn't strong enough to hear any bad news.

When they wheeled me down the hall for the surgery to remove the bit of rusty ladder sticking into my leg, I was lying on my side and Laurence was with me, telling me everybody could see my butt. I was laughing so hard I was crying.

Not a bad way to go into surgery.

"By the way, you did have a tetanus shot when you were here last time," Laurence was saying to me. They were the first words I heard when I was brought back to a room after the operation, after spending a bit of time in recovery when I came to. "You kept mentioning that you had tetanus when you were all doped up before the surgery. So it was a pretty good thing you nearly drowned before, 'cause I am here to tell you, that pipe was *rusty*. I'm having it nicely framed in a shadow box for you."

"They didn't cut my leg off," I said. I looked down.

"No, we've all decided that there's been too much cutting of things off around here lately. All further amputations have been postponed." Laurence looked exhausted. He shook his head. "Bad joke. Sorry."

"When was the last time you slept or ate anything?"

"If you count burnt coffee and six apple Danish as eating, then about ten minutes ago," he said. "I think I'm crashing from the sugar rush." He wasn't talking about my leg.

"What was the damage, Laurence?" I said. "Just tell me. Please. They didn't have to amputate it, so I can handle anything else. I just need to know." I also needed water. I looked around for the side of the bed, but moving my head made me nauseous.

"I'll field that one," someone said. A doctor with a round

face and a nice smile was there. She poured me some water and helped me drink it. "How do you feel?"

"Better," I said. "I don't have a pipe rammed through my leg, and I'm not sitting at the bottom of a hole. Things are looking up." She told me that I was lucky. The pole had missed my femoral artery and my sciatic nerve, and it had only "scraped" the femur. They had cleaned out the wound and packed it, and would leave it open for a few days to make sure there was no infection. Then they'd sew me back up. I was going to recover. While I might need some physical therapy and help walking for a while, the word "recover" was the one I was most interested in.

"The fever?" I said. "I had a bad fever when I was down there, and my throat was killing me. Even before I went down, my throat was hurting."

"She's hung up on tetanus," Laurence informed the doctor.

"You probably would be too, if you'd been impaled on a metal ladder in a hole in the ground," the doctor shot back, and I grabbed her hand. She squeezed it. She was motherly. She reminded me of my sister-in-law Marie, but with fewer frills. "You're fine for tetanus. Your infection from your last visit with us seems to have returned a bit." She was looking at the chart at the end of my bed now, having extricated herself from my hand with a kindly pat. "You were given a scrip for antibiotics?"

"I didn't get much chance to take them," I said. "This all happened pretty fast."

"Yes," she said. "You've really been through it, Danielle."

"Call me Danny," I said. My eyes were heavy. I was so tired, and, really, I didn't feel at all well.

"Get some rest," she said. "We're confident you're going to be fine. The next day or two might be the worst, but I think you're probably a tough young woman." I tried to smile, and I wanted to assure her that whatever happened in the next two days, it would definitely not be worse than the time I spent in that bunker. "I want you to sleep, and I want your brother to sleep, too." She was looking at Laurence intently. She grabbed a thermometer thing from the wall and, without asking him, stuck it in his ear. It beeped a couple of times.

"You're running a bit of a fever yourself," she said. "I assume you're not leaving her side, so I'll get a bed or a cot brought in here, whatever we can manage."

"Thank you," Laurence said, adding no wisecracks whatsoever.

And then I slept.

When I woke up, the curtains were wide open to a sunny day.

My leg hurt. A lot. But otherwise, I felt good. No fever. No headache or sore throat. And no drug cravings. And Laurence was sprawled out in a hospital bed that had been pushed against the window, snoring.

Count your blessings, Dr. Singh had told me. I had so many to count, at that moment, I nearly didn't know where to start. I wanted to call Dr. Singh. I would ask the nice doctor if she could get Dr. Singh's phone number for me.

A nurse came in and took my vitals, and I wouldn't let her speak above a whisper. I wanted Laurence to sleep as long as he could. She told me I was doing well. She asked about my pain level, and I told her I could manage it for now. She told me it was better to suppress pain than to manage it if it got to full throttle, and she told me she was going to give me some pain meds. I asked for some food; I realized I was ravenously hungry. Not for anything with meat – I was definitely going the vegetarian route, at least for a while – but I was fantasizing about a cold glass of milk. Milk and scrambled eggs and toast and water and juice and a really crisp apple.

I wanted to ask her about everyone. Dave, and Ned, and Dickie and Mary. I was ready to hear now, or at least I would be when I ate something. Instead, I asked her if anyone had been to visit me.

"I just came on shift," she said. She was a short, efficient-looking brunette who looked like she knew her job. She was probably a few years older than I was, and while she was friendly enough to me, I had a feeling that on the job she wouldn't be someone you'd want to cross. I liked that in a nurse. Hell, I liked that in anyone.

"It's early," she said. "We don't allow visits until after 10 a.m. Docs are still doing rounds. I'll see what we can scrape up for breakfast. We decided not to wake you two." I thanked her, and a couple of minutes later, a younger woman in different scrubs brought me a cup of tea with two packets of honey, and told me breakfast would be along in a minute. I decided I could get used to this, and then I realized that I also needed the pain meds and was glad the nurse was getting some.

After eating scrambled eggs and jello – no milk, no toast, no apple, not so soon after surgery, they said – and having another lovely dose of pain management, I drifted away again.

I didn't have any answers yet, but that was okay. I wasn't going anywhere.

* * *

The next time I opened my eyes, Dave was sitting next to my bed, reading a battered copy of *Today's Parent* magazine.

"Something I should know?" I said. He startled and dropped the magazine into his lap. "Any little Daves running around?" I didn't even know his last name. And even if he told me, I didn't know whether I would believe him. And yet I'd trusted him with my life and, more importantly, with my family's safety. Bizarre.

"I had no idea breastfeeding could be so complicated," he said. "Painful, even."

"Me either." I smiled at him. He really did have an Al Pacino–Michael Corleone thing going on.

"Somebody break your jaw?" I said.

He shook his head. "No, but Jonas has informed me of the *Godfather* thing, if that's what you're thinking. He sends his love, by the way." He lowered his voice. "Best if he and Bert and Lydia don't come down here just now."

"I get it." I could imagine the media and police were camped out somewhere nearby. There was no TV in this room, for which I was grateful. I sat up a bit and winced.

"Is it bad? Should I get a nurse?"

"No, stay there," I said. "Where's Laurence?"

"Gone to the house to have a shower and get changed. I said I'd stay until he gets back." He leaned forward. "I suppose you want to know what happened."

"You mean, why I got imprisoned in a hole in the ground for – wait a minute – how long was I down there, anyway?" It was starting to fade a bit. My sense of time felt distorted.

"About ten hours," he said.

"That's all?"

"I'm sure it felt like more." He cleared his throat and helped himself to my water. "First of all, Dickie and Mary are both alive."

"Oh, Jesus, thank you." Somehow, I felt sure that the fact that no one had said anything meant no one wanted to tell me they were dead.

"Mary was arrested. She's facing a lot of charges. I don't know what they are yet." I opened my mouth to speak, and he held up his hand. "Danny, I don't know how much time we're going to have privately, so let me just tell you what I know quickly, okay?"

I nodded.

"Dickie Doyle lost one finger and three toes. And as I'm sure you saw, part of his scalp."

I swallowed drily. Dave poured me some water. From what I had seen through my fever, I thought Dickie had lost his whole foot. Three toes was, in context, good news, I supposed.

"It wasn't really a scalping. Apparently –"

I held my hand up. "Can I hear about that part another time?" I felt a bit sick. I'm not usually so squeamish, but I didn't want to think about it.

"Sorry. Anyway, he's going to be okay. Physically, anyway. Mentally, he goes between lucid and off in la-la land, apparently." That fit with what I remembered from him being in the hole. "But he says it was Pamela who initially took him. Though sometimes he says it was Rose, so…"

"I can see how he thought that," I said. "I mean, if he was having issues with reality. You saw her in that nightgown, running through the trees."

Dave nodded, and winced a bit. "He said it was Pamela and Des Murphy who did the, uh, damage to him. He was in Mary's basement for a day or two. He did say Mary tried to help him."

"Oh my God," I whispered. "How did Mary get involved in this?"

"Through her husband, I suppose," Dave said. He paused. "Can you imagine having Pamela for a mother-in-law?"

"Oy," I said. My brain was spinning.

"Mary has first-aid training. She saw to his wounds as best she could, I'm sure, but she didn't have proper equipment or anything."

I swallowed. "Did he get anything for the pain?" I tried to imagine going through what Dickie had gone through. Having skin peeled off, toes cut off, a finger. Not to mention the scalping. And enduring the horrendous pain that would come after, without anything to take away the pain.

No wonder he had looked like a monster, crawling at me in the hole. He must have gone somewhere very deep in his head to escape that level of torture.

Dave shrugged. "No idea, Danny. I'm sure more will come out at trial."

"Tell me what happened when I was in the hole. Tell me about Des."

Dave shook his head and looked at his feet. He couldn't look at me. "I wasn't being careful. I thought the threat had passed. Pamela and Geoffrey were dead."

"It's not your fault," I said. I wanted to reach out and touch him, but I didn't. I should have.

Des tasered him, Dave said. He was surprised I hadn't heard it, the sound of the taser. "He punched me a few times, knocked me out when I was on the ground." When he came to, he was handcuffed to the woodstove at Dickie's cabin, his legs duct-taped together.

"So he, what, carried you to Dickie's?" Dave was slight, but dead weight is dead weight.

Dave shrugged. "Probably a fireman's lift," he said. "Des is pretty big, and it's not that far."

In the cabin, Des was pacing, he said, and he helped himself to a beer from Dickie's fridge.

"It was him," I said. Dave looked at me. "That first night when Laurence and I went to Dickie's cabin and he had been taken. It must have been Des who had been cooking the steak and drinking the beer."

"Or Pamela," Dave said. He told me that Des kept saying that he should burn the cabin down, with Dave in it. He was frantic, talking to himself, mostly too low for Dave to hear. "I kept waiting for sirens. Ned would have gotten out of the area pretty quick, and called 911. And even if he had gone back to the safe house to get the others, I knew at least one of them would probably go to Dickie's to find me."

"And you don't know how long you were unconscious," I said. He shook his head. "So what happened to Ned? Is he okay?"

"He's fine. Furious, but fine." As soon as Ned had pulled onto the road, Des had pulled him over with flashing lights, but no siren. He had taken a decommissioned police vehicle, Dave told me, so he couldn't be traced.

"Smart," I said.

"He is," Dave said. "He's a torturing, murderous hillbilly, but he's not stupid."

I grinned at Dave, and he smiled back for a second. It looked like it hurt.

"He tasered Ned in the car and stuck him in the trunk, and drove it off the road somewhere. He knows those woods; he knew where there was space to pull into the bush and leave a vehicle. Left Ned in there to suffocate, or die of thirst."

"He couldn't risk anybody calling for help and finding us in the hole," I said. I wrapped my arms around myself. For a while, I'd been sure that I would never get out of there, that in a day or two our bodies would have been found buried alive. "So how did you get away? And Ned?"

At that moment my hospital door opened a bit. A hand with flowers pushed through, and someone said, "Knock, knock."

Ned came in, one arm in a sling, the other holding an obscenely large bouquet.

"I was just getting to that part," Dave said, grinning, indicating Ned.

"Good," Ned said. "I haven't missed the entire storytelling session." He came over and kissed my forehead. "You're a sight for sore eyes, Cleary."

"Yeah, yeah. Listen, fuckwad, that hole was more than fifteen feet deep," I said. I ignored the flowers.

"Oh, no way, that had to be thirty feet," he agreed. "Cripes, you gave us a scare when that ladder gave out." He plonked himself and the flowers at the end of my bed. Dave was looking at the floor, trying to hide his stupid crooked grin.

"Wait," I said slowly. "Were you guys trying to get me in that hole?" Maybe they thought I'd be safer down there or something. My mind was going overtime all of a sudden.

I wanted my brother.

"What? No." Dave looked at me.

"I just knew you wouldn't get going on that goddamn ladder if I told you how deep it was," Ned said. He pulled an apple out of his pocket and took a big bite of it, then seemed to realize he might be being rude. "Want some?" He held it out to me. I shook my head. He shrugged and took another bite. "I knew it was rickety, but not *that* rickety. You must be heavier than you look." I stared at him, then at Dave, until they both started laughing. Ned kept on chuckling, that helpless tears-from-the-eyes laughter.

I wasn't laughing. I was too busy trying to stop myself from leaning over and punching him.

"So sorry, Danny," Ned said. "I'm still punchy. I'm not as young as I once was."

"You can say that again," Dave said. "Remind me to fire you one of these days."

"As if. Imagine how bored you'd be." Ned looked at me. "Seriously, I am so sorry this happened to you. If I had any idea that ladder was that close to giving out, I wouldn't have sent you down there. I'm just not that good with the whole 'damsel in distress' thing."

"I'm sorry? Who the fuck do you think you're calling a damsel in distress?" My leg hurt. I was fine before, but seeing Ned made me remember falling into the hole, and I found myself so angry that I was almost near tears.

"Not you, Mary. Mary!" Ned put his good hand in the air. "Mary was the damsel in distress. I just... I should have just picked her up and carried her, but she was cringing when I tried to touch her at all, and backing away from me."

"You should have just carried her up," Dave said. "That error in judgment could have cost Danny her life." He was serious now. His words were even and quiet, but he was definitely serious. "As it is, it cost her a lot of pain, and now a lot of recovery." Dave was pale. The bruise on his jaw stood out like a big purple rose.

"It's okay," I said. My anger was gone as quickly as it had come on. If I had made a mistake like that, it would make me feel like hell, even if I tried to pretend it didn't. "Besides, if I hadn't fallen down there, if you had just gone down and carried Mary out, you might not have seen Dickie at all. He was way off in the back corner somewhere. He didn't make himself, uh, seen, right away." I tried to forget how he looked, blood all over his face from his head, crawling toward me in the dark. "I had a fever, and when Dickie came crawling out of the depths of the hole toward me, I thought he was an animal. I thought I was going to end up like Sarah." I paused to collect myself. I had tears in my eyes, and I didn't want them to fall. I continued. "Luckily for me, he wasn't some bloody monster who'd come to eat me alive. He was too busy trying not to die from thirst and blood infection."

We were all silent for a minute.

"Well, Jonas says that hole was probably either an old hiding place for slaves, like we talked about, or it could have just been somebody's root cellar at one time. Anybody living closer to the lake wouldn't have been able to dig a proper one close to the water line." Ned was serious now. He looked chastened. He had gone down into the hole; he would have an idea of how horrible it would be to be trapped down there.

"So," I said. I tried to sit up a bit, and the pain from my leg made me feel nauseous for a second. I closed my eyes. "Who rescued you from the Jeep, oh great adventurer?"

"I rescued myself, chiquita," Ned said. "Well, no. To be honest, the good people of the local fire service rescued me." I looked at him, eyebrows raised. "Murphy, the fucking idiot, didn't think to take my cell off me when he put me in the trunk. I called 911. Easy peasy."

"How did he even know we were there?" I said. "At the hole, I mean?" I was wondering if he'd gone to check on Dickie and Mary, see if his prisoners were dead yet.

"Oh, he had come out to Dickie's to look for Pammie and old Geoff," Ned said. "He'd gone to the house, and they weren't there, so he went to Dickie's. He saw the tape was off the door, and he went into the woods, 'cause we all know Pamela was the local wood nymph." Ned finished his apple and chucked it into the trashcan. "Crazy as a fucking loon, that woman."

"He found their bodies," Dave told me. "And he immediately thought that somehow Dickie or Mary had gotten out or – whatever, I don't know. But I guess he waited till Ned had gone and went tearing after him."

"The old divide and conquer," Ned said. "Bastard knew he couldn't have taken us both."

"Wow," I said. "Just… wow."

"You said a mouthful there, Danny girl," Ned said. He stood up. "I'm going to love you and leave you. There's a very sexy medical type around here who's keen to get me alone."

"He needs his arm x-rayed," Dave explained to me.

"How did…" I started, but Ned interrupted.

"Oh, this? I fought the good fight after Murphy tasered

me. He wound up breaking my arm to get me in the trunk." He looked proud of himself.

"Phffft," Dave said to me. "It's probably just bruised. Go get it x-rayed, Romeo. I'll come and find you."

Ned kissed my forehead again, and left us alone. With the door open.

"Wait a minute," I said. "How do you know all this?"

"Oh, as soon as Murphy heard the sirens coming to get Ned, he took off. But I guess he knew he wasn't going to get very far, or maybe he just didn't want to be on the run for the rest of his life. Anyway, apparently he just took himself down to the detachment and turned himself in. Sang like the proverbial canary."

"And the cops told you all this?"

"Some of it," Dave said. "I have friends." He tapped the side of his nose and winked. I just shook my head. How Dave knew things and who his friends might be, I would probably never know.

Des Murphy. The kindly man I'd compared to my own dad. "What made him do it? I mean, has he done anything like this before?"

"Well, his wife died not long ago. Cancer," Dave said, catching my look. "Natural death and everything. That's stressful, and I'm sure his lawyers will say it was a precipitating event, made him lose his mind. And who knows, maybe they'd be right. And of course his first love, Rose, had died a while ago, and I guess when Pamela showed up around here, they started plotting against Dickie." Dave got up and started looking in the cabinet and closet for something to put the flowers in. "Murphy really hated Dickie. Rich guy shows up married to the girl he loved as a kid, the one who got away?"

"Des talked about his wife as though she was still alive," I said. Dave shrugged. "So Des had a hard-on for Dickie. But why all the others? Sarah, and Evan?"

"Oh, that was all Pamela," Dave said. "With help from her son. From what I can tell, Murphy just had it out for Dickie, wanted him to suffer."

"Poor Mary," I said.

"Danny, Mary could have turned them all in, anytime she wanted. For whatever reason, she chose not to. Loyalty to one's murdering family does not come above the lives of innocent people."

"I know," I said. And I did know, and if this was all true, then Mary did deserve to pay the price. But I had a good sense of how much she loved Geoffrey. "I just think she couldn't bear to see her husband in a jail cell. And nobody is saying she did any of the..."

"Wet work?" Dave said. "No, Murphy hasn't said anything about Mary having hurt anyone herself. And, of course, she hasn't opened her mouth." He found a dusty glass vase at the back of the small closet, filled it with some water from the bathroom sink, and stuck Ned's flowers in it. "There."

"Thanks," I said. He'd actually done a good job arranging them.

Dave sat on the bed and grabbed my hand. "Danny," he started to say. "When I was tied up in that cabin, I thought I would go insane. I was so worried." I squeezed his hand and willed him to stop talking. I'm not ready, I thought. I don't know if I'll ever be ready.

Just as I was about to open my mouth to say something inane and probably regrettable, Maureen the nurse came in to give me pain medication and check my leg. I could have kissed her, and not just because my leg really did hurt. Dave said something about checking in the next day, and slipped out.

The nurse bustled around me, not speaking. She was gentle as she changed the dressing on my leg as I let myself cry for a few minutes. She helped me into a wheelchair so I could go to the bathroom, and tucked me in expertly when she helped me back into the bed. The doctor had been in while I was sleeping, she said, and was happy with my vitals, but I had to be prepared, she said.

"You're going to have pain for a while," she said. "I don't know what you've been through, other than the basics. But I do know that you were at the rehab centre when all that shit started to go down." Of course. Everyone would know about that. "Were you in for opiates?"

"No," I said. "Crack. Opiates were never my bag."

She nodded. "Good. I'm not one of those people who think that if you're addicted to one thing you'll be addicted to everything. You are going to need drugs for a while. You won't get better unless you learn to walk without pain." I wasn't sure what she meant, but it didn't matter. She was giving me another IV dose, and I just wanted to sleep, and wake up when my leg was better and this whole mess had blown over out there.

"Thank you," I said, as she let herself out of the room.

"You're welcome, Danny," she said. "Get some rest. Ring if you need me."

I decided that Maureen would also have to join me in Toronto. I floated along on my little morphine cloud and thought about Maureen taking care of me, and Jonas hanging with us and the boys. A little while later Laurence came in and gave my hand a squeeze, but he didn't ask me to talk. He lay down on the other bed and started to read, and I slept.

I dreamed I was back in Toronto, but Ginger was there with me, and she was curled around me, telling me everything was okay, and if I didn't want to, I didn't have to do anything again except sleep.

THIRTY-SIX

The police arrived later, in the form of Staff Sergeant Lester. I immediately recognized him as the surly cop who had been at Rose's the night Sarah had found Evan's body in the basement. When all of us – Sarah Gilbert, Laurence, me, Aussie Rules/ Ned and the other residents, along with Janet and assorted and sundry police – had sat in the kitchen, shaky and afraid.

And Des Murphy had come in and diffused the situation, as Laurence was tearing a strip off this guy.

"Good afternoon, Ms. Cleary," he said. "We've met before." There was a constable behind him, a younger man who kept bouncing on the balls of his feet as though he was either nervous or badly needed the bathroom.

"Hi there," I said. "I remember." Laurence had gone to get me a doughnut, making noises about being an errand boy. But it was a nice evening, and he needed to get out of this hospital room for a bit.

Plus, I really wanted a cruller.

"Do you mind if I sit?" He indicated the chair Dave had been in earlier.

"Please do," I said. I amazed myself. So polite. Maybe

morphine was the drug for me, after all.

"Thank you." He sat down and made himself comfortable, then opened his notebook.

I was ready for this. I had already spoken to the criminal law partner of my lawyer in Toronto, Linda Patel, and I knew what I was going to do.

Tell the truth. That was the plan, anyway. Or at least, as much of the truth as I could tell without landing myself in prison.

"Ms. Cleary, before we begin, my colleague and I would like to audio record this chat. This will save you from having to give another statement on video at a later date when you're out of hospital, unless we have other things to follow up on."

"Certainly," I said. "But perhaps your colleague could come and sit down instead of standing in the doorway. You're making me nervous," I said to the young man. I smiled at him. "Please, why don't you sit on the other bed, or find a chair."

"The lady is right," Lester said. "Morriss, take a load off." The other cop smiled, and for a second he reminded me of Colin, Mary's nephew, whose blood and brains had been splattered all over me not long ago. I felt so tired again suddenly. For half a minute I thought about asking Lester if we could do this tomorrow.

"I have heard that Sergeant Murphy has confessed," I said. "Is this true?"

"It is," Lester said. "We're not on audio yet, so if you have any immediate questions, I'll answer them if I can. Once we're on audio, I'll ask the questions, if that's okay." He paused. "Ms. Cleary, I would like to apologize to you for my demeanor when we first met. I had an impression of you based on information I had which was, I think, incorrect, or incomplete. I've done my homework, and I talked to Detective Belliveau, in Toronto."

"Oh, how is he?" I said. "I was thinking of calling him. He'll be worried."

"Well, your name hasn't been released to the news organizations, nor will it be if we can help it," Lester said. He kind of snorted, and said, "Even Des Murphy made sure your name wasn't released. For what it's worth, you were never a target." He told me that Belliveau had told him about Michael Vernon Smith and what my family and I had gone through. And how I was probably number one on Smith's hit list, if he ever decided to come out of whatever rock he had crawled under. And apparently Sergeant Lester and Laurence had gone for coffee together when I was sitting in the hole.

"Your brother told me I was so rude, I was the only cop he trusted for sure," Lester said, and I laughed.

"Well, he's a good judge of character," I said. "I, however, am not. You know, I really liked Des Murphy. He even reminded me of my dead dad. When he was alive, I mean."

Lester sighed. "I'm not going to pretend that I was his biggest fan," he said. "He was a bit too old-boys-club for me. But, until this, nobody ever said he wasn't a good officer." We were both silent for a minute.

"People, huh," I said. That's me, a philosopher if ever there was one. My leg was starting to hurt, and I was so tired suddenly. I wanted to sleep until there was no sleep left in me. I didn't feel like talking, but I wanted to get all of this over with and go home, back to Toronto and Darren and the boys. "So it was Pamela who did most of the, uh, killing? That's what I heard, anyway."

Lester nodded. "There were aspects of this whole situation

where Pamela and Des Murphy seemed to have been operating with what you might call a grudging cooperation. But Pamela was more interested in the drug users, the situation at Rose's Place. Murphy was more focused on Dickie Doyle. And we think – well, I think – that Murphy used Pamela's, uh, mental illness, to his own ends. And Pamela used her son." He paused. "We still aren't sure of how much of a role he played. But we will be."

I nodded. "Listen, why don't you turn on your recorder thingy. I'll tell you whatever I know." I tried to get more comfortable. "I'm not sure how long I'll be of any use to you. I'm in some pain, and I keep falling asleep every five minutes."

"Bet you're glad to be in a bed," Lester said.

"Detective, after the couple of weeks I've had, being in a bed, no matter why I'm here, is a miracle." I wished Laurence would get back. I wanted that doughnut. And coffee. Coffee would be nice.

I told Lester the story, in broad strokes. Unlike my time dealing with Michael Vernon Smith's family in California and Toronto and Maine, my motives for coming to Nova Scotia and Rose's Place were honest, real, and without guile. And while I believed that Pamela knew that I would probably be the one who found the hand in the mailbox that started all this off, she'd only known that because she knew I went for a run every morning, and that checking that mailbox was part of my routine. And she'd approved of my routine. She thought I was a "good girl." I told Lester about Evan's head being tossed at me in the woods outside Dickie's, about Laurence and me finding the body in the cabin. I told him about being shot at in the dining room, and grabbing Colin's gun to keep the shooter from getting too close and picking us all off, one by one. I told him about finding Sarah

Gilbert's body when I was going to get some food and things for Laurence and me.

I spoke quickly, and didn't add too many details. This part of the story I had told before, and as I spoke, I realized that, really, I hadn't done anything wrong. I hadn't broken anybody's bones, or looked for any trouble. Not really. I had given a cop a good shot in the gonads, but he'd had it coming, and under the circumstances it didn't seem like anybody was bringing it up. No, until I went into the woods with Dave and Ned, I'd pretty much been reacting, instead of seeking out trouble.

I explained that Dave was some kind of security expert, or private investigator, or bodyguard, but I truthfully said that I didn't know his last name. I didn't know his company's name. And I hadn't asked him to come here.

"He showed up at the hospital when I was here the last time," I said. "After those fishermen rescued me." I told Lester about Dave posing as the flower delivery guy, because he asked how Dave had made contact. I didn't tell him that I was going to call Dave anyway. And I was clear that Dave had said that we shouldn't trust the police because it didn't seem like all of this could have been done without at least one member of the local detachment knowing more than he should. At the very least.

Lester asked where we all stayed, and I said I had no idea how to get there. That was my first lie, and even that was a half-truth. I'd been driven in and driven out at night. Once each, on a road I'd never been on before. I probably could find it again, but Lester didn't need to know that.

Laurence came in halfway through, and Lester briefly paused the recording to get up and shake his hand. He asked if

Laurence would mind leaving us in the room while we did the interview. Laurence turned to go, but I asked for my coffee and cruller before he did. We continued.

I told Lester about having dinner with the people Dave worked with, but I did not mention cocaine.

I told Lester about going into the woods to look for an underground structure of some kind with a metal detector, but not that Dave and I had broken into Dickie's cabin.

I told him that I saw a woman in a white nightgown in the woods, but not that I'd seen her from Dickie's cabin. Or, in fact, that I had thought for a minute it must be Rose Doyle.

I told him about us watching Pamela shoot Geoffrey, then shoot herself, and what I could remember about what she'd said. Lester knew about the cell dead zone around Dickie's cabin, so he didn't ask why we didn't call the police immediately.

I told him about Ned finding the hole, and finding Mary in it, and how we needed to get her out right away, afraid we wouldn't be able to find it quickly again, and our view that Mary needed to get out as soon as possible.

And finally, I told him about seeing Dickie in the hole, and asking him about the tattoo, and Dickie saying that Des had done it.

"You were right there when Des talked about finding that tattoo," I said to Detective Lester. "He seemed really shaken."

Lester nodded. "I'm sure he was," he said. He put his hand in the air, indicating that I should shut up. "Thank you, Ms. Cleary. Those are all the questions we have for now. We appreciate your patience. For the tape, the time is now sixteen forty-eight, or four forty-eight p.m." Lester turned off the recorder. "Sorry about that. We like to keep all the information in the interviews on point, and do the questions before or after, like I said."

Detective Lester hesitated. He told the other cop he could go visit his wife. The cop smiled brilliantly at both of us, and nearly ran out of the room.

"She just had a baby," Lester said. "She's right here in the hospital. He's supposed to be on leave, but everybody's been called back in." He moved to the edge of his chair, like he was going to get up in a minute.

"You know, in my experience there's a difference between killers like Pamela Carlisle, and killers like Des Murphy. Pamela spent much of her life institutionalized. Until now she had no criminal record – well, only minor shoplifting charges, misdemeanors during periods when she was out of hospital – but she was, to quote my grandmother, crazier than a shithouse rat."

"I like her," I said, and Lester gave me a look. "Your grandmother, I mean."

"Yeah, I miss her like crazy," he said. "But then you have your killers like Desmond Murphy. Pillars of the community. Would give you the shirt off his back, rescue your cat from a tree, and give you half his last meal. But there was something in him. Something broken."

"Hard to believe this was his first episode like this," I said. "I mean, you're describing a kind of serial killer like Ted Bundy or BTK. Has anyone checked on any missing persons or his travel habits?" I was picturing a swath of dead people up and down the east coast.

Lester shook his head. "No. I actually do think that, I don't know, after his wife died he had some kind of break, some kind of psychotic break or something. His loss was so great, and it broke him. And he focused on the man he thought brought all this bad luck into his life, from Rose Carlisle appearing again and, who knows, maybe tempting him or reminding him of what he had lost, to going through his wife's long struggle with cancer and her death."

I was silent for a minute. "It sounds like you feel sorry for him," I said.

"I do," he said simply. "I think he belongs behind locked doors for the rest of his life, probably, but in a way that makes me feel more sorry for him. He's sick. And between you and me, he's being totally honest with us. He's telling us everything."

"As far as you know," I said.

"As far as we know," he agreed. I adjusted my position on the bed and winced. "I've kept you too long," he said, as though I was going anywhere. I felt him wanting to say something else.

"Out with it, Staff Sergeant," I said. "We're besties now."

"The only other person I've heard actually use that word is my twelve-year-old daughter," he said.

"I like to stay current," I said. There was something he didn't want to tell me. I felt a sense of dread creeping up my neck. I looked carefully at Lester, and he was another one who seemed like he could use a good night's sleep.

"Dickie Doyle released himself from the hospital earlier today. There was nothing anyone could do. He should have been under a psychiatric hold, aside from anything else, but with his physical state, the psychiatrist hadn't got around to doing the formal paperwork. And while his wounds look awful and he should be in hospital, they couldn't legally, physically stop him from leaving. And he was bound and determined." He looked at his hat. "We simply don't know where he is."

"Oh, you have got to be fucking kidding me," I said. All this time, and staying here to find Dickie, sitting in a hole because I hadn't taken the opportunity to drive back to Toronto, and Dickie disappears. Again. I felt very sorry for Dickie, and I loved my brother. But I was not going on another Dickie Doyle hunt.

"I wish." We sat in silence for a minute, and I could almost smell Lester's brain working. "Off the tape now, Danny. Do you swear you don't have any more information on Dave and his people?"

"I don't," I said. "I know how it sounds. Trust me. But after what we went through last fall, I just trusted him. And he wrote to me when I was in Maine, a sympathy letter about my husband." I pushed my fingernails into my palm to stop my voice from breaking. There. Better. "But the postmark was obscured, and all I have ever known him by is Dave." I paused. "I know it's shady, and too James Bond to sound real. And there are members of my family who disagree with me about this. But I do think that he's on the right side." I hoped he was. I really did. My brain felt fried – too full and too tired to make any more sense of anything.

If it weren't for the fact that I was avoiding any exposure to the media, it would have been a perfect time to watch some mindless television.

Lester said his goodbyes, and said he'd be in again to check on me when I felt a bit better. He said they'd keep me in the loop, as much as they could. He was on his way to the door when I stopped him. "Hey," I said. "Thank you."

"For what?"

I hesitated. "For calling Paul Belliveau," I said. "For trusting us."

As soon as he left, I rang for Maureen and when she arrived, I asked her to send my brother in if she saw him. She asked how my pain was, and I lied. "Fine," I said. "Still good." In truth, my leg was throbbing. But I didn't want to zone out and drift off just yet. I had to talk to Laurence first.

They were bringing dinner trays around. Laurence walked in as I got mine. A banana and a spinach omelette. And jello.

"I'm vegetarian now," I told Laurence when he turned up his nose. I pushed it away. "Close the door again, will you?" He did, and came back and sat on my bed with me. I gave him a quick nutshell of my interview with Lester. I was glad I didn't have to break the news that Dickie had done a runner; Laurence had already heard.

"There's something very wrong with Dickie," he said. "This is not the man I know."

"Knew," I said. Gently. "He's a sick, broken man, who was being mentally tortured, seeing what he thought was his dead wife running around near his house." I leaned back, letting go of Laurence's hand. Sitting up wasn't my favorite position.

I was tired of thinking about all of it. As far as I was concerned, I had found Dickie. I had done what I set out to do. Lester seemed more than capable of handling things from here on out. "Laurence, you may have to just accept that Dickie is lost to you now, as a friend. We have both done more than our fair share here."

"Danny, you definitely have. As soon as you're well enough to travel, we're getting you back to Toronto. Darren and the boys are fixing up a room for you, and we'll be getting a physical therapist. Whatever you need."

I nodded. What I needed was to have my family around me, and to sleep for a year.

"But I'm going to stay here for a while longer," Laurence continued. He grabbed my foot under the sheet and squeezed it, causing me to jump. "Be quiet. I'm not doing anything dangerous. But one thing I can do for Dickie is to help get his affairs in order so that he can at least live comfortably. Check into selling Rose's Place, for a start. And if he's able to – if we find him, whatever – I can find him somewhere safe and secure to live. Make sure he has help." He looked at me. "Dickie's lawyer contacted the police a couple of days ago. Dickie has a living will, and I have power of attorney."

"Don't you have to sign something saying you agree to that? While the person is compos mentis?"

"I did. After Rose died, when Dickie was buying the property and so on. He said I was the closest thing he had left to family, and he didn't want things to go to hell if anything happened where he couldn't make decisions for himself." He ran his hand over his face. He had shaved at some point, which made him look younger, but I had sort of liked the scruffy look on him. "I'm sure he'll be easy enough to find."

"Dave's crew will help you," I said.

"If necessary." Laurence was not happy with Dave and Ned. Not at all. No matter the reason, they had left his little sister badly injured in the bottom of a hole. "I'm going to get a hotel. I was thinking of staying at Rose's, though. I don't want any journalists or kids or whatever breaking in and photographing everything for some tabloid TV story."

"The Murder Rehab," I said.

"Drug Den of Death," Laurence said.

"Annapolis Valley Amputators." I grinned. "Don't be a putz. Hire security."

"Yeah. I did. We'll see. For now, though, I'll stay here." His fever was gone, but I was paying extra for a private room, and under the circumstances, I'd like to see anybody try to tell me I couldn't have my brother stay there with me.

"Good."

Laurence went and propped the door open again. Nurse Maureen had complained about how much I had the door closed. Neither of us wanted to cross her.

A minute later, Debbie MacLean walked in, out of uniform, carrying a pizza box. Laurence had mentioned that she'd stopped by a couple of times when I was sleeping, but this was the first time I'd seen her.

"Dinner," she said. "Half vegetarian, half pepperoni and anchovy."

"Pepperoni with anchovy? You're sick," I said with approval.

The three of us ate and joked about the hospital staff, and nobody talked about death or killing or people being buried in holes.

And I did my very best not to think about what could have happened to Dickie Doyle.

THIRTY-SEVEN

Four days later, I was released from the hospital, with crutches and a prescription for a small number of painkillers. As the surgeon promised, they kept me in as long as they could, but I wanted to get home, to Toronto, to all the boys. But I'd decided to stay for a few days to be in the Valley with Laurence, who was busy with lawyers, an industrial cleaning crew for Rose's Place once the police released it, and real estate agents. Then Laurence would get me on a plane to Toronto, and I would be met at the airport by Darren and the boys.

Dickie Doyle was, somehow, and against everyone's predictions, in the wind. He had left the hospital in a wheelchair, holding two crutches, and had been helped into a taxi by a driver. The driver told police that he dropped Dickie off at a bowling alley in New Minas, a little town close by. He remembered, he said, because he couldn't figure out how the man was going to bowl. The security camera outside the bowling alley was on the fritz, and he never showed up on the camera inside.

He hadn't walked in, and despite a thorough interview of each and every cab company within thirty miles – not as many as one would think, apparently; there wasn't a lot of call for taxis in the Valley – no one had picked up any fares from there that day.

Someone had picked him up. He had no cell phone with him. But somehow, someone had picked Dickie Doyle up from a bowling alley in a small town, and spirited him off somewhere. His bank accounts hadn't been touched, and his credit hadn't been accessed.

Laurence was worried, but as he said, he was just going to focus on getting Dickie's affairs in order, so that when he was found, things would be taken care of. It was all he knew to do. And while I was curious, and worried, I had had enough of searching for Dickie Doyle to last me a lifetime.

Laurence had rooms for us at a local hotel, but he had stayed at Rose's overnight for the last two days of my hospital stay.

And me? Well, I was full of offers of hospitality.

Dave, Ned et al. were still at the safe house. Laurence had met with them a couple of times. He heard them out, about what happened the night I went into the hole, and he said he was convinced that everything was on the up-and-up, that neither of them had any choice in how things had played out. But as much as his rational brain told him that they were on our side, that they hadn't done anything to hurt me, because of them I had fallen into a deep hole in the ground and suffered what could have been a life-threatening wound. Laurence was not in a particularly forgiving mood.

I had my own reasons for not wanting to stay at the safe house. I was petrified that Dave would make a profession to me that I wouldn't know how to handle, and I also knew that I had feelings enough for Dave that I didn't want to screw it up by doing or saying the wrong thing to him if he did.

As far as I was concerned, staying at the safe house was not an option, as much as I wanted to. Jonas would be so much fun, and his cooking would help get me better. And I'd have a chance to talk him into leaving Dave's employ and coming to live with me and the boys in Toronto.

But Laurence had told me that Dave had made it clear he wasn't going anywhere until I would see them, or at the very least until I left the Valley and went back to Toronto. He had sent more flowers and a simple note asking me to stay with them during my recovery. He reminded me that Lydia was a nurse.

He added a smiley face, but didn't sign the card.

Debbie MacLean wanted both Laurence and me to stay at her place on the lake. It was June, and the weather was now unseasonably warm. She had moved in there herself for the summer as she did every year, subletting her apartment in Wolfville to a visiting professor who was teaching summer school at Acadia. She'd been in to see me every day, usually bringing food and books. We'd had the talk, one night, about the fact that she was embarrassed about kissing me. I told her not to worry, but even if I were more inclined toward women, that she should think of me as a newly fixed puppy: sore, a little sulky, and uninterested in sniffing anybody. But she made me laugh, and it was nice to have a female friend. Especially a female friend who, like me, would rather fight than shop. And Debbie said that if and when I was ready, she would take me to visit Mary in jail.

She had refused to say anything to defend herself, and she hadn't sought bail.

I was talking to Dr. Singh on the phone once a day for a little while. I would be ready for things eventually, but I was taking a break from sadness. That's what I was trying to do, anyway. Skype with the boys and Darren, talk to my brother Skipper and his wife Marie on the phone – she always talked about what she was cooking, which helped my appetite – and now that I was out, lie in the sun. Read books. Go to physical therapy.

Not do drugs. I was having crack dreams every night in the hospital, dreams where I was sitting with my old partner in crime from my drug days, Gene, and no matter how much I pulled on the pipe, I wasn't getting any smoke into my lungs. And in the way of dreams, I knew that if I just found the perfect rock, the perfect little crumb of crack on my living room floor or in the cushions of the couch, my problems would be over. I would get high, the angels would sing to me, and nothing bad would ever happen to anyone I cared about, ever again.

I would wake up from these dreams sweating, my blanket on the floor. I was happy to be awake, happy that I wasn't smoking crack, but it made the craving for the real thing almost unbearable in the mornings.

In the end, Debbie talked me into staying at her place. Laurence said he'd stay too, if Debbie was offering, but that he would still be at Rose's a lot. He and Debbie had become tight friends while I was missing, and I think a part of him was disappointed that I wasn't going to jump in her bed and marry her.

The morning I was released, Laurence picked me up in his rental – he still had the SUV – and I had the fun of getting into a car for the first time with my leg the way it was. I was just glad it was my right leg.

"Really, Danny, if you loved me at all, you would take up

with Debbie," Laurence said as we finally pulled away from the hospital. "I am tired of being the only homosexual Cleary."

"You know how I feel about sexuality," I said.

"Yes, I know, the Kinsey scale, and you're more on the straight side. Well, I don't know about that. You look more like a dyke, you know."

"I know," I said. "But don't be so shallow."

"Debbie's a cop. It would be so nice to have a cop in the family, the way you carry on." It was a gorgeous day. I took off the cardigan Laurence had made me put on before I left the hospital, as though I was an old lady about to catch a chill.

"It would," I said. "In fact, I think that should be your mission. To marry a cop, I mean."

"Not me," he said. "I'm going to marry Antonio." I looked at him.

"You are?"

Laurence glanced over at me. "Beanpole, please."

"Oh," I said. Laurence had never even lived with one of his boyfriends. He liked to say that his obituary would describe him as a "confirmed bachelor" like they used to say in the old days, code for gay men. "Well, probably Darren should."

"Yes!" Laurence drummed the steering wheel. "That is exactly what he needs! I'm going to start looking for a cop for him as soon as we get back to Toronto."

Laurence had taken a leave of absence from his network. He said it was a long time coming; he'd been working too hard for too long, and he didn't care what it might mean for his career at this point. "I've got stock," he said, "and a golden contract. Life is short. I should spend some time with the nephews." Matty and

Luke were excited about the prospect of having Big L coming to stay. For whatever reason, Luke had taken a particular shine to Laurence, and Laurence was the only one other than Darren who could reliably bring Luke out of his shell.

"Ask Paul," I said, referring to my guardian angel, Detective Paul Belliveau. "He'll hook Darren up."

"Genius idea, Bean. I'm going to get on the blower with him tonight." He looked over at me. I was rooting through the glove compartment for sunglasses.

"Debbie took your stuff to her house," he told me again. I could tell he was a bit nervous, bringing me back to the lake, back to the cottage where I had found Dickie's severed finger in a box outside the back door. Back to the lake where I had been buried alive a week earlier. "How's the pain?"

"I can deal," I said. I could. I'd enjoyed the morphine cloud at the beginning when I needed it, but I'd been on Percocet for a few days now, and it was nice to get my cognitive functioning back, slowly. I'd asked Laurence to hang onto the Percocet for me, just on the off-chance I took an emotional nosedive one of these days and decided it would be a good idea to get high. "I'm still supposed to be in rehab, don't forget." I needed sunglasses. I love the sun on my skin, but I have the photosensitive eyes of a vampire. I put my hand up before he could say anything. We'd been circling around the issue for days. "A sober living companion. Seriously. No more rehab. It doesn't work, anyway."

Laurence kept his mouth shut, and I was thankful for small mercies. I turned the radio up, and we sang together. Wilson Phillips' "Hold On" was playing.

"Fuck, but we're good," I said when the song ended.

"Damn straight," Laurence said. He sounded like Mary for a minute.

I wasn't going to think about Mary right now. Mary, lying on the dirt floor of the bunker, taking sips of water from the bottle Dickie had in his hand.

"Step on it," I said. I stuck my head out the window and closed my eyes. And swallowed a bug. Laurence laughed as I choked, and I thought, okay. Today is a good day. We're alive, and we're safe. And if I can, I'll try and help Mary. She tried to help me, and I will try to help her.

"I want to sit on the dock and get some sun," I said.

"Really? You want to go near the water?"

"No point in being scared of everything, Laurence. Que sera sera."

Debbie was unloading groceries from the back of her Honda when we pulled into the driveway.

"Let me help you with that," Laurence called out the window. He jumped out and trotted toward her.

"No, that's okay," I yelled to him. "I can get out of this ridiculous vehicle on my bad leg by myself, you fucktards." Debbie and Laurence rolled their eyes at each other and came over to the truck to help me out.

"She's going to drive you crazy, Debs," Laurence said. Debs? I thought.

"I'm regretting it already," Debbie said.

"You two should take your act on the road." I was happy. I figured, okay, we're going to have some fun. But my leg was also telling me that the time for sitting up in the truck and not keeping it elevated was over, for now. Laurence saw my face, which even I could tell had probably gone a bit gray as I struggled with righting myself on the crutches.

"Come on," he said. "Let's get you settled, princess."

"I hope one of you clowns went to the liquor store," I said. "This is my vacation." And of course that made us start to laugh – some vacation – and I started to fall off the crutches. I'm elegant that way. Debbie caught me handily. She was strong, at least as strong as I was. Or used to be. "One of these days, I'm going to stop getting in trouble," I said. I was out of breath, trying to make it to the back door. "I'll have a quiet life. I'll take up knitting."

"I knit," my brother piped up. "It's very relaxing."

Debbie had set up the room off the living room as my bedroom. It obviously was usually a study, or a den, but there was a real bed set up, and a couple of books and things were sitting beside it. A small rolling cart was at the foot of the bed, with some neatly folded clothes and toiletries on it. A vase of lilacs was on the windowsill.

"Laurence did it," Debbie said. "Well, most of it."

"It's wonderful, you guys. Thank you." I was so glad to be there. I sat heavily on the bed. Debbie went to get me some water, while Laurence showed me where all my things were, unpacked and easy to get to.

"And look," he said. He opened the drawer in the little table next to the bed, "a corkscrew, and a screwdriver!"

"Aw," I said, "that's very sweet. My StabbyScrew."

"That sounds fairly disgusting," he said. "But I know it'll make you feel better." He lowered his voice. "There are tools everywhere.

And she said that's nothing – she has a whole woodworking studio in the garage." He shook his head. "Lesbians."

"Teach her how to knit, why don't you," I said.

"What's this, now?" Debbie brought both of us bottles of water, and there was a nice bottle of wine. On a tray. With three glasses. "Are you casting aspersions on my sexual orientation?"

"I just don't know how you could want to have sex with women, but otherwise you're perfect, my dear." Laurence kissed her cheek, and she reddened. He picked the bottle of wine up off the tray. "Especially now. Sancerre!"

"I have no idea what that means, but I'll have a glass of wine," I said. "And maybe one pill."

"Bean, you may have two. Every four hours."

"With wine?" Debbie said. Her eyebrows were somewhere at her hairline.

Laurence and I looked at her. He shook his head sadly. "Oh, Debbie. You haven't spent much time with Danny yet. But you'll learn, my dear. You'll learn."

"I have a high tolerance," I said. "A glass of nice white wine and a couple of Percs? That's a healthy, balanced lunch, compared to the way I was living a year ago."

Debbie and Laurence moved chairs around and we all sipped wine. There was a large window in my room, looking over the lake.

"Listen, you," she said to me, pointing at me with her wine glass. "Go to town on the wine, or your prescribed painkillers, or whatever. But no crack here, *capiche*? No cocaine."

"Debbie, unless you plan to go and get it for me, I have no way of getting anything of the sort."

She looked uncomfortable. She looked like she wanted to say something.

"Out with it," my brother said.

"I saw your chart and the police report on the incident," she said. She twirled the wine glass around in her hand nervously. "You had cocaine in your system when they brought you to the hospital. They tested you for everything before your surgery." She looked at me. "We're friends. I trust you. I gave you the key to my gun safe, for God's sake, which obviously could have gotten me fired. Could have landed me in jail, actually, and still could if you decided you wanted to snitch on me." I made a sound with my mouth that indicated how likely that would be. "But this whole thing has scared the shit out of me, to be honest. And even though I know there's no more danger, the whole thing was around drugs. I know Dickie Doyle is your friend, Laurence, but, frankly, since his escape from hospital I'm not convinced he didn't have some part in what happened. I know that wherever he is, he's a mess. And sick. Possibly dead by now."

Laurence shook his head.

"I'm sorry, I didn't mean to – look, all I wanted to say is that my life is usually pretty boring, you know? Good boring. I mean, the job has its share of adventures, but nothing like what happened."

"And thank God for that," I said.

"Exactly. And while I've never had any huge issue with drugs, other than the people who traffic them, this whole thing has put the fear of God into me. I don't let any of my friends smoke weed anywhere near me anymore."

"I'm surprised you ever did, you being RCMP," Laurence said.

"Well, I've always been careful not to be in the room. But sometimes I still feel that there's something out there in the woods, and… I just don't want drugs in here," she finished lamely. She gazed out the window.

"Debbie, don't worry," I said. "I know what you mean. I do. And yes, I did have a quantity of cocaine earlier that night. It was my birthday." I didn't tell her that Dave had procured it, and that he and Laurence had already discussed the fact that they were going to monitor me with it, until we found Dickie. She might have been a friend, but she was still a cop. And I didn't want to get Dave in any more trouble.

"I slipped up once. Once. There was a lot of stress. A lot of stuff going on. I'd just nearly died in the Bay of Fundy. It is not going to happen again."

"Okay. I believe you," she said after a pause. "Let's eat."

"You eat a lot," I said. "You must have the metabolism of a mouse." She was strong, but very lean.

"I love food," she said. "I don't know why I don't gain more weight. My parents were both kind of big. I'll be one of those people who balloon at forty."

Laurence went to help her in the kitchen, and I sipped my wine, looking at the lake.

I knew what Debbie meant about the woods. I had no morphine in my system and had only taken one Percocet, six hours earlier. I was clear, and the thudding in my leg reminded me that I was not hallucinating.

But as I looked at the lake, I saw someone in my peripheral vision, at the edge of the woods. Someone looking at the cottage.

But when I swung my head around, they were gone.

My heart was pounding, and I knew as certainly as I was sitting there that it wasn't over.

It wasn't fucking over.

THIRTY-EIGHT

Debbie and Laurence brought in tuna sandwiches and potato salad cold from the fridge, and the three of us ate and drank wine, and the whole time my brain was clicking. Should I tell them? Debbie was a cop, and I knew she had at least one gun. But if there was someone there, I didn't want Laurence going running into the woods.

And really, wasn't it more likely that I imagined it? It had only been a week since I had witnessed Pamela shoot her son and then herself, and then I had my ordeal in the bunker with Dickie and Mary. Things had been playing at the edges of my vision down in the hole, and I had put it down to fever, but what if I was having some kind of visual hallucination or something? A brain tumor? Or, I could be going crazy. I felt full of death, and I felt cheated of the normal life I had been starting to plan. Des Murphy had reminded me of my dad.

Dr. Singh had said that maybe I'd wanted to trust Des like I had trusted Paul Belliveau in Toronto. Paul had risked his life to save mine, and he had been a protective father figure at a time when I really needed one. And she had also reminded me that it was only just over six months since my twin sister had been murdered. I had never been one to think about my emotions much; I'd always led with my fists. But I also knew I'd had enough trauma to last me a lifetime.

So, either I had a brain tumor, I was crazy, or there was someone lurking in the woods watching me, us, again. Or still.

Crack, please. Really. I closed my eyes and inhaled, imagining I was sucking crack smoke into my lungs.

"Danny?" Debbie said. "Are you okay?"

"I am," I said. "I think I just hit a wall. I think I need a pill. Or two."

Laurence took the pill bottle out of his pocket and put two in my palm as he took my plate. I was surprised to see that I'd eaten everything on it.

"We should leave her to sleep," Debbie said. "You remember where the bathroom is down here?"

"Yup," I said. "Thank you so much, Debbie."

"I'm doing a shift tonight. I was supposed to have it off, but somebody called in sick. I'm so sorry, I'm going to have to leave you. Are you staying?" she said to Laurence.

"I was going to take a quick run to town, check on a few things. But I'll be back in a couple of hours." He looked at me. "Will you sleep? Will you be okay?"

"Yes, I'm going to sleep." As they were walking out, I asked Debbie if she had a pen and some paper. "I like to make lists sometimes, when I can't sleep. It calms my brain down. Dr. Singh said it's good for me." She said no such thing, and I rarely made a list that didn't involve eggs and bread, but whatever.

Half an hour later, both cars had pulled out of the driveway. I hopped over to the door, nearly crashing into the furniture, and, not for the first time in this cottage, stuck a chair under the handle. Foolproof against homicidal killers, as everyone knows.

I lay back on the bed, glad to be alone despite everything, and finished the wine, feeling it mix with the painkillers. I curled up with the sun warming a cozy spot on the bed, and drifted to sleep.

I woke up to a phone ringing.

The phone in the kitchen. The only phone, as this was the area with the famously poor reception. The dead spot. Well, I supposed so.

I debated getting up and trying to get to it. I hate the sound of a ringing phone; it's so intrusive and jarring. But I had a feeling the phone had started ringing in my dream, so it would probably stop before I could get to it. And with all the furniture in my way and my lack of skill on the crutches, I doubted I'd make it. And besides, it was obviously not going to be for me.

It was nearly sunset. I had slept for hours. I might have just gone back to sleep, but I needed to use the bathroom, and I knew it would take me a while.

My leg felt okay, and when I got off the bed I tested some of my weight on it. Not great, but it was the first time I'd felt like it might actually heal someday. It had been the most painful injury I'd ever received, and something about its placement – so high on my leg, so close to my core – had made me feel more vulnerable than anything else ever had.

Between one crutch and my good leg, I made it to the bathroom off the back door.

Of course, it had no shower. I was going to have to attempt the stairs tomorrow.

I looked in the mirror and thought maybe I looked better than I had. But that was probably the lack of fluorescent lighting; every day in the hospital I'd felt like I looked worse than the day before. Luckily, I wasn't particularly vain.

I went back into the living room and looked out over the lake. The sunset was beautiful and looked oddly like a winter sunset. Maybe it was the lack of city smog, but I spent a minute getting lost in the blues mixed with the pink and orange. Then I moved to the window and, with difficulty and feeling like I was going to keel over, I closed both sides of the curtains.

I wanted to go home. I wanted to go back to Toronto. I wanted to feel safe.

I felt safe when I was taking action. Not safe, exactly, but in control and completely in the moment. No busy brain getting in the way. But right now, I was literally and figuratively hobbled, and feeling like I was either going crazy or being watched. Possibly both.

I wished Laurence would get back. I started toward the phone to call his cell, when I remembered us giving our SIM cards to Jonas back at the safe house. I didn't have my cell, not that it would work here anyway, but even if Laurence had his phone back I didn't know the number off by heart. I relied on my contacts list.

Jesus, what a lazy race we'd become.

I made my way back to the bedroom and closed the curtains there too. I couldn't see anyone now, but the light was nearly gone.

I sat down on the bed and picked up the pen and paper

Debbie had left. I decided to write things down. I made myself comfortable, pushing the pillows behind me. Just as I touched the pen to paper, the phone rang again. Of course. Not five minutes earlier.

I decided to try, at least. It could be Laurence.

By the time I made it halfway across the living room again, the phone had stopped. And I remembered that it was an old-fashioned wall phone, with no call display. I sat on the old La-Z-Boy near a small bookshelf, the closest seat to the phone.

I rifled through. Some very old Harlequin romances – Debbie's mother, I supposed, or stepmother, depending on when she came into the picture. Probably not young Debbie, figuring out she was a lesbian and devouring the most hetero kinds of books on the market. Telephone books going back to 2001, for whatever reason. A few more recent bestsellers, airport-type books.

And on the bottom shelf, what looked to be high-school yearbooks. Debbie's parents probably went to the same school that Rose did. Probably everybody around here did, actually. I debated going into the bedroom to get my paper and pen, in case I could find anything interesting and make notes.

I sat for a minute, frustrated at the fact that a simple act like going into the next room to fetch a pen could possibly turn into such a decision. I felt a surge of anger again, at Dave and Ned, and even right now at Laurence. He should be back by now.

Then I realized I did helpless and sick about as well as a man does, and I told myself to deal. I may have called myself some names while I was at it. On top of everything, I was a bit premenstrual. Hormonal and feeling helpless: my favorite combination.

I grabbed the few yearbooks that were in the bookcase and

took them back into the bedroom. One trip, instead of back and forth; and if the phone rang, I'd let it ring.

I noticed the bottle of Sancerre had a bit left, and once I settled myself back on the bed, yearbooks and paper in my lap, I took a swig from the bottle.

1992. Same year as the one Dave and I had seen at Dickie's. Dave had gone back in for them, in fact. If he had found anything exciting that we hadn't already seen – i.e., Des Murphy was the captain of the hockey team – I probably would have heard about it, despite my moratorium on any news.

I love other people's photo albums and yearbooks, almost especially if I don't know them. I find myself making up stories about the people in the pictures. I find it relaxing. Going through people's underwear drawers? You can keep it.

I read a few of the grads' write-ups, all in the same prose style as Rose's had been. Seemed like about half or more of the kids had plans to go off to university. I studied pictures of the Chess Club and the Badminton Team.

Really, it wouldn't matter what year or what school you were looking at, the Chess Club always looked the same, full of kids who were unpopular in high school but who would more than likely be successful in life.

Finally, I turned back to the grads again, and searched for Murphy.

Desmond Murphy came screeching into the world on December 8th 1974. He tells us he was a preemie baby, which some of the girls of the grade 12 class might not find surprising!

I raised my eyebrows. How did that get by the staff censors?

His love of fast cars and fast women came to an abrupt halt when he and Rose Carlisle knocked each other out during Co-Ed Volleyball in grade 10.

Yeah. Fast cars and fast women, all before grade 10.

Not only has Des been captain of the hockey team since grade 11, but some say he may have even broken the speed of sound at Ferryman Lake in his souped-up dinghy. His favorite subject is Phys Ed, and his dream is to marry Rose and coach other people's rugrats. His other dream is that he keeps his hair until he's at least 30. Dream on, Des!

Handsome kid. Same cleft chin. Hair that was already starting to recede; no wonder he was worried about being bald by thirty. I leafed through a few more grad pictures, then went to the sports teams and extracurricular activities.

One was labelled "Fall Clean-Up," and showed a bunch of fresh-faced kids raking leaves.

One was Des, clowning around with Rose Carlisle. She was laughing, ducking from him slapping her butt or something, the way it looked. She was thinner than I had expected she would be; she was one of those girls with a full face but a slim body.

They looked happy.

I saw the hockey team photo again, and had a quick look at the girls' teams. I checked basketball and volleyball first. She was tall, but Rose was obviously not a sporty girl in school. I couldn't find her in any of the club photos. Well, she wound up at Bennington. She probably spent her time studying, when she wasn't attached at the hip to Des.

I found only one more picture of Rose.

There were a few pages of candid shots of the kids around school, set on the page at jaunty angles, showing how much fun the students and staff got up to. Rose was at her locker, leaning with one hip holding her up, reading a book. I couldn't see the cover. There were two girls standing beside her, but she didn't seem to even notice them. The other two girls were mugging for the camera and sticking their bellies out. There was something off about the picture, and I flipped back to it.

The other two girls were sticking out their bellies. Rose wasn't.

Rose was pregnant. From what I could tell, quite pregnant. I was no expert, but maybe six months? Not like she was about to drop, but not like it wasn't noticeable either.

Rose and Des had a baby.

I forgot how to breathe for a minute, and then I headed for the phone.

I moved carefully through the space, cursing myself for not leaving a lamp on. I didn't know the layout well enough to risk crashing through and falling.

I wondered if Debbie's gun safe was open, or if I could find the key. Or if I could even make it up the stairs just now.

I stood with my hand on the phone, and realized I had no one to call. I didn't remember Laurence's number, and I could go and look up Debbie's RCMP detachment, but what was I going to tell her? "Get back here immediately, Rose and Des Murphy had a baby"?

In that moment, I didn't have a single phone number in my memory bank. Even Darren's was gone, not that I was going to call him.

Dave. I had Dave's number, as permanent as it could be, tattooed into the design on my inner left thigh. And I didn't even have to look: as soon as I remembered it was there, I remembered what it was.

Instead of getting Dave on the phone, a woman with a prim English accent answered, "Pemberly's." At least, that's what I thought she said. I was so shocked that it was a woman's voice that I was startled.

"Oh," I said. "I'm looking for Doug Douglas, please." Our code name, since our time in California.

"He'll call you back very soon, Miss Cleary," the woman said. She hadn't paused to do a search of which weird made-up-on-the-spot alias he had used with each person who might call him. "I'm to tell you that he's helping the police with their investigation, but all is well, and he'll check in the minute he's free."

"Free? Do you mean they're holding him?" Who the fuck was this guy?

"Not unless something has changed in the last thirty-five minutes, no," the woman said. "He's just doing the second part of his videotaped statement." Well, she was certainly forthcoming, if she was telling the truth.

"Listen, please," I said. "I don't have a phone at the moment. I mean, I'm on a landline; I'm staying at a friend's cottage. I was released from the hospital today."

"Yes, we're aware," she said.

I paused. "Who are you people, anyway?"

"Dave will explain, Miss Cleary."

"What's his last name?"

"Miss Cleary, I'm going to have to direct you to speak to Dave again."

I sighed. "You do realize how bizarre this is, right?"

"I do," she said.

"What did you say when you answered? Pemberly's?"

"It doesn't matter, Miss Cleary. We'll answer differently next time."

"What's your name?" I said to the woman.

"Astrid," she said. There was the briefest of pauses between us, and then she said, "It really is."

Finally. I believed her. She was human.

"Astrid, listen to me. I am at Constable Debbie MacLean's cottage, her family cottage, on Ferryman Lake. I can't even give you the phone number here because I don't have it. I don't have my phone, and the number isn't written here."

"Are you alone?" she wanted to know.

"I really hope so," I said. "You're, uh, apprised of what's been happening?"

"Yes," she said crisply.

"Constable MacLean is on shift, and my brother is quite late getting back. I'm not particularly mobile at the moment, as you obviously know. Several hours ago, I thought perhaps I saw someone at the edge of the woods, but I could have been mistaken. Debbie – Constable MacLean – mentioned something about thinking it too, that someone was still out there." Fuck, I sounded like one hysterical chick. "I don't have a weapon. Astrid, look. Do you believe in intuition? Instinct? A sort of, ha, almost psychic, sixth-sense kind of thing?"

"Not usually," she said, "but I believe in yours." She was so brisk, so matter-of-fact and unwavering in her responses, I knew exactly why she worked with Dave. Or, more to the point, why Dave would want her working with him.

"I feel as though something is wrong. I feel as though we've all missed something."

"You feel as though you may be in danger?"

"Yes." I didn't hesitate.

"I'm sending someone else to you," she said. "Someone else you know."

"From the… team?"

"Yes, but we don't mention names, except mine and Dave's," she said. "In the meantime, you know what to do."

"Uh-huh." I did.

"When help is arriving, they will sound their horn, long and loud, from the road, so you know they're coming and you know it's them."

Loud noise. Announce it's them, and also possibly scare any bad guys away.

Or draw attention from me to them.

"Thank you, Astrid," I said.

"I'll be speaking with you again," she said. "Good luck, Miss Cleary."

"Call me Danny," I said. I didn't want to hang up.

"Good luck, Danny. Call back at any time." She hung up.

I hung up, and flicked the kitchen light off. The entire cottage was in darkness now. I had memorized the placement of a few things while I was speaking with Astrid. I hopped to the knife drawer and felt around, gingerly. I found a knife with a large handle and slid it into my back pocket, thankful I had changed into a pair of Debbie's jean shorts. Right now, pockets were my friends.

A baby born in 1992 would be in his or her mid-twenties by now.

I thought I heard something, and realized it was just the wind.

I felt for the stove, making as little sound as I could. I took the handle of the cast-iron frying pan that I'd seen there. I weighed it in my hand, getting used to its heft. It would do. I put it down quietly for a minute, as I took four ibuprofen from the bottle I'd taken from the bathroom. Laurence wasn't back with my pills. I dry swallowed them, two at a time, keeping my ears open and my eyes trained on the outside.

It was now full dark outside, and having the lights off inside not only made me less visible to anyone outside, but it helped with my night vision. If I had to go from a bright kitchen into a dark room or outside quickly, I'd be blind.

I found a bar of hard soap by the sink, and I broke off a little chunk, smearing it into the skin on my face and neck, hoping it would be greasy and slippery. It was the best I could do with no Vaseline at hand. Fighter's trick: having a greasy face helps punches slip and slide off you if they don't land perfectly, and it can help with bruising.

I was busy putting a few other things in my pockets when I saw the light flashing. A little flashing red light, somewhere by the phone. It was like the flashing light on a smoke detector when it's losing its batteries.

I held my breath and listened. No one could have come

downstairs without me hearing; I remembered that the stairs were pretty creaky.

I slid my body weight along the counter to avoid putting much weight on my bad leg, but I couldn't move soundlessly at the moment. It wasn't going to happen.

I was back at the phone. The flashing light was coming from what I had assumed was a small stick-on light source over the phone. I had those in my apartment in Toronto as nightlights. But it wasn't a light.

It was a camera.

Someone, somewhere, was watching. After a moment of feeling around under the phone and the counter, I found what I was looking for. Jonas had shown me examples of these on my tour of the safe house.

A bug. And not the creepy-crawly kind.

My heart was beating double-time. I headed for the back door, opened it, and threw one of my crutches outside. I let the door bang shut, and stood inside by the wall, and waited to see if someone outside would come running at the noise. My mind was racing.

Someone was recording what went on here. I knew that these devices could have been placed there by Geoffrey when he was doing his errands for Mother Pamela. Maybe they didn't trust Debbie, or Pamela just wanted to keep an eye on all the cottages around Dickie's. Or someone else was recording us, someone who was still watching from the woods.

I tried to slow my breathing. I didn't have all the facts. I knew it couldn't be Debbie; she was inside with Laurence and me when I saw the figure in the woods earlier in the day.

Something had been eating away at the back of my mind for days. I just needed to get to it. I had filed something away. I had either heard or seen something that my brain had stored as a red flag, but I couldn't remember what. Whether it was the meds or lack of them, my mind was blank of anything but the desire to flee. Inside the cottage, I felt like a sitting duck, being watched and heard, and I couldn't bear it. I had to get out of the cottage, and get into the woods and hide until Dave's people arrived.

I might be heading into the woods where someone had been watching me. But despite my injury, despite everything, action was a lot more natural to me than sitting around waiting.

I opened the door and went outside.

THIRTY-NINE

I threw the cast-iron pan a few feet down onto the ground so I could negotiate the stairs from the back door with one crutch. I was putting weight on my leg now. I had to. And I was relying on adrenaline to help me with pain.

There was no point in trying to be quiet now. I just had to move. I had to assume there was a camera showing angles from the back door, if there had been one in the kitchen.

When I was off the steps, I picked up the pan and chucked a crutch as far as I could into the trees. I made my way toward where I'd thrown it, moving more quickly than I had since the night Dave and I had run through these woods. A bolt of pain shot up from my leg and made everything on my right side hurt. Even the roots of my teeth hurt.

I grunted, but I didn't stop.

I passed the outbuilding, Debbie's garage/woodworking studio. There was a padlock on the door. I could see that well enough from here. I headed to it.

The padlock was rusty and barely functional. Two decent whacks with the cast-iron pan broke one of the sides of the shackle in half.

I leaned against the door and listened. I thought I heard a car in the distance, but I couldn't be sure. It could be Dave's crew, or Debbie, or some random stranger. Or even the wind, which was picking up. I hesitated for a second. I didn't particularly want to be in the woods if a storm started. And I really didn't want my leg to open up and get infected, again.

I went inside the building, and shut the door behind me.

What I wouldn't have given for a headlamp or a flashlight. I wasn't going to risk turning on the lights. There was a large window at the far end, the lake end, and two smaller ones, high up, on either side. At the far end, from the little I could see in the dark, there might have been a few tools and some wood.

But what really had my attention was right in front of me.

A vehicle covered by a tarp. A pickup-sized vehicle. I lifted the tarp. It was a truck. It was black, or maybe midnight blue; too hard to tell in the dark. But I would have bet cash money that, until not long ago, that truck had been canary yellow. I didn't even bother to check if the windows were tinted. I might not be able to tell in here, and besides, I knew.

"I knew you'd find it," a voice said from the dark. "I just thought you'd wait a day or two before you made it out here to snoop around, so I could get a chance to have a talk with you."

Debbie was standing in the open doorway. I hadn't heard her over the crinkling of the tarp, the wind, and the beating of my heart.

And in that moment, I remembered what my mind had stored for me.

When Laurence and I had come to stay here the first time, when I was searching the cottage like a crazy woman and one of us had to go into the basement to turn on the water, Debbie had phoned and walked us through it. And at some point recently, she had made a comment about how it wasn't necessary to go into the basement with an axe. She had made a joke about it, telling me that her place was safe.

But I had never told her about how scared Laurence and I were that first night here, and how she had phoned – at exactly the right moment – to tell us how to turn the water on, and that I was going to go down into her unknown basement with the axe that was hanging on the wall behind the door. Unless she had seen it as well as heard it, she wouldn't know that. I hadn't told her. I was sure I hadn't told her.

Debbie talked about both her parents being big – the later picture I had seen of Rose indicated she was a heavier woman, and Des certainly was. She was about the right age to have been born when Rose was seventeen or eighteen.

Debbie was the daughter of Desmond Murphy and Rose Carlisle. The daughter they had given up for adoption. Pamela's granddaughter, and Geoffrey's niece.

I looked at her. She was in uniform. She had a gun at one hip and a tactical baton at the other. She was a few years younger and as tall as I was, and trained.

I had a badly injured leg, a crutch, and a cast-iron pan, which was on the ground somewhere here.

Hoo boy, I don't fancy her chances, Ginger's voice said in my head, and I laughed.

"I love your laugh. I really like you," she said. "I was hoping we were going to have some time in the next days, so I could talk to you. I don't think I did anything you wouldn't have done.

That's one of the reasons I talked to you that day at Rose's. I knew what you did for your family, Danny. I knew you killed people for your family. What makes us any different?"

She seemed sincere. She seemed like Debbie. And I didn't want to have to try to fight her. And that's if she would even fight, and not just shoot me.

"At the moment, I'm really not sure," I said. "But first of all – where's Laurence? He said he was going to be back here in a couple of hours."

"He's fine. He got hung up at Rose's," she said. "He found a bunch of teenagers in the basement, taking selfies and drinking. He called us, and they put him through to me. He tried to call here, but I told him I'd take a run out here and check on you. It's a remarkably quiet night, other than that, and I'm covering for someone else. Easy to get a bit of time off."

"Oh," I said. That could be true. She sounded like she was telling the truth. And, oddly, I didn't think she would lie to me now. "I found the yearbook. I saw the picture of Rose pregnant. Was that with you, then?" I leaned against the truck, facing her. I was up by the cab, and Debbie was standing by the end of the truck, pacing a bit.

"Yeah. Rose Carlisle and Des Murphy were my parents."

"Well, that's where you get your height, then."

"Yup." I could tell she was smiling.

"So why MacLean?"

"I was adopted. Rose's father made her put me up for adoption. And my dad's parents wouldn't let him fight it. And then Rose's father took her down to the States, and she was only a kid. Eighteen is only a kid, right? She had a chance to start a new life, and she took it." She looked at the ground. She seemed like a child suddenly. She wanted to believe that neither of her parents had wanted to abandon her. "It was fate, though, that Des and I both ended up back here. I mean, after Depot…"

"Depot?" I said.

"RCMP training, in Regina," she said. "Anyway, I was posted up north, and then it was just a fluke I got sent back here. We move around a lot, but we can ask for assignments. Doesn't mean we get them."

"And you wanted to be home," I said.

"Wouldn't you? It's paradise here."

I decided to let that one pass. My plans for buying a summer home in the area had long since evaporated. Along with my desire for meat. Or lobster.

"Anyway, Des had moved around a bit but he's been with H Division – here in Nova Scotia, I mean – for a long time. But the fact that we wound up at the same detachment? And then I find out he's my dad?" She shook her head like she couldn't believe her luck.

"When I met him and spent some time with him, he reminded me of my own dad." I sounded like I was being honest, because I was.

"You had both of your parents, Laurence told me. That must have been nice."

"It was," I said. "I was really lucky."

"Until you weren't," she said. But she sounded gentle, sad. "You lost yours, and I found mine."

"And Pamela, your grandmother," I said. She nodded. My eyes were adjusting to the dark. "And your uncle, Geoffrey," I said.

"I really liked Geoffrey," she said. "He was sort of a tortured soul, you know? He had some issues with mental illness when he was younger, and it made him very sensitive to other people. You know what I mean. He was the kind of soft-hearted lug who always took in strays."

I felt so odd. I felt like I was having a good, honest conversation with this woman. She didn't seem crazy, and she didn't seem like a killer. Like someone who could tie a defenceless young woman to a tree and let animals feed on her.

"Did you grow up okay? I mean, were your adoptive parents good people?"

"Oh, absolutely. I love them. They had a farm. They were an older couple. They had another adopted girl, a few years older than me. We had a few cows, horses, chickens."

"Where are they now?" I was really hoping she wasn't going to say tied to trees somewhere, or in a hole in the ground in some random forest.

"Boca Raton," she said, and I laughed, and then so did she. "They're fine, Danny. They don't even know I was looking for my birth parents, or that Des found me."

I hoped for their sake that they stayed in Boca.

"Actually, you know my sister," she said. "My adopted sister. Janet? She worked at Rose's."

"Janet is your sister?" Wispy Janet, who wouldn't say boo to a goose? Who Laurence had given money to clear out of the area, after we had all been shot at in the dining room.

Who had told us that she had been a bit afraid of her little sister.

I wanted to ask Debbie everything. I wanted to know how

much of a role she had played in the killings. And a part of me didn't want to know.

"Janet still lives on the farm, when she's not living at Rose's Place," she said. "She was another one."

"Another what?"

"Addict." Debbie was pacing a bit, between the end of the truck and the wall. "Pamela didn't mind her, though, and Des would never have hurt her. She didn't do anything wrong. She got herself cleaned up and tried to help people."

"Yes, she did."

"It's a good thing they didn't know about your fall off the wagon," Debbie said. "I wouldn't have wanted to be in your shoes."

"Well, somebody did knock me out and tie me to a pier when the tide was coming in, Deb," I said. "I didn't exactly get away unscathed."

Debbie looked at me. I couldn't see her face clearly, but she had stopped pacing. "Look, I'm sorry, but I did that. Or part of that."

Here we go. I waited for the car horn to sound from the road. Wasn't it taking an awfully long time?

"Okay," I said. My voice was so calm and even. I amazed myself. "But why?"

"If Mary hadn't freaked out, none of it would have happened. But Pamela said she heard Mary tell you to run. Things weren't finished yet." She looked down at her feet, and for a minute, she looked like a kid who knows she's done something wrong. "What else could I do?"

"I don't know," I said. "Not knocked me out and tied me to a pier to drown?" I had been convinced I was going to die. And this woman had put me there. I felt it again, for the first time in a while, the rage that seemed to take me over, seemed to get rid of any fear I ever felt.

"Danny, I had just been getting to know my father, and my grandmother, and my uncle. I wasn't in on all this at the beginning. I mean, trust me, I heard about Dickie Doyle early on, as soon as I met my dad. Des blamed Dickie for Mom's death." Mom. Des was Des, but Rose was Mom. "She would have been fine, everybody would have been fine if he hadn't brought her back here and thrown all these memories in everybody's faces."

"I thought she got addicted to pain pills after a riding accident," I said. I was trying to keep my voice steady. I didn't want her to feel the change in me.

"There was no riding accident. She was just depressed, and became an addict."

That could happen. I was walking proof. But right now, I didn't care.

"So Pamela was the one who knocked me out?"

"Yes," she said. "I was with your brother, remember?" Right. Debbie had taken Laurence to get his clothes from Rose's Place, to get groceries. "I didn't get there until later."

"Then were you the one with the brilliant idea to drown me slowly? And I mean, torture me until I drowned. I was unconscious; if you had wanted me dead you could have just tied me up and thrown me in the water."

"I really didn't want to do that, Danny. But Pamela was so keen on having her way, and really, we didn't have a boat, so anything else would have been too much trouble."

Too much trouble. "I see," I said.

"For what it's worth, I hated that," she said. "But Des said it was also stupid for me to have given you the key to my gun safe, that if you told anybody I would lose my job. I love my job."

"Your job," I said. "Your job?"

Keep it together, Danny. Help is on the way. Keep her talking.

"Des and Pamela – well, neither of them had anything against you. And, God knows, I didn't. If you hadn't come to Geoffrey's house that day, everything would have been fine. But things had gotten a bit out of control. Des was really worried about me. He never wanted all of that to happen."

"He stopped my friends from helping me when I was in that hole," I said. "He was going to let me die down there. And he's confessed to things that you did, I assume."

"Well, he did want to put the fear of God into Dickie," she said, "ruin the reputation of Rose's Place, and scare Dickie into leaving." She was pacing again. "But Pamela – well, she was a force of nature." She sounded proud. Proud of her batshit crazy grandmother.

"He sounds like a good dad," I said gently. "It wasn't his fault that you were put up for adoption."

"He is a good man," she said. "When I was cutting the R tattoo off Dickie, Des walked in and saw, and he actually had to go throw up." She stopped pacing, and I could see her smile in the last of the light coming through the windows. "Pamela blindfolded him first, because she wasn't sure she wanted to kill him or whatever, and she didn't want him to know about me. Anyway, I was doing it, and Pamela had put a sock in Dickie's mouth to stop him screaming too much. I mean, my God, Pamela was the least squeamish person I've ever met – next to me – but Des? I can't believe he's been a policeman for this long."

I tried to smile a bit. "What about Sarah? Was that Pamela, or…?" Or you, I wanted to say, but Debbie answered quickly.

"Well, I was the one who took her, but after that it was all Pamela. Sarah came with me. I mean, I'm a cop."

"But Pamela told you to do that? I heard she had a pretty strong personality."

Debbie nodded. "She had a list, yeah. I just wanted to get the weekend over with, to be honest. I had been hearing about nothing but the fucking Apple Blossom festival from Pamela for months. And I was really tired. I've got insomnia issues," she said to me, like we were confessing intimacies to each other over a bottle of wine. "Between that dude from Halifax, the one you found at Dickie's, and Evan, and Sarah, and Dickie – I got, like, no sleep that weekend."

Sleep. The poor dear.

"And me," I said. "That was the weekend you guys tied me to the pier, don't forget." I made myself sound light.

"Right?" she said, as though I was confirming how much she'd had to do, how tired she must have been. "Anyway, I'm glad that's over with. I miss Pamela and Geoffrey, but I'll still be able to visit Des."

"He really protected you," I said. "You were lucky." Debbie was getting closer, inch by inch, as we talked. I had stopped fully listening to her. I was doing some math in my head. "So he painted the top of the cabin for you when you met him and told him you were gay?"

"It's ugly as shit, right? But that's the kind of dad he was."

"He still is. He's still protecting you, Deb." She looked at me, and I knew she wasn't getting closer because, oh, maybe she wanted to try to kiss me again. She was going to kill me, and she didn't want to have to fire her gun. She would probably have to write a report about firing her weapon on duty. And she had made clear how important her job was to her.

I steeled myself, put my hands in my pockets casually, and took a deep breath. "Listen, you crazy bitch. Your job is to uphold the law. Instead you committed some of the most heinous acts I have ever heard of, because, what, your grandmother – who never had a hand in raising you, so it wasn't like you were brainwashed at a young age to be the fucking psychopath you are…" Debbie took a step toward me. "Your mentally ill grandmother persuaded you to start killing people horribly, innocent people, because Rose Doyle became an addict and overdosed?"

"Danny, you should stop now." Her voice was even, but perhaps for the first time I started to feel the presence of real crazy in the room.

I wasn't sure if it was coming from me or her.

Debbie was absolutely still, arms at her sides. I could no longer see her face; she was standing in darkness. I continued.

"You have ruined countless lives. All the families of the people you killed, everyone who loved them, just because you happen to have been born into a fucked-up gene pool with some kind of lovely combination of mental illness and psychopathy. And you're worried about keeping your fucking *job*? Bitch, you belong in the ground. Not in a hospital. Not breathing air in a jail cell. You belong tied to a tree so the animals can eat you slowly. Preferably while I watch."

It worked. Instead of taking out her gun and shooting me, she ran at me.

It was slow motion. I didn't feel the pain in my leg. I didn't feel anything but the pounding of blood in my ears and the knowledge that I was going to bring this psycho bitch down, or die trying.

I stood perfectly still as she ran at me from fifteen feet away, her upper body forward to take me down to the ground.

When she was in full throttle, before she could stop or change course, I put my weight on my good leg, my left leg, and let myself fall to the ground, reaching out to the side.

Debbie fell over my leg and my crutch, knocking me on my back. Within seconds, she had me pinned, as I knew she would, her legs straddling my thighs.

Fast, faster than she could think, faster than she could start to lean forward to strangle me, I stabbed her with both hands. Once in the top of her inner left thigh with the knife I'd pulled out of my back pocket, and once in the top of the right thigh with the screwdriver from my other pocket. I did it hard, as hard as I could. The fabric of her uniform trousers looked thick, and I had to make sure I hit the femoral artery on at least one side.

There was a horrible pause.

She looked down at herself, at the sharp objects impaled in her thighs. She looked confused. I wished I could see her legs better. Then I saw the blood, which was pulsing out of her with every beat of her heart.

In seconds, the front of her pant legs was soaked.

She started to lean over, to try to claw at my face. She was looking at me in the eyes, as though she was confused that I had betrayed her. I could have eased her onto her back and whispered a couple of nice words to her as she lost her blood. I could, at least, have eased her way out of this world in a way that would maybe have comforted her in her last second.

Instead, I flipped her off me, ignoring the fire in my leg. I held her hand onto the ground. "Look, Debbie," I said. My voice was almost cheerful. "Watch." And, with her arm pinned to the ground and her eyes on it, I removed the knife from her thigh, raised my arm high in the air, and with all my strength, brought it down on her wrist. The knife wasn't sharp enough, or big enough. It took me three blows to separate her hand from her body, but I did it quickly.

She died screaming.

Good.

"Damn straight," I said out loud.

"Danny," someone said, and I looked up.

Laurence was standing in the doorway. He had seen, and he had heard.

But he was my brother, and he came to me and held me, no matter what I had done. Which, perhaps, is what Debbie had done with her own family.

Laurence managed to lift me off her, and he put me down feet away and held me as I threw up. Neither of us spoke.

Then a car horn sounded, a long, loud honk from the road.

FORTY

Dickie Doyle was arrested and charged for the murder of Constable Debra MacLean. He confessed freely, and instructed his counsel not to seek bail.

When Dave and Jonas showed up at Debbie's cottage that night, Dickie came out of the woods. He had been watching. He had been watching, he said, for a while. He didn't believe that Rose was dead, but he did realize that at some point Debbie MacLean had hurt him badly. He didn't say when or where. He seemed to think Pamela had cut off his tattoo, so perhaps Debbie had been responsible for one or more of his other injuries.

He wanted to make sure, he said, that she didn't hurt anyone else. He would never tell anyone how he had gotten from the bowling alley to the lake, what he had survived on, or who, if anyone, had helped him.

It was Dickie I had seen from the corner of my eye the day I killed Debbie, when I was in my room and doubting my sanity. He had been sleeping in the woods, he said, during the time when Debbie and I had been in the garage. The car horn on the road woke him up, and he emerged from the trees to find Dave, Jonas, and Laurence arguing about what to do about the gory scene they'd all found in Debbie MacLean's garage.

I could possibly have gotten away with self-defence. And it would have been true, in fact if not in spirit, but Debbie's severed hand might have caused some raised eyebrows.

I sat on the floor of the garage, not really paying much attention to any of them. I had gone somewhere in my head that it would take me a while to come out of. Laurence talked to Dickie as he came out of the woods, but the situation was time-sensitive – Debbie MacLean was officially on duty, and her location could be easily traced by the RCMP. Dickie left them to it, hobbled into the garage, past me, to Debbie's body. Before anyone could react, he gathered up the tools I had used to stab Debbie, making sure his fingerprints were on the weapons in her blood. He kneeled in the blood pooling around her, smearing it over himself.

"Danny was afraid, and she came out to the garage to hide. Debbie came in and attacked her. Danny fought back, but Debbie overpowered her. There's blood on the back of you, on the back of your head," Dickie said to me. He was emotionless, and the men just stared at him. "I was watching, then I came in and we all wrestled. I killed Debbie. I cut off her hand." He looked at me and smiled gently. "Let me do this for your brother," he said. "So many people have died because of me. You very nearly died."

I couldn't speak yet. I wouldn't speak for another day. Laurence tried to talk him out of it, but Dickie wouldn't listen.

"It doesn't matter what you say. This is what happened, and this is what I will tell the police. They will believe me. You know they'll believe me."

Jonas called the police, and they all came. Everyone came.

I got separated from Laurence for a time, but he found me and held my hand. I didn't want him to. I didn't want anyone to have to touch me.

Dickie was right, of course. The police did believe him.

I was hospitalized that night for observation. I was unresponsive, and they thought I was in shock, and might possibly have a brain injury.

I didn't. My head was as hard as always. But they decided to keep me there for another day to make sure my leg was healing after my ordeal in Debbie's garage.

I started speaking the next night, when Laurence brought Mary to my hospital room. Dickie had paid for a good independent criminal defence counsel for her, and she was out pending review of her charges. I hadn't wanted to see Laurence the day after it happened. I was too ashamed about what he had seen, and I was still terrified at myself, at what I had done.

It would take time, and a few good Skype chats with Dr. Singh, before I started to get back to normal. Whatever normal is for me, which I am coming to accept is not what is normal for most people. And I'm having a lot of help accepting that. Sometimes I can even embrace it.

But seeing Mary was what I needed most, before I could start to feel human.

She walked into my room with Laurence, and shooed him out when I started crying at seeing her. She didn't quite look like herself, not fully. The trauma ran pretty deep with her as well. But she was wearing heels and lipstick, and that was a long way from how I had last seen her, curled up in a hole in the ground, waiting to die.

It had only been a year, Mary told me, since Pamela and Debbie had come into her life. She and Geoffrey had been together for ten years by then, and she knew all about his history with mental health and his ongoing struggles. She filled his prescriptions for him when he couldn't, and, as she said, she had gotten him the job as handyman at Rose's Place long before Pamela had shown up with her burgeoning plans.

"What did they used to say about the Nazis? They were just following orders?" Mary was clutching my hand, trying to explain. "But Geoffrey didn't know. Not until it was too late. He really didn't know."

"Why did he think he was putting hidden cameras in the residents' rooms?" I said. "Mary, I believe that you didn't know. I have to believe it. But what did he think he was doing?"

Mary let go of my hand then, and I realized she had known about them as well. "We thought it was about making sure people were staying clean," she said. "To help people. Pamela said we would be saving people's lives. It was just to make sure people weren't using." She was pleading with me to believe her. "It was supposed to be helping people. Geoffrey had lost his only sister. You have to understand what that did to him."

I nodded. I had more than a passing knowledge of how that felt.

"And Pamela – well, you never met her, but she was sort of bigger than life." I didn't tell her that I was there when Pamela had killed her son and then herself. Maybe someday I would, but I wasn't able to, not then. "Geoff had no family left other than me, and all of a sudden his mother shows up, and it turns out he has a niece too! He was away in hospital when Rose was

– well – when Rose had Debra. He never knew." She looked like she wanted to smoke. "Oh, Danny. And Debra was a police officer, and she was so nice, and at the beginning it was – well – it made Geoff so happy."

"I can understand that," I said. I couldn't imagine not having family, so having one show up and actually liking them would be a rush.

"After Rose died, we didn't see much of Dickie. He would drop by once in a while, but we could never count on it. He was Geoff's brother-in-law, but they didn't have anything in common, and I don't think Dickie could stand to be around us. Around anybody that reminded him of Rose."

She stood up and walked around. "I feel like I'm going to go crazy without him, Danny."

"Mary, I have to know. I won't tell the police, I promise. But please, what part did Geoffrey play in the – well – in the killings?"

"None. Really, he didn't. And once he realized that his mother was a fucking lunatic – and I don't mean mentally ill, I mean a fucking crazy person – he wanted to go to the police. That's when things went bad. That was during the festival weekend, when she shot Colin. That's why, by the way. She thought I would tell Colin about the cameras, and he knew she was staying in our basement. She was sure he knew that she had killed that man whose body you found at Dickie's cabin. And poor Evan." She was crying now. She sat back down at the foot of my bed. "That was my fault. If the cameras hadn't been there, she wouldn't have known Evan was selling a little pot."

"So she shot at us in the dining room to make sure you didn't talk?"

"We didn't even know it was her, until that day," Mary said. "We really didn't. We didn't know it was Des either. We were like everybody else."

"She was a good shot," I said. "Oh, fuck. I'm sorry, Mary."

"Colin was a good boy. A good man," she corrected herself. She took Kleenex out of her bag and wiped her face. "And, if you can believe it, when they first started working together, he used to have a crush on Debra." She looked at me. "He was the only one who didn't seem to know she was gay."

"Considering that Debbie was police and her father would do anything to protect her, going to the authorities might have been a bad idea anyway."

"I suppose so."

"Who was the one who put you in the hole? Pamela?"

"No, it was Des Murphy," she said. "I don't even think Pamela knew about that. You saved my life, Danny. You saved my life."

"No, I didn't. Some friends of mine did. They found the hole."

"Yes, that Australian fellow from Rose's," she said. "I didn't realize you two had become friends."

"Sort of, yes." I didn't explain. She obviously didn't remember that he didn't have an accent when he came down into the hole, and it didn't matter.

"I'm going to go to jail," she said. "I deserve to." She took a compact out of her purse and reapplied her lipstick, her hand shaking slightly. I handed her some tissues and she accepted them automatically. "I don't even mind, not really. With Geoff gone, and seeing what I saw... well, I don't deserve to be around good people." She shook her head, trying not to let the tears come. "Our Colin, killed by my mother-in-law, a woman I had living in my home. I might as well have pulled the trigger."

I couldn't think of a single thing to say. I knew exactly how she felt, and, in a way, she was right. How do you come back from this? How do you make your life normal?

"Will you write me letters?" she said. "In jail. I want to hear all about your nephews and your brothers and your crazy life."

"I will, Mary," I said. "I promise I will." Mary stood to leave, and I stopped her. "The night Colin died, Laurence and I drove past your house. I thought I heard men screaming. There was a police car at your house."

"Pamela, that would have been," she said. "Pamela and Des Murphy. He was livid. And Pamela – well, she had a voice like a foghorn. Just as much man in her as woman, I always thought." She got to the door and turned around. "I'll tell you one thing, Danny. As sure as I am fucking standing in this room with you, I am glad that woman is dead. I just wish I had gotten to see it. And I wish someone else had killed her, that she didn't get a chance to die by her own hand. I don't care how crazy she was, she deserved to go out harder. You know what I mean?"

"Yes," I said. "I do." I wished I didn't know, but I did. But it made me feel a bit better about Mary's chances in prison, hearing her say that. She had a core of steel that I hadn't really seen until now. Turns out Mary and I had more in common than I'd thought.

She clip-clopped back over to the bed in her heels, leaned over, and hugged me hard, saying nothing, then left my room without looking back.

FORTY-ONE

One week later

Laurence dove elegantly into the lake from the wharf, and swam back to shore. The sun was just past being directly overhead, so it was very early afternoon, but I was the only sober person on the beach. Even my brother had had a few beers before swimming. He was taking me back to Toronto the next day, and, between them, he and Dave had decided that we were all going to spend the day at the public beach across the lake from both Dickie Doyle's and Des Murphy's cottages.

"Pretty fly for a white guy," Jonas called out, as Laurence did his best Daniel Craig/James Bond impersonation, walking through the water toward the beach.

"You missed a spot," I said. Jonas was putting sunscreen on my back. "I thought you said you weren't much of a drinker. I feel like I've got more sand on my back than sunscreen."

"We're celebrating," he said. "And besides, that's how you know I'm not much of a drinker. I had two vodka lemonade things and my head is spinning." He patted my back like he was finished, and flopped back in the sand.

"Oh for fuck's sake, eat something," I said. I was feeling both happy and yet discontented, elated that we were all safe, but haunted by what had happened. I couldn't settle on an emotion, and more than anything I wanted to wear myself out with exercise until my brain stopped. I wanted to swim, but I was forbidden to, as the wound in my leg had opened up again during my fight with Debbie. And as all these people were here because of me, because of my family's problem, I had volunteered to be the designated driver. Unfortunately, my leg was healed enough that I could drive, and the Tahoe could seat all of us. I rummaged around in the cooler next to me and pulled out a bottle of water and a veggie wrap and passed it to Jonas. "Eat this."

I knew on the trip back to the safe house I was going to feel like a harried bus driver after a field trip with rowdy ten-year-olds.

And I didn't know why we had to come to this beach. It was Nova Scotia. The whole place was water. But Dave and Laurence had insisted, and I had caused everyone enough trouble. I was going to be gracious.

I tried.

I settled myself down into the sand. I loved the feel of it, the heat of it. It was a perfect day, 27° Celsius, no wind, no clouds. I was wearing one of Debbie MacLean's bikinis, the one I had grabbed the first time Laurence and I had stayed there, but it didn't bother me. She was dead. She didn't need it. Dr. Singh said that the fact that I was having these mood swings was natural, after everything. But Dr. Singh didn't know what had happened in that garage across the lake a week ago. I could never tell her; as far as she and the rest of the world knew, Dickie Doyle had killed Debbie.

The only people who knew the truth were right here on this

beach with me. Laurence, Dave, Ned, Jonas, Lydia, and Bert. I had agreed with Laurence that we would tell Darren when we got back to Toronto.

And Ginger knew. I knew Ginger knew, and I hadn't felt her near me since that night.

Dave came from somewhere behind me and settled himself in the sand next to me. I could hear Ned, Lydia, and Bert whooping as they played some form of one-armed volleyball further up the beach, in concession to Ned's cast. Jonas had set up a little sound system on overturned milk crates, and Dire Straits was blasting loud enough to wake the dead.

Needless to say, we had the place to ourselves.

"God, that is one ugly building," Dave said, and I looked across the lake at Des Murphy's striped second floor.

"He meant well," I said. I didn't move from my position, and I was glad my eyes were hidden behind oversized aviator sunglasses. I watched a bead of sweat make its way down Dave's bare back. I felt his eyes on the mandala tattoo on my thigh. I'd never told him that the emergency number he'd given me was there, inked into the intricate design, and I was confident that he wouldn't be able to tell. Still, I subtly shifted my legs, suddenly self-conscious.

I couldn't wait to get back to Toronto. And yet I didn't want to leave this beach.

"Your brother tells me you really like this Dr. Singh," Dave said, and not for the first time I wondered if he could read my mind. "You're going to keep up with her when you get back?"

"Yeah," I said. "Skype."

"And you're going to hire someone to stay with you, keep an

eye on you? The sober living whatsit?"

"I think so," I said. "I'm actually not craving it right now. Crack, I mean. Or coke." I didn't realize it until I said it, but it was true. After Mary's visit, after getting one more night of sleep, I seemed to have forgotten about why I had come here in the first place. "This was one hell of a rehab."

"That's good," Dave said. "But still, once things are back to normal…"

"I know," I said. "But I have no idea what normal is going to look like for me. I feel different now. I've got some things to figure out." I felt like an awkward teenager and a very old person at the same time.

We were both quiet for a minute, and I could hear Jonas snoring on the other side of me. "We're not just talking about drugs, are we," Dave said. He lay back and rested his weight on one elbow, his head in his palm, looking at me.

"Don't be such a smart-ass," I said. "You know I'm not." I couldn't help smiling, but I was trying not to. That was the thing with Dave: He could snap me out of my own head, my own stupid mood, just by being there.

"Well, while you're getting your head back on straight, I want you to think about one more thing," Dave said, and for one crazy second I thought he was going to make some grand romantic gesture, and I stopped breathing.

Again: Thank God for sunglasses. I must have looked like a deer in headlights.

"I want you to come work with me," he said. "When you're ready, I mean. I talked to Laurence about it, and he thinks it's a good idea too. Well, he almost does. I had to talk him into it."

"Oh, so you asked my brother for my hand in… employment?" I said. Then I wished that I could swallow my words and rewind two minutes. That, or die of mortification on the spot. Either/or.

Dave just grinned and scratched his ear. "We all want you to be okay, Danny. It's going to take a while for you to heal."

"I'm tougher than I look," I said. "I'll get my head together eventually." Work with Dave and his people. Do what they do. I was petrified, excited, and vaguely nauseous.

"Oh, I know," Dave said. "Frankly, the way I see it, your leg will take longer to heal than your head will. You just need to accept who you are, Danny."

"Really? Who am I?"

I heard an engine out on the lake, and turned my head toward it.

"You're a warrior," Dave whispered in my ear. "You're better than fearless. You do what the strongest people do; accept that you have fears, and leap in anyway." He got to his feet and held his hand out for me, to help me stand. A speedboat was slowing toward the dock.

Laurence was jogging up the beach toward us. "Come on, you lazy so-and-so. You may not be permitted in the water, but we arranged for a ride on it." Dave woke up Jonas, and the others were already running toward the dock. Jonas and Dave kept me steady on the sand, and with more than my usual share of F-bombs as they insisted on hoisting me down into the boat, I managed to secure a place in the bow. Ned was insisting he was going to do a touch of one-handed waterskiing.

The boat's operator was a guy in his early twenties, whose favorite word seemed to be "groovy" and who was almost a caricature of the laid-back water rat. He insisted we all wear life jackets – if he lost a passenger he would be "so bummed" – but it was no surprise when he passed around a joint two minutes after we left the dock. The water on the lake was calm, almost like glass, and schools were still in session for another week or so. We only passed one other boat, a guy fishing, who raised a lazy wave in the air by way of greeting.

I was glad I was in the bow. I didn't have to smell the weed – I always hated the smell – and while I was purely happy that these people were with me, I didn't want to talk. Behind me, I could hear Laurence's booming laugh as he and Jonas were riffing about something, and Lydia was shrieking at Ned's antics on the waterskis. We circled the lake, stopping for Ned a couple of times when he fell.

This was perfect. This was what I needed. This lake wasn't evil. This place, this province wasn't cursed. I wasn't cursed. I was with people I trusted, whose company I enjoyed. I was going home the next day to see my nephews and my brother. Count your blessings, Dr. Singh had told me. I was trying.

After an hour or so, we came around the other side of the lake, near the Murphy cottage, and Dickie's. I wasn't going to look – I'd seen them; I'd been facing them all day – but something made me turn my head.

Just a flash, ephemeral as smoke. Two women in white, both with long black hair, shimmering in the sun.

"Pamela," Laurence said quietly.

I turned around. "And Rose," I said. He'd seen it too. I grabbed my brother's hand.

"Poor Dickie," he said quietly, and I nodded.

"You two kids want to let us in on what you're talking about?" Dave said.

"Not really," Laurence said. "Dave, my friend, you wouldn't understand."

"It's a Cleary thing, honey," I said to Dave, and then turned back around to face front. I hadn't meant to call him honey. I could hear Jonas ostentatiously whistling to himself, pretending he hadn't heard anything.

And I was happy. I felt Ginger's breath in the breeze that cooled my face, and I was happy.

And maybe, just maybe, when I was healed, when my head and heart and body were healed, I would work with Dave. I'd caused a lot of damage. I could never bring Ginger back, or Jack, but maybe I could do something in this world that could stop other lives from being destroyed. Perhaps my soul would never be clean, but I was pretty sure my conscience would be.

Dave had called me a warrior.

I wasn't, not yet. But maybe I could be.

ABOUT THE AUTHOR

Barbra Leslie lives and writes in Toronto. Visit her at www.barbraleslie.com, or follow her on Twitter:

@barbrajleslie

For more fantastic fiction, author events, competitions,
limited editions and more

VISIT OUR WEBSITE
titanbooks.com

LIKE US ON FACEBOOK
facebook.com/titanbooks

FOLLOW US ON TWITTER
@TitanBooks

EMAIL US
readerfeedback@titanemail.com